William Black

Briseis

A novel

William Black

Briseis
A novel

ISBN/EAN: 9783337049065

Printed in Europe, USA, Canada, Australia, Japan

Cover: Foto ©Andreas Hilbeck / pixelio.de

More available books at **www.hansebooks.com**

B R I S E I S

A Novel

BY

WILLIAM BLACK

AUTHOR OF

"A PRINCESS OF THULE" "HIGHLAND COUSINS"
"THE HANDSOME HUMES" ETC.

ILLUSTRATED

BY W. T. SMEDLEY

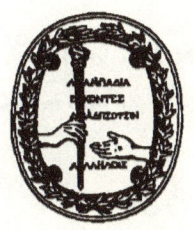

NEW YORK
HARPER & BROTHERS PUBLISHERS
1896

CONTENTS

ILLUSTRATIONS

BRISEIS

CHAPTER I

AT SANCHORY ON DEE

Away up on the heights of Scoulter Hill, overlooking the wide and wooded valley of the Dee, a tall and slim young woman lay at full length on the heather, her interclasped hands beneath her head, her large, dark, foreign-looking eyes fixed lazily and dreamily on the slow-moving heavens. And she was singing to herself—in a kind of absent undertone : probably she was quite unconscious that she was following these idle words—which as likely as not were of her own haphazard composition :

> O Love went sailing along the sky
> On the soft white clouds, so far and high ;
> 'O yonder's the world for which I'm fain—
> The wild gray waves and the driving main.'
> 'O dear little Love, much better you'd be,
> If you'd clip your wings and come down to me !'
>
> Poor boy, he was beaten and battered sore—
> Tossed by the surf and flung on the shore :
> 'I told you, you wretch, 'twould happen ; but now
> Here are handkerchiefs cool to bind your brow ;
> And you'll fold your wings and creep close to me,
> And I'll hide you safe from the angry sea.'

She turned her head a little. And if she had chosen,

1

she might have gazed abroad on a sufficiently spacious
and varied panorama—the fertile pastures of Glen Dye
—the outskirts of Glen Tana Forest—the vast, undulating billows of the Grampians, shining here and dark-
ened there with sunlight and velvet shadow; while on
the remote horizon-line rose the peaks of Loch-Na-
Gar, the snow on them of a dim and burnished gold
through the distant haze.   But perhaps before her
mental vision there was a very different scene.   Perhaps she had transported herself back to her island
home in the Saronic Gulf; perhaps she found herself
once more under the cool shade of the olives, looking
across the great plain of waters—the blazing blue of
the summer sea all twinkling with innumerable little
flashes of white foam; on her right the lonely shores
and precipitous cliffs stretching away down to Cape
Colonna; far in front of her the bold cimeter-sweep of
the Bay of Salamis; beyond that again the palely violet shoulders of Corydallus, and these but the beginning of a mountainous semicircle coming round to
the scarred and gray-green slopes of Hymettus; then
in the midst of the extended plain a mass of rugged
rock rising faint and visionary into the vibrating air,
and, higher still, on the summit of the plateau, certain lofty and saffron-tinted pillars telling of a ruined
temple—the famous temple once the home and shrine
of the Maiden Goddess, Pallas Athene.   It is a spectacle that the merest stranger cannot contemplate
without profound emotion; but in the case of this
Greek girl—this Briseis Valieri—now lying supine and
abstracted on an Aberdeenshire hill—there were many
added and personal associations and affections and
memories; for she also — for a time, at least, during
her days of schooling and school-friendships—she also
had been a Maid of Athens.

Of a sudden she was brought back to herself and her actual surroundings.

"Briseis! Bry! Bry! Where are you?"—she heard the remote call for her.

And then she rose quickly to her feet—her slender, tall, symmetrical figure showing dark against the sky —and looked all around. On this solitary open space of silver-lichened rock and herbage no one was to be seen; but presently, beyond the adjacent larch-wood, and not far from the base of an ancient tower, she had found the object of her quest—the figure of a little, elderly man, who appeared to be frantically gesticulating. At once she set off to rejoin her companion, her long limbs and her free and agile step taking her over the heather as if she had been a young fawn. And even before she drew near him her eyes were full of a smiling and kindly interest; for those dark and lustrous eyes of hers had this unusual faculty, that even while the rest of her features were apparently quiescent, they of themselves could express pleasure, and good-will, and gratitude—and even on occasion mirth and mockery, for she was by nature a daughter of the laughter-loving Aphrodite. But now, as she rapidly approached, this smiling curiosity gave way to a vague concern and wonder; because she could see that her uncle was strangely agitated. He held up his hand.

"Not too near—not too near!" exclaimed this small, nervous-looking man, who nevertheless had apple-tinted cheeks and bright gray eyes. "Briseis, I tell you this is a day of days for me—a day of days, indeed!—you will remember it all your life when you come to understand. Do you know what that is?"

She followed the direction of his finger, and saw on the ground in front of him some scattered patches of a white, waxen-looking flower, which she thought might be one of the stitchworts or some such thing—for notwithstanding her long spring and summer and autumn rambles with this devoted enthusiast she had not picked up much botanical lore.

"It's the *Silene alpestris!*" he said, excitedly. "Don't you understand? That is one of Don's 'reputed discoveries'!—but perhaps Sir Joseph Hooker, in the next edition of his *Flora,* will be so exceedingly kind as to transfer it from the Appendix and place it in the body of the book! Yes, yes; it's all very well for the younger men to make fun of me, and call me the Marquis of Clova, and say I shall never die happy till I rehabilitate the whole Don family. But what is that before you? I ask you, what is that? There it is!—staring you in the face—the *Silene alpestris*—one of Don's 'reputed discoveries'! There it is before you—growing wild on an Aberdeenshire hill—and not so far away from Clova either. I tell you this will make some of them open their eyes—"

Naturally enough the young Greek girl stooped to secure for herself one of those starlike blossoms—if only for the purpose of closer scrutiny—but instantly he gripped her by the arm and checked her.

"No," said he, peremptorily, "they are too precious. Perhaps to-morrow or next day, when I have everything ready, I may take one or two specimens to forward to the Linnæan Society, and the Royal Botanic Society, and the Andersonian at Glasgow; but otherwise they must be left to spread and flourish as much as ever is possible. I tell you, if I were that young Sir Francis Gordon, I would fence them round, so that not a single tourist should get near them. But in the meantime, Briseis—in the meantime, come away down—I must send some telegrams off—come away down

"SHE FOLLOWED THE DIRECTION OF HIS FINGER"

to the inn, and I will dictate them to you. Don't you think Professor —— at Oxford will stare—don't you think so?—ah, don't you think so?—but come away, Bry—I shouldn't wonder if I could show you the plant figured in Loudon or Robinson, and then you will be convinced—"

"Oh, but I am delighted, uncle!" said the young girl—and now all the beautiful, pale olive face was aglow with sympathetic pleasure. "I am delighted! And is it so great a discovery? And will they give you more honor?—and print your name in more Transactions?—and make you a Fellow of more Societies? Oh, but indeed I am delighted! I must write and tell my cousin Calliope—"

He laughed aloud, in a half-hysterical fashion—he seemed hardly to know what he was doing or saying.

"And sooner or later, Bry, you will discover that in this country we say Callīŏpe, not Calliŏpe—"

"In Athens we used mostly to call her Opĕ," said the young girl, without taking any offence, and still regarding the waxen-white flowers with the greatest interest.

"But come away—come away now," he said, hurriedly. "I must send off the telegrams at once." Then he paused. "No. Stay a moment. Kneel down."

She was a biddable creature, and her dress was of a rough and simple material: she did as she was told.

"Is it some form of worship, uncle?" said she, with the soft dark eyes smiling.

"Examine now," he said. "Examine closely; and when we go down to the inn, if I can find for you a figure of the plant, you will see how they correspond. Observe now—the flowers panicled, rather large, and of a glossy whiteness—each petal with four notches—

the calyx erect, with blunt teeth as long as the petals
—stem simple, few-leaved, about six inches high—"

She had risen to her feet again.

"But I do not need to be convinced, uncle!" she
exclaimed. "When you tell me, that is enough.
Surely there çan be no better authority than yourself,
after you have given your whole life to the study?—"

He slung his vasculum over his shoulder; he put his
hand in affectionate fashion within her arm; and together they proceeded to descend the hill—down
through the larches that were moving and whispering
in the light and varying breeze.

"You see, Bry," he continued, in a grave and matter-of-fact manner (for he would not betray too much
exultation), "this Scoulter Hill is very well known as
the habitat of many rare or at least uncommon plants;
and among them is the *Linnœa borealis*. Not that the
Linnœa is so very rare, but the fruit of it is—very rare
indeed: Hooker says he had to take the description of
it from Wahlenberg. Well, you understand, I have
never given up the hope of some day stumbling on
a branch of the *Linnœa* bearing fruit—even in the
spring or early summer—for it is an evergreen shrub
and tolerably hardy—and in a sheltered place in the
woods there might always be a chance of the fruit
hanging on through the winter. And I was pottering
about"—here he began to talk a little more quickly—
"I was pottering about. I had no thought of Don, or
of the Don family, or of the scepticism that has re-
jected so many of their discoveries. I was not thinking of any *Silene*, or any of the disputed Saxifrages, or
anything of the kind; it was the dark green leaves of
the *Linnœa* I was looking for; and not very anxiously
either. Then of a sudden"—and now he was speaking in an eager, half breathless way—"of a sudden I

saw something: it was like a slap in the face: for a
second my eyes seemed quite bewildered. For I knew
—oh yes, I knew instantly what it was!—I knew the
gap that the stranger filled; and the oddest thing happened—all in the flash of a moment it appeared to me
as if I were answering back to this authority and that
authority—this one in Edinburgh and that one at Kew
—as if I were saying to them: 'Ah, perhaps you will
now be a little less ready to add "not confirmed"
when any one sends you the report of a discovery from
Clova or from Dee-side; and perhaps you will be less
distrustful about Don's contributions to the British
flora; and perhaps, considering the height and the
whereabouts of Scoulter Hill, you won't find the
phrase "a garden escape" sufficient to account for
everything.' Briseis, I think they will open their eyes
a little!" he went on—and he laughed in his nervous,
excited way. "They will begin to doubt their doubts
—and that's the fact. They will begin to think that
a thorough search of the whole of the Clova mountains
might be more serviceable than dismissing every un-
confirmed discovery with contempt. The rehabilita-
tion of the Don family? Well, I never thought that
necessary—and I never proposed it to myself as an object—never—but still—but still—"

And so he continued talking, garrulous and restless
beyond his wont, while they held on their way down
into the valley, and crossed the Dee by the gray stone
bridge, and went along and into the village of Sanchory. It is a quiet and still little hamlet, with one
large and wide main thoroughfare, a straggling row of
houses on each side of the spacious street, an inn, a
church, and a number of small villas scattered about
among gardens. But it is these gardens, especially in
early summer, that redeem Sanchory from what other-

wise would be its commonplaceness of look; for wherever
one turns—glancing down a lane or over a wall—there
is a profusion of vivid, luminous, trembling leaves and
branches; and always through the young translucent
green of this immediate foliage there is visible here
and there the deep, soft rose-purple of the distant
hills.   As old John Elliott and his niece Briseis now
walked up to the Gordon Arms, there was a hot glare
of sunlight abroad, and the wide thoroughfare was
quite empty.

That was a busy afternoon for both of them.   For
what with his anxious temperament and the greatness
of the occasion, the old botanist's hand was rather
shaky, so that it fell to his niece's lot to take down
from his dictation the telegrams to one or two learned
professors and the letters to certain familiar friends
which he composed as he paced up and down the
small room.   And then again at dinner—these preliminary announcements having been got rid of—he was
still unusually talkative, and apparently he was very
happy; he said some pretty things about the young
lady's looks and the neatness of her dress; and he was
generously insistent that she should share with him
the small bottle of claret which was his modest daily
allowance.   She only shook her head, however.   She
was ready enough to fill his glass for him—but her
own remained empty: she was like Fair Annie in the
old ballad—

> ' O, she has served the lang tables,
>   Wi' the white bread and the wine;
> But aye she drank the wan water,
>   To keep her colour fine.'

Nay, rambling on from mood to mood, he at length
grew remorseful.

"Briseis," he said, "I do think you are the most admirable companion that God ever created. Nothing comes amiss to you; whatever happens, it is always for the best; I never saw such content, such good-will, such a kindly disposition. But all the same—all the same I am convinced I ought not to allow you to sacrifice yourself in this way. It is pure selfishness on my part. You should be living in Edinburgh or London, seeing young people of your own age, mixing in society, going to theatres and concerts and dances. You should not have elected to join my wandering life; you should have gone to your Aunt Clara—" —

Her eyes—those lustrous, dark, expressive eyes—looked amused.

"Uncle, uncle," she said, "you are not going to forsake me, are you? I know well enough what every one else would say of me. They would say that I was useless and lazy and idle, and that I had no right to shirk my part of the work of the world, and go away and lie on a hillside, doing nothing but drink in the sweet air. And all that would be quite true. But then, it is for you to defend me. You are my ally. You should tell them that I am not entirely useless; for if I were to let you go away into these lonely places all by yourself, some day or other the Elfin Queen would be carrying you off into captivity and keeping you hidden for twenty long years—"

"There is another thing too," he proceeded, still harping on these hesitations. "There is your music. They tell me that your natural gift is quite wonderful —your facility and touch on the piano quite wonderful; and that you ought to go into training at the Royal Academy of Music, to perfect your technique—"

"*Eucharisto!*" she exclaimed, laughing, yet not at all scornfully. "For what would the next step be?

1*

Why, if I succeeded, I should have to play in large concert-rooms, and earn much money. Many thanks, yes !—but the little money I have is sufficient for my wants, and I do not even have to trouble with a banker, since you are so kind as to look after it for me. And as for the concert-rooms, and meeting people, and making acquaintances, well, I do not like town life at all. It does not interest me. The air stifles me. It is different when I am wandering among the valleys and the mountains with you, uncle—ah, and such splendid wanderings !—from Clova up to Atholl, from Atholl to Braemar, from Braemar all along Dee-side. *Sas hupereucharisto !* — but I have no ambition to appear at St. James's Hall !"

"As you please, Briseis, as you please," he replied, thoughtfully; and seeing that he had finished dinner, she now went to the mantel-shelf and filled his wooden pipe, and brought it over to him, along with the matches. And then she turned the conversation back to the great discovery of the morning—so that he had soon dismissed these passing clouds. Nay, he grew garrulous and exultant again; and would have her fetch this or that botanical cyclopædia, to convince her who was already convinced. There could be little doubt but that the plant they had found on the summit of Scoulter Hill was in reality the *Silene alpestris*, the Alpine catchfly.

Nevertheless, that same night, when all the little village had sunk into slumber—Briseis too, most likely, for she had for some time been gone to her room—the outer door of the Gordon Arms was stealthily opened, and a small, dark figure stole out. It was late; but there was still a pale and steely glow up in the north-western heavens; and this half-light produced a kind of wan grayness on the wide thoroughfare and on the fronts of the houses: the trees alone were black. The profoundest silence reigned; not a horse whinnied in its stall; not a dog barked a false alarm. And through the sleeping hamlet this small dark figure—which was that of the old botanist—pursued its noiseless way, eventually passing into the road that leads down to the bridge over the Dee. Then, as he went on, there came a murmur into the stillness of the night—an eerie sound—the sound of some unseen thing in this world of all-pervading death—the low-murmuring voice of the river. He crossed the bridge; but he could only listen—there was no glint of water underneath. Then on again into the strange peace and hush of the country: it seemed to him as though he could have heard the faintest click for miles away, the silence was so absolute. Nor was there any sign or symptom of life; not even a rabbit scurried away from beneath the hedge-rows; he was the sole occupant of this mute and inanimate universe, in its dusk of metallic gray.

But when he entered the woods, and proceeded to follow as best he might the ever-ascending path through the trees, even that faint guidance from the western skies was denied him, so that he had to remove the cap from the dark-lantern that he carried, letting the ball of orange fire glare out on the phantasmal stems of Scotch fir and larch and spruce. Slow progress, perhaps, as he toiled up the winding track, with the spectral limbs and branches starting out here and there from the surrounding gloom; but there was something in his heart and brain that had to be satisfied; there could have been no sleep for him that night while any nervous and torturing dread might keep suggesting that he had been the victim of an extraordinary hallucination. And at last he emerged from the black ob-

scurity of the trees; there was a colder breath of air stirring; he found himself on the open plateau of heather
and rock; and if the lingering twilight in the north-
west was fading down into the transient darkness of
the short summer night, at least he had with him this
blazing will-o'-the-wisp that swung in his hand as he
warily went forward.

Warily indeed he went; for though the bull's-eye of
the lantern glared fiercely enough, the light that it
shed on the herbage was pale and ineffectual, and revealed almost nothing of color. But at length, after
much searching, he came upon patches of small white
dots. He knelt down — as Briseis had done. He
brought the lantern close—and peered—and examined
— just touching here and there with a finger-nail.
And finally he rose to his feet again, with a sigh of
immeasurable relief and satisfaction.

"There is not a shadow of a doubt!" he said to himself. "And to morrow—or the day after to-morrow
—some folk in the south will be opening their eyes!"

CHAPTER II

THE GORDONS OF GRANTLY

ON the following morning old John Elliott conveyed to his niece, with his usual shy and sensitive round-aboutness, that he would rather be left alone. He had to prepare the more formal communications respecting his discovery to be sent to certain learned Societies—especially with the view of showing that, from the position of Scoulter Hill, the *Silene alpestris* he had found there could not possibly have been a garden es-cape. But, he added, when these memoranda had been roughly drawn out, perhaps Briseis would be so kind as to copy them for him in her neat and accurate handwriting? And in the mean time she might go and amuse herself in exploring the surrounding neigh-borhood.

Well, she was nothing loath; for in truth she was an idle wretch, as she herself had admitted; always glad to get into the open air; content to have nothing to do but gaze abroad upon wild flowers, and clouds, and hills; and more than content when she chanced to have a box of chocolate-creams in her pocket. So she put on her black straw hat with its spray of crimson blos-som; and she took her crimson sunshade with her, lest the direct rays in the valley should prove too oppres-sive; and a few seconds thereafter she was march-ing along the wide, empty thoroughfare, leisurely enough, yet with the bold freedom of step that

her long legs gave her.　And she was repeating to
herself:

> 'Down Dee-side rode Inverey, whistling and playing,
>   He rapped loud at Brackley gate, erc the day's dawing:
> "O Gordon of Brackley, proud Gordon, come down;
>   There's a sword at your threshold mair sharp than your
>   own." '

For this was a country-side haunted everywhere with
historical and legendary associations; and while her
uncle was entirely engrossed with his botanical pursuits she had had plenty of time for the reading up of
the old ballads; and it was with the intensest interest
that she had come upon or hunted up this or that
place mentioned in those wild tales of love and sorrow
and tragic farewell, of war and hatred and passionate
revenge.　The two of them, uncle and niece, had been
down in Glen Prosen and Glen Shee, where 'the gallant Grahams' assembled:

> 'In Glen Prosen we rendezvoused,
>   Marched to Glen Shee by night and day,
> And took the town of Aberdeen,
>   And met the Campbells in their array.'

They had come round by Atholl:

> 'As I went in by the Duke of Atholl's yett,
>   I heard a fair maid singing;
> Her voice was sweet, she sang sae complete,
>   And the bells o' the court were ringing.'

She had seen the ruined castle of Inverey, and the
remaining stones of Brackley; she had crossed the
fatal burn of Corrichie:

> 'Mourn ye Hielands, and mourn ye Lowlands,
>   I trow ye hae mickle need;
> For the bonnie burn o' Corrichie
>   Has run this day wi' bleid.'

But perhaps it was the pathetic story of the two Gordons that kept most frequently recurring to her brain, now as she got away from the village, her tall, slim figure erect, her light and easy and graceful step taking her quite rapidly enough out into the open country:

'"Arise now, gay Gordon!' his lady 'gan cry:
"For there is fierce Inverey driving your kye."
"How can I go, lady, and win them again,
When I have but ae sword where he has got ten?"

'"Arise, now, my maidens, leave rock and leave fan;
How blest had I been had I married a man!—
Arise, now, my maidens, take lance and take sword:
Go, milk the ewes, Gordon, for I will be lord!"

'Up sprang the brave Gordon, put his helm on his head,
Laid his hand on his sword, and his thigh o'er his steed;
But he stooped low and said, as he kissed his proud dame—
"There's a Gordon rides out that will never ride hame."

'There rode wi' fierce Inverey thirty-and-three,
And nane wi' the Gordon save his brother and he;
Twa gallanter Gordons did never sword draw,
But against three-and-thirty, woe's me! what were twa?'

But here she stopped, in her idle and absent repetition. For she had arrived at a field of young corn, and somewhere over her head there was a lark pouring forth his melodious silvery trills, and she wanted to discover where he was. Yet in vain did she endeavor to pierce the blinding white spaces of the sky; he was nowhere visible; though all the listening air was filled with those pulsating floods of song. So she carelessly wandered on again, not heeding much whither she went; keeping by the outer edge of the corn-fields, now and again skirting some strip of copse or spinney, and gazing with delight into the dim recesses, for all around the foot of the trees were masses of a heavenly blue—not the purple-blue of the wild hyacinth, but the clear, intense, ·pellucid blue of the germander speedwell. And then, as she still held onward, it seemed to her as though another sound were invading —or increasing—the silence of the summer morn : a sound hushed and remote — a murmur constant and unvarying—and more voluminous than the soft stirring of the leaves around her. Had she then, in this for- tuitous fashion, drawn near the river? But why not? On Dee-side all roads, paths, and byways eventually lead to the Dee.

Of a sudden she came upon the verge of a steep bank, which was crowned by scattered clumps of Scotch firs; and there before her, stretching away over to the high and wooded slopes on the other side, was the broad bosom of the stream, the swaying and hurrying current sweeping round the dark brown pools with an easy oily swing, and then breaking away again into the open shallows, racing and chasing, sharp-glinting and shimmering in the glare of the morning light, while a great breadth and blaze of quivering diamonds lay immediately under the sun. Then, after some little survey, she pitched upon a sheltered nook for herself; and it was through a perfect paradise of wild flowers that she descended to the river—through masses of gorse and broom, with heartsease, dog-violets, yellow bedstraw, speedwells of various kinds and hues, and glossy and golden celandine all basking in the heat. It was a gracious bower she had chosen for herself, by the side of an alder - bush, and overlooking a rather deepish bit of the water; and here with much com- placency she sat herself down to listen to that monoto- nous, dreamy, drowsy sound, and also to the music of a thrush that was carolling clear and high from among the neighboring leaves. This was a beautiful world she found herself in; and she had it all to herself.

The river glanced, and chased, and swung along; the gorse burned in the sunshine; the pervading stillness seemed only to be intensified by that universal murmur and whispering. And it was in a kind of half-somnolent mood that her purposeless brain went back to the story of the two Gordons who were so foully done to death by Inverey and his three-and-thirty men:

'"O came ye by Brackley, and what saw ye there?
Was the young widow weeping and tearing her hair?"
"I came down by Brackley; I looked in, and, oh!
There was mirth, there was feasting, but naething o' woe.

'"Like a rose bloomed the lady and blithe as a bride,
A bridegroom young Inverey stood by her side;
She feasted him there as she ne'er feasted lord,
Though the bluid o' her husband was red on his sword."

'O there's dule in the cottage, but there's mirth in the ha',
For the twa bonnie Gordons that are deid and awa';
To the bush comes the bud, and the flower to the plain,
But the twa gallant Gordons come never again.'

And she was thinking that when next her uncle and herself were anywhere near Glen Muick she would like to go and see Auchoilzie, where the two brave Gordons were slain: she was thinking of that, or perhaps of something else, or perhaps of nothing at all — when—

When suddenly a silver-white object leapt into the air away on the other side of the river, falling again with a startling splash on to the surface of the oily, smooth, brown pool, and instantly disappeared. She stared in astonishment. What was the unknown creat-

ure that had so marvellously shown itself in this solitary world that she had thought was tenanted by herself alone? Then she reflected: the Dee was a noted
salmon river—that must have been a salmon! And
then again, as she regarded with the most eager interest that smooth stretch of the stream, she perceived something — she perceived some faint semblance of a thread — a gray gossamer line only just
visible against the herbage of the opposite shore. Instinctively her eyes followed upwards: the next moment she became aware that this long line ended
in a fishing-rod, and that the fishing-rod was in
the hands of some one—gentleman or gamekeeper—
who was coming rapidly along her side of the river,
reeling in as he advanced. Very well. She would sit
still and see the novel sport. For there is not much
doing with rod and reel in the arid channels of the
Cephissus, nor yet where the washerwomen of the
Ilissus ply their calling in the turbid pond once the
Fountain of Callirrhoë; nor were the fishermen of her
island-home of Ægina likely to find a salmon in their
nets. She would wait and look on. Here was a tale
to carry back to her uncle.

But her equanimity was of short duration. For, to
her dismay, she observed, by the manner in which that
gray thread was cutting the surface of the stream, that
the fish must be making straight in her direction; and
presently, as the tightened and straining line was actually forcing its way in among the branches of the alder-
bush, she beheld beneath her feet an olive-green creature that had come sailing into the pool, and was now
hanging there almost motionless, its tail alone slightly
moving, its head boring down. What to do she knew
not. She had a terrified sense of being in the wrong
somehow—she ought not to be there—her intrusion

could but make mischief—and was there not enough
peril brewing with that taut line working in among the
alder leaves? Breathless, bewildered, she regarded
that creature in the deeps below her, not with a
pleased interest, but a shrinking alarm; and at length,
overcome with this nervous apprehension, she could
sit still no longer; she swiftly and stealthily struggled
to her feet, and retreated up the bank, glad to find a
place of shelter behind a clump of Scotch firs. When
she ventured to peep forth to see what was going on,
she perceived that the fish had headed out again into
midstream, while the fisherman seemed to be doing all
he could to pull him away from the proximity of that
dangerous bush.

Now when the fascinated eyes of Briseis Valieri had
been fixed on the mysterious object that lay suspended
in the pool, she had assumed that it was a large salmon;
but it was nothing of the sort: it was a small grilse of
about six or seven pounds; and when a grilse of that
size is inclined to be lively, it forms an excellent imitation of an electrical battery, that keeps sending continuous shocks not to the wrists only, but to the very
innermost soul of the angler. Of course Briseis, from
behind the firs, could only in part make out what the
beast was after. First he held steadily over to the
other side, until the weight of the long and bellying
line gave him pause. Then he appeared on the surface, lashing and splashing with head and tail, and
churning the water all around him; and in these fitful
glimpses he was no longer of a dull olive green but of
a brilliant silver and purple. Then he disappeared;
and the attaching gray thread remained motionless.
Then with an appalling rapidity he shot right in the
direction of his captor, who was seen to go backward
along the bank as best he might, while he frantically

reeled in until the top of the rod had resumed its curve. Then the indomitable small creature made over to the other side again, and for a few seconds he lay there and sulked. Then he began to move—slowly—slowly —until there was a sudden slackening of the line, and a sinuous flash of splendor sprang into the air, coming down again with a crash. All this was very well, and very heroic; but these successive discharges from the electrical battery were diminishing its power. After that last flourish the gallant little grilse grew more and more amenable; he suffered himself to be towed nearer and nearer; the angler took from his pocket a bright metal instrument and adjusted it; he shifted his rod to his left hand, holding it high; he watched his chance—then there was a cautious stoop—a quick gleam of the gaff—and the next moment the flapping and struggling fish was on the bank. The absorbed spectator behind the trees imagined that this vicissitudinous fight must have lasted an hour: in reality it had occupied precisely eight minutes.

And now that she could breathe a little more freely she thought she would step forth from her hiding-place, and walk along the bank, and apologize to the angler for her untoward presence. Whether he were gentleman or gillie she could not make out as yet; for he wore the ordinary costume—knickerbockers, shooting-jacket, and stalker's cap; and he was stooping to fix a bit of string to the grilse, for the easier carrying of it home. But the moment he became aware that she was coming his way, and evidently with the intention of speaking to him, he dropped the fish, he most respectfully raised his cap, and even made some show of advancing to meet her, to await her commands. He was a tall and firmly built young fellow of about five-and-twenty, well-featured and pleasant of look, with clear gray-blue eyes that seemed all the clearer because of the light yellow sun-tan of his complexion. He appeared a little surprised—and no wonder: for apparitions such as he now saw before him are not common on Dee-side.

As for her, she went forward without the least trace of shyness; no touch of added color was visible in the pure, pale, transparent olive of cheek or forehead. It is true, her eyes seemed to bespeak a little favoring consideration; but that was only natural—as she was a culprit.

"I wish to ask your pardon," she said, with great sweetness—and surely since ever the world began no more musically-toned voice had ever reached a young man's ears—"I wish to ask your pardon, sir, if I have done any harm. I had no idea you were fishing—"

"Oh, but it's quite the other way round!" said he, promptly, and even anxiously. "Quite the other way round, I assure you! You did me a very good turn indeed; I am exceedingly obliged to you. Your getting up on the bank frightened the fish out into the stream when he was very nearly breaking me in that alder-bush. I am extremely obliged to you—"

The Greek girl's dark and lustrous eyes, with their highly curved, wondering, attentive eyebrows, looked pleased.

"That is fortunate — very fortunate indeed," said she, with a smile of thanks. "But I will not run any such risk again. I will keep away from the river—"

"Oh, I hope not!" he protested. "Why should you? What possible harm can you do? For one thing, this isn't fishing weather at all. I was not even trying the ordinary pools; I was merely putting a fly over one or two of the runs; as you see, I did not think it

worth while to bring a gillie with me. You must not
dream of keeping away from the river !—"

Shyness and embarrassment?—they were certainly
not on her side. It was he who was disconcerted and
bewildered; the splendor of her eyes abashed him;
this slim slip of a girl, in the sweet graciousness of her
self-possession, was stronger than he; he hardly knew
what to say next. And yet he had to make some desperate effort, or in another moment she would be away
—vanishing out of his life as though she had never
existed.

"I hope you won't think me rude," said he, "but—
but there are few visitors coming about these parts at this
time of the year; and I wonder whether it could have
been you that I saw yesterday, from a distance, going
into the Gordon Arms, along with an elderly gentleman. For the day before I had a note, dated from the
inn, from a Mr. Elliott—"

"That is my uncle," said she, simply.

"And I was very glad to give him any permission
he may have thought necessary—" he was continuing,
when she interrupted him.

"Then you are Sir Francis Gordon?" she said, her
face lighting up with interest.

"Yes—"

"Oh, but I must thank you ever so much for the
very kind and friendly note you sent to my uncle. He
would have written to you himself, but he has been so
busy yesterday and this morning—"

"I am sure there is no occasion," said he—and perhaps the subtle freemasonry of youth was already establishing itself between these two; perhaps for the
moment they had forgotten town proprieties; surely,
it seemed natural enough and right enough, strangers
as they were, for these two young folk to be tarrying

and interchanging a few half-hesitating words here
on the banks of the cool-murmuring stream, in the
blaze of sunlight, among the wild flowers of the early
summer. "Nor was there much need," he went on,
"that your uncle should ask permission to go through
the Grantly woods. One thing is very certain: it is
the people who have the courtesy to ask permission
who can be trusted everywhere not to do any injury—"

"Oh, I assure you," said Briseis, "that my uncle is
most scrupulous—most scrupulous, to the smallest particulars. If we are away for the whole day, and have
our scrap of luncheon on some hill-side or on the bank
of a burn, he has every little bit of wrapping-paper and
every little bit of string carefully buried, so that not
the least trace shall remain."

"If they were all like that!" said he, ruefully. "I
wonder if the tourists and excursionists know how
many private parks and grounds are closed against
them that might otherwise be open to them but for
their thoughtless behavior? Why, later on in the year,
when a band of excursionists comes out from Aberdeen
to this neighborhood, what do they immediately set
about?—putting their dogs to hunt the rabbits, breaking off branches from the flowering shrubs, and strew-
ing the place all over with empty lemonade-bottles,
and paper bags stained with strawberries. It is ignorance of course. They don't know any better. But it
is distressing to go about the next morning and see the
litter they have left behind them—even on the lawn
seats and the terraces—everywhere about. Naturally
the gardeners complain; it is all added work to them;
and they would have me adopt a policy of rigorous
exclusion. I don't like to do that either. I don't
want to play dog in the manger. I'm sure those people would be heartily welcome if they'd only be a

little more considerate — if they could be got to understand how unfair it is—" Then all at once he
jammed down his helm and was off on another tack:
this was not the way to entertain a young lady. "It
has just occurred to me, Miss Elliott," said he—and she
did not care to correct the little mistake—"that I
could get much more extended permission for you and
your uncle if you were remaining in this country-side.
I could get you letters that would make you free of
the forests, and would secure for you help rather than
hindrance from the keepers—"

"Indeed, we have always found them most civil,"
she answered him; "though sometimes they have
seemed anxious that we should go away down to the
valleys again—"

"That may have been when you were getting too
near the sanctuary," said he. "But if I get you those
letters, you would find both keepers and watchers only
too ready to be your guide. Will you allow me? If I
can get one or two for you by to-morrow afternoon,
may I call with them?"

"Oh, thank you, it is so very kind of you—my uncle
will be so much obliged to you!" said she. And then
she gave him one of her sweetest smiles — with her
eyes; and a little bow as well; and turned away and
was gone: leaving him standing there as if he had
been in dreamland, and vaguely wondering why he
had been such an immeasurable fool as not to have
offered to shake hands with her on parting.

When Briseis returned to the inn, she told her uncle
of her having met Sir Francis Gordon of Grantly, and
of the young man having promised to bring along one
or two letters which might be of use to them when
they happened to be in the neighborhood of the deer
forests.

"Civility," said the old botanist, "is the best pass-port everywhere. I have never found it fail. In all my years of wandering in Scotland I have never had to bandy a word with any one, when once I had explained my errand, and asked for information as to where I should be doing no harm."

Nevertheless, when on the following afternoon young Gordon drove up to the inn, and alighted from the dog-cart, and was shown into the room where uncle and niece had been respectively writing and reading, Mr. Elliott was profuse of thanks for those talismanic missives that had been procured in so remarkably short a space of time.

"Oh, that is nothing—that is but a trifling courtesy to one of your name and lineage," said this young Frank Gordon, who had a most pleasant and modest manner. "No doubt they were very glad to be of the slightest service to you; there are few families in Scotland better known or more respected than the Elliotts of the Lea."

At this the old botanist blushed slightly, and glanced furtively towards his niece; for the fact is he had not told Briseis that in writing to Sir Francis Gordon for permission to explore the Grantly woods he had contrived to mention his kinsmanship with that famous house, as some kind of voucher for his petition. But Briseis did not notice; she had turned to this young stranger, who seemed so kindly intentioned, and so anxious to win favor.

"Oh, and I am very proud of the name too," said she, smiling, "though I myself have no right to it."

Frank Gordon looked perplexed, and even a little embarrassed; but of course he could not put a question. It was old John Elliott who interposed.

2

"My niece," said he, "is an Elliott only by her mother's side—my sister, poor thing."

And as these tentative explanations appeared to involve some trifle of constraint—pointing to the absence of any formal introduction, and so forth—Briseis herself resolved the situation by asking their guest whether he would not have some tea. He thankfully accepted; and for the moment the difficulty was got over; though he was all the time conscious that he did not even yet know her name.

He staid an indefensible length of time; for they were practically strangers to this district; and he had plenty to tell them about where they ought to go and what they ought to see. And for the most part he addressed himself to the old botanist; when in the course of talk he had to turn to this beautiful Greek creature, it was in a diffident sort of way; he seemed afraid of the glow of those splendid black eyes. And yet, afraid or not afraid, nothing would satisfy him but that uncle and niece should come out the very next day to have a look over Grantly Castle.

"It isn't much of a show-place," said he, "though the excursionists from Aberdeen appear to think it is. And if we cannot let you see a Fairy Flag, such as they have at Dunvegan, or a Brooch of Lorn, such as they have at Dunollie, still there are a few things might interest you; aud besides that, the Castle itself is a very good specimen of the Scotch baronial style of architecture. You might pass an hour or two—"

Old John Elliott looked timidly and inquiringly towards his niece; and she responded frankly enough—

"Oh, thank you very much; we shall be delighted: my uncle deserves a rest after his labors of the last two days. And what hour will be most convenient for you?"

"No, no; what hour will be most convenient for you? The gardens are freshest in the morning, of course. But perhaps it will be better to leave it this way: 'Come as soon as you can, and stay as long as you can'—and that's a Dee-side welcome."

Thereupon young Gordon got up to say good-bye; and this time he did not forget to shake hands with the Greek girl; while she did not hesitate to bestow on him a look of great sweetness, as if to thank him again for his kindness to two strangers. There was some final understanding that they were to go out to Grantly Castle on the following morning.

He drove rapidly home, paused for a second to let the groom get to the cob's head, then he descended, and walked into the big stone-paved hall. On the table there were a number of letters lying; and these he carelessly took up, to look at the envelopes. But one of them appeared to arrest his attention; the address was in a foreign hand:

À Son Altesse Royale, le prince de Monteveltro:
Chez Monsieur,
M. sir Francis Gordon,
Grantly Castle,
Aberdeenshire,
Ecosse.

He turned from the table, and sent his voice echoing through the hollow-sounding hall:

"Aunt Jean!—are you anywhere about?—Aunt Jean—are you there?"

"Here I am, laddie: what is't you want?" a voice answered him; and presently, at the top of the wide oaken staircase, there appeared Miss Jean Gordon. She was a tall and fair-complexioned woman, rather elderly and rather plain, but with cheerful and good-humored eyes.

"Didn't you see this?" he said to her, holding out the letter. "Does it mean that the Mater is coming on here at once, just as I had got everything ready to go up to London?"

He advanced to the foot of the staircase; she came down the steps, and took the envelope from him, and regarded it.

"No, no," said she, "there must be some mistake. Your mother's last letter to me was from Nice; and she said they meant to go straight through to London, to Thomas's Hotel, and would be there for a considerable time. This must be the blundering of some courier or valet—"

He received the letter back and looked at it thoughtfully.

"I never know what that excellent step-papa of mine may be up to," he observed. "He may be wanting to escape out of the hands of the diplomats and seek sanctuary here — for himself and his two black poodles." Then of a sudden he changed his tone. "Aunt Jean," said he, "we are going to have two visitors here to-morrow—two strangers to the neighborhood, who would like to look over the Castle and about the grounds. And I didn't ask them formally to lunch; but to-morrow, when they are here anyway, and when it's about lunch-time, I mean to propose it promiscuous-like; and of course they will stay. And I wish you would see that McKillop sends in plenty of flowers for the table—and for decoration all about—plenty of them—plenty— Confound him, he's nothing but an old miser—"

"Is she so very pretty, Frank?" Aunt Jean inquired, with a demure smile.

"Who told you there was a 'she' in the case?" he demanded, loftily.

"There usually is," said Miss Jean Gordon. "Especially when a young gentleman is so particular about flowers for the luncheon table."

"Very well, then, Aunt Jean, I will tell you honestly: she is just about the most beautiful creature you ever beheld; and I don't see why you shouldn't be as much interested in her as I am; I don't see why you should think there's nothing in the world worth admiring except old china and old lace. You know, Aunt Jean, I'm not much given to rave about young women; but you should see this one; why, she bewilders you—"

"She won't bewilder me," said Aunt Jean, shrewdly.

"She is a Greek girl," he continued—and it seemed to afford him much pleasure to stand there and talk eagerly about the marvellous stranger. "I gathered as much from her Christian name—which isn't Christian, by-the-way, but pagan. A Greek goddess she is! —in figure, and height, and symmetry; but not of the severe type either—oh, no!—most womanly and winning in expression. Beautiful?—but wait till you see! What I can't understand is why she should have remained unmarried! She must have seen lots of men —in her own country—in England—even wandering about on those botanizing excursions with her uncle— men presumably with eyes in their head—"

"She may not wish to be married," retorted Miss Jean, rather tartly. "Why should she? They say that a woman ought to marry in order to have an object. Well, when she does, she generally gets one!"

Jean Gordon—Jean Gordon! But now she was moving off—for the dressing-bell was beginning to sound; and she was as particular about the punctuality of dinner as though there had been twenty guests staying in the house.

CHAPTER III

But next morning found old John Elliott in an apprehensive, restless, fidgety mood; nay, he was inclined to be peevish and fretful.

"I'm not used to going among strangers, Briseis," he said. "I don't like it—it worries me—"

"Why, uncle," she remonstrated, "didn't you hear Sir Francis say there was no one staying at the Castle —no one except his aunt, who always lives there—"

"And it is too far for you to walk, along a dusty road," he continued, plaintively. "Even if they have a dog-cart at the inn here, there would be the cost of it—for what?—the expense of a dog-cart—for what?"

Now part of this conversation had been overheard by the servant-lass who was bringing in breakfast; and she, with the friendly familiarity of the Scotch domestic, made no scruple about intervening.

"I beg your pardon, sir," said she, "but there's a wagonette and pair come in from Grantly, sir, and they're in the stable-yard, and the coachman says Sir Francis ordered him jist to wait for your convenience, sir."

"Oh, well, I suppose we must go," the old botanist said to his niece, though with evident reluctance. "I suppose there will be no further letters until the afternoon post—"

"Uncle," she answered him, coaxingly, "you must

give those people in the south a little time. In the
case of the Societies you could not expect an answer
until after their next meeting, when the various Sec-
retaries will be asked to acknowledge your communication—"

"But there were the telegrams to my personal
friends—"

"And what could they reply?" she went on, in her
persuasive and musical tones. "No doubt they were
very glad to learn of the discovery; and no doubt they
thought you were very lucky. Of course you will hear
from them sooner or later, when they have leisure to
write; but in the mean time you must have a day or
two of idleness; and then we will set to work again—
that is, you will set to work, and make more wonderful
discoveries, and I will tramp over the hills with you,
and wish I could be of some help."

It was difficult to withstand the subtle and singular
charm of her voice; he usually yielded, and yield he
did on this occasion; so that about eleven o'clock the
wagonette was brought round to the front of the inn,
and uncle and niece went out and took their places.
Then ensued a most blithe and inspiriting drive along
the valley of the Dee, the winding road giving them
occasional glimpses of the broad-sweeping and glancing stream, or again plunging them into scattered
woods of larch and birch and pine. Then they came
to a lodge gate and entered; the wagonette rolled
smoothly along the wide carriageway; until of a sudden
Briseis grasped the arm of her companion, who had at
the moment been plunged in profound meditation:

"Look, uncle, look!—isn't it noble!—isn't it splendid!"

And yet this tall and gaunt keep was not imposing
by reason of its spacious dimensions, though otherwise

it was picturesque enough. The structure was lofty
in proportion to its restricted base; the windows were
for the most part narrow, deeply-recessed, scattered
unevenly here and there; the surmounting angle tur-
rets had conical roofs suggestive of French Gothic;
the gables showed 'corbie-steps'; and crowning all, up
against the blue and white, a weather-cock was perched
airily on a tiny golden ball. A building of solid and
severe aspect, perhaps; but the surrounding grounds
were more modern and more cheerful — the trim terraces, the grassy slopes velvet-smooth, the long range of
greenhouses, the blazing masses of color in flower beds
and plots, the partition-walls smothered in the dark
green foliage of apricot and fig, the sunlit woods trend-
ing down to the river. From this high plateau, indeed,
there was a wide-stretching view, not the least conspicuous feature being Scoulter Hill with its ruined
tower, far away in the silvery west.

And here was the young laird coming bareheaded
down the steps to receive his guests; and up there at
the hall door was Miss Jean Gordon, her shrewd eyes
not too evidently scanning. The welcome that the visitors now received was of the most friendly kind — in
its Scotch fashion almost too insistent—for who wanted
cake and wine and fruit at this time of the day?—and
who needed rest after so pleasant a drive? — in truth,
Briseis, who was ever hungry and athirst for sweet air,
and sunshine, and open landscape—Briseis so avowedly
lingered without—gazing abroad on the variegated garden, and the glimpses of the river through the trees,
and the rising and swelling uplands beyond — that
young Gordon was forced to alter the form of his invitation.

"Perhaps you would rather stroll about for a bit,"
he suggested, "and have a look at the greenhouses?"

"Oh, yes; wouldn't you, uncle?" she made answer, promptly. "They are such beautiful gardens! I have not seen any gardens like these since we were at Drummond Castle in Perthshire."—And if the young laird was in any way proud of his paternal inheritance, that was a compliment surely!

So the four of them set forth on a sauntering perambulation, walking two and two for convenience' sake; they passed under the canopied vines, house after house; then out again, and through part of the 'policies' skirting the woods; then back into the basking and brilliant garden. And while the old botanist was descanting to Miss Jean on the origin of this or that cultivated plant or shrub, young Frank Gordon, with a shy ingenuity, was putting questions to his companion, about herself, her knowledge of Scotland, her pursuits, while also he was incidentally telling her a great deal about his own occupations and plans. Briseis listened with a smiling acquiescence; she did not say much, but her eyes were amiable; and whether she spoke or was silent, she seemed to be drinking in the beauty of the things around her with a constant and perhaps half-unconscious delight. The fragrance wafted hither and thither, the warm sweet air, the sunshine and azure sky, the radiant glow of color in the garden, the stir and silver-glancing of glossy leaves: these were happy surroundings — for a gracelessly idle creature, whose chief and distinguishing faculty appeared to be that of enjoying every minute and second of her life.

Then, as they chanced to be walking along one of the upper terraces, Frank Gordon pulled out his watch.

"Just luncheon-time!" he cried. "Come away in —Aunt Jean will tell you that starvation and fainting fits are not allowed at Grantly."

2*

It was not a very sumptuous banqueting-hall they
were ushered into—this long, low apartment, with its
wainscot of panelled oak and its five or six plain windows; but it had some interesting family portraits—
the men of them appearing by their uniform to have
been mostly admirals and generals; and it had several
fiery and fuliginous battle-pieces, chiefly of naval engagements; while the luncheon table was set forth in
quite a bright modern way, with an abundance of flowers. And perhaps Jean Gordon, who sat at the head
of the board, was listening to the old botanist's tale of
his many experiences in the wilder parts of Scotland,
or perhaps she was only perfunctorily heeding him; at
all events, she beheld what she had never beheld before, and that was the assiduous and diffident and respectful court that her nephew was paying to this Greek
girl with the gracious ways and the resplendent eyes.
Well did the amused Miss Jean know that this was not
at all the young man's ordinary habit. She was acquainted with him. She had studied him—in no unfriendly fashion either. And she had heard tell of him
at Oxford too: how that even during Commemoration
week those pretty pieces of femininity who come fluttering from college to college like so many butterflies appeared to have no attraction for him whatever. Nor
could it be said that this was owing to cruel neglect on
the side of those young persons; they seemed willing
to accord him a fair share of notice; for he was exceedingly good-looking, and he was merry and pleasant-
humored and ever ready for a frolic; but somehow his
soul was rather set on sports and athletics; and when
these happened to fail him, a pipe and a meditative
stroll along the tow-path appeared better to suit his
fancy than consorting with muslin. But now—but now!
Jean Gordon's demure eyes saw a good deal more than

they seemed to see. Not that there was any intentional sentimentalizing on the lad's part; no trace of such a thing was in his nature; the frank and open good-comradeship he was ready to offer to any one whom he chanced to meet and like was not of a kind to lead to the little appeals and secret understandings of sham love-making. Indeed, what Miss Jean chiefly remarked on this occasion was that the young laird was clearly so well pleased by his companion of the moment that he was rather tempted to let his boyish gayety get the better of him; and that again and again he had to recall himself, resuming that attitude of shy deference that became him very well in the presence of this beautiful stranger. Good-comradeship was all very excellent in its way; but this Greek girl was too august somehow —too serene and remote—in spite of the sweetness and charm of her manner and the unmistakable friendliness of her regard. So, notwithstanding that he was by birth and lineage and personal temperament one of 'the gay Gordons,' he subdued himself and kept himself humbly respectful; he was like a school-boy waiting upon a great lady; and when she turned her glorious eyes upon him, his own rather shrank away from that overpowering bewilderment. Jean Gordon thought that the young laird of Grantly had met with his match—and more than his match—this time.

And then he would have his guests go for a stroll round the hall, to look at the old armor and the stags' heads; and many a tale he had to tell of both; with now and again an anecdote of this or that one among the more noted of his forebears. Perhaps he did not treat those ancestors of his with the reverence which their deeds of love and valor and their territorial designations demanded; but it is the way of youth—especially of a modest youth—to make light of such things;

and there was not much boasting or showing off about
this young man. He pretended not to remember whether it was a head of seventeen or of eighteen points
that caused the Duke of Gordon, when he discovered
what a magnificent stag he had shot, to exclaim, in
despair, "And now there is nothing left for me to live
for." He did not know where Glenlogie was, or even
whether there was such a place, though Briseis herself
could quote for him a couplet out of the old ballad:

"He turned about lightly, as the Gordons does a';
'I thank you, Lady Jean; my love's promised awa'.'"

"And are all the Gordons as light of heart as that?"
asked this tall young Greek creature, with her inscrutable, enchanting smile.

"Oh no," he made answer, almost bashfully. "It
is impossible to say how those epithets got attached to
the different families in the north—I suppose through
the chance of alliteration mostly—the gallant Grahams,
the gay Gordons, the fighting Frasers, and so on. And
if you know that very ballad, Miss Valieri, you will
remember that Glenlogie was not so hard of heart after
all; for he married 'bonnie Jeanie Melville, who was
scarce sixteen years old.'"

And so they wandered about the dim, stone-paved,
hollow-sounding hall, examining claymores, dirks, targes, and old powder-horns, trying to make out the
phantom figures in the breadths of faded tapestry, and
telling or hearing about all kinds of people and places
and things—about the Queen's coming to Balmoral on
the following week; about the Farquharsons of Dee-
side, and the Lindsays, and the Irvines of Drum; about
Lord Lewis Gordon and the '45—

"O send Lewie Gordon hame,
And the lad I daurna name!"

But in course of time the old botanist grew more and more abstracted; it was clear to Briseis that he was thinking of the afternoon post, and of the expected communications from the south; besides, both of them knew that young Gordon was going up to London by that night's mail-train. And so, in spite of many protests, and with many thanks and good wishes, the visit came to an end; the wagonette was brought round; and Frank Gordon and his aunt Jean stood at the top of the steps watching their departing guests until a curve in the drive hid them from sight. And then it was that the young man turned to his companion.

"And now, Aunt Jean? What do you say now?" he demanded, with something of triumph in his tone.

But Aunt Jean did not answer him at once. She regarded him for a second, curiously.

"I have often wondered, Frank," said she, "what kind of woman would prove attractive to you. And—and I'm glad it's that kind."

There was a flash of boyish delight in his eyes; but at the same time he said, reproachfully:

"Why, you talk as if there were whole heaps of them! You talk as if there were a whole race of such women. Come, now, Aunt Jean—honestly now—honestly—did you ever in all your life come across any girl or woman half as fine and wonderful as that one—so perfect in her manner—so winning in her disposition—and so extraordinarily beautiful too—"

Aunt Jean smiled.

"Lad, laddie," she exclaimed, "I am saying nothing against her! Nothing of the kind! I would rather be on her side. If it comes to that, I will say this for her, that she has the most bewitchingly musical voice I ever heard in my born days. And when she was going

along the terrace I thought she walked just as a swan
swims—breasting the air, as it were—as graceful a
thing as ever I saw—"

"Didn't I tell you! didn't I tell you!" he cried,
eagerly.

"A strange girl, too," said Aunt Jean, thinking
back, "with her modest little apologies for being at
once useless and perfectly happy. Well, I could not
say it to her face, but indeed I was thinking it all the
time, that there were plenty of women useless enough
who could not make you pleased and satisfied-like with
just looking at them. A rare, fine creature that, or
my name's not Jean Gordon." Aunt Jean was silent
for another second or so. "And there's one thing I
would say to yourself, Frank, my man : If you have a
thought of bringing some one home to this old house,
you'll not find me in the way, nor will she ; neither the
one nor the other of ye ; I'll just pack up my bits of
things and be off to Edinburgh—there's the Carmi-
chaels—the Ramsays—there will always be a corner for
me somewhere—"

But at this a prodigious blush overspread his handsome, boyish face ; and in his embarrassment he could
hardly win to articulate utterance.

"Aunt Jean !—why—what—what are you thinking
of ? Do you imagine—I could have any such fancies
in my head ?—a mere stranger—a perfect stranger like
that—though I thought you would be interested in
her—yes, I certainly thought that—and I wanted to be
civil to the old gentleman— But how can you imagine
I had any fancies of that kind—"

"I don't know—I don't know," Miss Jean answered,
cautiously. "She is just winsome enough to turn any
lad's head, and that's the truth ; and there would be
no great madness about it, either, as far as I can make

out; for you don't need to marry for money, Frank; and the Elliotts of the Lea are as old a family as the Gordons of Grantly. So give me notice when ye please—"

"Oh yes," said he, and he put his hand within her arm to lead her into the house again. "Precisely. Just so. And what would Grantly be without Aunt Jean?"

Well, she patted the hand that lay on her arm; for she was very fond of this lad—and very proud of him too, though he hadn't done much to speak of, as yet.

"It is very generous of my young lord," said Aunt Jean, half laughing, "to talk like that to his humble dependant. But she knows her place; and when the bride comes home, all she'll want will be just to get a kiss from her—and then off by train to Edinburgh town." And then Aunt Jean, who was not an effusive sort of person, abruptly said: "Frank, laddie, mind you see that Wentworth puts your Tam o' Shanter in your travelling-bag, for there's nothing so soft to the head when you're in a railway carriage."

Meanwhile old John Elliott and his niece had been driven rapidly away towards Sanchory; and when they at length arrived there, and entered the inn, and opened the door of the parlor, his first and eager glance was directed to the sideboard, where a number of letters and newspapers lay extended in a row. And he would have gone quickly forward to examine these and seize his own, but that at the same moment he became aware of the presence of a stranger in the room—some one seated in the dusk between the two windows—and to his amazement he found Briseis exclaiming:

"Why, Aunt Clara! And you did not let us know you were coming!"

And in his inordinate surprise he even forgot the coveted letters.

"I hope there's no ill news, Clara," he said, with sudden and nervous apprehension.

This Mrs. Alexander Elliott who had now risen to receive their greeting was a middle-aged woman, rather short and stout of figure, but with a pinched and care-worn face, her hair gray or yellowish-gray, her eyes somewhat sad and tired, and yet shrewd enough, her mouth thin-lipped and resolute. She gave one the impression of an indomitable, unjoyous kind of little woman, who had come through many trials, and was not even yet likely to give up in despair.

"No, there's no ill news, Uncle John," said she; "at least I hope you'll not regard it that way. And you'll have to forgive me for appearing intrusive and importunate. I know how difficult it is to write and explain; and when you have written and tried to explain, it's so easy for the answer to be put off and put off, or forgotten altogether. So I thought I would come right through and see yourself, as soon as I could find out where you were—"

"Is it about money, Clara?" John Elliott said, timorously.

"It's about Edward," she replied. And then she went on quickly and anxiously: "You know how I have slaved and toiled, on poor enough means, to give those three boys a fair start in the world—perhaps even to the neglecting of the girls. Have I not done everything for them? Did ever any mother do more? I led or followed them into every one of their studies, keeping pace with them, and night after night, when all the house was asleep, sitting up hour after hour, just to get a bit ahead of them, and be able to coach them for their examinations. And I'm sure the girls have helped too—making their own dresses as well as they could—and scrimping themselves of their pocket-money. Not but that we've had our reward in one way. Look at the result—though perhaps it is not for me to boast. There's John at Sandhurst, doing splendidly; there's Alexander on the *Warspite;* and now there's Edward, who has a grand prospect before him, if ever there was one. For he has just passed his University Certificate Examination, and that would enable him to enter at Caius College, Cambridge—it's Caius most of the medical students make for, I believe —and he would have no bother about matriculation; then if he did anything near as well at Caius as he has done at King's College—followed by some practical work at the hospitals—he would make just an invaluable junior partner for some well-known doctor; indeed I may say he is universally popular owing to his pleasant manners and his cleverness. But then, Uncle John, three years at Cambridge—"

Uncle John had been growing more and more uneasy; he knew what was coming. And yet he could not but listen with respect to this piteous appeal from the poor mother.

"Two hundred and fifty pounds a year at least," she continued; "perhaps two hundred and eighty—though he is a most considerate and economical boy; and how am I to provide that without the help of one or two relatives? And I know I ought not to come to you; you have been so generous to me so many times before; but here is a very special juncture—it will be the making of Edward's career—if you can find it in your heart to help us—"

"But, Clara," said old John Elliott, nervously and hurriedly, "it is impossible !—quite impossible—I'm very sorry—you know I should be only too glad to do anything for you and yours—but there are circum-stances—the plain truth is, I have not the means. But —but why don't you go to Sir Patrick ?—he is the head of the family—"

"Sir Patrick Elliott ?" said she, with a touch of scorn even amidst her plaintive suspense. "I know him. I know what I should get from him. I should get a grandiloquent lecture, and a civil good-day—" ·

And now it was that Briseis Valieri interposed.

"You won't think me too bold, Aunt Clara, will you ?" she said, in her soft and persuasive tones. "But I often reproach myself with being so idle and useless ; and now you might give me the opportunity of being of a little help. Shall I show you how simply it could be done ? The money that my father left me was put into the India Three-per-cents ; then my uncle here heard of some American railway bonds, quite safe, that were paying six per cent.; and after he had consulted with one or two people—to make sure, you know—we changed the money over to the American bonds, so that my income was actually doubled. Now, Aunt Clara, if you were to take the half of the capital—if that would be of use to you in my cousin's education—don't you see that I would have exactly the same income that I had before the change was made ? Is not that quite clear ? I should be none the worse—you would be all the better—"

So far John Elliott had listened, with symptoms of an ever-increasing distress becoming visible ; but now he could bear the situation no longer.

"Briseis," said he, in the strangest way, "you don't understand about such things. You can't understand about them at all. There are some circumstances that I must explain to your aunt. Would you mind—would you mind leaving us alone together for a few moments—"

She looked from one to the other in mute astonishment. But she said, as she moved to the door—and her parting look was surely one of exceeding kindliness and good-will :

" At least you will remember, Aunt Clara, that the half of what I have is yours, if you will take it : the rest is quite sufficient for me."

The moment she was gone John Elliott rose from his seat and began pacing up and down, in great agitation.

" That is a noble-hearted creature, John," his sister-in-law began to say, " though of course one hesitates about accepting such an offer from a mere girl—"

" Clara, she has not a penny !" he broke in, excitedly. " Not a penny ! And it's all my doing. I advised her. I heard of these railway bonds through Philip Murray —you remember Philip Murray in Edinburgh ; and he had made ample inquiries—a First Mortgage it was— the Denville Valley First Mortgage Guaranteed—and he was so convinced of its safety that he put £8,000 of his own money into it. Well, I laid the matter before Briseis ; I thought it was a good chance for her ; and she assented only too readily ; the fact is, I don't suppose she cared one way or the other ; she has no thought for money matters—her wants are so simple—"

" And do you mean to say that her little fortune is entirely gone ?" his sister-in-law demanded of him, staring at him in a blank kind of way.

" Clara, it's a terrible thing even to speak of !— terrible !—I that should have been the first to protect her, since she chose to join my wandering life. The bonds are still quoted—yes—but they are valueless : no one would touch them. They were 108 when we bought them ; now they are down at 17 or something of the kind ; but they are quite unsalable ; nothing has ever been paid on them after the first six months, and nothing ever will be paid on them, so it is said. Of course Briseis does not know. She thinks the six per cent. interest is still being paid; and probably imagines that a considerable portion of it is being stored up for her; hence her offer to you—which was generous all the same. And she must not know, Clara!—she must not know!—"

"Then she is dependent on you for her support!" exclaimed Aunt Clara, her eyes still staring.

"I give her what money she needs—it isn't much," he said, in a more resigned way. "And I may explain to you that my own means are still further crippled; for I put a small sum into the Denville Valley Mortgage along with hers; and that's gone too. So you see, Aunt Clara, it is impossible for me to do what you ask. I'm very sorry. I've always heard that the boy was clever and brilliant, and likely to do well. But after all, the three years at Cambridge are not an absolute necessity—"

The startled and expectant look had faded out of Aunt Clara's eyes; there reigned there a sort of hopeless rumination; and she was silent. But at length she said:

"You may as well call Briseis in again, John. She shall hear no word of all this from me."

When the young girl returned to them she was much astonished to learn that Aunt Clara was on the immediate point of departure. No, Aunt Clara could not remain a day or two with them, nor would she even stay to dinner; her time, she said, was at the moment extremely precious; she must make haste back again to the south. And what surprised Briseis still more was that no reference of any kind was made to her offer. Even if a refusal had been decided on, she might fairly have expected a word of thanks? On the contrary, a complete and incomprehensible silence prevailed with regard to the business that had brought Aunt Clara all the way to Sanchory; and in a few moments further she was in the fly that was to take her to the station, on her way to Aberdeen and London.

CHAPTER IV

Now Briseis was well aware that, the moment this poor, distracted Aunt Clara had gone, her uncle would plunge into the correspondence awaiting him on the side table; accordingly she turned to the window; and there as it chanced she encountered a spectacle that entirely suited her humor, the idle wretch that she was. For just beyond the pavement, in the wide, empty, sunlit thoroughfare, two small boys were playing marbles; and though of course she knew nothing of the mysterious fascination of commies, jarries, whinnies, and chenies (if these be the terms fashionable among the Aberdeenshire youth), she could at least guess at the fluctuations of the game, and she could watch the eagerness of the urchins with a vaguely sympathetic interest and with a serene good-nature in her smiling eyes. She was thus employed—and it was an employment completely in accord with her indefensible disposition—when her uncle mentioned her name.

"Briseis," said he—"Briseis—I have something to tell you—that—that may surprise you a little—"

She turned quickly; she found that he had drawn in a chair to the central table, and was seated there with one arm hanging down, an open letter in his hand; and then she noticed that the usual fresh tints of his complexion had given place to a curious ashen-gray hue. It was wonder rather than fear that possessed her : what further astonishments had this day in store for them ?

"And yet it is not of much importance—perhaps—perhaps not of much importance," he went on, in an absent kind of way, as if he were thinking of a hundred different and distinct things. "A good deal of trouble, of course—but with a little patience it can be set right—in time everything will be set right again, and no harm done—"

"But what is it, uncle?" she demanded.

Then he looked up, in his anxious, apprehensive way.

"Now you must not be angry, Briseis," said he. "You must not make too much of it. Only a bit of a practical joke, after all. There's no harm done—not much harm done—a little trouble, and it will be all set right—"

"But I don't understand, uncle—"

"The *Silene alpestris*," he said—and he seemed to talk as if there were some kind of weight on his chest. "You know the *Silene alpestris*, Briseis—well, it appears that two or three of the young fellows in Edinburgh had got to hear that I was likely to be round by Dee-side this summer—and—and of course they made sure I would be up Scoulter Hill—and so they got some seed of the *Silene alpestris*—sent to Austria, perhaps, for it—or perhaps got it from some garden —and they sowed the seed on the top of Scoulter Hill. Nothing more than a kind of joke, you know—nothing more—nothing more. No doubt it will be a little awkward—a little humiliating—to take back my imagined discovery—"

And then she understood—and her face grew quite white.

"The hounds!—the sconndrel hounds!" she said—
and her voice was vibrating with passion. "If I were
a man, I would lash them! I would take a horsewhip
and lash them!—"

And then in the blindness and bewilderment of her
indignation she seemed to look all around for help. To
whom could she appeal? Who would come forward to
take her part? Who, for her sake, would exact vengeance for this cruel trick that had been played on an
unoffending old man —an old man of exceeding sensitiveness of mind? Oddly enough, at this moment,
and if only for a moment, her thoughts involuntarily
turned to Frank Gordon of Grantly. But of course
that was out of the question. Young Gordon was almost a stranger, notwithstanding the marked friendliness he had shown them; besides, he was probably by
this time on his way to London. And meanwhile old
John Elliott had risen from his chair and was walking
up and down the room, showing a good deal more of
perturbation in his manner than he allowed to appear
in his pacific words.

"No, no, Briseis," he was saying—while he nervously clutched the letter that had brought the news—"you
must not be angry. You must not make overmuch of
it. You see, I was too certain. I had convinced myself that no garden escape could have found its way to
the top of Scoulter Hill; and I carelessly imagined
that that was enough. The possibility of a trick did
not occur to me. But where is the harm done? Of
course I shall have to write to the various Societies,
and explain. I dare say most of the people know that
I have never been in the habit of proclaiming false discoveries, or jumping to rash conclusions. I have never
laid myself open to suspicion before; and this time it
is hardly my fault—it is hardly my fault, Bry, is it?"

"Your fault, uncle?" She burst out crying; and turned away to the window again. "If—if I were a man—if I were a man—I'd let them know whose fault it was! The hounds—the cowardly hounds!—"

He went after her and took her gently by the arm—his own fingers trembling a little.

"Come, come, now, Bry," he said, "you must not make too much of it. It was only a kind of joke, you know, among two or three of those young fellows in Edinburgh. And there can be no permanent harm done. The Linnæan and the Andersonian and the rest of them are well aware that I have never tried to push myself forward; I think they would give me credit for that; they will not accuse me of having claimed the discovery with any intention of deceiving. I think they would tell you that what little work I have done has been done in a quiet way; I have never pushed myself forward; I don't think they will suspect me of having tried to snatch false honors. Come, Bry, you must not pay too much attention to a mere trick of this kind—"

She pulled herself together—and dried her eyes.

"Quite right, uncle," she said, firmly. "It is too contemptible a thing to be thought twice of." And then she added, cheerfully: "Why, what a long time we have been in-doors, on such a beautiful afternoon! Let us get out—let us go for a stroll somewhere: uncle, you can attend to the rest of your correspondence and papers when we come in again."

For it was she who would play the part of comforter—perceiving clearly enough how deeply he had been struck; she was talking blithely to him as she fetched him his hat and cane; she opened the door for him, and together they passed out. And yet amidst all her forced vivacity they had not left the inn a dozen yards before

she became conscious that a change had come over
Sanchory on Dee. It was not the same place, somehow,
that it had been an hour before. There were the familiar features, to be sure—the sunlight of the wide, open,
empty street, the dark blue-gray stone of the old-fashioned houses, the glancing and shimmering of the
yellow-green foliage, with now and again a glimpse of
the soft, ethereal rose-purple of the western hills.
Yet this was not at all the same Sanchory through
which they had driven on their return from Grantly
Castle—her heart full of gratitude because of the kindness shown them by the young laird and the gentle-
mannered Miss Jean. And perhaps Briseis too had
been looking forward with quiet satisfaction to this an-
ticipated correspondence. She liked to see her uncle's
name in printed Transactions; she liked to see his contributions to botanical lore suitably acknowledged;
these were modest honors and dignities in a harmlessly
simple life. But now—well, the little hamlet of Sanchory seemed all different now: something had changed
its aspect.

As for old John Elliott, he walked on as one in a
dream, apparently paying no heed whither they went.
But of a sudden he stopped. Right in front of them
was the stone bridge spanning the Dee; and beyond
that was the road leading to Scoulter Hill.

"Not that way—not that way, Briseis—some other
way—let us take some other way."

She guessed what this shrinking reluctance meant;
and immediately she turned. But when they had re-
traced their steps towards the village, he said:

"I think I would rather go into the inn, Briseis. You
see, I must begin and write out those explanations—"

"Oh no, uncle, no, no," she pleaded. "Leave that
till to-morrow. "What is the hurry?"

"I would rather go in, anyhow," he said, in a tired fashion.

Indeed, he seemed all broken down and disheartened; and sometimes he sighed heavily, as though the mere act of breathing gave him pain. And yet when they had returned to the little room, he did not resume his seat; he kept restlessly moving hither and thither, staring absently into the grate, or out of the window, or at the sideboard with its unopened newspapers; and hardly listening to the attempts that Briseis made from time to time to break in upon his reverie. Then dinner was served; and he took his place at the table; but she could not induce him to touch anything, though he made a pretence.

"Uncle," she remonstrated, "you must really eat something, or you will be ill."

"Oh, I am doing very well, my dear—I'm doing very well," he said; and then: "Briseis, you don't think they will suspect me of having intended to deceive them? They wouldn't think that, would they?"

"How can you imagine such a thing, uncle!" she exclaimed. "And why should you worry about a mere trifle? The explanation will clear it all away."

"I should have been more careful," he said, breathing heavily. "I should have doubted. Hooker is very explicit about the *alpestris*—'One of Don's reputed discoveries; never confirmed.' I was too eager. And now some of them may be thinking that I was trying to palm off a sham discovery on the Societies, and that I have been found out—"

"And those that are so base as to think that, what is their opinion worth?" she demanded, scornfully. But he paid no heed to her: he was absorbed in his own self-torturing thoughts.

Ere long he complained of being tired. It had been

a fatiguing kind of day, he said; he thought he would get off to bed at once; and so he bade her good-night, and left.   Then, that she might not disturb him, she also stole up-stairs to her room, which was next his, and in silence made ready for the still hours of sleep. But very soon she discovered that he had not gone to bed at all.   As she lay and listened, she could hear him walking to and fro—perhaps framing the apology that he would have to send to the various Societies, perhaps merely brooding over the underhand blow that had been dealt him.   Her heart was full of grief, and sympathy, and burning indignation; but what could she do?   And in time the healthy constitution of youth claimed its rights; her eyelids closed; and her spirit was free to wander away into the poppyland of dreams.

Next morning, when John Elliott came down, there was a worn and shrunken look about his features, and his eyes were wearied.   He took his accustomed place at the breakfast table; but in spite of all her entreaties he could not be persuaded to eat anything—he had half a cup of tea, that was all.   Yet he declared there was nothing the matter with him; only, he had not slept very well.   Then he regarded her in a curiously timid and furtive manner.

"Briseis," he said, hesitatingly, "I—I would not like to cause you any inconvenience.   Perhaps I have not always been considerate; perhaps I have been so engrossed in my own pursuits — selfishly engrossed — that I have forgotten to try to keep you interested as well.   And Deeside is a picturesque neighborhood—oh, yes—there are many places you could visit yet—and Loch-Na-Gar always looks fine when you climb up one of the other hills.   I—I would not like to inconvenience you, Briseis—if you would rather stay and see something more of this country-side—"

"What do you mean, uncle?" said she, promptly. "Do you want to leave Sanchory? For I can be ready in ten minutes."

Then he confessed that the district had grown distasteful to him somehow; he had lost interest in it; would she go with him in to Aberdeen, where they could mature their future plans? And this Greek girl, idle and easily good-humored and pleasure-loving as she might be, had nevertheless her wits about her; she divined readily enough why he wished to get away from this neighborhood, so she said at once and with much cheerfulness:

"Uncle, I will make a bargain with you. If you will remain here and try to eat at least that one piece of toast, I will undertake to have my small belongings packed in less than a quarter of an hour." And therewithal she went off to her own room.

And thus it was that by the very next train they left Sanchory and made their way in to the Granite City, where, for the sake of economy, they took lodgings instead of going to a hotel. Their rooms were over an old curiosity shop—a storehouse of all sorts of miscellaneous oddities—dirks, claymores, cutlasses, ostrich eggs, stuffed birds, Delft-ware, eighteenth-century tea-caddies, and the like; and among these Briseis would sometimes linger, examining; but generally she was more intent on taking her uncle for circuitous walks in the environs of the town, chatting to him the while, and trying to rouse him from the fits of brooding into which he had fallen. Frequently they went out by St. Machar's Cathedral, and over the Old Brig of Balgownie, and then back by the seaward road, with its glimpses of the blue-green water and the white line of foam curling up on the sand. But very soon he began to restrict these excursions. They grew shorter and shorter, until at length he would rather sit in-doors, in an arm-chair, silent, his head downcast—and well she knew what was gnawing at his heart. Then one evening he said to her:

"Briseis, surely it's very cold—very cold. I'm all shivering. I don't understand it."

Indeed, he was visibly trembling with this attack of chills, though there was an unusual flush of color in his face. Well, she was not much used to dealing with illness of any kind; but she did what she thought best; she got him to bed at once, and sent for a doctor. The doctor's report was reassuring. There was some degree of fever, no doubt, and an abnormally quick pulse; but there was little immediate cause for alarm; perhaps she had better get in a trained nurse; and with proper care and precautions all would come right.

The following day there was a different story to tell. Old John Elliott lay breathing laboriously, utterly exhausted, dozing sometimes, yet restless and nervously sensitive to the slightest noise, and muttering to himself on occasion, whether incoherently or not she could hardly make out.

"Has he been in any trouble of late? Has he had any mental worry?" the doctor asked.

"Oh yes—yes, indeed," she said; and her hands were clinched behind her back—as if that could prevent the tears welling into her eyes.

"This nervous fever is sometimes serious," said the doctor, guardedly. "And you are young to have so much responsibility thrown on you alone. Has he any other relatives about here?"

"You do not think there is any danger?" she exclaimed, in a low voice—with a quick look of unimaginable dread.

"Not yet—not yet," said he. "I will tell you before you need send for any one."

And so a day or two passed without apparent change, the fever running its usual course. But one afternoon, while Briseis was seated by the bedside, patiently watching, the old botanist suddenly flung himself out of his comatose trance, his eyes all burning and brilliant with excitement.

"Briseis, Briseis," he said, or gasped rather, in an eager, breathless way, "haste now—haste, haste!—telegraph—telegraph to them to keep back the papers—they must not be read—keep them back from the meetings—there will be time yet if you telegraph at once—keep them back—tell them—explain—it was all a mistake—I never tried to cheat any one—I never made false claims to discoveries—never—never—"

She laid her cool hand lightly on his hot forehead.

"That is all right, uncle—the explanation has been made—they understand perfectly—"

"I never thought of imposing on them," he panted. "But—but if they wish to remove my name from the lists of membership— well, I cannot object — that is quite just—though I did not wish to deceive any one—"

"No, no, uncle—they understand perfectly—they understand you were not in the least to blame," she said, softly and smoothly—and if ever there was persuasive charm in the music of a human voice, it was in hers. So that in a little while the hectic fire appeared to fade out of those restless and eager eyes, and he had relapsed into a kind of dozing state, while the fell disease continued its work.

But later on in the evening he began to talk again, in a less excited mood.

"Briseis, I want to tell you something. Your aunt Clara seemed to reproach me—and quite fairly, too—yes,

yes, quite fairly. I should have put the little money I inherited into some business, or tried some profession. But, you see, it was this way. When I was a lad I was allowed to do pretty much as I liked ; and what I liked most of all was to go wandering away among the hills, with a vasculum slung over my shoulder. The hill-side was my love. The other young fellows, they would talk about girls ; but I never had any thought that way ; and the young women seemed to have some sense of it ; they had never a word or a look for me. Well —I was content—when I was away by myself—in Glen Rosa or Glen Sannox. Briseis," he continued, in this hard-breathing, rambling, confused fashion, "before I was out of my teens I had some fairly good things in my herbarium—the *Drosera*—I mean the *anglica*—and —and the *Hypericum dubium*—and the *Saxifraga stellaris*—the *Pinguicula alpina*—and many another—I cannot remember at the moment—"

"Of course not, uncle," she said, her voice tranquil and soothing. "Why should you trouble yourself ? I know how valuable your collection is."

"But this is what I meant to tell you—Briseis ; it is a kind of explanation—and—and perhaps an excuse," he went on. "When I was quite a lad, I discovered among the slopes above Gourock a little dell in which the *Osmunda regalis* was growing in great luxuriance. The *Osmunda* is rare on that coast—and—and I was proud of my discovery—and kept the secret to myself ; and many a time I used to go and sit in the little hollow, under the birch-trees, and listen to the trickling of the burn. And then—well, you see, I was foolish and romantic—and my only love in those days was the hill-side—I took it into my head that I would spend a night in that dell, with the *Osmundas* as my only companions. It was not a cold night either ; but I found

the ground very hard and damp before I could get to
sleep. I remember the stars through the birch-trees
overhead. I thought I could hear the sea, too, along
the shore—though I was some distance up the hill-side,
and in a hollow, too. I remember the stars well—I lay
and looked up at them—twinkling white and clear
through the branches of the trees. And there was the
sound of the burn close by—not two yards away from
me. I had no wrap of any kind—a boy is careless of
such things, you know—but anyhow in time I got to
sleep. Well, the weather must have changed during
the night; for when I woke, just about daybreak, there
was a fine, thin rain falling, and I was wet through to
the skin, and shivering with cold. And I was miles
and miles away from home. You may guess what
followed—rheumatic fever—and all its worst consequences; so that from that hour my life was broken."

He tried to raise himself a little, so as to address her
more directly; but he fell back, through sheer weakness.

"Do you understand now, Briseis ?—do you understand why I have kept out of the struggle, and been
like an Ishmaelite wandering in the desert ? It is only
within the last few years that I have had anything like
health, and that with constant watching. But, all the
same—your aunt Clara was quite right in accusing
me—"

"Uncle, I do not accuse you !" she said, passionately. "Not I !—and I wonder who knows you better
than I do ? If every one were living as blameless a life
as you have lived, I think it would be a considerably
different kind of world !"

"Ah, but your aunt Clara was right," he insisted,
in this painful fashion. "I should have given a better
account of my stewardship—I have been selfish—and
absorbed in my own pursuits—" But at this point he

3*

seemed inclined to turn away his head; and instantly
she was silent—scarcely daring to breathe, indeed; all
the desire of her being was that beneficent sleep should
descend upon him, to still that troubled brain.

Another day or two passed; the fever showed no
signs of abatement; but now, strangely enough, his
confused mutterings had no reference to his concern
about the Societies and what they might think of his
alleged discovery: mostly they were about the botanical wanderings of his youth—Glen Rosa and Glen Sannox in Arran, the hills above Lochgoil, Ben Lomond
and Ben Voirlich, the winding shores of Loch Achray,
the 'banks of Allan Water,' the far Braes of Balquhid-
der.   Sometimes he knew that Briseis was by his side;
sometimes he did not; he would frequently talk as it
were to one of his boyish companions—talk of his
tramping through a rainy day towards Aberfoyle, or
his waiting for the steamer at the breezy quay of
Greenock.   And pervading these reminiscences and
rambling confessions, there was the greatest self-depre-
ciation and gentleness; he seemed to have treasured
no recollection of any harm done to him by any one;
there was no aggression or resentment; rather a kind
of gratitude towards all the people whom he had encountered in his journey through the world.

Then there came one evening—Mrs. Alexander Elliott, who had been urgently telegraphed for, was in the
room, and so also was Briseis, stricken faint and numb
with long tendance—on this evening he appeared to
waken out of the profound coma that had followed
upon the violence of the fever.   And now there was
no unnatural glitter in the eyes; no hectic color in the
pinched and wan face; he regarded these two with a
calm recognition.

"You will look after Briseis, Aunt Clara," he said,

in a voice that was just audible and no more. "She will be grateful to you for your kindness—she has a heart of gold. And Briseis—my dearest—oh, indeed, my dearest—remember this—you must not think too hardly—of the young fellows—who played that trick on me. They—meant no harm—meant no harm—only a frolic of youth—I am sure they meant no harm."

He relapsed into silence. But a second or two thereafter there came a sudden change—and Aunt Clara sprang to the bell.

"Send for the doctor!—send for the doctor at once!" she cried in her frantic alarm.

But there was no need to send for any doctor. Old John Elliott had quietly passed away, and was now free from all earthly cares and wrongs. And perhaps —who knows?—there may be rare plants to be sought for among the lonelier of the high hills of Heaven.

CHAPTER V

AUF DER HÖHE

ONE evening early in July Sir Hugh and Lady Adela Cunyngham entertained a distinguished company at their house on Campden Hill, the dinner being given in honor of the Prince and Princess of Monteveltro; and although the party was rather an elderly one, being chiefly of a diplomatic character—Ambassadors, Ministers, Attachés, and the like—nevertheless a corner had been found for young Frank Gordon, as was but natural, seeing that he was the only son of the Princess by her former husband, when she was Lady Gordon of Grantly. Likewise Lady Adela had been considerate enough to provide the boy with a companion more of his own age—a Miss Georgina Lestrange. Now this Miss Lestrange—who generally was called Georgie by her intimate friends—was a ruddy‑haired, rebellious‑nosed, fresh‑complexioned, merry-eyed lass, who wore a pince-nez; and being of a lively and audacious spirit, she opened the ball at once, the moment the people had taken their seats.

"I've heard a good deal about you, from Lady Adela," said this frank young damsel; "and I've often wondered why you didn't go into the great world of state affairs, when you have such opportunities. Your mother the Princess is quite an important person in Eastern politics, isn't she?"

"Yes, I believe she is," he made answer, with rather

significant emphasis on the *she*. " As for the Prince,
his chief ambition seems to be to get his two black
poodles to sit up on their hind legs, each with a pipe
in its mouth."

"Then, if that is his disposition," continued this
bold young creature, " all the more reason why you
should go and make a name for yourself. What is the
use of salmon-fishing and shooting rabbits ?—"

" Would you like to know how many thousand
spruce and larch trees I planted last year ?" he demanded—for even the most modest youth does not
liked to be trampled upon.

" Oh, but what is that — when you have great
chances ! If I were a man, I should like to know that
I had done something—something to distinguish me
from everybody else—something that people could remember me by. Oh, I beg your pardon—really—
really, I beg your pardon—because of course you have
—you have, at all events. You rowed in the Oxford
Eleven, didn't you ?"

" Well," said he, ingenuously, " there weren't quite
so many of us as that ; but we managed to beat Cambridge all the same."

She looked puzzled for a second.

" Oh, how silly of me—how very silly ! Only eight,
of course." And then she sheered off—her conversation taking the form of a series of rambling questions,
that hardly waited for an answer. " It's an awfully
pretty table, isn't it ?—maiden-hair-fern goes so well
with silver, doesn't it ? And I'm certain there's nothing suits a dinner table so well as candles ; they are so
soft and quiet ; don't you positively detest the electric
light ?—it's only fit for gin-palaces. And don't you
think it is much better to have the Hungarian Band
out in the garden rather than in the hall ? They play

awfully well, don't they? That's Waldteufel — the
'Pluie d'or'—I simply worship Waldteufel.   Oh, I
forgot.   When I mentioned the electric light, I did
not mean in a garden; in a garden it's quite charming; when you get out after dinner you'll find all the
grounds lit up.   For you don't mean to hide yourself
away in the billiard-room, do you?—on a night like
this it will surely be ever so much nicer for you to
have your cigarette in the open air.   And mind,
there's a treat in store for you; don't forget to ap-
plaud; the band has been instructed to play Sibyl
Bourne's 'March.'   You know, she is just wild to get
it adopted by the band-masters of the different regi-
ments—the 'Soldiers' Marching Song' it is, when it's
sung; and I fancy she hinted something about it to
the Duke of Cambridge, and to Sir Evelyn Wood
when he was at Aldershot; but nothing seems to have
come of it—"

"I'll tell you what Lady Sibyl ought to do," observed young Gordon to this loquacious maid.   "She
ought to approach my august step-papa, and suggest
that the 'March' should be adopted as the national
air of the Principality of Monteveltro."

"Oh, my good gracious, Sir Francis, what a splendid
idea!" she cried, eagerly.   "What a perfectly ripping
idea!   I will tell Sibyl the moment we leave the room.
Or I wouldn't mind making the suggestion myself.
Only—you see—I don't quite know—"   She glanced
towards the personage seated next to Lady Adela
Cunyngham : he was rather stout and elderly, good-
natured - looking, with a long mustache carefully
waxed at the drooping ends.   "Faut-il le monseig-
neuriser ?"

"Oh, you needn't be particular," said the Prince's
step-son, smiling maliciously.   "Get him into a good-

humor by asking about his black poodles, and you might even call him Monty or Veltry. He's a very good kind of chap; but I think the Principality bores him. He would rather sit on a bench in the Prater, and have his poodles go through their performances—"

"What an awfully handsome woman your mother is," said Miss Georgie. "And so distinguished-looking. I don't wonder at the influence she is said to have. They tell me it was she who really planned out King Milan's return to Belgrade."

"Yes, but her life isn't altogether roses," responded young Gordon. "I'm always wishing she would catch her dress on the door."

"On the door?" said the ruddy-headed lass, turning and staring at him through her pince-nez.

"Well, I should have a chance of firing off Lord Palmerston's epigram—don't you remember?—when the Princess of Servia met with that kind of accident —'Vous voyez, Princesse, c'est toujours la Porte qui vous incommode.' Rather neat, wasn't it? But even that isn't as good as what the Attaché said—I forget his name—when the Shah of Persia was over here. His Majesty on some evening or other had been refreshing himself a little too freely, whereupon this gay youth remarked: 'Oh, every one knows the French proverb—La nuit tous les chats sont gris.' He made a reputation on the strength of that—it went the round of every court in Europe."

"But tell me now about Monteveltro," she said— after she had been talking to her other neighbor for a little while. "I am really quite ashamed—I hardly even know where it is—"

"Very well," he answered her, obediently, amid this prevailing hum of conversation, while the Blue Hungarian Band outside in the garden was playing softly and melodiously Batiste's Andante in G. "As you are sailing down the Dalmatian coast—"

"That sounds rather wicked," interpolated the impudent minx, demurely, though probably he did not hear her.

"—you come upon the entrance into a long inland gulf—something like a Norwegian fiord, only the mountains are higher, and brighter in color—in fact, as you go winding round promontory after promontory the whole thing looks like the drop-scene of a theatre. Then at the head of the gulf the steamer comes to anchor, and directly rowing-boats put off from the shore —the most gorgeously painted boats, and the men and women exceedingly picturesque—and they want you to buy Albanian embroidered jackets and waist-belts of leather and cornelians. Then you jump into one of the blue and red boats and go away across the green water—it's all exactly like a theatre—and you land at Dattaro, a clean-looking, white little place. Clean-looking, yes; but, oh mong jew !— Have you been to Constantinople ?"

" No."

" Then you don't know the slums of Galata and the dogs. Venice, perhaps ?"

" Oh yes, I have been to Venice."

" Then you remember the short-cut between the Rialto and the Riva degli Schiavoni—past the Post-office, I mean—and there is a corner of the canal just before you reach the Bridge of Sighs—"

" I know it well—oh, don't I !" said Miss Georgie, in a sad kind of way.

" But if you were to take a year of that corner and compress it into five minutes, you would hardly match the odors of Dattaro. Never mind. You are soon away from the little seaport, and driving up the most

amazing road that was ever cut—a zigzag up the face
of the mountains, but it's more like going up the side
of a house. Very well. You have six hours of that
dizzy climb, and then you arrive at the capital of
Monteveltro. It's the remotest, strangest-looking little place, away up there in the mountains : there's the
Palace, and a Monastery, and a Telegraph office, and
the house of the British Chargé d'Affaires—by-the-way,
he has an excellent tennis-lawn, and it's the oddest thing
to see the ladies of his family, English girls, dressed as
you would find them in Surrey or Sussex, playing-lawn-
tennis with the young Monteveltrin officers in their
embroidered caps and jackets and long riding-boots.
Because of course there's an army—a mimic army—
comic opera kind of thing—only, the fellows can fight
—oh yes, they can fight—perfect devils for fighting :
it's my step-papa's younger brother, Prince George, who
commands them ; and I can tell you they make it particularly warm for the Albanian brigands, who are continually coming across to plunder and kill the inoffen-
sive peasantry. Very brave fellows indeed, and very
proud of their independence : if either Turkey or Austria were to try to annex Monteveltro, there's not one
of those hardy mountaineers who wouldn't die at his
post rather than surrender—there would simply have
to be a universal massacre—nothing else."

"Oh, that is very interesting, very," said she. "And
I suppose when your mother married the Prince, it
was considered she had made a very proud alliance."

Now he was a most modest, and ingenuous, and
courteous youth ; but this unhappy remark seemed to
nettle him a little.

"Well, I don't know," said he, with some trace of
reserve. "I don't know. There are several of the
Gordon families who can trace their descent back to

the daughter of James I. of Scotland, who married the
son of the second Earl of Huntly ; and if there is to
be any claim on account of birth and blood, I think
that may rank as against a twopenny-halfpenny Eastern prince, who only lives by the sufferance of his big
neighbors——"

" Oh, of course, of course !" said the penitent Miss
Georgie, with a quick flush springing to her forehead.
" I ought to have known, of course. But I'm making a dreadful fool of myself this evening. I generally
do, in fact. Have you heard that Madame Albani is
coming to sing to-night ? And Lionel Moore—and
his awful pretty wife—Nina Ross she is called on the
stage, you know ; Lady Rosamund is painting her por-
trait for the next Academy—that is, if they'll accept
it ; and Sir John Mellord has been so kind and generous in giving her all the hints and assistance that he
can. Oh me," continued Miss Georgie, with a sigh,
" it must be delightful to belong to such a clever family. It's really horrid to be stupid. You cannot imagine how horrid it is unless you are out-and-out
stupid. Of course I don't think the public have taken
up Lady Adela's novels as they ought to have done
—you have no idea what trouble she expends on
them—I know something about it, for now and again
I am her model—I shriek, and fling myself on a couch,
and she describes it so as to get it natural—but it does
disarrange one's hair so—if you have to be in a tempest
of passion—and tearing things. And after all the
flattering mention that has been made about her books
by the newspapers—well, at least some of the newspapers. It's too bad. It isn't fair. I think the public's an awful fool : don't you ? Why, in Lady Adela's
books, on every other page, you come across people
you can't help recognizing—and the talk is real talk—

just what people say— But I will tell you about that
later on." For at this moment a mysterious signal
went round the room; all simultaneously rose; the
ladies left singly or with an affectionate arm linked in
arm; and on this occasion at least the Porte did not
incommode the Princess of Monteveltro.

Somewhat later in the evening Lady Adela received
a more numerous company of guests—a quite notable
assemblage, indeed : the Russian, Austro-Hungarian,
French, Italian, and United States Ambassadors, the
Portuguese, Danish, and Norwegian Ministers, the
Swiss and other Chargés d'Affaires, were all present,
with a goodly sprinkling of our own statesmen and
politicians ; and it is to be presumed that in the brilliantly lit drawing-room the conversation was not altogether about the recent proceedings in the Bulgarian
Sobranye when from time to time one could listen to
Madame Albani singing the 'Piano, piano,' from *Der
Freischütz,* or Mr. Lionel Moore (the accompaniment
played by his wife) giving 'On Lido Waters' in his
rich barytone voice. But there was something besides
that. At the further end of the long room the tall
French windows stood open ; there was a little stone
balcony ; there were steps leading down into the garden; and any one descending these found himself in a
kind of fairyland, for the black trees and bushes were
all bestarred with colored Chinese lamps, while the
electric light shone in the more open spaces. And as
Miss Georgie Lestrange was about the first to suggest
that the cool air outside would be preferable to the
hotter atmosphere in-doors, and as it chanced to be
Frank Gordon she was talking to, he promptly acqui-
esced ; so she went and got a lace scarf to throw round
her head—a delicate piece of adornment that neither
destroyed the symmetry of her costume of cream-hued

brocade nor yet altogether hid her extremely pretty
Venetian necklace of filigree gold and pale coral.
Then those two—though they were not quite the first
to make the experiment—passed out from the yellow
radiance of the drawing-room, and went down the
steps, and began a perambulation of the shubberies,
which were all festooned with parti-colored lanterns,
while the Hungarian Band, under the blue-white glare
of the electric light, was playing, with exquisite finish
and charm, Thomé's "Simple Aveu."

Now Miss Georgie Lestrange happened to be in a
particularly merry and mischievous mood, as they wandered through these alleys, listening or not listening
to the music ; and amongst other things she was de-
cribing to him certain aspects of the Grosvenor Square
Ladies' Athletic Club—for example, the shyness of
the novices over their unaccustomed attire, the desperate valor of the elderly matrons, and the like.

"But are you a member ?" he said, interrupting
her suddenly.

"Oh yes ; I have been ever since the Club was
started," she answered him.

"Well, that would be an interesting sight—that
would be something to see !" he exclaimed, with innocent fervor.   "In all London nothing more interesting—"

"Why, what do you mean ?" she demanded. "The
very idea of such a thing ! Of course no gentleman
is ever admitted !"

"But if it came to that," said he, boldly (for she
had been bearing rather hardly on him with her quips
and cranks)—"if it came to that, and if you would
take me, I could go dressed up as your waiting-
woman."

"What—you ?" she retorted, laughing.   And then

with her forefinger she made a dainty and dexterous little movement as if she were painting something on her upper lip. "I'm afraid you forget a trifling detail that would rather interfere with your disguise."

"Oh, but I'd soon have that removed," he declared, "if there was a chance of my being allowed to penetrate into these mysterious arcana."

"Not to be done, Sir Francis—not to be done," she replied, decisively. "You would make as tall and as ungainly a waiting-woman as Prince Charlie did; and the Grosvenor Athletic Club is not like the Isle of Skye—you would be found out in a moment. But I'll tell you now—"

Here she paused; for the Hungarian Band had begun to play Mascagni's well-known Intermezzo, and she listened for a second or two to the familiar strain. Then she resumed:

"I'll tell you now: if you would like to see a Ladies' Club, why not come and have some tea to-morrow afternoon at the Hypatia? It is to-morrow afternoon that we receive visitors; and you'll find Lady Adela there, and Sibyl and Rosamund Bourne as well—almost certain—"

"It's extremely kind of you—I shall be delighted!" he responded at once. "But—but the Hypatia, did you say? What kind—"

"Oh, well, you know," she proceeded to explain (but in a half-absent sort of a way, for the band was playing most beautifully), "it's supposed to be a club for authoresses and lady journalists, and so on—rather advanced, you know—rather emancipated—they thought of calling it the Forward Club—the equivalent of the German Vofwärts, don't you see?—and then they considered that that name might be misunderstood—Forward might be taken to mean something else—don't you think so ?—"

" Well, the Hypatia is a very pretty name," he replied, discreetly.

" Of course you are supposed to have done something to qualify for admission," she continued; "but really it's not so difficult to get in, if you have a friend on the Committee; and Miss Penguin has been so extremely kind—"

" Miss—?"

" Miss Penguin. Oh, surely you must know! The poetess—she writes under the name of Sappho—"

" I'm such an ignorant brute," he pleaded.

" And she was so kind about getting Lady Adela and her sisters into the Club—and poor me too," said the ruddy-haired damsel, only half listening to the music. " You see, I wouldn't for worlds say anything against Adela Cunyngham, but the truth is, she is just mad to find her name in the papers; and there's a lot of writing people at the Hypatia; and naturally she thinks, when they get to know her, they will make little paragraphs about her. Of course it's quite horrid the way the public have taken so little notice of her novels—awfully clever they are—oh, just everybody you know in them—you can go from page to page recognizing this one and the other—most awfully interesting. And Lady Adela does like to see her name mentioned in the papers; I must admit that. It's rather a weakness of the family, don't you know—Adela the author, and Sibyl the musician, and Rosamund the painter; but what I always contend is that if you want to get yourself advertised, if you really want to keep yourself before the public, you should recommend a soap. It's so simple! Lady Adela goes to this Hypatia Club, and pays court to all sorts of women whom she doesn't know in the least, and otherwise wouldn't want to know; and sometimes, but very seldom, they give her a bit of a paragraph—nothing to speak of. But now, if she were to recommend a soap, her name would be in every newspaper in England! And it's so easy! They would say: 'Lady Adela Cunyngham of Aivron Lodge, Campden Hill, writes— *Your soap is the most fascinating I have ever tried.*' Don't you see? Then she would get her name in big type into all the weekly illustrated papers; and people would say, 'Well, but who is Lady Adela Cunyngham?' —and other people would say: 'Oh, don't you know? She writes novels. She is the authoress of so-and-so.' And that would secure her fame. It would draw attention to her work. Then she wouldn't be dependent on that horrid creature Mr. Octavius Quirk and his gang of self-puffers to give her a little contemptuous cold encouragement now and again when they're not engaged in bepraising each other. I'm for soap. Don't you think it's reasonable? Isn't it more independent? I wouldn't ask horrid, ugly men to my house, in the hope of getting a favorable notice of my new book. And I wouldn't go to the Hypatia Club either, talking to inky-fingered young women, and secretly looking forward to small paragraphs. Lady Adela is really the dearest creature in the world; but she does strive a little too much for notoriety. I don't think it's dignified; I don't, really. Do you?"

This was an unexpected gybe; and the swinging over of the boom (so to speak) rather frightened him.

"But—but—" he stammered, "how can there be any harm in belonging to the Club you mentioned— why, you yourself are a member, you said—"

She burst out laughing.

"Oh, I go there for fun. Sometimes it's awful fun. The discussion nights, especially—"

"And what do you discuss?"

"Well, we generally discuss Man; and I can tell you we give him what for. Then there's education—and stupid things of that kind—"

These glades and alleys were becoming almost crowded, so many people were lingering about in the cool air of the summer night; and as he did not know at what moment this talkative young person might consider it her duty to go and join one or other of the nebulous groups, he thought it better to clinch the bargain about the Hypatia Club by asking the number in Suffolk Street, Pall Mall, and the hour at which he would be expected to make his appearance on the following afternoon. She told him.

"And mind you put on your best bib and tucker—metaphorically speaking," said she, saucily. "For they'll write paragraphs about you."

"About me?" he said, in astonishment. "Why about me?"

"Because it's their business! Literally their business. They live by it. Oh, I know the kind of thing that will appear—among the little snippets divided off by three stars: 'Sir Francis Gordon of Grantly does not at all look the tyrannical landlord he is reported to be—' By-the-way, are you a tyrannical landlord?"

"I'm not a landlord at all!—nothing to speak of, at least. I keep nearly all the farms in my own hands."

"Very well," she went on, with much complacency. "'Sir Francis Gordon of Grantly, who is well known as the crofter's friend—'"

"Bless my soul, there's not a crofter in the whole district!" he exclaimed.

"What does that matter? One must live. But

don't be alarmed, Sir Francis. They're not so bad as they're painted. And it's generally the people who want paragraphs who get paragraphs. I'll protect you as well as I can." And with that the engaging nymph put her hand on his arm, and said she would like to be taken back to the drawing-room now ; Lady Adela might notice their lengthened absence ; besides, she wanted to see and hear something of the great folk assembled there.

It was between two and three in the morning that Frank Gordon set out on foot for his rooms in Jermyn Street : this invariable walk home was about the only exercise that the busy life of London left him. And if the pert and charming young lady who had been doing her best to entertain him was pleasing herself with the idea that she had secured another captive, she was —on this occasion, at least—mistaken. As he passed along by the sombre spaces of the Parks, he was thinking of some one very different : he was thinking, and quite involuntarily and perhaps unconsciously thinking, of a Greek girl — so sweet, so serene, so self-possessed, so bland in the smiling of her dark eyes. And perhaps, in a vague kind of way, he may have been speculating as to the direction in which those two, uncle and niece, might now be distantly wandering —whether they were searching the lone hills around Glenavon, whether they were following the windings of the silver Spey, whether they were on remote 'Loch Loyal's side, or up by Mudal Water.' He did not know that the old botanist had gone on a far wider quest ; and as little did he dream that Briseis Valieri, become a mere slave and drudge, was here in this very town of London.

CHAPTER VI

Now Sir Francis Gordon of Grantly had about as much courage as most people (the Gordons have never been conspicuous for cowardice); but it must be admitted that when he entered the door of the Hypatia Club, in Suffolk Street, Pall Mall, and beheld a dim vista of feminine forms, an indefinable apprehension occupied his mind. However, here was the hall-porter, and him he was glad to recognize as a man and a brother; and he inwardly blessed the little page-boy who took from him his hat and gloves and cane. Then, just as he was hesitating at the very last moment as to whether he should not turn and fly, he became aware of the figure of a young person on the staircase—a figure gracefully clad in biscuit-colored Indian silk, and surmounted by a portentous Gainsborough hat; and at the same moment he was conscious that Miss Georgie Lestrange was laughing at him. The ruddy-haired damsel descended a step or two.

"Aren't you awfully frightened?" she said.

"I am," he said.

"Well, come up into the drawing-room. They really don't bite.

She led the way into a spacious suite of apartments; and presently he found himself in the midst of a large assemblage of fashionably dressed ladies, who did not in any wise differ, as far as he could see, from the ordinary folk that one would expect to meet at an afternoon reception. Moreover, they did not take any notice of him; apparently they were chiefly concerned in worshipping at the shrine of a well-known actor, whose benevolent airs of patronage might have made a cat grin its ears off. So gradually, while the vivacious Miss Georgie kept talking to him, he began to recover his nerve.

"When does the shocking begin?" he said.

"What shocking?" she demanded.

"Well, I wanted to be shocked," he went on. "And there isn't anything. They're mostly pretty women, with very pretty dresses. Don't they ever — do something—to—to make a stranger jump?"

"Of course not!" said she. "Why, what did you expect? They're just like other people—"

"You hinted that they were rather advanced—emancipated—"

"Oh, well," she confessed, "you might once in a blue moon come upon an elderly lady wearing divided skirts—"

"And is that all? Is that all? Divided skirts? That's nothing. I wear them myself."

"Come away now, Sir Francis, and talk to Lady Adela, and Sibyl and Rosamund Bourne—I can see them in the next room—and we will all go down and have tea together. And if you would only take that detestable creature, Octavius Quirk, and fling him out of the window, I would give you an additional slice of bread and butter."

Young Gordon did not wish to throw anybody out of the window; but he went with her to seek Lady Adela Cunyngham and the Ladies Sibyl and Rosamund Bourne; and the three tall and handsome sisters he found paying assiduous and humble court to about as

ill-favored a person as he had ever encountered — a
podgy person, of unwholesome complexion, with eyes
the color of boiled gooseberries—who was explaining,
with a sort of feebly boisterous glee, how he had just
been appointed to the control of the literary department of an important morning paper.

"The fact is, Lady Adela," he was saying, when the
playful Miss Georgie and her companion drew near,
"the Editor doesn't care a hang about literature; all
his interests are in politics and the Church—the House
of Commons debates and the Ecclesiastical Intelligence
—ecclesiastical intelligence !—why don't they read
Gibbon ?—and then as the Manager is entirely occupied with his Special Correspondents and his foreign
news, the two of them between them have agreed to
hand over all the books to me. And I can tell you
I mean to make some of those fellows sit up ! There's
a great deal too much of mutual puffery going on—"

At this moment Miss Georgie's mischievous eyes became demure and inscrutable ; she dared not laugh ;
she would not offend one from whom Lady Adela Cunyngham was always expecting a little judicious help.

"—especially among the bardlets—the small poets
—who keep bandying verses the one to the other.
And some of them in Government offices, too !—
pocketing the public money — and scrawling their
wretched sentimental trash on her Majesty's stationery,
with her Majesty's pens and ink. I tell you I mean to
make them hop !—like a hen on a hot girdle—"

"Oh, Mr. Quirk," said Lady Adela, "I'm sure you
wouldn't do anything unkind !"

"Well—well," he said, doubtfully shaking his head
—his extremely unprepossessing head—"that is as it
may be. I intend to keep my section of the paper
lively. The public doesn't read books ; but it does

delight in slashing reviews; and it shall have them. And I am going to start a literary *causerie* as well: some of those pretentious dolts who pose as wits and philosophers—philosophers catching at the coat-tails of Comte—a lot of those fellows want taking down a peg—several pegs—"

"But just think, Mr. Quirk," Lady Adela pleaded, "about the reviews: you might be doing an irreparable injury to some poor struggling aspirant—"

"Then let them stop struggling and aspiring," he said, with his boisterous hilarity. "We have quite enough authors already, of recognized position. You yourself, Lady Adela, have acquired your status: you are no longer an amateur."

Of course that clinched the matter: Lady Adela, looking as proud and pleased as if she had been presented with the Crown of England, had no further thought for the poor struggling aspirant. And meanwhile young Gordon, who had been eying with a vague curiosity this mouton-enragé sort of a creature, and who was not much interested in his shop-talk, had been inwardly saying to himself: 'My fat friend, it would do you a world of good if you were made to crawl six miles up the Corrieara burn, with a rifle in your hand. And perhaps two or three days' starvation wouldn't do you much harm either.'

Then they all went down to the rooms on the lower floor; and they were lucky enough to secure a small table for themselves; and they had tea, amid the moving and murmuring crowd; while Frank Gordon, glancing round him from time to time, so far from finding anything to shock him (he rather wanted to be shocked, the scoundrel), thought he had never seen anywhere a more pleasant-looking, intelligent-looking, and well dressed set of folk. And then Miss Lestrange said to the lady who was presiding at this little festivity :

"Addie, listen. Do you think it would be a dreadful breach of confidence if I showed you some lines that Miss Penguin dashed off yesterday morning, when she was in here ? You know, I rather think she likes these pieces handed about — especially when they're just a trifle strong—I mean, when an editor would probably fight shy of them—"

"Come away with it, Georgie," said Lady Adela, laughing. "Never mind about Miss Penguin."

"Oh, but really I think the little piece is very fine," replied Miss Georgie, with much seriousness, as she dived into the recesses of her purse. "The fact is, what she aims at is passion—passion—passion. She declares there is no passion in our modern literature—"

"Let's see what she has to say for herself—"

At this point Miss Georgie found the fragment of paper she was seeking ; and it was handed round ; and when it arrived at young Gordon this was what he read :

> *We stagger through blunders and errors—*
> *Be it ill—be it well :*
> *Till we come to the lightnings and terrors—*
> *And we quail not at Hell !*

"Yes, it's rather choice," he observed, with a critical air.

"Oh, there's no impressing you," said Georgie Lestrange, impatiently, and she snatched back the paper. And then she smiled. "Well, Sir Francis, if Miss Penguin turns up this afternoon, I will introduce you to her. And you mustn't mind much what she says. The truth is, since some brute of a man threw her pet pug overboard — it was somewhere in the Black

Sea, I believe — she has been just a wee, tiny bit cross with things in general. But she means well; and she's a dear, unreasonable, quixotic kind of creature ; and be sure you remember that she writes under the name of Sappho."

Georgie was as good as her word; for hardly had they risen from the table, after their brief refreshment, when she exclaimed,

"Why, here is Miss Penguin just come in !"

And the next moment young Frank Gordon found himself being presented to no less a celebrity than the poetess of fire and fury, of spasms and gasps. She was a somewhat elderly and rather dowdily dressed woman, who had a baleful eye ; and the meaning of that aggressive eye he was soon to discover ; because it now happened that certain friends of Miss Lestrange came up to claim her, so that he was left at the mercy of Sappho.

"Hadn't we better go into the court-yard ?" she said, abruptly. "It is pestiferous here."

This was a command rather than an invitation ; and meekly he followed her through the open French windows. The stone court-yard was a bare-looking place ; but there were a few scarlet geraniums in pots, and there was some ivy on the wall.

"Have you read my 'Mirrorings'?" she demanded forthwith.

"Well—eh—not yet," he said, in utmost trepidation. "I have not been so lucky. But—but I have heard that the poems are very beautiful—full of fervor—"

"They are not poems," she observed, calmly (and he wished the paving-stones would open and swallow him up). "The book is a novel. And it is a novel of fashionable society as it exists at the present day ; and I wished to ask you if the picture is not a true one."

"Oh, but I am not a fashionable person at all !" he exclaimed, with momentary relief. "Far from that. I know hardly anything of London life. My interests are all in the country—"

"But you must be well aware of what is going on," she said, with a severity that brought him to his senses, and scattered to the winds his trembling subterfuges. "You go enough into society to know what exists there. And it is time that some one should speak the truth. It is time an exposure should be made."

And from this starting-point she proceeded with such a denunciation of the vices of fashionable society as nearly took his breath away ; and not only that, but she appeared to hold him responsible for this appalling condition of affairs. At first he only mildly protested.

"Miss Penguin," he said, "how can you believe such things ? And how can you know ? I must put it plainly—how can any unmarried woman know ?"

"The married women of my acquaintance are my authority !" she retorted.

And with that she made a statement still more sweeping and preposterous than any of her previous allegations. It shall not be repeated here, for the simple reason that the morbid imaginings of a neglected and elderly and ill-conditioned spinster would be interesting only to doctors — as the symptoms of a familiar disease. Young Gordon could but say :

"Oh, that is absurd. Pardon me, but it is quite absurd. I have as wide a circle of friends and acquaintances as most people ; and I am certain no such state of things exists—there may be isolated cases here and there, of course. Why, even if the men were so base, do you imagine their wives would allow such a system to continue ? — they could not be kept in ignorance !"

"Oh, I dare say their wives are just as bad as they are!" she answered him, tauntingly.

Now at this there arose in Frank Gordon's heart something that was not to be repressed; he tried to choke it down, but he could not; for it seemed to him that all the women whom he knew and honored—all the mothers and wives whom he knew and honored—were being slandered by this frowzy fool, this Sappho of the Seven Dials.

"If these are the stories," said he — and he averted his eyes, for he knew that they were hot with indignation—"that the married women of your acquaintance tell to you, an unmarried woman, I can only wonder amongst what set of people you live."

Then he checked himself hard. Her language had been brutal; but he had no right to reply with brutality. And at this moment a heaven-born inspiration sprang into his brain.

"Oh, Miss Penguin," said he, with affected cheerfulness, "do you know that Mr. Octavius Quirk is here ?— and he has just been given the control of the reviews of a daily paper; and I suppose he must be forming a staff of contributors. Wouldn't you like to talk to him about it ? Shall I go and fetch him to you ?"

"Oh, will you—will you ?" she said, eagerly; and without another unnecessary word he left.

As he was passing through the first of the lower rooms, he came upon Miss Georgie Lestrange, who turned aside from her small coterie to find out how he had been getting on.

"Why did you introduce me to that woman ?" he said, rather angrily. "She's a brute !"

But at this juncture Lady Adela Cunyngham came up.

"Sir Francis," said the tall, and smiling, and comely

4*

young matron, " would you like to join in a little bit of a frolic ?"

His mood changed in a moment—he had a quite boyish love of diversion.

" Certainly—certainly !"

" Well," said she, " this is what I propose. Sir Hugh has gone down into Devonshire ; and I have just discovered that Georgie, and my sisters Sibyl and Rose, have no engagement whatever for to-night ; and my idea is to have an evening in Scotland."

" What ?" he said—fearing she had gone mad.

" We will have all the shutters shut," she went on ; " and all the lamps and gases lit ; and I've telegraphed home to see if they can let us have dinner at seven— with cockaleekie, if possible ; and we are all to be in tartan things, or at least homespun ; and we are to imagine ourselves in Strathaivron—at the lodge, you know—with the guns, and the keepers, and the ponies, and the panniers just come down from the hill—"

" Delightful—delightful !" he cried, with enthusiasm. " What a grand idea ! And so awfully good of you to give me a chance of joining in ! But, Lady Adela, if you don't mind, I would rather have twenty minutes at my rooms, to change these hateful garments for something more sensible—"

" Why, we're all going home now for the very same purpose ! You come along as soon as you can, Sir Francis. It's getting late, you know. And we must not have the cockaleekie cold."

Sad it is to say that he forgot all about the perfervid Sappho whom he had left pacing the solitary courtyard ; and he never bestowed a thought on Mr. Octavius Quirk ; he went out, and jumped into a hansom, and drove to his rooms in Jermyn Street, and there he quickly exchanged his town costume for Norfolk jacket and knickerbockers. Then he got into another hansom, and was rapidly conveyed out to Aivron Lodge, Campden Hill.

And here the drawing-room, with the shutters closed, was all lit up; and Lady Adela, and her sisters the Ladies Sibyl and Rosamund Bourne, and Georgie Lestrange, were disporting themselves in such scarves or bodices of tartan as they had been able to find—Miss Lestrange, indeed, had a dark blue Tam o' Shanter curbing her rebellious ruddy tresses; and each of them had at her neck a brooch of cairngorms or a ptarmigan's foot set in silver. Young Gordon of Grantly threw himself on to a chair.

"Lady Adela," said he, in an exhausted kind of fashion, "will you forgive me if I don't dress for dinner tonight? I'm completely done. We've had an awful stalk. Three hours up the Corrieara burn before we could get to leeward of the beasts; and then the stag I hit disappeared; we hunted and hunted; and do you know where we found him—about an hour and a half ago?—why, he had been able to run as far as the Black Rocks, and then he had tumbled dead, and rolled right down into Glen Shuna. We found him in a peat-hag—his feet sticking up—"

"You are a lovely liar," said Miss Georgie Lestrange, half audibly; and then she went over to the piano, and sat down, and sonorously struck two handfuls of keys. What was this?

'Cam ye by Athol, lad with the philabeg,
   Down by the Tummel, or banks of the Garry?
   Saw ye the lads wi' their bonnets and white cockades,
   Leaving their mountains to follow Prince Charlie?
      Follow thee, follow thee, wha wadna follow thee?
      Lang hast thou lo'ed and trusted us fairly:
      Charlie, Charlie, wha wadna follow thee?
      King o' the Highland hearts, bonnie Prince Charlie!'

She sang with extraordinary spirit, whatever a trained musician might have thought of the quality of her voice; and this first verse was greeted with cheers of approval and encouragement.   And then she went on:

> 'I'll to Lochiel, and Appin, and kneel to them;
> Down by Lord Murray and Roy of Kildarlie;
> Brave Mackintosh he shall fly to the field with them;
> These are the lads I can trust wi' my Charlie!'

But so infectious was the martial call that they all broke out into the chorus:

> 'Follow thee, follow thee, wha wadna follow thee?
> Lang hast thou lo'ed and trusted us fairly:
> Charlie, Charlie, wha wadna follow thee?
> King o' the Highland hearts, bonnie Prince Charlie!'

In the midst of this tumult the door was opened.

"Dinner is served, your ladyship," said the grave and unseeing butler.

So they all stopped, and burst out laughing; and Lady Adela drove the younger folk into the dining-room, herself following last with Frank Gordon.

The soup was cockaleekie; and if there is any form of food more nutritious, and appetizing, and wholesome, then one person who has wandered about the face of the earth a little bit is ignorant of it. But it was not of the viands they were thinking.

"Georgie," said Lady Adela (in grave continuation of the make-believe), "do you know what Honnor has done to-day?"

"I know what she did in the morning," said Miss Georgie (who also was a tolerable liar), "for I went up to the Geinig to share her lunch with her—not much of a lunch either—biscuits, an apple, and a bottle of milk—and she had got a fifteen-pounder out of the Horseshoe Pool. But it's no use speaking to her—she's just daft with pride about her new waders—" Here the fair damsel suddenly turned to the guest of the evening. "I wish to explain, Sir Francis, that although Honnor Cunyngham—I mean Lady Rock-minster—goes fishing in waders, she preserves perfect decorum ; for she wears a skirt over them—a simple skirt, that doesn't drag, don't you know. And when she has them on, she's as fond of the water as a New-foundland dog ; yesterday she wouldn't let old Robert pull the ferry-boat across—she got hold of it by the bow, and dragged it over to the other side—"

"Well, really," said Lady Adela, in a most serious manner, "we must have something done at the Bad Step. It is getting to be a more breakneck place than ever, for the shingle is gradually falling to the foot of the precipice ; and how Honnor can clamber down, with a long salmon-rod over her shoulder, I don't un-derstand. She won't let old Robert carry anything now—except the lunch-bag and the gaff—"

And so they chattered on—these happy children—up here on the still heights, with all the great mur-muring world of London quite forgotten. Then, when the simple banquet was over, young Gordon rose.

"I'm going to propose a toast," said he, "and in Highland fashion. I want you all to drink with me to the health of the Lady of the House !"

He got up on to his chair, and placed one foot on the table ; the three girls, giggling over the difficulty of the performance, followed his example, holding their glasses very shakily ; Lady Adela, blushing a little, remained seated. And then he called to them : "*Suasa! suasa! Nish! Nish!* To the *Baintighear-*

na!" * He tossed off the claret; he threw the glass over his shoulder, shattering it on the floor; and the three merry maidens did the like, though they seemed rather glad to get down from their unstable position. And then Lady Adela stood up, shyly, and made a pretty little bow.

"It's awfully good of you," said she. "I'm sorry I can't make a speech. I'm awfully sorry. But if you will allow me, I will propose another and a more important toast that I think will appeal to you—if you recall bygone days it will appeal to you—maybe— maybe it will even raise a lump in your throat—as it's like to do in mine—well, I can't say more—but—but —Here is to Bonnie Scotland!"

At this there was a perfect whirlwind of cries.

"The land of the hills and glens!"

"The land of the heather!"

"Strathaivron—and all the friends who have been with us there!"

Then again Lady Adela interposed.

"Sib," she said to her sister, "you know, Scotland isn't all skylarking. Come away now, and play something for us—'Caller Herrin,' perhaps."

So they all of them trooped into the drawing-room, and Lady Sibyl got her violin out of its case, while Lady Rosamund sat down to the piano. There was a little tuning; then the air began; and the two sisters played very well, for amateurs; as clearly as might be the vibrating strings of the violin spoke their pathetic message:

> 'Buy my caller herrin,
> They're bonnie fish and halesome farin',
> Buy my caller herrin,

* Up with it, up with it!—Now, now!—to the Lady of the House!"

New drawn frae the Forth.
Wha'll buy my caller herrin,
They're no brought here without brave darin'.
Buy my caller herrin,
Ye little ken their worth.
Wha'll buy my caller herrin—
O you may ca' them vulgar farin':
Wives and mithers, maist despairin',
Ca' them lives o' men.'

But no sooner had Lady Rosamund risen from the piano than Georgie Lestrange took her place.

"Oh, that kind of thing will never do!" she exclaimed (though her own eyes were brimming with tears), and thereupon she dashed into the lively strains of

' Hey, Johnnie Cope, are ye waukin yet,
And are your drums a-beating yet?
If ye were waukin, I wad wait,
To meet Johnnie Cope in the morning!'

She suddenly stopped. She pretended to hear something. She ran to one of the windows.

"Listen, you people, listen!" she cried. "It's Roderick—and Colin—they've brought home the stag!" Then she called out into the dark: "How many points, Roderick? Twelve points? A Royal? Well done! And why are you so late? Couldn't catch the pony? Wasn't it hobbled? But it had to be chased all the same? And you couldn't stop it till it got down to the Glaisyer burn? And in the dark the strapping of the stag on to the saddle wasn't easy? Well, I should think not! Now you go round to Jeffries and tell him that you and Colin are to have an extra glass of whiskey to-night; and I've no doubt, seeing it's a Royal, that Sir Francis will give each of you a couple of sovereigns in the morning. And in the mean time," continued this giddypated lass, turning to her audience, "ladies and gentlemen, since there are just enough of you for a reel, we must celebrate the coming home of the stag."

She went quickly back to the piano, and again struck her hands on the keys. What the frantic reel or strathspey was they did not stay to consider; the well-known air had all of them at once to their feet, facing their partners; and before they knew what they were about these laughing folk were going through elaborately intricate evolutions, with many a wild 'hooch!' thrown in to stimulate Georgie's intoxicating music. It was at this point that the drawing-room door was opened, and once more the calm-visaged butler made his appearance.

"Lord Rockminster," he said, in an absent kind of fashion.

There advanced into the room a portentously tall man—a man in his way just as handsome as his three beautiful sisters; and when he had recovered from his momentary bewilderment, and when the confusion had been quelled, he said:

"Very sorry to interrupt; but I've some news — I hope for every one of you. I've been writing and writing for the last fortnight; but the final telegram only came this evening. I've taken Glen Skean Castle for the autumn. Now, look here, Addie, to begin with you: Cunyngham is perfectly well aware that the Strathaivron moor must be let alone for the next two years—it will take all that time to recover. So I consider that he and you are booked. I won't take any refusal. And you, Miss Lestrange—may we count on you?"

"The prospect is just heavenly!" said Georgie, with her eyes gleaming delight.

" You, Sib ?"

" Of course !"

" You, Rose ?"

" Me, too, please !" said the youngest of the sisters.

" As for Gordon," continued this tall person, who was generally known as ' Rock,' " we simply can't do without him on the Twelfth ; and besides, there are two beats on the Skean — with a sprinkling of forty-pounders, I am told ; and he can exchange with Honnor just as they may choose. And then I'm going to ask the Prince and Princess, if they haven't gone back to Monteveltro. What do you say as regards yourself, Gordon ?"

" I'm on—awfully good of you," was the instant response.

" So that's all settled," said Lord Rockminster, placidly. " And now, drop your tomfoolery, and let's go into the dining-room, and have some cigarettes, and soda-water, and things."

What time that party broke up (for they were not yet done with Bonnie Scotland) it is needless to inquire ; but at last, at the door, the ladies came along to bid Rockminster and Frank Gordon farewell ; and the younger of the two men said :

" Lady Adela, I really don't know how to thank you. It has been the grandest night I ever spent in London."

" And about the maddest, I should think," said she, laughing, as she gave him her hand.

CHAPTER VII

A GREEK SLAVE

"Now, Briseis, dear," said Mrs. Alexander Elliott to her niece, as these two were seated in the somewhat dusky dining-room of a large house in Devonshire Place, Regent's Park, "you must not think me unfeeling if I try to explain a few matters to you, though no doubt you are tired after so long and fatiguing a journey. You see, it is absolutely necessary. I fear you did not pay much heed to what Mr. Murray the lawyer told you; you were so completely overcome by what had happened—naturally; you did not seem to understand that your little fortune was as good as gone; and not only that, but your uncle appears to have been eating into his own small capital to give you the six-per-cent. interest regularly, and keep you in ignorance. Well, he has made you what reparation he could; he has left you every penny he possessed; though I did think he was going to do something for Olga and Brenda—if it was impossible about Edward—"

"Aunt Clara," cried the girl, "my cousins shall have the money!—they must take the money. I can earn my own living. I can go back to Athens—and teach English—"

"Leave me a little self-respect," said the pale-faced, anxious-eyed widow, with some semblance of pride. "You were confided to my care; and I have always endeavored to do my duty. And sometimes the struggle has been a hard one—yes, sometimes very hard—harder than you might imagine. But now, Briseis, I wish to explain further : the interest on this money that your uncle has left you will not do much more than keep you in clothes, with a trifle for your pocket—and so far you are independent ; while here is a home for you, and a hearty welcome ; only, I—I was going to make an appeal to you—whether you would mind lending a hand about the house—"

"I will do anything—anything, Aunt Clara—and be delighted !" cried Briseis, most cheerfully. "I have been so idle and useless—nothing but amusement. Tell me what I can do !"

"Of course I would not ask you to do anything menial ; but it is different when family affection is the motive—"

"Tell me what I can do !"

"Well, for example," continued Aunt Clara, rather apprehensively, "there are your cousins Olga and Brenda : they are the dearest and sweetest girls ; but their temperaments are extremely sensitive ; and they have to be studied, in the smallest particulars, or some serious illness might ensue. Each of them has to have a cup of tea taken to her room every morning at seven—"

"I will take up the tea to them !" exclaimed Briseis —as if it were a privilege.

"Oh, would you ?—would you be so very obliging ?" said the widow, with the somewhat sad and yet resolute face showing instant relief. "That will be so good of you ! And then at nine each has her breakfast in her own room—and it is such a busy hour—there are so many of us—"

"But I will carry up breakfast to them !" said Briseis, with the beautiful black eyes wondering. Was this all that was to be demanded of her ?

Of a sudden the door was thrown open, and there marched into the room a flabby-faced, flaxen-haired girl of about eighteen, whose naturally pallid skin was flushed with anger and vexation.

"I will stand this no longer," she said, hotly. "I will not be insulted by lodgers. Either they leave the house or I do. Why should I be insulted by lodgers? What else are they? Oh, yes, I know! Young ladies of good family, who are to be introduced to polite society—and this big house is kept up on their account—and every one put to the greatest inconvenience and worry—"

"My dear Olga!"—but no heed would she take of the feeble protest.

"Young ladies of good family! Country bumpkins who come to town to be taken to a few concerts and private views! And I will not stand it any longer. I will not be insulted—I will not—I will not! I will not be told that I have the temper of a hedgehog! That Bingham girl—that cat, Ada Bingham—must leave the house—or I do!" And therewith she flounced out of the room again, slamming the door behind her.

The poor mother was all trembling. Presently she said, in a limp kind of way:

"It's so dreadfully inconsiderate of any one to cross her, if you think of her sensitive temperment. If she was as dull and commonplace and thick-skinned as most girls, I dare say she wouldn't mind; but now this will just break her down. I know what she will do; she will go straight to her bed, in complete collapse; and every hour she will have to have scrambled eggs and tea sent to her—keeping a maid coming and going the whole day long. It's so inconsiderate of Miss Bingham. And yet I cannot afford to quarrel with her. I must find some means of soothing Olga's wounded feelings—"

"Shall I go up to her room, Aunt Clara," said Briseis (who was insensately anxious to be of use, no matter in what direction), "and try to pacify her?"

"Oh, no—oh, no!" exclaimed the mother, in great alarm. "She would fling things at you—I mean—I mean, she might not understand—she wants some one who knows her ways. And I suppose I must go now and see about the scrambled eggs."

As she said this, she sighed, and rose from her chair. But the next moment all her countenance lighted up with an expression of the greatest kindness and affection; for there came into the room—or rather hobbled in on crutches—a poor small lad of twelve or thirteen. This was the only one of her cousins whom Briseis had not as yet encountered; and she had no sooner set eyes on him—regarding his friendly glance, his modest demeanor, and the gallant effort he made to shake hands with her, despite the crutches—than she knew that here was a little gentleman. She took a liking to him from the first instant.

"Cousin Briseis," he said, eagerly, as soon as his mother had gone away to look after the afflicted Olga, "you are from Greece: have you seen the Plain of Marathon?"

"Oh, yes, many a time," she said, in her pleasantest manner; and she could be extremely pleasant, both with voice and looks. "When you go up Pentelicus—you know that is where the quarries are, where they got the marble for the temples on the Acropolis—you look right across the Plain of Marathon."

"And Salamis?" said this poor chap with the pinched features and the wide-staring blue eyes.

"Oh, yes; you can see the Bay of Salamis from any of the heights about Athens. Quite close by."

"And Thermopylæ?"

"Ah, that's much further away—and one doesn't often go round by that part of the coast."

"I suppose you haven't been as far as Troy?" he said, with the same wistful, imaginative intensity. "You couldn't tell me what the country is like?"

"Well, I have sailed past it," said she, good-naturedly; "but there's not much to be seen from the steamer. First you come in sight of Mount Ida—"

"Many-fountained Ida!" he exclaimed, breathlessly.

"—that's inland from Cape Baba. And then you have Tenedos on your left—Tenedos is a yellowish-looking island. But the shores of the Troad are ruddy, as far as I remember; and what you chiefly notice are a number of queer little wind-mills—attached to the wine-presses, you know—"

"Briseis," said he—for his mind was extraordinarily alert, jumping from one subject to another with astonishing swiftness— "what is the meaning of 'Zoe mou, sas agapō'?"

"That is 'My Life, I love you!' But you seem to have read a great deal, Adalbert."

The boy's lips quivered, and his eyes filled.

"What else have I had to do, Briseis?" he said, looking down. "I have never been allowed to go to school—I have never had any games." But the next moment he had plucked up his courage. "Briseis, do you know the story of General Gordon at Khartoum? They say that when he knew he was going to be killed, he put on his full uniform, and took no weapon of any kind with him, no revolver or sword, and he went and stood at the top of the staircase, and waited for them, and faced them in that way when they rushed in." He looked at her for a moment. "I believe you could have done that, Cousin Briseis."

"What?" she cried, in amazement.

"You know, you are very pretty," he said, in a simple and yet earnest kind of fashion. "You won't mind my saying it—for I'm only a boy—and I want you to be a chum of mine; but there's something more than that about you. I think you should have a gold helmet on your head—and you should have a double-handed sword—and you could hew them down!"

"I?" said she, laughing outright. "I? Why, I jump on to a chair if I catch sight of a mouse!"

"That's different," he said, doggedly. "That's different. I believe you would have held a shield in front of Horatius when he kept the bridge. Of course you must be brave. You have been brought up within sight of Salamis, and Marathon, and Thermopylæ. Of course you must be brave. I think you could stand at a door, with a double-handed sword in your hands—if you were defending any one you cared for—and it would be a bad lookout for the other people—"

"Well, well, Adalbert," said she, with the beautiful, soft, dark eyes smiling, "who would have thought that I could be so ferocious? I'm afraid you haven't guessed rightly this time. It won't be long before you find out what a coward I am. Only, you and I are going to be chums—that's agreed."

Just then Mrs. Elliott returned—despondent and almost despairing.

"Oh, it's dreadful!" she said. "The poor darling child is quite broken down. And Miss Bingham refuses to send a single word of apology. And that means a maid's services lost for the whole day." But at this she pulled herself together—for she was a woman with many cares, who had little time for repining. "Briseis," she said, "would you be so extremely kind as to take Adalbert out now, for a turn in the Park? He generally goes out at this hour—I am so sorry to

trouble you — but things seem to be going against
me—"

"Why, Aunt Clara," said Briseis, at once jumping
to her feet, "you should have told me before !"

And away she went to fetch her hat. When she came
down again she discovered what was expected of her.
There was an invalid-chair in the hall, and the poor
lad was waiting. She did not hesitate for a moment.
She got the chair out and on to the pavement ; she
assisted her cousin to his place ; she carried back his
crutches into the house ; and then she set forth, she
pushing the chair, while he directed its course. It
never occurred to her to ask whether this was a menial
task or whether the motive was family affection ; and
as little did she stay to consider whether the people in
the Marylebone Road might fancy she was a nursery-
maid in charge of a perambulator. She was happy in
having something to do ; and she was interested in this
small gentleman, whose intrepid valor, unluckily, had
all to be of the subjective kind—a mere mirror and
reflection of what he might have wished for in actual
life.

And then the day was quite cheerful—for London ;
a breezy day with blue and white skies shining down
through the prevailing pale mist ; and when they had
passed in by York Gate and entered upon the winding
avenues of feathery ash, and sturdier sycamore, and
tall, rustling, swaying poplars, throughout this world
of leafage there was a perpetual soft murmur as of the
sea. Then they made their way to the lake ; and there
was a shimmering silver on the water, with olive-green
reflections under the banks ; and there were bobbing
ducks and stately swans ; and all the busy life of the
small boy-mariners adventuring their tiny craft on the
bosom of the rippling and glancing main. Not at all

"'ONLY, YOU AND I ARE GOING TO BE CHUMS'"

a dismal place—for London; and her crippled cousin seemed to know its quietest nooks and recesses; presently they had drawn up by a wooden bench, where there was comparative solitude, and she could sit there while he talked to her.

"Cousin Briseis," said he, "you are an Elliott too, you know; did you ever hear of the Lion of Liddesdale?"

She confessed her ignorance.

"Well, if you will look in the pouch at the back of the chair, you will find a volume of ballads; and in it is 'Lock the door, Lariston'—I wish you would read it aloud to me—it sounds so much better when you hear some one else repeat it."

She did as she was bid; she searched in the cunning receptacle, that she discovered to be filled with books and magazines, chiefly of wild adventure; and at last she was ready to begin her recitation:

> 'Lock the door, Lariston, lion of Liddesdale—
> Lock the door, Lariston, Louther comes on;
>   The Armstrongs are flying,
>   The widows are crying,
> The Castletoun's burning, and Oliver's gone.'

She did not in the least know what the story was about; but as she proceeded she could see that this poor lad's sensitive physique was all tremulous with excitement, and his look was keen and exultant.

> 'Why dost thou smile, noble Elliott of Lariston?
> Why does the joy-candle gleam in thine eye?
>   Thou bold border-ranger,
>   Beware of thy danger,
> Thy foes are relentless, determined, and nigh.'

Nay, as she finished—

5

'See how they wane, the proud file of the Windermere,
   Howard, ah ! woe to thy hopes of the day,
         Hear the rude welkin rend
         While the Scots' shouts ascend :
"Elliott of Lariston, Elliott for aye !"'—

he turned to her, his face quite pale with emotion—

"Are you not proud of being an Elliott, Briseis ?" he
demanded.

"I had never read the ballad before," she said, more
calmly.

"And you have such a beautiful voice !" he exclaimed.
"You could read anything—I mean, you could put the
right sound into it. I can hear your voice now—ringing. It is wonderful. Briseis—if you don't mind—
there's Campbell's Poems in the bag there—if you were
to get them out—I think you are the only one I ever
knew who could recite 'Ye Mariners of England'—
would you mind ?"

She hunted about, and found the book.

"I hope I am not troubling you too much," said the
small gentleman. "I only want you to repeat one
verse. It's 'Britannia needs no bulwarks'—"

And so she pronounced the lines—as nobly as she
could :

'Britannia needs no bulwarks,
No towers along the steep ;
Her march is o'er the mountain-waves,
Her home is on the deep.
With thunders from her native oak,
She quells the floods below,
As they roar on the shore
When the stormy winds do blow ;
When the battle rages loud and long,
And the stormy winds do blow !'

"But you make one mistake," said he, rather disap-
pointedly. "It should be wīnds, not wīnds. Am I

bothering you too much, Cousin Briseis—will you read
it again ?"

She was a most biddable creature. Again she read
the verse, this time altering her pronunciation to give
the sonorous wĭnds :

> "As they roar on the shore
> When the stormy wĭnds do blow ;
> When the battle rages loud and long,
> And the stormy wĭnds do blow !"

"Isn't it splendid !—splendid !" he cried, his frail
frame almost panting with enthusiasm. "And aren't
you glad you are of English blood ? And Greek blood,
too, of course. Briseis, tell me about Greece. Were
you ever near the island that Ulysses came back to,
when his dog recognized him ? That was—well, I forget—but his dog knew him—"

"Oh, that was Ithaca—Thiaki they generally call it
now : I used sometimes to go and stay there for a week
or two with a cousin of my father's—"

"And what is it like—what is it actually like now,
Briseis ?" he said, with his eyes again grown eager and
visionary.

"Why, the most beautiful island you ever beheld !"
she went on, only too glad that she could amuse him.
"Very mountainous in most parts—with sheltered bays
down at the coast—and gardens round the villas—and
white terraces—and olive groves along the hill-slopes.
I used to climb up through these olive groves until I
could get a wide view of the other islands ; and it was
just like fairy-land, the color was so fine and clear—
you would think everything was transparent, though
here and there was a sprinkling of tall black cypresses.
And then you can't imagine how intensely blue the sea
is—and you watch the gayly colored boats with their

double sails like the wings of a bird—and sometimes the sails are white, but mostly they're a rich ruddy brown. I never did get so high up as the summit of Mount Ætos—that is where the ruins are that they call the Castle of Ulysses; but I may be more fortunate some other time; and then I hope you may be there too—"

She suddenly stopped—and a flush of frightened embarrassment sprang to her-forehead. How could she have been so heedless and cruel as to talk to this poor maimed lad—even in the innocent prattle with which she had sought to entertain him—of any attempt on his part to scale the rough slopes of Mount Ætos? However, if he had taken notice, he would not reveal the fact. He betrayed neither mortification nor resentment. He only said, gently:

"I think we ought to be going back now, Briseis. Mamma does not like any one to be late for luncheon."

They did get back in time; and a very queer meal that luncheon proved to be. First of all, just as Briseis had assisted her cousin Adalbert to get into his chair at the table, there came into the dining-room the younger sister, Brenda—a stout, lumpish girl, with yellow hair, white eyelashes, and about the sulkiest mouth that mortal man or woman ever beheld. She had met Briseis before, so she passed on without a word. Then Mrs. Alexander Elliott appeared, followed by three young ladies — three pleasant-complexioned, rather countrified misses, who, as they were introduced to the foreign stranger, wore a look of unaccountable shyness, not to say dismay. What that extraordinary expression betokened Briseis could not imagine; but she was soon to learn. Meantime they all took their places; and then ensued a period of constrained waiting, almost in silence. The anxious mother kept glanc-

ing nervously towards the door ; the maid at the sideboard was evidently listening. And at last, after a
considerable delay that every moment became more de-
pressing, there lounged into the room, with his hands
in his pockets, a tall, cadaverous, supercilious-looking
youth, who lazily strolled along to the chair at the
head of the table, without a syllable of apology to any
one. It was his mother who spoke for him.

"You must excuse Edward," she said in a low voice
to Briseis. "He is so busy with his studies. And he
does not like us to begin without him."

Then the frugal luncheon was served ; and again
Aunt Clara turned to Briseis — this time talking in
tones that all should hear.

"Do you know, Briseis, I have been told that you
are a most accomplished linguist ; and I am sure you
will agree with me that there is nothing more valuable,
for a young girl going into society, than fluent French
—not the French of the school-room and grammars,
but the French that people actually speak. And it has
occurred to me — you are so friendly and obliging—
that if our conversation at lunch-time were to be ex-
clusively in French—"

"What rot !" muttered the medical student at the
head of the table.

"—and if you would be so kind as to suggest any
more correct phrases or elegant idioms to the dear
girls there—"

The fear on the faces of the three young ladies deepened to fright ; and now Briseis understood. It had
been the dread of having to talk to her in French that
had been at the bottom of their incomprehensible shyness when they came into the room. Nevertheless,
Briseis bravely buckled to her task ; she tried to en-
courage them ; she asked them, in sufficiently simple

phrases, about their pursuits and occupations, and so forth.   Each of them kept her eyes resolutely fixed on her plate, doubtless hoping that one of the others respond ; and as all three were of the same mind, the result was a most ghastly stillness.   At last Mrs. Elliott made a piteous appeal to Miss Bingham, who had caused the tragedy of the morning.

"Ada, why don't you answer Miss Valieri ? You need not fear criticism. You know French well enough —only, of course, you have not had much practice."

And then, indeed, the poor lass — with her face grown all rosy-red—made a desperate plunge.

"Je suppose, mademoiselle," said she, in a gasping sort of way, "qu'on parle Français à la cour d'Athènes ?"

Briseis politely informed her that no doubt that must be so sometimes ; but that the favorite language of the Court of Athens was English.

The next girl was not to be outdone :

"Comment prononcez-vous, mademoiselle, le nom de l'île où vous etiez née—Ægina, ou Ægeena ?"

In reply the obliging Briseis (if she was inwardly laughing, she made no sign) gave her the modern Greek pronunciation of the name of the island—which the wise virgin was too prudent to attempt to repeat.

Then the youngest must have a try as well.

"Dans les rues d'Athènes, mademoiselle—est ce que vous avez le—le—le lit électrique ?"

There was a prevailing puzzlement for a brief second, until Miss Ada rather angrily nudged her young neighbor.

"La lumière—la lumière !" she said, under her voice.

But the youngest was so overcome with confusion that she did not seek to retrieve her blunder ; she collapsed into an ashamed and hopeless silence. The other two, however, having gained a little courage, went on with their Ollendorfian questions; while Miss Brenda remained sulkily apart, and the medical student, muttering in half-heard English, grumbled about the hardness of the cold boiled beef.

Immediately lunch was over, the company broke up, the young ladies dispersing to their several rooms to get ready for a walk in the Park, accompanied by Miss Ada's maid—for Miss Ada's parents were kind enough to let her have a maid all to herself. And then Mrs. Elliott asked Briseis to go with her to the drawing-room, where they found themselves alone.

"I think you will soon begin to perceive how I am situated, Briseis, dear," said the much-enduring widow. "I have a hard fight to make both ends meet; but then, as I often say, I have my reward; there are few mothers have such reason to be proud of their children as I have of mine. At the same time, it is a hard struggle. It takes a great deal of planning, and management, and tact—especially as regards the servants; they know they have too much work for their number; but I cannot afford to engage more; and yet I must keep up this big house—with its large drawing-room—for my receptions; and also for—for—these young ladies who stay with me. But I was speaking of the servants: well, they have to be treated with the greatest consideration, or I don't know what might not happen. For example, I never ring the bell in this room. That would bring a girl up to see what was wanted; then she would have to go down to fetch it; then a third time coming up, and a fourth going down again. Whereas, if you go to the top of the kitchen stair, and call to them, you get what you want at once, and they don't keep grumbling."

"I quite understand, Aunt Clara," said Briseis, after this ingenious preamble.

"And that is what I was coming to," continued the harassed widow, with rather a timid and apprehensive look; "you see, the maids sit down to their dinner presently, and they do not like being disturbed. I was thinking—whether you would mind going and asking cook to prepare some more scrambled eggs and tea for poor dear Olga; and then, when they are ready, I'm sure you wouldn't object to taking them up to her room. It is more than an hour since she has had anything; and the poor darling is quite upset if she thinks she is neglected. It preys on her mind so; and the worry simply destroys her nerves — something quite dreadful might happen—"

"Oh, I will go at once, Aunt Clara!" said Briseis— for of course this was no menial duty; the motive was family affection.

"And now I can get off to my tradesmen's books," said Aunt Clara, at once hurrying away.

So Briseis went down and saw the cook, and ingratiated herself with that important person, and finally obtained the wherewithal for Miss Olga's repast. Then she proceeded up stairs to her cousin's room. She knocked at the door.

"Come in!—oh, it's you? Put the tray down on that little table, please."

The flabby-cheeked girl, with her dull straw-colored hair dishevelled on the pillow, was lying in bed, reading a ladies' paper that appeared to consist chiefly of fashion plates and advertisements; and as soon as she had issued her orders she resumed her devotion to those luxuries. But the next instant she had changed her mind.

"Has that cat Bingham been turned out of the

house?" she demanded, turning her vindictive gray eyes upon Briseis.

"I believe she has gone for a walk in the Park, with the others," was the placid reply.

"I did not ask you that—I asked you whether she had been turned out of the house—yes or no!" she said, with considerable insolence.

"Now, Olga, be reasonable—do be reasonable!" Briseis pleaded. "Think what that would mean to your mother; for the others would most likely leave as well. And I'm sure Miss Bingham did not mean any harm—"

"I will not endure being insulted," she said, fiercely. "I don't care whether they all leave or not—a blessed riddance! I will not be insulted by a cat like that!—I will not!—I will not! And here I remain until Miss Bingham sends me a formal apology. And if she doesn't, very well, then I shall be ill. I know it. It has happened before—I shall be ill—and then what will they do?—"

"Come, come, now, Olga," her cousin said, in answer to this threat, "be reasonable. And I am quite sure Miss Bingham will say she is sorry she vexed you. There's another thing I meant to tell you. I haven't had time to open my trunk yet; and all my few belongings are in it; among them some embroidered silk kerchiefs that my mother gave me when we were in Broussa—of the strangest colors they are, and yet very beautiful—and I am sure they would interest you—and you might choose one for yourself if you wished. Will you come to my room and look at them?"

The coverlet was whisked aside in a moment; and as soon as Miss Olga was on her feet, she undid the buttons of her white dressing-gown, which forthwith dropped on to the floor. It was now manifest that she had

5*

never really gone to bed at all ; she had merely slipped this upper garment over her ordinary costume, and hidden herself beneath the coverlet.   And it was in her ordinary costume that the still impenitent Olga now followed her cousin to her room.

That was but one of the many events of the day, so far as Briseis was concerned ; but there was an abundance of others ; the next of these being her endeavor to propitiate the reluctant Miss Bingham.   Thereafter, all through the afternoon and evening, her time seemed to be continually under requisition ; she was asked to do this and do that, always as a favor ; until her final task turned out to be going to Brenda Elliott's room and reading to that sulky damsel until she fell asleep.

But at last she was enfranchised, a little after eleven o'clock—she having arrived in London that morning at a quarter to eight ; and then she got away to her own small chamber, and went to bed happy (perhaps with some occasional back thoughts not quite so happy); for at least she had tried to do her best—and that in a right cheerful frame of mind.

CHAPTER VIII

BY MOOR AND RILL

It was early morning on the Twelfth of August—a golden morning that spread abroad a soft and wistful radiance, so that all the surrounding landscape seemed ethereal and dreamlike : the deep, wide valley—the winding waters of the Skean, here a flashing silver, yonder a pale turquoise—away on the other side yellow-green slopes, with tiny white dots telling of crofters' cottages—above these the purple shoulders of the distant hills receding into the cloudless sky—and then, still further away, towards the east, and south, and west, rampart upon rampart of giant mountains, grown almost visionary in the pellucid atmosphere—it was on this still, placid, golden morning that the Prince of Monteveltro, his host Lord Rockminster, Sir Hugh Cunyngham of the Braes, and young Frank Gordon were strolling up and down the terrace in front of Glen Skean Castle, each of them smoking a cigarette. The Castle was a large gray building, or rather pile of buildings, of quite modern date—though the square towers, the machicolated walls, and mullioned windows sufficiently revealed the origin of its architecture ; it was picturesquely situated, on a high plateau overlooking the broad and fertile strath ; while at the back it was sheltered from the western storms by a belt of dark green pines. There was not much sign of life about, though occasionally the glimmer of a skirt crossed the inner recesses of the hall.

Monseigneur appeared to be a trifle uneasy and impatient; now and again he twisted the waxed ends of his long and drooping mustache; he kept glancing from time to time towards the portico, where no carriage was as yet visible. At length he threw away his cigarette.

"When do we go?" he said, in excellent English. "Is it not time to start?"

"There's no hurry," said the tall, and handsome, and lazy Rockminster, in his impassive way. "The wagonette will be round shortly; but the keepers and the dogs won't be up at the moor yet awhile."

"It's the greatest possible mistake," said Sir Hugh —a short, powerfully-built, clear-eyed, brisk-looking man, with plenty of decision about his mouth—"the greatest possible mistake to make too early a start on the Twelfth. The birds should be allowed to have their breakfast comfortably, and get settled down in the heather. Faith, they'll lie close enough to-day! Awful hard luck on the dogs. No scent. It's going to be a regular scorcher!"

At this moment a rumble of wheels was heard, and the next moment a wagonette, drawn by a pair of beautiful bays, appeared at the end of the drive, and presently was pulled up in front of the portico. There was a little commotion—for the women-folk of the party were now coming out to the hall door; and thus it was that Lord Rockminster managed to get a side-word with young Gordon of Grantly.

"Look here, Gordon," said he, so as not to be overheard, "when we begin work, what do you say as to our order of march? The Prince tells me he knows nothing, absolutely nothing, of grouse-shooting—never saw a grouse. Shall we put him in the middle, and you and Cunyngham on the outside—to retrieve mistakes ? I sha'n't bother you much — I don't care about it—I may as well be a middle-man—"

"Oh, but you needn't be afraid of my step-papa !" Frank Gordon said. "Not a bit! He's a rattling good shot—a nailer!—when he knows what kind of thing he has to expect. And that's what he doesn't know here ; he'll want a friendly lead ; and if you don't mind I'll look after him. Of course he may be a little bit nervous at first. His great ambition in this country is to do everything correctly, as an ordinary English gentleman would. You see, he is quite familiar with the silly burlesques of the foreign sportsman in England that appear in plays and comic magazines— idiots in *Der Freischütz* costumes, who shoot sparrows with rifles.; and all that rubbish has made him desperately anxious to be just like everybody else. Look at his get-up now—how's that ?"

And indeed the Prince's attire was severely accurate, from the deer-stalker's cap and belted Norfolk jacket to the knickerbockers of homespun, the greenish stockings, the brown gaiters, and nailed shoes. But by this time all the ladies of the house had come out into the portico ; and a very charming group they formed, in their costumes of lightest material and brightest color ; a kind of flower garden they seemed to be, on this shining summer morn. Then one of them—a ruddy-haired young creature wearing a pince-nez—as the sportsmen were getting into the wagonette, stepped forward, and there was a propitiatory smile on her pert and pretty features.

"Monseigneur," said she, holding up between thumb and forefinger a small glittering coin, "you must take this with you."

He could not refuse to accept the new sixpence ; but he was somewhat bewildered.

"That's for good luck," Frank Gordon explained. "Put it in your pocket, sir, and you'll have all the best chances; you'll have everything your own way."

But that was not in the least Miss Georgie Lestrange's idea; for she, blushing a little, passed round the wagonette, giving to each of the others one of these brilliant talismans; then the coachman removed the brake, there was a fluttering of handkerchiefs from the front of the portico, and soon the wagonette had disappeared from sight.

The route to the moor lay at first alongside the steep banks of the river Skean; and down through the hanging birches and the tall bracken they got glimpses of the deep gray chasms and the still brown pools—for there had been a long drought, and the stream had dwindled away almost to nothing. Here on board the wagonette there was not much mirth, or even talkativeness; there was rather a sort of subdued-excitement; even to an experienced sportsman the morning of the Twelfth brings an unusual sensation; for one thing he cannot forecast whether he is going to shoot well or ill. Then they left the densely wooded valley, and gradually ascended until they had reached a height almost on a level with the distant Glen Skean Castle; a gate was opened, and they entered upon a rude track apparently leading up into the mountains: they were now within the outskirts of Corriefruin deer-forest.

"A forest?" cried the Prince, with his eyes staring. "Is that what you call in Scotland a forest?"

It was a still and sombre scene—that vast extent of bare and undulating moorland, seamed and scarred with deep peat-hags half filled with stagnant water; then far away beyond this voiceless plain rose the almost precipitous slopes of the lower hills; and above these again the sterile peaks of Aonach Môr (the Great

Solitude), with a glimmer of snow among the less-exposed crevices. Not a sound came from this barren wilderness; not a living creature moved—for the deer, in the settled fine weather, had withdrawn to the seclusion of the higher valleys; a brooding solitariness seemed to have gained possession of this lonely world, on which it seemed a kind of sacrilege to intrude. Yet here was a fair summer morning: what would such a place be like on a wild night of storm, with the winds sweeping over the desolate waste, and the thunder rumbling along the glens, and the shafts of splintered lightning striking down from the crags of Aonach Mòr, and startling the black heavens and the black earth into a sudden and lurid life?

And so they made their way into this silent domain —the horses dragging laboriously—until, after two or three miles, they arrived at a long, low building of wood and zinc that had been erected as a temporary stable, and also for the convenience of luncheon parties; and here the occupants of the wagonette got down and proceeded on foot. They had not gone very far, however, when it became evident that the still air and the ever-increasing heat in this vast hollow between the hills were beginning to tell on Mgr. le prince de Monteveltro; perhaps fashionable life in Vienna and Buda-Pesth had got the hardy mountaineer out of proper condition; at all events, when they at last did join the picturesque group of keepers, gillies, ponies, and panniers waiting for them by the side of the track, instead of taking his gun from the youth who had been specially told off to wait on him, the Prince sat down on a big stone, and mopped his forehead, and brought forth his pocket-flask.

"Get me some water," he said, panting, to young Angus.

The lad took the cup, and went down to the trickling little burn, and brought back some water; the Prince put a dash of whiskey into it; and he was just about to drink it off when—

When a most terrific explosion took place—and that apparently quite close by the very stone on which he was sitting: an indescribable *kr-r-r-r!* that might have shattered the nerves of the Sphinx; and the next moment a reddish-brown object was seen to be darting away over the heather with a swiftness as if all the fire-engines in the universe had got compressed into its whirring wings. Frank Gordon had been leisurely putting cartridges into his gun; he had but half a second in which to snap together barrels and stock and take aim; there was an echoing report; and the gay muir-cock, now a considerable distance off, came plumping down. Very neatly done; for it was a nasty cross-shot; and, moreover, he had been taken unawares. By this time the Prince was on his feet again.

"Why," said he to the head keeper, "that bird must have been hiding there since ever you came!"

"Yes, monsenior," replied the tall, grave, respectful keeper, "they whiles lie like that. And maybe there's one or two more about. It you'll put cartridges into your gun, I'll lowze the dogs."

So they formed into line there and then — young Gordon on the extreme left, Sir Hugh on the extreme right, the Prince and Lord Rockminster (the latter with his gun over his shoulder) between; the grave Malcolm uncoupled a brace of extremely handsome setters, that joyously set to work; and the whole party moved warily forward. It turned out, however, that the grouse which had so startled the stranger-guest had been a kinless vagrant; they descended into the

channel of the burn and up the opposite side without
finding anything; and as the dogs were now ranging
freely, they stepped along with more confidence.

Then of a sudden one of the setters, that happened to
be right in front of the Prince, stopped short and rigid,
with eager nostrils and outstretched neck.

"Have a care, Wallace, have a care!" muttered the
keeper to the other dog, that now also stopped, watching its neighbor with half-frightened eyes.

Monseigneur glanced towards his step-son as if to ask
what he should do; and the answer was a wave of the
hand telling him to follow the setter; for the beautiful
silken - haired animal, trembling in every limb, was
cautiously drawing on. All the guns were now moving
slowly forward; the keeper had stolen up, to encour-
age the dog by patting its neck; and the profound
silence was full of a restrained expectancy. Then a
wild rattle right in front—a ball of feathered lightning
had sprung from the ground and was whizzing along—
the Prince put up his gun quickly and fired—and the
grouse came tumbling on to the heather, with a single
rebound simply by reason of its own weight. At the
same moment another bird got up some distance off
and disappeared over the top of the knoll—and they
could hear the warning *uk—uk—uk! — come back—
come back—come back!* that he directed to his late companion. Nay, they were to see him again; for while
Malcolm was picking up the dead bird, which was a
hen, the cock-bird, having made an unseen détour, returned to the crest of the knoll, and fluttered down
among the heather, where only his small head, with
its bright eye and scarlet markings, was visible. And
now, if ever there was temptation to shoot a sitting
bird, it was on this occasion—if one could avoid sym-
pathizing with the faithful spouse who had again faced

danger in order to see what had happened to his mate ;
for it was perfectly obvious that, the moment he was
off again, he would drop down behind the hillock and
get clean away. So once more Monseigneur turned
with an inquiring glance towards his step-son—who
instantly warned him, by gesture of head and hand,
that no such thing was to be done ; while almost simultaneously the grouse settled the matter in his own
fashion, for he simply dropped away from his exalted
position, and vanished. Perhaps they were all just
as well pleased that he had not fallen a victim to con-
jugal fidelity.

And so they shot their way along these lower slopes,
keeping well aside from the Forest ; and as they were
now on better ground, the fun waxed brisker and
brisker. Moreover, the birds lay very close ; sometimes
the dogs ran past them altogether ; and as it was impossible to say from which mound or dip a bombshell
of a covey might not suddenly burst, scattering to every
point, there was no lack of watchful exhilaration. As
for Monseigneur, he acquitted himself admirably. Of
course they did not expect him to observe the niceties
of the game ; they did not expect him, when a covey
hurtled itself into the air, to single out the old cock ;
they looked after that themselves as well as they
could ; and left him to his discretion. *Kr—kr—kr!*
—went the throbbing ·wings ; crack !—crack !—crack !
—went the guns ; and as only smokeless powder was
used, they could easily see what execution was being
done. The bag mounted up apace, as the gillie with
the pony and panniers came along to pick up the
spoil.

There was one drawback—nay, there were two ; and
both told desperately on the poor Prince, who was somewhat corpulent. The first was the overwhelming heat,

that seemed to deprive one of the power of breathing; the second was a plague of midges, these demoniacal insects alighting on any unguarded portion of wrist, or neck, or forehead, and leaving a most vexatious wound, especially if one happened to be of a stout habit of body. Monseigneur suffered inconceivable torment. For even when they came to a hollow down which trickled a small streamlet, and when he would go to the burn-side to get some water (some whiskey and water) to slake his overmastering thirst, then in this sheltered place the midges would attack him more venomously than ever, even creeping under the peak of his cap and getting among the roots of his hair. He rubbed his forehead hard with his handkerchief, and that only produced more pain; he drank more whiskey to still the fever in his blood, and that appeared to create a kind of delirium of despair; his companions could hear him muttering, they knew not in what language; until at last, from the crest of a slope, there broke upon their sight a beatific vision—a long and narrow table placed outside the stables, and abundantly set forth with cold meats and cooling drinks, while something very like a pail of ice stood by.

"Thank God!" said the Prince of Monteveltro—and no one could object to that pious ejaculation.

And here were the Ladies Sibyl and Rosamund Bourne and Miss Georgie Lestrange, who had driven up in a landau hired from the Skean Bridge Hotel; and these three were engaged in decorating, with such wild flowers as they could find—milkwort, tormentil, grass of Parnassus, and the like—the snowy cloth that concealed the rude construction of the table; while for a centrepiece they had got a dish of freshly cut heather and sweetgale.

"Why, where's Addie?" said Rockminster, speaking

of his sister, Lady Adela Cunyngham. "And Honnor?" he asked again—speaking of his wife.

"Honnor," said Miss Georgie, who was the know-all of the family, "is hurrying through her household affairs to see if she can get an hour on the river, though everybody maintains it isn't a bit o' good. And Adela is busy with her proofs—those fearful proofs! Why, she tells me they keep her awake at night: she lies and recalls page after page, dreading to think what she may have passed. I declare it's too bad of the printers," continued the bewitching young damsel of the pince-nez, as she graciously accepted a slice of galantine. "Do you know what they made her say in her last book?—her heroine had to die of an overdose of opium, and they printed it opinion."

"A book might die of an overdose of opinion," observed Lord Rockminster, in his dispassionate way, "but a heroine couldn't very well, could she?"

"The worst printers' blunder I ever heard of," Miss Georgina went on, in her demurest manner, "appeared in a Plymouth paper. The report began: 'Last evening a banquet was held on the body of a dead seaman that had been found washed ashore at Prawle Point. The coroner, in his opening remarks—'"

"Georgie, you're horrid—you are positively horrid," Lady Rosamund broke in.

But at this moment Monseigneur jumped to his feet, panting and gasping, and frantically rubbing forehead, and ears, and neck.

"I can stand it no longer," he exclaimed. "These brutes are perfectly maddening!—"

"They are pretty bad," said Rockminster, calmly.

"Here!" the Prince called recklessly to the footman who was doing duty as butler. "Bring me a tumbler half filled with whiskey—quick, if you please !—quick, quick !"

The glass was brought, and at once he dipped his table-napkin into it, and began to sponge his face all over, until he was fairly dripping with the fiery fluid.

"I don't think you'll find that of much use, sir," said Frank Gordon to his step-father. "I've tried it myself. They seem rather to like whiskey."

"But I have got something," put in Georgie Lestrange. "I thought they might be plaguing us when we sat still." And away she tripped to the landau, returning therefrom with several layers of a fine silken gauze. "You must cut off just what you want," she said, addressing the company generally, "and tie it round your head, or fasten it on with a hat. And mind you take plenty, and leave it loose, or else the little fiends will bite through."

And thus it fell out that this luncheon was partaken of by seven white-headed ghosts, and that not without difficulty, for they had to be careful about raising their silken veil. But very soon it appeared that Monseigneur was impatient to get on again ; he seemed to have some frenzied idea that in movement he might escape from this insufferable cloud of persecutors, which, gauze or no gauze, managed to sting him about the wrists and along the junction of his cap and forehead ; so the men of the party rose, and lit their cigarettes, and presently had summoned the keepers and gillies, leaving the three young ladies to dawdle over the fruit, and biscuits, and iced claret-cup.

Now what happened on this afternoon will never be accurately known ; a vague secrecy was maintained by every one concerned ; but it is to be suspected that the hapless Prince, completely overcome by the unendurable torture inflicted by the midges—and also being

entirely ignorant of the strength of Highland whiskey
—it is to be surmised that he may have paused somewhat too frequently by the side of the babbling little
mountain rills, to seek a desperate relief.   At all
events, when they did get back to the Castle, and
when, in his half-demented condition, he had called
his valet to him, he declared that nothing would re-
duce the fever in his veins but an extremely hot bath;
whereupon that was immediately prepared for him;
while the other men went away to their own rooms, to
change and get ready for dinner.   So that a considerable interval occurred; and it was not until about an
hour thereafter that Lord Rockminster, happening to
come along by the top of the hall staircase, encountered the Prince's valet, who appeared to be agitated.

"My lord," said this pasty-faced person, with his
eyes starting out of his head, "I—I hope there's
nothing wrong—but—but the Prince has been in the
bath-room for such a long time—and I can't hear a
sound—would your lordship mind—"

His lordship was a man of few words: he at once
went along to the end of the corridor in which the
Prince's apartments were situated, and there he
knocked at the bath-room door.   He thought he
heard some mumbled sound in reply; but was not
sure; accordingly he knocked again.   This time there
certainly was no answer; so he tried to prize the lock;
and these efforts failing, he was driven to use his
shoulder as a battering-ram; and as he was of great
muscular strength and weight, the door eventually
flew open.   It is a matter for devout thankfulness that
on this occasion he was not accompanied by the Presi-
dent of the State Council of the Principality of Monteveltro and his colleague the Minister for Foreign
Affairs.   For Monseigneur lay supine in the bath, his

head resting on the canvas belt at the upper end, each hand helplessly clutching on to the enamelled zinc.

"Can't get out," he said, with a humorous smile. "Sides of the bath too zlippery—very zlippery. Never mind. Quite comf'ble. No mizzjehs here. Quite comf'ble. Sides of the bath awful zlippery—"

Rockminster had recognized the situation at a glance.

"Oh, come along, Monseigneur, you must get ready for dinner!" he said—and he and the valet together managed to hoist the luckless Prince out of the bath; and they clothed him in his dressing-gown, and conveyed him into his bedroom, which fortunately was just next door. "Now you lie down for a while," Rockminster said to him. "And I will send you up some strong tea. You needn't hurry—I will put dinner off till nine o'clock."

Strangely enough, some hour and a half thereafter, when the house party had assembled in the drawing-room, there was no one more sedate, and calm, and outwardly self-possessed than the Prince of Monteveltro. His forehead, indeed, showed what merciless treatment had been dealt him by the midges; but neither in his manner nor in his speech (except, perhaps, in a certain pretentous and cautious solemnity) was there any trace of the wild relief he had sought for by the margin of the rippling burns; and as he took his hostess in to dinner—Lady Rockminster was a handsome and distinguished-looking young matron, with chestnut-brown hair and clear hazel eyes—he comported himself with an excellent dignity and gravity. Then they all sat down.

All save two. For this dining-hall, quite modern as it was, had been constructed and decorated in Elizabethan fashion—oaken panels, tapestry, large mullioned windows, and so forth; while at the further end, above the immense fireplace, there was a small pillared gallery, in which were visible a harp and two music-stands. And as the guests below took their places, the Ladies Sibyl and Rosamund Bourne came into the gallery, the former carrying her violin; and Lady Rosamund sat down at the harp; and presently these two began to play, very softly and gracefully, a cavatina of Lady Sibyl's own composition.

"Awfully good-natured of them, isn't it?" said Georgie Lestrange to her neighbor, young Gordon of Grantly. "I call it a great compliment, don't you? I hope the Prince will be pleased—"

"Aren't they going to have any dinner?" said the young man, with tender compassion in his heart.

"Oh, they'll get something—or they've had something," continued the ruddy-haired lass, with blithe indifference. "That isn't the point. Sibyl is awfully proud of this cavatina, don't you know, and she wants us to hear it effectually. Rather nice, isn't it? Sounds very well from the gallery, doesn't it? I think it's a beautiful room, don't you? And how handsome the Princess is looking to-night—so commanding-looking, so capable-looking—and yet as merry as any one: don't you think so? Scotch eyes, I should say; nothing foreign about her appearance at all. I wonder what rent Lord Rockminster pays for the season—a ripper, I should imagine. Oh, by-the-way, Sir Francis, I suppose you've heard that Lady Rockminster has arranged a little dance for to-night—the keepers, and gillies, and Highland maids—in the pavilion—just to give the Prince some small idea of what happens when a stag is brought home; for I suppose the Prince and Princess won't be able to stay until the stalking begins. And I have been wondering," proceeded the wily maiden, in her artless way, "whether any of us will be expected to join in—perhaps for a single reel. I'm rather timorous about it, don't you know—of course, I've often danced a reel, in a scrambling kind of fashion; but I never feel safe unless I have a partner who can pilot me through—"

" Will you let me try ?" he said, promptly.

" Oh, I didn't mean that," she made answer, with a pretty and ingenuous blush. " But we'll see what Lady Rockminster has to propose."

The pavilion of which she had spoken was a large temporary structure of wood and canvas that had been erected in the grounds a year or two previously on the occasion of the visit of certain members of the English Royal Family, and had been allowed to remain; and when Lord and Lady Rockminster's guests, rising from dinner, proceeded to thread their way through the dark shubberies, they found the great tent brilliantly lit up, and the entrance all hung round with festoons of heather. Nay, the merrymaking had already begun; supper was over, and the tables had been cleared away; Ronald the piper, in all his kilted bravery, was up in front of the platform; and the lads and lasses were stepping out to the lively strains of 'Lord Breadalbane's March.' But directly that Ronald caught sight of the visitors he changed his tune; the pipes broke into a spirited reel; almost instantly there was a transformation of the nebulous company into definite groups; then at a given signal away they went in swift and gliding and sinuous movement, until the laughing partners faced each other again, to do their best with pointed toe and uplifted finger and thumb. All this gay turmoil—the stirring music, the rapid evolutions, the joyous 'whoop!'—was not long in throwing its irresistible seduction over certain of the visitors; a 'foursome' was speedily formed—Miss Lestrange and young Gordon of Grantly, Sir Hugh Cunyngham and his sister-

6

in-law, Lady Rosamund ; and off they went—figures of
eight, facing to partners, and round again in nimble
manœuvres—as dexterously as any. And Ronald the
piper blew and trilled, and trilled and blew, and trilled
and screamed and blew, as though he would have all
Glen Loy, and Clunes, and Achnacarry know what
doings were going on in Glen Skean.

But of a sudden Lord Rockminster—who was merely
a spectator—became aware that the Prince was missing ;
and as he had not been able to keep an eye on him
during dinner—for the Princess of Monteveltro was
a brilliant and fascinating talker, and kept her host's
attention fully occupied—he grew somewhat anxious.
He looked about, and moved about, discreetly ; and at
length, to his amazement, he perceived the Prince, at
the other end of the pavilion, in a corner all by himself, engaged in executing a series of the most extraordinary springs and gyrations, both hands held high
in air. For it appeared that he had found a partner,
and he was imitating as best he could the steps and
gestures he had observed in use among the general
assemblage ; and as this fancied partner happened to
be no other than his own shadow on the canvas wall,
the most beautiful time was kept, and Monseigneur,
proud of his own performance, and proud of the responsive accuracy of his visionary companion, beamed
with a bland delight. Rockminster caught him by the
arm.

"One moment," he said. "Sorry to interrupt. Awful
storm threatening. You'd better come away with me,
and we'll get back to the Castle while there's time."

The Prince of Monteveltro was a peaceable, good-
natured-man ; he suffered himself to be led off, and
fortunately there was a door at this end of the pavilion ;
while they had no difficulty in finding their way back

to the Castle, for now there was a ghostly white moon shining from over the crest of Ben-na-Vân, and all the paths and terraces were of a silver gray. Hawkins, the pasty-faced valet, was quickly summoned ; the Prince was easily persuaded to go to bed, when once they had got him smuggled up into his room ; and then Lord Rockminster left to return to the pavilion. There was no great anger and reprobation in his heart ; rather he had a kind of sympathetic pity for an innocent and unsuspecting stranger, who had fallen a victim to the sweltering heat of Highland glens, to the relentless ferocity of Highland midges, and to the insidious dangers of loitering by little Highland rills.

And yet in throwing out threats of a possible storm, Rockminster had not been altogether romancing. When the ladies had retired to their apartments for the night, he strolled into the billiard-room, to smoke a final cigarette.

"I say, Gordon," he observed, in his laconic way, "have you been looking at the glass since lunch-time ? Down a good half-inch. And there's a double halo round the moon. And the trees are beginning to talk. I rather fancy something's going to happen."

CHAPTER IX

"WITH HEY, NONNY, NONNY"

AND something did happen. For towards midnight a wind began to come up out of the west, moaning across the solitudes of the forest; the trees around the Castle were no longer talking among themselves, instead there was an angry and ominous portent in the swaying branches; presently the first heavy drops came pattering on the window-panes; and then, after a wild and spectral glare that lit up all the dark, the growl of the thunder went booming along the hollow glens, followed by rain that came down in sheets, and continued to do so, hour after hour. Blissful tidings, no doubt, for the half-dozing salmon-fisher; for of all the rivers in Scotland none rises more quickly than the Skean; and so it was that he who looked abroad on the next morning—on the tossing and dripping branches of beech, and ash, and rowan, on the stormy sunlight flooding the wide strath, and on the hills grown a heavy purple under the surcharged skies—found also that the stream was careering down in full spate, its ruddy-indigo surface streaked here and there with threads of foam. Everywhere motion, and vivid color, and restless, incessant, fugitive life and change: the startled curlews calling from the distant slopes, the peewits wheeling and circling with sudden alterations of flight, the swallows darting hither and thither over the oily eddies of the pools. All the world was transformed, and full of an eager activity; all shining brilliantly, too, after this new baptism.

And here was Miss Georgie Lestrange flying through the house, from corridor to corridor, knocking at the rooms she knew.

"Honnor! Honnor! Haven't you heard? The river has risen two feet; and Malcolm says you ought to get down at once, before the spate becomes too heavy."

And again—at Lady Rosamund's chamber:

"Rose!—Rose! Do you know what you are missing?—the most wild and beautiful pictures you ever beheld—changing from minute to minute—Landseers —Peter Grahams—MacWhirters—on every hand. Come along!—the clouds are down almost to the foot of Aonach Môr, and Ben-na-Vân looks thirty miles away —you never saw such splendid effects of sunlight and mist—get up, you lazy!"

And again—at Lady Sibyl's room:

"Sib!—Sib!—it's monstrous you should be so late! Now is your chance for your storm-symphony, if ever there was one—you should hear the river thundering down through the rocks—and you should hear the fir-woods on the hill. Wake up out of your snoozling! I declare if only I had a broomstick I could go whirling across the whole breadth of Inverness-shire in about five-and-twenty seconds!"

The next person she encountered somewhat moderated her mad enthusiasm: it was young Gordon of Grantly, who was on the terrace outside, engaged in fixing together an eighteen-foot rod. Here in the early light he looked a wholesome kind of a lad; and the clear gray-blue of his eye and the sun-tan of his fair complexion caught the open glow of wind and weather, for he wore no overshadowing cap on his head.

"Oh, Sir Francis," said she—after salutations—"of course you are going down to the river. And are you taking the Upper Beat, or the Lower Beat?"

"The Upper, I believe," he answered her. "Malcolm is waiting to go to the Lower Beat with Lady Rockminster. I understand that is the arrangement."

"Then you will have that extraordinary old man with you—what is his name?"

"Tod—John Tod—and as ill-conditioned an old scoundrel as ever came up from the south country to malign the gentle Highland folk." Young Gordon could talk a little more freely now, for he had taken the last of the bits of silk thread from between his lips.

"Because," said Miss Georgie, in a very shy and ingenuous way, "I have been quite anxious to see this side of the river—the Upper Beat, I mean; and I have never dared—and for a very good reason. Do you know the forester's cottage just beyond the burn? Well, there's a bull there; and not more than three weeks ago he hunted a man up a tree, and kept him there for over an hour. Of course I daren't go near such a beast; and he roams wild all about the neighborhood, so they say; but if you and the old fisherman are going up that way, and you would let me walk with you until I was well past the cottage—then, you see—"

And naturally he pitied her soft embarrassment, and hastened to assure her that he would be delighted if they could be of any assistance whatever to her: only, what time would she be ready to start? Whereupon the young lady with the pert nose, and the pince-nez, and the tangled golden-red hair blurted out a still more audacious proposal.

"I've been trying to rouse this household up," said she, "but it's no good at all. And it's past the proper breakfast hour : what do you say — shall we go in and forage for our two selves ?   We are quite entitled to do it ; and Hallett is a great pal o' mine : he'll look after us—you'll see."

So this impudent boy and girl went boldly into the dining - room ; and rang for tea and boiled eggs ; and began to cadge for themselves from off the sideboard. And meanwhile the fisherman, John Tod, had turned up in the portico : an extraordinary - looking, black-a-vised, elderly man, whose broad and stooping back, and long arms, and short legs gave him something of the appearance of a gigantic crustacean.   He was mutter-ing to himself, too, as he began to overhaul the cast-ing - lines, the reels, and salmon - flies that Frank Gor-don had left lying on the table : it was clear that this Dee - side tackle did not wholly commend itself to his professional mind.

And then, when all was ready, away through the wild, wet world went these three ; with the sunlight showering diamonds on the leaves of the birches, and the river roaring down between the steep banks, and the far cloud-wreaths, sweeping in from the Atlantic, intertwisting themselves along the lower hills, darken-ing here and lightening there, and occasionally show-ing, through the higher mists, a pale silver thread — a mountain-torrent sprung into existence after the long night's rain.   Miss Georgie was in the happiest of spir-its ; she had forgotten all about the bull; perhaps there was no bull ; at all events, when her companions left the pathway and plunged into certain woodland glades to make down for the stream, she unconcerned-ly went with them, laughing and talking the while. These glades, by-the-way, were not a bit like Scotland ; they rather resembled the Forest of Arden, as it is pre-sented on the stage — wide-branching oaks, tall ferns, masses of meadow-sweet, and the like; while as for the Rosalind who walked by his side—but indeed she was too slight and slim for the part—there was not much of the swashbuckler about this light-hearted little Rosalind with the ruddy hair. And now they were come to the nearest of the swift-rushing pools.

Here Miss Lestrange contentedly sat herself down on a big stone at the foot of an alder-tree, in placid expectation. Nor had she long to wait for the performance to begin; for young Gordon — not wading very far in, because of the height of the water — had only made one or two casts when, just as he was about to recover his line, there was a ringing whirr of the reel; he stumbled backwards (nearly throwing himself into the river) so as to preserve the strain; and Miss Georgie clapped her hands in delight.

"Well done!" she called to him. "A thirty-pounder? I'll bet you, a thirty-pounder!"

And in truth this invisible creature, so great was the force of the current, did pull like a thirty-pounder; but that was only for a couple of seconds; the next moment there was a gleam of silver in the air—and a sea-trout of little over a pound and a half had flashed into the sunlight, and splashed again into the hurrying stream. The angler turned to the young lady, and there was a rueful smile on his face.

"How's that for a thirty-pounder?" he called to her.

"Better than nothing!" she replied, courageously. "I must have a bit of it for breakfast to-morrow."

The sea-trout got short shrift; it was hauled in by brute force, knocked on the head, and thrown contemptuously on the shingle; while in a minute or two the long line was again going whistling out. But the body of water in this pool was too great; in vain he thrashed and better thrashed — always with a careful

eye towards the shallows; his assiduous labor met with
no reward; and at last he reeled up, and returned to
the pensive maiden at the foot of the alder-tree.

"Oh, for rain!" said she, looking at him imploringly as he drew near. "Why doesn't it rain! Why
doesn't it pour a deluge!"

"What do you want rain for?" he demanded.

"To drown the midges! Oh, they're dreadful! Rain,
rain!—come rain!—come rain! Just look at this."

And therewith and piteously she held out her two
wrists, where undoubtedly there were a number of tiny
swellings between the delicate blue veins. Of course
he expressed his sorrow; but what else could he do?

"I've got a little bottle of eau-de-Cologne with
me," said Miss Georgina, rather timidly, "and if you
wouldn't mind taking my handkerchief, and soaking
it, and trying whether that would be of any use—"

Well, he was not accustomed to wait upon damsels
in distress; but this seemed a simple matter; and accordingly he took her handkerchief, and steeped it,
and tenderly and softly bathed those grievous wounds.
It did not occur to him to reflect (1) that she might
just as well have done this for herself; and (2) that
if she had been looking forward to midges—as the
bottle of eau-de-Cologne appeared to suggest—she
might have adopted the precaution of putting on a
pair of gauntleted gloves. No matter: she expressed
herself as profoundly grateful; and then they set out
on their travels again, this time in the direction of the
Linne nan Nighean,* where there might be a more
practicable chance.

And as they proceeded through this tangled wilderness—the breckans breast-high, the dells of meadow-

---

* Pronounced *Leeny nan Nyean*—the Maiden's Pool.

sweet scenting all the humid air — Miss Georgie was
amusing him with her gay and careless prattle; nor
did she pause for an instant to receive answers to her
artless questions.

"I do hope Honnor will get a fish — don't you?
She's awfully nice—isn't she? And there's a firmer
vein of character in her than in Lady Adela and her
sisters; you wouldn't find Lady Rockminster paying
court to all sorts of nobodies in order to get paragraphs
about herself put into the weekly papers. It's a little
undignified—don't you thing so? But all the three
sisters are just wild after notoriety—there's nothing
they wouldn't do to bring themselves before the public
—they would take an engagement at the Folies Bergère
—to shoot glass balls—any mortal thing. Mind, I'm
saying this in strict confidence—you understand? I
wouldn't say it to any one else; of course not. And
at the same time, you know, in spite of that one little
weakness, they are the very dearest people—so generous—they would do anything for you; besides, they
are so bright, and clever, and perfectly accomplished—
why can't they be satisfied with themselves?—without
little newspaper notices about their books, and their
pictures, and their music? And I'm certain these
caravanserai dinners—that's what Sir Hugh calls them
—ill-dressed women and ugly men—are just as often
thrown away as not. I am convinced of it. Do you
suppose Miss Penguin goes to Aivron Lodge to help
Lady Adela with her novels? Not likely! She goes
there for her own purposes—wants to get glimpses of
fashionable people, so that she may lash the whole
tribe of them for their fearful iniquities. Poor old
thing, I suppose she's rather dotty on the crumpet—"

"What?"

"Slate off, don't you know? Oh, by-the-way, Sir

Francis," continued this debonair lass, but somewhat more demurely, "Miss Penguin has just sent me the new number of the *Unmuzzled Magazine;* and the first article in it is from her pen. Well, it is—yes, it is—precisely so—"

"What do you mean?"

"There's some plain talk," she observed.

"You must let me see it!"

But at this she burst out laughing.

"Show such a thing to you, Sir Francis?" she cried. "To an innocent boy like you? I couldn't accept the responsibility! Why, do you know the title of her essay?—'On the Radical Incompatibility of the Sexes.' And do you know how it begins?—'Let the reader imagine for a moment what Eve must privately have thought about Adam'—"

"Oh, that's nothing," said he, lightly. "I can imagine, too, that Adam had his own little opinions about Eve, when he was smoking his pipe in a quiet corner—"

"Ye'll begin jist here, sir," said John Tod, in a fine, broad, Lowland accent; and with that the colloquy ended.

They were now at the top of the Linne nan Nighean —a long, wide, deep pool formed by the junction of the rivers Skean and Rua. And indeed it was an extremely picturesque scene that Miss Georgie found before her—after she had, so to speak, evaded the bull; for the Rua was roaring and racing over its shallows of yellow-red gravel; the darker Skean went headlong by, tossing tawny wavelets here and there; the enormously tall larches on the opposite bank swayed in the varying gusts; while now and again a burst of sunlight broke over the brilliant green pastures. But Miss Georgie, when she had called aloud for the rain to come and destroy the midges (which it cannot do) had not counted on her prayer being so speedily answered ; and she had not observed that in the wild mist-land heavy masses were trooping up from the Atlantic, each with a wine-stain of shadow underneath it as it stole along the darkening hills. And then this darkness increased ; there was no longer anything of azure or indigo in the further reaches of the river ; the gloom deepened and deepened ; until all at once the storm burst—in torrents of rain that thrashed the surface of the stream into a white smoke, and that even drowned the rush and roar of the Rua channels. Miss Lestrange fled and took shelter under some thick alder-trees ; and, after a brief space, young Gordon, unable to withstand this whelming downpour, laid his fishing-rod on the bank, and made for the same cover.

"Why have you no water-proof ?" she demanded, in panting and breathless and reproachful tones.

"Because I can't be bothered with it," he answered her. "It makes casting too hot work. Why haven't you one ?"

"Oh, this cape will keep out anything."

They were silent for a minute or so—while the wind howled, and the rain tore the river into a silver-gray spindrift. At length Miss Lestrange said, in a most pathetic way—

"I shouldn't mind—I really shouldn't mind—if it didn't trickle down my neck."

He turned to her.

"Why don't you put up the collar of your cape, then ?"

"Because my back-hair is all wet, and if I put up my collar, it would only be more miserable." And then she said—oh ! so sweetly, and shyly, and prettily : "Sir Francis, I am quite ashamed to trouble you again —but would you be so very kind—so awfully kind—as to take my handkerchief, and see if you could dry my hair a little, and then perhaps I could put up my collar? I can't get at it very well myself—would you be so awfully kind?—here is my handkerchief—"

"But it is soaking wet, with the eau-de-Cologne," said he, "whereas I happen to have two with me, both perfectly dry. And if you don't mind my making the attempt—"

Nevertheless this new service she had required of him was a very different matter from merely sponging a few midge-bites. It was with something more than timidity that he approached the unwonted task; when he had to fold back an inch or two of the cape, and when he could not choose but notice the beautiful pure whiteness of her neck, and the pretty waifs and wisps of the dishevelled ruddy-golden hair that clustered around it, a kind of sensation of awe and fear came over him; nay, it was literally with half-averted eyes that he proceeded to do what he could, while she kept murmuring—"So sorry to trouble you—awfully good of you—I'm ever so much more comfortable already." And then, when he had in a manner finished, he folded a dry handkerchief into a band, and put that round her neck, and raised the collar, and asked her to fasten it in front, so that at length she was quite secure and warm and happy. By this time the sudden storm was perceptibly lessening; the clouds were lifting, and there was a gleam of silver here and there, though nothing of blue had come back to the river; presently the pasture-lands on the other side of the stream shone out with a vivid and golden radiance: it was time for him to be back at his work. And perhaps—though the Gordons are not supposed to be deficient in courage—he may have felt a certain subtle relief in being once more on the bank, with the long line whistling out.

There are experiences—a thrilling, inadvertent touch or two, for example—which are bewildering, and even alarming, to a modest youth.

What happened next was this : Miss Georgie had wandered on a few yards to have a word with the black-a-vised and round-shouldered gillie when all at once she saw Frank Gordon stagger back in a wild endeavor to keep his line taut, while he was reeling in in a frantic manner, the mere haste and desperation causing an occasional bungle. For the fact is, the fish he had hooked had run directly towards him ; and for a flurried second or two there was extreme danger ; but rapid manipulation — or perhaps a change in the salmon's tactics—soon restored the safety-giving curve to the top of the rod : they could all of them breathe again, for the moment at least.

"And—and what is it, John ?" she said, almost in a whisper—and with her eyes intent. "A salmon ?"

"Weel, I didna get glint or glimmer," said John, composedly, "though I jalouse it's but a bit sea-trout, being so near the bank. Ay, and where is he off for now ?—what ails the crayture ?—fegs, he'll find oot what a Skean spate is like, if he makes for the middle." But as John stared and stared, he became more interested, and even excited. "Losh bless me, d'ye see yon ? That's nae sea-trout—that's a fish !—ay, and a heavy fish—d'ye see'm makkin steady across, and him wi' the whole wecht o' the Skean on 'm ! Ay, and borin up a' the time—borin—borin—the dour rascal that he is—dod, if he keeps on that gait, a' the tackle in Scotland winna hand him—"

And now a startling thing befell. Her eyes had been fixedly watching that thin gray thread of a line as it slowly cut its way through the swinging torrent ; but it was fifteen or twenty yards higher up stream that a huge fish—looking about as big as a pig—threw himself out of the water, and fell again with a mighty souse.

"Oh, John, is he off!" she exclaimed in heart-broken accents.

"No, no, he's no off," replied John, "but soon he will be. Eh, my, my, a fine fish—a grand fish!—five-and-thirty pounds, I'm thinking—a fine fish—and nae chance wi' him ava—"

"But no chance?" she demanded, in almost feverish agitation. "There must be a chance! I tell you, Sir Francis must get that salmon—he must get him—eh, he must get that splendid salmon—or—or I declare I shall cry with vexation—"

"Ye needna fash," said John, in a more resigned way—the resignation of despair. "Sir Francis is doin' his best, but it's no a bit o' use. There's thirty yards o' a bagging line ahint that fish, wi' a' the wecht o' the water on it; and there's forty yards oot forbye; and how is onybody to pit a strain on 'm? It's the spate that's pitten the strain on—and it's the spate that 'll—ay, I thocht sae—"

At first she did not understand what had taken place, for the long and heavy line, held by the current, had not released the top of the rod; but the next moment she perceived that the angler was quietly reeling up. She ran to him.

"Oh, Sir Francis, is he gone?"

"He's gone, and no mistake," was the sufficiently cheerful reply. "I had little hopes of him, so long as he kept away to the other side, and would go boring up stream. I had no control over him—"

"It is enough to make one cry with disappointment!" she exclaimed, almost stamping the ground.

"Oh, you get used to these things in salmon-fish-

ing," he said, placidly. "And now we'll move on
and see if there's any better luck waiting for us at the
Mill-dam; or perhaps we might go right up to the
Priest's Bridge Pool, for it's a pretty place to have
luncheon—"

"Oh, luncheon?" said she, rather drawing back.
"I was quite forgetting. I shall have to go away
home now—"

"You can't."

"Why not?"

"Because of the bull."

"Oh, well—" She hesitated—and it was a winning
kind of hesitation. "If you could spare me a biscuit
—just one biscuit," she said, with a most becoming
bashfulness.

"But your luncheon is in the bag!" he informed
her. "I made sure you would come up the river with
us, if there was any amusement going on—not that
there's much; and I told Hallett; and I myself saw
the packets put in—"

"Oh, then, if I may!" said she, promptly and
blithely—and there was no more talk of a return to the
Castle during the remainder of this day's excursion.

The Priest's Bridge Pool—which they arrived at
after a devious meandering by ferny glades and through
copses of oak and hazel—lies in a long and deep hollow; and here the waters of the Skean, having come
dashing, and boiling, and foaming through the narrow
and rocky chasms above, collect themselves, and (in
ordinary seasons) begin to moderate their headlong
pace. The banks are lofty and steep; that on the
north covered with heather and short birch-bushes;
that on the south with hanging woods that descend
almost to the river's edge. And here, on the trunk
of a felled tree, young Gordon discovered a comfort-

able seat for his fair companion, while he proceeded to help John Tod to get out the contents of the luncheon-bag. This done, John withdrew to a little dingle hard by, where unseen he could hastily get through with his mid-day meal, the sooner to reach the far more important solace of a smoke.

And thus it was that these two young people, seated side by side on the trunk of the felled ash, found themselves practically alone in this strange and solitary world—alone with the wet and silent woods, the surging and swinging river, the steep banks of heather and green birch burning in the sunlight, the silvery cloud-phantoms of the sky, and the mysterious distances of unnamed hills. And it may have been some sense of this isolation and remote seclusion that made Miss Georgie begin to talk of the crowded gayeties of the London season now left so far behind.

"Just to think," said she—as she briskly munched her sandwich of salmon-and-lettuce-leaf, and daintily sipped her claret and water—"just to think that it is only a matter of weeks since you and I were in the big whirl—and meeting very often too—I don't know how it happened we were always coming together—at dances, dinners, theatres, garden parties—the Academy Soirée, the Grosvenor Club—up at Lord's, too—and several times in the Park, and once or twice at the Zoo—why, we were meeting everywhere : it almost looked like a fate, didn't it ?"

"Oh, yes," he added, inadvertently—for a fish had shown itself at the end of the pool.

"Ill-natured people," continued Miss Georgie, with her eyes downcast, "might have said there was more contrivance than accident in it—mightn't they ?"

"Oh, yes," he answered her—still watching for the fish.

"I wonder if you recollect that night at Lady Coltsborough's, when Cardinal Pepys took Madame Varitza in to dinner ? I've never seen such a tall combination of color at any table—the Cardinal's gorgeous scarlet robes and Madame Varitza's white satin dress embroidered with silver, and her jet-black hair—rather a startling combination, wasn't it ?"

"Oh, yes ; oh, certainly," he replied ; and then he got quickly to his feet. "You won't mind," he said, "if I go along and put a fly over a fish I have seen gambolling about down there ? You keep on with your lunch—I shall be back in a few minutes."

Now if Miss Georgie was at all inclined to be vexed and cross over his desertion of her, she soon had her revenge. For young Gordon, beginning well up, and working down to the fish, was wholly absorbed in his occupation ; and the nearer and nearer he got to the spot where he had seen the salmon leap, the more and more careful and concentrated he became ; so that what now occurred could hardly have been guarded against. For he had just made a good long cast, and was allowing the fly to come quietly across the water, when out of the smooth-rolling flood there suddenly and silently arose an awful and terrifying object that had been hitherto quite invisible. It was a branch of an oak-tree sweeping down with the current; and the moment that Gordon saw this hideous thing going right on to his line, he made a violent effort to jerk the fly into the air. But in vain. He was fast. Then he tried another sharp tug, to see if the leaf or leaves would not come away : they would not. Then he attempted to haul by main force that brutal branch in to the side ; this also was clearly hopeless, by reason of the strength of the stream. Nay, there was nothing for him but to run madly along the bank, reeling in a

yard or two when he had the opportunity, while he
kept yelling—

"John !—John !—where the devil are you !—bring
the gaff, man !"

Indeed it was Miss Georgie herself who had to rout
John out of his secret shelter ; and then he, too, set
off in pursuit, with his unwieldy, crablike movements ;
but eventually they did get hold of that maleficent
branch, and managed to drag it ashore, and release the
fly, without much harm being done. Then Frank
Gordon came slowly back to his companion.

"Nothing but mishaps to-day," he said. "This
pool's spoiled, at any rate ; so we may as well go down
to the Mill-dam now."

"Oh, do you think I have brought you bad luck ?"
asked Miss Georgie, with the air of an erring and re-
pentant child.

"You ?" he made answer. "I should think not !
Besides, what does it matter ? There are other things
than salmon-fishing—and the whole of this morning
has been delightful !"

"It's rather nice of you to say so," remarked this
demure maiden, as she moved aside to let John pack
up. "I thought you cared for nothing but fishing
and flies."

At a somewhat late hour that afternoon the Prince
and Princess, the Rockminsters, and Sir Hugh were all
of them seated out on the terrace, having tea—Lady
Adela and her sisters had doubtless been detained in-
doors by their earnest devotion to literature and the
arts. This side of the Castle, facing east, was now in
cool, clear, silver-gray shadow ; but beyond the plateau
and the policies all the wide valley was filled with a
warm and mellow radiance ; for away in the west—
over Loch Eil, and Morven, and Arisaig—the heavens

had entirely opened, and the golden-white light was streaming across the hills by Glen Loy and Clunes, and even touching here and there a shoulder or peak of the lofty Aonach Môr. And it was amid these pleasant surroundings—and with the grateful hush of the evening not far distant—that the Princess was entertaining her friends with an account of the celebrated dinner at which the young King Alexander of Servia, then a boy of seventeen, tricked his grave and elderly Ministers and threw off the yoke of the Regency. Of course she must have had the main story at second-hand ; but she was able to embellish it with many particulars derived from personal knowledge ; and a very amusing tale it turned out to be—how the unsuspecting Regents and Ministers sat down to dinner ; how, while they were at the soup, their houses were occupied by soldiers ; how, midway through the banquet, guards were placed outside ; and how, as dessert was about to be served, the youthful Alexander rose and announced to his guests that he rather wanted to be King on his own account now, and that he would be much obliged if the Regents would forthwith resign. Then consternation—refusal—the doors thrown wide, and the officers and soldiery calling " Long live the King !" while the point to be considered by the Regents and Ministers was whether they should rush out into the corridor to meet an almost certain death, or whether they should sit quietly down and go on with their fruit, and cigarettes, and coffee and cognac. The Princess was making maliciously merry over this legend when of a sudden the expression of her face slightly changed.

For beyond the carriage-drive there was an extended avenue of ash and rowan ; and as this part of the roadway was out in the open it was barred across by bands of alternate sun and shade. And into this picturesque

setting came two figures, followed by a third; the two
leading figures — a tall and handsome young fellow,
and a laughing-eyed lass — looking rather well in the
glow of light.

"Lady Rockminster," said the Princess, with something of a calm air, "has Miss Lestrange been away all
day with Frank?"

"I suppose so," was the answer, "for I saw them
start in the morning. And she has had distinctly the
best of it."

"In what way?"

"Well, he can have had but little fishing, the river
being so high; while she has had a fine picnic excursion."

At this moment the two young people came up; and
Miss Georgie was easily persuaded to take a seat at the
tea-table; while her companion had to give a report
of the persistent ill luck of the day. Then he left, to
get his brogues and waders hauled off; and as he was
going, his mother called to him—

"Frank, I see there's a letter waiting for you from
Grantly. If Aunt Jean has anything to say that concerns me, don't forget to let me know."

Aunt Jean, however, had but little news to send
from Dee-side. What held his prolonged attention
most was the postscript—

"P. S. No, I have never heard of the old botanist
and that beautiful Greek girl you have asked about
once or twice. Of course I assumed that I should
meet them again; for you said they were going to
ramble about the neighborhood for some time; but
they seemed to have disappeared altogether, leaving
no trace behind. I am sorry—I was interested in both
of them.—J. G."

CHAPTER X

FROM MORN TILL EVE

OLGA ELLIOTT flounced up from the piano, and went and threw herself on to an adjacent couch.

"Bother that trash!" she said, impatiently. "Brilliancy — delicacy of touch — expression : rubbish ! I can't play; and I never shall be able to play; and I don't want to be able to play. You sit down yourself, Bry, and bang; hammer as badly as you can manage —and Ma 'll think it's me. Oh, I suppose you consider it's my duty. It's my duty to practise so many hours a day—and read 'Paradise Lost'—and darn my own stockings—and twenty dozen other things. But I know what all these duties are; they're simply a lot of ridiculous nonsense invented by the elderly people to keep the younger people within strict bounds. And I'm not going to be kept within strict bounds; I must have my freedom; I mean to have my whack, if I can get it. Sounds selfish ?—but it's honest. You've got to fight for your own hand in this wicked world. It's all very well to say, 'Do unto others as you would that others should do unto you'; that's all very fine; but I want to see the others begin. They don't appear to be in a hurry, do they ? Now Bry, I wish you'd sit down and bash away at the piano—or else Ma 'll be here."

She had hardly uttered the words when the door was opened; and Mrs. Alexander Elliott, finding Briseis standing irresolute by the piano, while Olga lay supine on the couch, looked reproachfully from one to the other.

"Really, Briseis," said she, "on a day like this—when every minute is of value—"

But the poor, tired widow with the care-worn face and sad eyes was no termagant, notwithstanding her thin and resolute mouth; besides, she was much too dependent on the alacrity and good-will of her niece to risk giving offence. So she altered her tone.

"I wish you would come down to the school-room, Briseis, dear, and help me with Olga's and Brenda's dresses that they are going to wear at dinner to-night. When Mr. and Mrs. Bingham come here this evening, I hope they will see that everything is done properly in the house. And you have such taste, Briseis, dear —such natural good taste—and you are so clever with your needle—and familiar with the best styles, in different countries—it will be so easy for you to plan out a few little alterations that will bring the dresses up to the present fashion. There's not much time, to be sure—it was so inconsiderate of Mrs. Bingham to give us such short notice—"

The clock on the chimney-piece struck a silver chime: the alabaster cherub, swinging in his golden swing, had arrived at the hour of half past ten. She glanced at the dial.

"But I must first go and take Brenda's temperature—"

"Mayn't I do that for you, Aunt Clara?" said Briseis, promptly.

"If you would—if you would!" said the much-harassed mother, and she handed over the little glass instrument to Briseis, who thereupon left the room. And then Mrs. Elliott went to her daughter, and patted the dull flaxen hair.

"I hope my pretty Olga isn't going to be ill too," she said, in caressing tones.

"Oh, no, Ma, dear," replied the pasty-faced young lady, with great suavity. "I had only one helping of toasted cheese at the end of dinner last night. But Brenda had two; and then she went to sleep, as usual; and only woke up in time to ring for her glass of port wine and biscuit; and then she went to bed—and I wonder her temperature this morning isn't 140."

"At six o'clock it was 100.2," said the mother, half absently. "And that's not very high. If there are any signs of a decrease, then we needn't send for Dr. Thomas—doctors' visits do mount up so!" She turned again to the procumbent damsel. "So you are resting, dearest, to prepare yourself for the bustle of the evening?" she said, affectionately. "Quite right—quite right. For my two bonny darlings must be at their very best and brightest to-night, to show the Binghams what happy companionship their daughter enjoys. And I shouldn't wonder if they asked us all to dine with them at the Langham—"

Miss Olga jumped up from her prostrate position—her gray-green eyes staring wide.

"Oh, would they? Are they likely to?" she exclaimed, eagerly.

"It is at least probable," said the mother. "But lie down again, dear one, if you are really tired; and send Briseis to me the moment she comes back with the report."

So in a little while thereafter Briseis found herself, in the so-called school-room, busily occupied in snipping, altering, and stitching at her cousins' dinner gowns; and very well content was she with the solitary task—solitary, because her aunt had almost immediately been summoned away by other domestic du-

ties. Moreover, she knew she had a free hand in these
embellishments. The two sisters were not likely to
complain, whatever she did. They had formed a dim
idea that she was endowed with a certain distinction
and refinement; she had seen far cities and stately
ceremonies; nay, had she not in her possession, at
this very moment, what was the very summit of their
souls' desires—a fancy dress? Again and again they
had begged her to show them once more this wonderful treasure—though it was only the festival costume
of a Greek peasant girl; and with longing eyes they
had regarded the pale blue Albanian jacket and its
elaborate silver embroidery, the head-gear of rows of
pendulous coins, the silken veil showing tremulous
threads of gold through the diaphanous texture, with
girdle, bracelets, and necklace all complete. When
they went out shopping together, her cousins would,
if somewhat reluctantly and sulkily, defer to her taste.
Not unfrequently they would ask her to choose for
them ribbons, neckerchiefs, gloves, and what not—
especially as she had a common trick of paying for
such trifles, out of her slender pocket-money. And
they were not likely to take umbrage at any of the
alterations she was now making : they would be satisfied to be spared the trouble.

At noon there came a slight tap at the door.

"Master Adalbert is ready, Miss," said the maid,
who immediately hurried on.

She went to the door, and found her boy cousin in
the hall.

"I'm afraid we can't go out to-day, Adalbert," said
she, "every one is so busy—"

"But look at this, Briseis—look—look!" he cried;
and he was regarding with an intense curiosity a fine
assortment of golf clubs, all burnished and shining,

7

that lay on the hall table, the shafts strapped up in the brown canvas bag. "I suppose they're Edward's," he added, wistfully.

"Oh, no, they're not," she answered him, in her gentle fashion. "They're yours."

"Why, what do you mean, Briseis?"

"They're a little birthday present I got for you," she explained, "only I did not expect them to be sent home so soon. You may as well have them now as to-morrow." '

He was an extremely sensitive lad. He could not speak. It was a brief twitching of the muscles of his face that told how hard he was trying to keep the water from welling into his eyes. And then, mastering himself, he pretended not to be overwhelmed by her kindness; he pretended to be wholly engrossed and delighted with the clubs.

"Look, Briseis," he said, as he undid the strap, and drew one after the other out, "aren't they splendidly made! Did you ever see such finish? This is the driver, you know—he's the fellow to send the ball whizzing!—one, two, three, four, five, six, seven, eight, nine, ten, you count, and then it drops—clean away over all the dangers. And this is the cleek—and this is the iron niblick—that's the one if you're in a fearful bunker!—and this is the brassey—and this is the putter—"

But at this point Mrs. Elliott, bustling through the house on her manifold errands, made her appearance; and when the whole situation was explained to her, she thought that Briseis might after all take her cousin out for a turn in the Park, if only for half an hour; so, in a few minutes, these two set forth together, the tall, slim, beautiful Greek girl pushing the invalid-chair as usual. And while as yet they were amid the noise of the streets, he was silent; but when they had crossed the Marylebone Road, and passed through York Gate, and entered into the quietude of the Park, he said—

"Briseis, I never thanked you for the clubs."

"Why should you?"

"I wanted to tell you something," he went on. "You are so different from any one else. You seem to know what other people are thinking; and you take the trouble to find out; and you think along with them. And that's why you bought me the golf clubs. It was to keep me imagining that some day I might be a golfer."

Now it was quite true that she had a profound sympathy with the pathetic enthusiasms of this poor lame lad—about golf, cricket, football, and all manner of athletic exercises; but she was not going to allow him —even at this moment of confession and almost of appeal—to assume that there could be anything fictitious or hopeless about his passionate interest in such affairs.

"And what better can there be than imagining?" she said, boldly. "Look at me. I can't play cricket. I can't play football. I have never even seen a game at golf. And do you think it probable I shall ever pull in a college boat at Henley? But all the same, merely through reading the accounts to you, I have become as deeply interested in them as any one—as even you yourself; I know the names of all your heroes; and I follow the doings of the various teams—why, I can almost understand a game at football now—from the report, I mean—"

"It's a shame I should ask you to read for me, Briseis," said he. "But this is how it is. If I read for myself, I see little except the newspaper; but when you read for me, I can make up the picture before my eyes—"

"Very well, then," said she, "and who objects to my reading to you? And do you think I don't like to hear of brilliant achievements—and all the people at Lord's clapping their hands at a good catch—"

"But I wanted you to know, Briseis," said he, still unsatisfied, "that I quite understand what you were thinking of when you bought me the golf clubs—"

"And you will hang them up on the back of your bedroom door," said she, cheerfully. "And every morning, when you awake, you will wonder whether Mr. Ball, or Mr. Horace Hutchinson, or Willie Park is likely to be out on the links, and what kind of weather they are going to have."

These brief excursions with her boy-cousin were the one break in the continuous drudgery of the long and dreary day—the one opportunity permitted her of getting a glimpse of the sky, the clouds, the trees, and the pale London sunlight shimmering on the placid lake. And by this time she and he had explored all the secret nooks and byways of the Park; and they had chosen their favorite retreats—one, in particular, fronting a kind of back-channel, where there was a wooden bench sheltered by bushes, and whither they could easily, when they chose, summon a congregation of clamorous ducks, that would come breasting through the rippling waters, and even waddle up the grassy banks in jealous competition for crumbs. But on this occasion they had brought no bread with them; so, when the invalid-chair had been placed by the side of the bench, Briseis took out a newspaper from the capacious pocket.

"Well, what shall I read to you this morning, Adalbert? There will be the First Round for the Association Challenge Cup—"

"No, no, never mind about that," he said, hastily.

"I've got something better for you, Briseis—something that will stir you; I found it last night in a volume of Tennyson that Miss Bingham lent me, and I copied it: if you take out my MS. book, you'll see it is the last piece. I want to hear you read it aloud—I know it will be splendid, Briseis—just splendid!"

She was a willing slave to this poor chap; she humored him, petted him, and obeyed his every whim; and if he was occasionally a little exacting she did not mind very much. She got out the copy-book, and turned to the last piece; and a single glance down the page told her something of the proud indignation of the opening verses, so that she was in a measure prepared when she began—

'My Lords, we heard you speak: you told us all
  That England's honest censure went too far;
That our free press should cease to brawl,
  Not sting the fiery Frenchman into war.
It was our ancient privilege, my Lords,
To fling whate'er we felt, not fearing, into words.'

He listened in absolute silence, though already he seemed somewhat breathless; but when she had finished the fifth verse—

'Shall we fear *him?* our own we never fear'd.
  From our first Charles by force we wrung our claims.
Prick'd by the Papal spur, we rear'd,
  We flung the burthen of the second James.
I say, we *never* fear'd! and as for these,
We broke them on the land, we drove them on the seas.'

—he could restrain his enthusiasm no longer.

"How grandly you read, Briseis — how grand—grand!" he cried. "You ought to be in a great hall —and multitudes—cheering you and cheering you—"

"But who are 'these'?" she asked—for her edition
of Tennyson did not contain this poem.

"'These'?" he repeated, triumphantly. "Why,
the French!

'as for these
We broke them on the land, we drove them on the seas.'

Yes; and that's what England could do again to-morrow, if there were need! But, Briseis," he went on,
"would you mind turning back a few pages, and
you'll find another piece called 'The Charge of the
Heavy Brigade at Balaclava'—I won't ask you to read
it all—I'm quite ashamed, you know, to trouble you—
but only one verse, the one beginning 'The trumpet,
the gallop, the charge'—for one of the three who followed Scarlett right in amongst the Russian cavalry
was an Elliott—Scarlett's aide-de-camp, you know—"

Again she followed his directions; and she knew,
rather than saw, that his face was mantling with color
and his large eyes 'glowering' as she declaimed the
swinging lines—

'The trumpet, the gallop, the charge, and the might of the
    fight!
Thousands of horsemen had gather'd there on the height,
With a wing push'd out to the left, and a wing to the right,
And who shall escape if they close? but he dashed up alone
Thro' the great gray slope of men,
Sway'd his sabre, and held his own
Like an Englishman there and then;
All in a moment follow'd with force
Three that were next in their fiery course,
Wedged themselves in between horse and horse,
Fought for their lives in the narrow gap they had made—
Four amid thousands! and up the hill, up the hill,
Gallopt the gallant three hundred, the Heavy Brigade.'

"For you are an Elliott too," he said—perhaps as a kind of vague apology for demanding so much of her.

But this breathing-space had to be curtailed, for they had come out late; and soon they were leaving these misty glades, and the wooded islands, and the shimmering water, and were returning to the roar of the streets again. They got home just in time for luncheon—which, indeed, was an ordeal that Briseis would fain have avoided; for she had not been living long in this house before it became apparent to every one that she had found favor in the eyes of the supercilious and cadaverous medical student; and the patronage that he bestowed upon her, especially at lunch-time, took the form of asking her incessant and idiotic conundrums, and propounding all sorts of fatuous quips and catches. Now conundrums only bewildered her; she never could find the proper answer; and especially was she unable to perceive the simian japes that depend for their point on an imitation of Cockney speech. Then the young gentleman who was dallying on his way to Caius addressed her and her alone; he would take no notice of the others at table; so that they were forced to become spectators—amused and malicious spectators —of her desperate embarrassment. Sometimes the face of the small lame boy flushed with anger; but he dared not dispute with his elder brother.

And on this morning, as usual, the lanky, gray-faced student had allowed the whole of them to take their places before he deigned to saunter in with his hands in his pockets; then, the moment he was seated, he called down the table to Briseis.

"Briseis," said he, "are you good at finding rhymes?"

"Oh, no—oh, not in the least," she answered, involuntarily shrinking back—for she knew that all eyes would be upon her, in wait for her confusion.

"You must try," he proceeded—but whether to torment her or to entertain her who could say?—"I'll give you three lines of a verse; and you must find the fourth; and the fourth must rhyme and scan with the second; only, you are limited to two words: do you understand? Now, listen—

> 'She took some tea—a pound of tea—
>   And put it in a kettle;
>   And then she went and boiled it—'

Do you understand? You've got to find a fourth line that will rhyme and scan with the second—seven syllables—but only two words, mind—only two words—"

"Oh, I'm sure I can't!" Briseis protested—conscious of the prevailing giggle.

"Well, I'll give you until to-morrow," said he, gayly, "and then, if you haven't the answer, there must be a forfeit. Always a forfeit in such cases; it's a law of the game; the forfeit to be named by the propounder of the riddle."

"Edward, dear," the poor widow put in, plaintively, "I wish you wouldn't worry your cousin so."

"But I must be off now, if you will excuse me, Aunt Clara," Briseis said, rising from her place. "There is so much to do to those dresses."

"My dear child, you have had no luncheon at all!" the widow cried.

"Oh, yes, yes," she made answer, blithely enough—and indeed she had had two spoonfuls of soup and a bit of bread.

She was glad to get back to the musty and dusky school-room; nor did her task seem so very monotonous, once she had got everything planned out, with only the mechanical sewing to be got through; for in this still seclusion there were many pictures rising before her brain, however she may have been occupied with the swift stitches—tremulous and nebulous pictures that came before her in an unknown and unsummoned fashion, and that carried her leagues and leagues away from this lonely chamber. The glancing blue waters of the Gulf of Aegina; the saffron-white columns of the Parthenon, dim and far on their high plateau; the steep slopes of Pentelicus, glaucous-green and scarred; the solitary Santa Maura, and the outjutting golden cliff that heard Sappho's farewell cry; Corfu, and the luxuriant palms and magnolias of Mon Repos; the brown plains surrounding Acro-Corinth; the ruddy soil, the rich vegetation, the forts and bastions bristling with cannon at the Euxine mouth of the Bosporus: these and many another magic-lantern slide passed slowly before her eyes as she worked on at Olga's and Brenda's gowns. Sometimes her ears deceived her; it was as if she could hear a distant singing—"When we set out from Megara—Megara—Megara"—and the white fustanellas were twirling about with frantic energy, and there were laughing faces under the tasselled caps, out there in the blaze of the sun. Or rather was it not the lapping of waves along the side of a boat—with the moonlight silvering all the wide bay of Phalerum—and Hymettus black against the stars—and some one, delicate-fingered, touching the tightened strings—while there stole into the listening air the low cadences of a love-song of Zante? Cape Colias gray and distant in the ghostly radiance—and all the long line of shore murmuring like a sea-shell—

"How are you getting on now, Briseis?" said Aunt Clara, bustling into the room. "My bonny darlings must come down and look at what you have done, just

7*

to make sure. I wish all our other difficulties could be as easily got over. What to do I hardly know. You see," she continued, and now she was regarding Briseis with something more of hesitation, "it is of such importance that Mr. and Mrs. Bingham should be favorably impressed with Ada's surroundings; and yet, if there is only the one maid waiting at table, I am afraid to think what awkwardness may happen. Of course there are the two; but one of them must—simply must —be told off to bring the dishes up from the kitchen to the hall table. Cook can't be expected to do more than her own work; she can't keep running up the stairs; and old Wilkinshaw is useless—she'd tumble and bring destruction on everything. Yet if it could only be managed that we had both the maids in the dining-room, what a relief it would be—even as regards the handing of vegetables—"

"But, Aunt Clara," said Briseis, glancing up from her needle—and there was usually a touch of wonder in the beautiful, dark, friendly eyes when she raised her head in this way—"why should you have any difficulty? Meeting those strangers wouldn't interest me, I'm sure: why not let me carry up the things from the kitchen to the hall table?—then you can have both maids to wait in the dining-room."

"Do you mean that, Briseis?" said Aunt Clara, almost too quickly. "It is so kind of you!—so thoughtful! —so considerate! And your own suggestion too— that makes it all the more good-natured; for of course I never would have proposed such a thing—not for worlds would I have proposed such a thing; but when it comes so naturally and spontaneously from yourself, why, then I say that I have no right to refuse such a— such a—magnanimous offer. Oh, I know. It isn't every one who would do it—and who would be the first to suggest it. Thank you, thank you ever so much ! And then, when it comes to dessert, you see, Briseis, you will have time to slip up-stairs, and get dressed, and be waiting for us in the drawing-room. For we must have you in the drawing-room—we could not do without you in the drawing-room, you know—you play so exquisitely. And, Briseis, there's still another thing: if you saw your way, in the general conversation, to bring in an occasional sentence of Italian or Greek—"

But at this the pale, clear forehead of the girl flushed a little; and Aunt Clara instantly perceived that she had made a mistake.

"Oh, I didn't mean pretence—I didn't mean any vulgar show-off," she said, somewhat hastily. "Far from that. For how could there be any pretence in your case ? Every one knows you are such a wonderful linguist; and how could there be any affectation in your making use of such phrases ? To Adalbert, for example : haven't I heard you and Adalbert talking Greek together ?"

"Adalbert," responded Briseis, calmly, "can say *nai, alēthōs—agapēte moi phile*—and a few words like that. But I am quite sure he is much too honest and straightforward to pretend to know a language that he doesn't know."

"Oh, yes, of course—you are quite right—quite right—certainly : only—only—I did so wish the Binghams to understand that their daughter was living among people of culture—though, as you say, one wouldn't have any pretence—oh, no—not on any account. But at least you will play for us, Briseis ?"

"Whatever you please, Aunt Clara !"

So Briseis was once more left alone, with her patient toil ; but she was gradually getting to the end of it ; and eventually—as the dusk of the autumn day was stealing over—she had finished; and Olga and Brenda were summoned. They condescended to express a cold approval. Nay, there was more than that; for having asked of their cousin what dress she herself meant to wear at dinner, and having been informed as to the share in that festivity that had been allotted to her, Olga at least showed some trifle of indignation.

"It's a beastly shame," said she, frowning angrily. "You're being put upon, Bry; and you don't see it. It's too bad—it's simply disgusting—the way Ned rots you at lunch-time. And as for carrying these things up from the kitchen, why wasn't Ada Bingham's maid turned on to it?—she can't always be frizzing the hair of that spitfire cat!"

"Never mind," said the sullen-mouthed Brenda—whose temperature was no longer alarming her—"you'll be able to snick the best of the pastry when it's waiting on the hall table."

And now Briseis, who was completely overwrought —for she had been at these unceasing occupations and employments ever since seven o'clock that morning— now she thought she might steal away to her own little den and lie down for a few minutes, before the labors of the evening began. But she had not taken into account the indomitable activity of her ubiquitous aunt.

"Where are you going, Briseis, dear? Will you come here for a moment? I've arranged the flowers on the dining-room table—in a kind of a way; but you have such excellent taste, you know—if you wouldn't mind putting a finishing touch—I shall just have time to dress now. And you might have a look round the drawing-room, too—do just as you like—just as you like—it's sure to be an improvement—"

Which was all very well; but in the ornamentation of her house Mrs. Alexander Elliott acted on these two fundamental principles—first, that each and every article in the drawing-room must be adorned with a large bow of silk ribbon, as if it were a white poodle-dog, and, secondly, that flowers, whether cut or potted, were simple, feeble, ineffective things, and must therefore be swathed round about with masses of satin, either pink or yellow. And as Briseis did not know how far she might dare to impinge upon these traditions, her tentative little efforts at decoration were considerably restricted; however, she proceeded as well as she could; and, in fact, had only done restoring some measure of freedom to the cramped-up flowers of the dining-room table when a ringing of the door-bell warned her to fly and seek shelter down in the kitchen.

The carrying up of the dinner dishes did not prove to be much of a hardship, after all; and when, at intervals, she caught some glimpse or echo of the rather funereal banquet going forward in the dining-room, she did not much regret being on the wrong side of the door. Then by-and-by dessert arrived; and this was the signal for her to get off to her own apartment, to dress for the later ceremony. When she descended to the drawing-room, she found herself alone; so she occupied the spare moments in loosening out a few of the bows of ribbon, and in shaking free some of the tied-up curtains.

Miss Bingham's papa and mamma turned out to be a rather distinguished-looking couple, both of them of a countrified complexion, with good manners, and considerable reticence of speech. But, well-bred as they may have been, neither could altogether conceal a slight glance of surprise when they were introduced

to Briseis Valieri.   Who was the mysterious stranger,
then, who had not been granted a place at the dinner
table ?   A niece ?   But she was so singularly unlike
the rest of the family ; she was tall—dark-eyed—and
gracious of bearing ; and when, at her aunt's request,
she went to the piano and began to play something—
soft and low, so as not to disturb the conversation—
Mrs. Bingham at least knew that that was no school-
girl's touch, no, nor any music-mistress's either.   And
then, when Briseis had done what had been demanded of her, she rose and retired into an adjacent corner,
where there chanced to be a small side table, and a
lamp, and some photographs ; and here no one inter-
fered with her ; indeed she even ventured to open
and read a note that had stealthily been placed in her
hand by the little lame boy.   It contained only these
words—"The line is 'On Popocatapetl'; but don't tell
Edward I told you.—A."   She had a vague impression
that this might refer to some one or other of the
medical student's fatuities ; but which of them she
couldn't recall at the moment.

The Binghams did not stay late ; but there was much
to do after they had gone ; and it was not until well
past eleven that Briseis was allowed to retire finally to
the solitude of her own room.   By this time she was
about done to death ; and perhaps inclined to be a trifle
hysterical after the long and unintermittent strain ;
and to calm herself she went and sat by the window
(the stars were faintly visible above the roofs of the
opposite houses) and repeated to herself—and repeated
more than once, too — Goethe's pathetic Nachtlied.
The translation (of the untranslatable) was her own,
and no doubt was bald and bare enough ; but she had
used the litte fragment ere now as a kind of spell or
charm in moments of despondency.

Over all the mountains
Is peace ;
Along the far summits
Hearest thou
Hardly a breath ;
The birds are hushed in the forest.
Wait thou only, and soon
Thou also-shalt sleep.

This time the charm proved to be of no avail. She was restless—nervously excited—sleep was out of the question—' ihr war, sie wusste nicht wie.' And at length, hardly knowing what she did, she went to the side of the bed, and threw herself on her knees, and laid her forehead on her clasped hands. It was an attitude of prayer—though this was a strange kind of prayer :

" Mother—father—uncle—where are you all ?" she murmured, amid wild tears and wilder sobbing. " Where are you ? Can you hear me ? Do you know that—that I am trying to do my best ?—I try—to do what you would approve—but—but I am so lonely—so lonely. Mother—mother—surely you can hear me—cannot you say something—to let me know—that you approve ?—"

But there was no answer from the wide, and sad, and silent spaces of the stars.

CHAPTER XI

A SECRET OF THE WOODS

Now no one who had met Miss Georgie Lestrange coming lightly down the staircase and across the hall of Glen Skean Castle, on this fresh, and brilliant, and sweet-scented morning, would have suspected that there was aught of evil, or mischief, or malice in her extremely pretty eyes. And perhaps there was not. Perhaps she had only the natural wish to get out-of-doors for a minute or two—to look abroad on the wide valley with its azure ribbon of a river, on the rose-purple slopes of heather stained to a claret color here and there by the passing clouds, and on the sunlight weaving silver into the mists of Aonach Môr. That was simple and natural enough. The dew was trembling and glinting on the grass; the rowan-trees were a glory of scarlet; the black shadows of the limes and beeches moved slowly, this way and that, on the vivid green of the lawn: there were plenty of things to engage her pleased attention, out here in the open air. But Miss Georgie did not at once step forth into the sunshine.

For it so happened that in passing through the portico she caught sight of the luncheon-bag, already packed and lying on the table; and as this bag was made of netting, the contents of it were for the most part visible, among those being a couple of small tumblers, one within the other for safer carrying. She paused only for a second; and even now there was no indication that any devilment had occurred to her nimble brain. Nay, it was with a fine affectation of carelessness that she went outside and looked all about her —her dark blue Tam o' Shanter set jauntily on the rebellious tangles of her golden-red hair. And then she passed across the terrace; and tripped down the wide steps; and strolled along to the nearest flower-plot, and proceeded to gather a few pansies. These pansies were of an uncommon kind—dusky orange and russet, with manifold streaks and blotches; and perhaps that was why she wanted them; at all events, when she had secured the little nosegay, she returned with it to the portico, and placed it for a moment on the table. Then, and more rapidly (and after a quick and furtive glance into the interior of the hall) she undid the clasp of the luncheon-bag; she took out the two tumblers, and separated them; she wrapped the paper round one of them and restored it to its place; the other received the tiny bouquet; and with that in her hand she walked into the spacious and empty dining-room, where breakfast was laid. This was but a trifling decoration to place on the massive Elizabethan sideboard, in front of the great salvers and tankards; nevertheless she seemed satisfied; and when she went out once more to the terrace, she was demurely whistling to herself as she walked up and down—with a watchful eye for any new-comer.

And that, as it chanced, was none other than Frank Gordon, who had been down to see what the river was like.

"I'm afraid, Miss Georgie," said he, as he came up, "it's no use your going with us to day. The water has dwindled away to nothing. Not a ghost of a chance—"

"But you said you would show me the big fish in

the pools above the Priest's Bridge," said Miss Georgie, in rather an injured fashion.

"Oh, well, if you like to go as far, for the pleasure of sitting and looking at them—"

"And the photographs," she continued. "You said you would help me to get some instantaneous views of salmon-fishing—you casting, you know, out at the end of the jetty—and John standing by you, with the gaff—"

"Oh, certainly, by all means," he said, "if you think it's worth while coming for that."

"And you promised to try the new rod the Prince has had sent him—"

"Take a salmon-rod out to Monteveltro!"

"But you promised. And besides," she added, triumphantly and conclusively, "the luncheon-bag is already packed for us—for some of the English servants have been allowed to go off to see the Highland Games at Fort Mary, and they did everything they could before they left. What time would you like to start?"

"Whenever you please."

"Oh, well, I'll go and get the plates put in my camera; and if we set out immediately after breakfast, I dare say there will be plenty of time for us to photograph all the way up to the Priest's Bridge."

It seemed a satisfactory arrangement; but it did not so entirely commend itself to all the members of this household. Some little while after the setting forth of this expedition, Lady Rockminster went along to her sister-in-law's boudoir, knocked, and was bidden to enter.

"Adela," said she, when she had shut the door behind her, "I want to speak to you."

"What is it?" asked Lady Adela in reply, looking up from her writing. She was dressed in a most charm-

" PERHAPS THAT WAS WHY SHE WANTED THEM "

ing tea gown : it was a compliment she paid to her work, and indirectly to the public.

"Do you know that Georgie Lestrange has gone away up the river again, with Frank Gordon ?"

"Yes ?"

"Well, that's nothing in itself, perhaps," continued Lady Rockminster, who seemed somewhat vexed, "but really the way she is going on is too bad—"

"She is a mischievous wretch," observed Lady Adela, calmly.

"It is really outrageous!" the tall and handsome young matron protested. "And I am certain the Princess is deeply annoyed, though she is too proud to say anything. Why, do you know that more than once I have caught the maids sniggering among themselves ? Now that is abominable. That is perfectly abominable."

"Really, Honnor," her sister-in-law retorted, "I don't see how you can blame Georgie for the bad manners of your servants. And as for her little frolics, what harm is in them ? It's only her fun."

"It's a kind of fun that sometimes has very serious consequences," said Lady Rockminster, impatiently.

Her sister-in-law laid down her pen.

"What is it you are afraid of, Honnor ? A boy and girl amusing themselves, like a pair of kittens : what harm can come of that ? Is it Master Frank you are concerned about ? Leave him alone : he can take care of himself—trust him ! He wasn't born yesterday. Nor was she, for the matter of that. Georgie has had at least one little affair of a more serious kind. There was Jack Cavan—the Cavans of Kilcrana—I never quite knew how that was broken off—"

"All the same," rejoined Lady Rockminster, "I do say that Georgie Lestrange is carrying things too far ; and I consider that you ought to interfere. I cannot. I am her hostess. But you are her particular friend—"

"And I will give you a very sufficient reason why I cannot interfere," Lady Adela made answer, with not a little dignity. "Are you aware that I am making a study of the situation ? These two are my models, at present. I am drawing from the life—"

"And do you mean to tell me," exclaimed Lady Rockminster, with only half-concealed indignation, "that you are ready to sacrifice the interests of your friend—that you refuse to warn her of her danger—because of the requirements of your novel ?"

Lady Adela Cunyngham was not in the least put out.

"My dear Honnor," she said, with much self-possession, "you mistake the point of view. I am trying to make my book a minute and faithful picture of English life as it is lived to-day, in all its varied phases; and I trust that the record may have a permanent value long after these temporary escapades are forgotten."

In asserting her position the authoress had become almost convincingly sententious: Lady Rockminster hardly knew what to say. She left the room wondering whether she herself would have to ask Miss Georgie to be a little more circumspect in her methods, or whether those gay cantrips were to go on entirely unchecked.

And at this very moment Miss Georgie Lestrange was out in the middle of the river Skean, cautiously making her way along a knifelike edge of rock, while Frank Gordon was by her side, splashing through the shallows, and holding on by her arm to balance her. Presently she stopped.

"I think we are far enough," she said, looking back

towards the bank they had left behind—where John
Tod was in charge of the little black box of a camera
perched on a big gray bowlder. "Yes, this will about
do. Now you get up on that stone."

He did as he was bid.

"You must reach over and grasp my hand," she
continued, "as if you were going to help me to jump
on to the rock beside you—do you see? And take a
firm grip—my fingers aren't made of whipped cream—
and that will steady us both. If we're all in focus, castle and hills and all, I think it will be rather nobby."

'Nobby' is not perhaps the word one would have
chosen; but there is no doubt she had planned this
composition with considerable skill. For here were
the foreground figures, out on the rocks amid the silver-glancing waters; and behind them was a still, clear,
tea-brown pool that made a perfect mirror for the overhanging rowan-trees and hazel-bushes; beyond that,
in the distance, rose the plateau on which the gray
walls of the Castle stood out from their background of
dark green pine; while over all towered the peaks of
Aonach Mòr, the threads of snow in the shadowed
crevices losing themselves in the hovering clouds.
That, at least, was what she had arranged through the
medium of the 'finder'; and there remained now but
to signal to John Tod to press the spring.

"Sure you won't wobble?" she said to her companion, as she reached out her hand. "Hold on firm
now. Sure you won't wobble when I cry 'Go!'?"

"I have braced up my nerves," he answered her.

"Go!" she called—and the sound rang clearly away
across the soft murmuring of the stream.

The next moment she had straightened herself up
again, still clinging to his hand; and then he stepped
down from the stone into the water, to pilot her ashore;

and in a little while they had resumed their leisurely pilgrimage along the river-bank.

It was quite wonderful the number of picturesque backgrounds that Miss Georgie managed to discover, on this idle morning; and there was no need to initiate John Tod into the mysteries of time-exposure, for the sunlight was vivid on bank and brae; so that here, there, and everywhere she was forming her little group of two, and having it snapped for her. But there was one spot in especial that she set her heart on; just below the Priest's Bridge it was—a deep and slumberous pool dark almost to an ebony blackness, on the further side a wall of water-worn rock with overhanging woods, on the hither side steep slopes smothered in heather and bracken and scrub-oak, while out into the glassy surface of the stream ran a small russet-yellow jetty, rudely constructed of split pine, for the convenience of the fisherman.

"Now, Sir Francis," said she, "you must go right to the end of the jetty, for your gray figure will do splendidly against the black shadow, and there will be the reflection in the water as well. You must take your rod, too, and pretend to be casting—"

"And you?" said he.

"Oh, I am coming out, too," she answered, blithely. "I am going to stand by you as your gillie, gaff in hand—"

"That's rather reversing the natural order of things, isn't it?" he made bold to remark.

"Now be a good boy, and do as you're told," said she, in a businesslike manner, as she proceeded to poise the camera. "This is the very last one I am going to take—and it must be perfect."

Of course the result of all these experiments could not be known until much later on; but in the mean time she seemed well content; and as they continued on their way up through the woods to the heights above the Priest's Bridge, she appeared to be in excellent spirits. And yet she said—as she absently plucked a bit of heather and began to nibble at it—

"It's horrid to have no soul—positively horrid. Don't you think so? I call it loathsome—distinctly loathsome."

"No soul?" he repeated in amazement. "Who has no soul?"

"I," she rejoined, deliberately. "I am conscious of it all the time I am with Lady Adela, and Sibyl, and Rose. Their aspirations, their passionate yearnings, their noble ambitions—all that arises from their having souls; they are in earnest, and enjoy a kind of spiritual exaltation; and I feel so awfully ashamed—and mean—and—and empty. I am convinced I have no soul; and it's really and truly horrid."

"Oh, but there are other qualities," said he, boldly (for he must needs comfort this poor creature in her vague despondency). "You wouldn't have everybody writing, and painting, and composing music? You wouldn't have the world filled with people of that kind? Surely there are qualities in human life quite as valuable as the enthusiasm of amateurs! There's cheerfulness, for example; and there's good-nature—and good-comradeship—and straightforwardness—and brightness—and merriment—"

"Oh, is that me?" she said. "Do you mean me? Really? Perhaps, after all, I may be a blessing in disguise!"

"I don't see the disguise," said he.

"Hm!—that's rather nice," she observed, reflectively; and by this time they were out in the open again—high above the Skean Narrows.

And then, and cautiously, he led her forward to the brink of the deep and sombre chasm; and, resting his hand on a birch-tree, he peered over, and continued his intense scrutiny, for a few seconds. Then he withdrew his head.

"I can only see two down there, but they are huge brutes."

"Where—where—where ?" she exclaimed, excitedly; and she also would crane her head and neck, gazing down through the bushes into the deeps of the river far below.

But at first she could see nothing at all—nothing save the dark, clear, still water, with here and there some faint indication of the gravel or rock at the bottom. She stared and better stared—eager—impatient—and then she uttered a slight cry.

"Oh, I see him !—I see him !—"

For a dull-hued, olive-green object, hitherto lying motionless above a flat yellow stone, had made a slight movement; there was an obscure gleam for the fiftieth part of a second; but that was sufficient to direct the eye—and now she could dimly make out the enormous fish, which was almost motionless again, and not too easily discernible unless one's attention were kept steady.

"There's another about a yard and a half further down," Frank Gordon said to her, "but he's closer in to the rock : you won't make him out until your eyes get better accustomed. In the mean time, what do you say to having lunch, just here ? You can sit and watch the fish : very likely you may see one or other of them throw himself out of the water—and these two are forty-pounders if they're anything."

Well, she was nothing loth; for the long rambling by glade and stream had made her hungry; John was summoned to bring along the bag; the little white parcels were opened; and there was a display of tongue and turkey sandwiches, vinegared lettuce, and other commodities. Then he drew the cork of the claret-bottle; and proceeded to remove the paper that ought to have enwrapped two tumblers. There was only one.

"Look at this!" he exclaimed angrily. "Did you ever see such carelessness! Hallett has sent us only one tumbler!"

Not the faintest tinge of color appeared on the shell-like purity of her forehead.

"Oh, really?" she said, with great sweetness. "But it doesn't matter, does it?"

"Of course it doesn't matter," said he, gloomily. "I can get the loan of the cup from Tod's flask."

This startled her : it was an unforeseen check.

"Oh, Tod's flask?" she repeated. "Some battered old zinc thing—why should you want to have that? Surely this tumbler can do for both of us? I am not too proud, if you are not."

It was a challenge—a command, rather.

"If you don't mind!—" he said.

"Of course I don't mind!" she said, with robust good-nature; and therewith they set to work on the small packets; and when it came to the question of claret, they drank alternately, like two love-birds, from the same cup. The familiar hobnobbing, here in these remote and sylvan solitudes, seemed to delight her; she picked the nicest sandwiches for him; she recommended this and recommended that; and finally, luncheon over, she cleverly pared an apple, and duly presented him with his proper half.

And yet she was not wholly happy. Ever and anon she had been glancing down towards the still pools at the bottom of the wooded gorge, where she could now

8

make out, not only the two large salmon, but three or four smaller ones, equally immobile in the shadows of the rocks.

"It's an awful swizz seeing those fish lying there, isn't it?" she said, somewhat enigmatically. "Makes you want to throw stones at them, doesn't it? They're no use to anybody, are they?" Then she looked him straight in the face. "Sir Francis," said she, "did you ever hear of such a thing as 'snatching' a salmon?"

"A shabby trick," he said, as he lit a cigarette.

"Oh, yes, that's all very well," she proceeded, undauntedly. "I know that snatching is considered to be very disgraceful—at least, that is what people pretend—and you wouldn't do it while there was a keeper or a gillie near by. But if I were a man, I would not be afraid of the opinion of keepers and gillies!"

"I am not afraid of the opinion of keepers and gillies," he humbly protested. "I am afraid of my own opinion."

"Oh, that is all quixotism," she insisted. "Now just let me count up the reasons why you should snatch one of these fish, so that we may take it home with us. First of all, I want to see how it's done: that's one reason. Then I know the housekeeper at the Castle, or the cook, or whoever it is, will be glad to have a salmon for the kitchen—that's two more: three reasons. Then the fish for the time being belong to Lord Rockminster: eight reasons. Are you counting? Then it's a secluded place: no one can possibly see us: twelve reasons. That's already twelve undeniable reasons. But the twenty-first, and the original and imperative one, is that I must and shall see how it's done!"

Now if he had looked any other way he might have been saved; but he looked the very worst way of all;

he looked at her eyes—and these were full of a malicious and audacious mirth.   He fell.

"Do you mean' it ?" he said.

"Of course I do !" she answered him.

"John !" he called aloud.   "Bring me my fly-book, and a small japanned box you will find in the fishing-bag, and the Prince's rod."

"Why the Prince's rod ?" she demanded.

"Do you think I would contaminate my own rod with any such iniquity?—whereas the Monteveltrin conscience won't mind."   Then, when John Tod had brought the japanned box, he opened it.   "I wish to draw your attention, Miss Georgie, to the fact that I have not a triangle in my possession : I shall have to make one by destroying three valuable flies."

"And why not?" said she.   "Haven't I given you thirty-seven strong reasons why it is right and just and absolutely necessary that you should snatch a salmon !—"

"Oh, let that go—let that go," he said, doggedly. "When one is embarking on wild wickedness, it's no good trying to salve one's soul with excuses."

He took three large Jack Scotts, and ruthlessly cut the dressing off them ; he placed them back to back, and bound them together with brass wire ; he affixed a bit of string and a leaden sinker ; he ran a piece of gut through the eyed shanks— But enough : the execrable implement was at length complete.   And by this time the Prince's brand-new rod had been put together.

"Now, John," he said, "you go away down to the water-side, and hide behind a rock ; and you needn't see what's going on till I yell to you to be ready with the gaff."

He himself descended the steep bank some little

way, clambering through tall heather, and broom, and birch; and ever at his elbow was Vivien the temptress, far more resolute and set on this atrocious enterprise than he was.

"Try for one of the big ones," she whispered eagerly. "Won't it be splendid to take a forty-five-pounder back to the Castle!"

Which was all very well; but the difficulty of swinging and pitching that unholy implement, in this narrow chasm, was much greater than she understood; besides, it is not suggested that he was an adept. At last, however, he managed to drop the triangle on to the smooth-worn face of the opposite rock—he kept jerking it slightly—and finally it flopped into the water, just beyond one of the great salmon. The next moment there was a vacancy where that fish had been. It made no wave; it showed no sudden flash; it simply vanished; and the yellow stone over which it had been hanging was a yellow stone, and nothing more.

"Sir Francis, swear for me!" said Miss Georgie, with her teeth set.

"We must try further down," said he, more camly. "But those rowan-trees are the very mischief."

They were the very mischief; for more than once he got caught up, and had to risk the whole of his tackle in hauling away the triangle by main force; but eventually most unmerited success crowned his efforts—he was fast into a fish, that first dashed up the pool, and then dashed down again, and then went to the bottom and dourly remained there.

This was but the beginning of the most desperate series of adventures that ever befell an unfortunate angler. To start with, he was surrounded with difficulties. He dared not move from his place, so sheer was the descent beneath him. Bushes hemmed him in on this bank ; on the other were overhanging trees. Worst of all, the long and dark pool, towards its lower extremity, narrowed until the water flowed between two almost contiguous walls of rock ; and it was a matter of certainty that if the salmon entered that channel, he would depart on a farewell voyage. And of course, as is the wont of salmon, as soon as this fish had tired of sulking, it was for the neck of that channel that he deliberately made. More and more strain was put on him ; and more and more strain ; and still the brute kept boring down ; ruin seemed inevitable—

When there was a most appalling crack : the rod had snapped clean in two !—half-way up the middle joint. Gordon (with an inward 'O mother of Moses, what's going to happen now !') had just time to seize the upper half before it slid down the slackened line, so that he now found himself with half a rod in each hand, the line being the only connecting link.

"Here," he said quickly to his companion, "take this—and reel up when I tell you—and let out when I tell you—"

With trembling fingers Miss Georgie received the lower half of the rod, and breathlessly awaited commands. The marvellous thing was that the sudden slackening of the strain had apparently altered the determination of the fish to go down the narrow channel : he began to come steadily back—while the fisherman; holding his half of the rod with the left hand, with the right pulled in the line through the rings.

"Reel up !—reel up !" he cried to his companion— and Miss Georgie, with her heart in her mouth, and her eyes hot as fire, and her fingers shaking, fought with the small horn handle as best she could.

"Oh, Frank," she said (not knowing what she said), "what's going to happen?"

"Yes, that's what I want to know," he answered her, grimly, with his eye fixed on the gray thread that was slowly cutting the water. "I never before played a fish with the top half of a broken rod. I suppose it's a judgment— Let out! let out!" he suddenly called to her—for now the salmon was making a vigorous dash for the head of the pool, and the poor, quaking lass had to let the line run free, though her knees were now almost unable to support her.

"Oh, what's it going to do!" she said, pantingly. "Oh, I can't hold this thing any longer—I cannot—I cannot—"

And then she uttered a piercing shriek. In her blind agitation and terror she had somehow managed to get the reel released from the rod; the moment it was loose it fell away from her tremulous grasp; and then in helpless dismay she saw it gradually and beautifully roll down the steep incline, ending by a splash into the water.

"Well, I think that has about settled the matter this journey!" observed young Gordon, with a rueful laugh.

But not yet. The crustacean gillie, his back bent double, came swiftly and crouchingly along; he caught the line and tried to jerk the reel to the surface; he failed at first, but ultimately, by gentler means, succeeded; and then he rapidly wound in.

"Will I fling it up t' ye!" he called.

"No, no!" she screamed in her alarm. "Keep it yourself, and do what Sir Francis tells you!"

"Slide the butt down to him," young Gordon said to her, quietly, and without even looking at her: all his attention was concentrated on the point where the scarcely moving gray thread met the mysterious brown deeps of the pool. "The butt," he exclaimed—"your end of the rod—let it slip down the line, and he'll get hold of it."

Then she understood; the butt was launched, and safely delivered; John Tod reaffixed the reel; and then stood awaiting orders—in the most astounding predicament that had ever fallen to his lot.

And what was the salmon about all this time? Well, the salmon, not knowing that a single decisive movement must almost certainly have ensured its escape, had again gone below to sulk; and there it had remained, perhaps trying to persuade itself that nothing had occurred. And then, getting tired of the monotony of this performance, it began slowly to return to the middle of the pool, while Master Frank pulled in the line through the rings, keeping such strain on as he dared.

"Reel in, John, reel in!" he shouted to his henchman underneath—so that the line between the two pieces of the rod should be kept taut. And again: "Let go!—let go!"—for the salmon had now taken it into its head to wander away down by the opposite bank, where the water was deep and black-brown under the smooth gray rock. And all this while the fish had not shown itself once: they could form no idea of its possible size.

"If we ever land this fellow," said young Gordon to his companion, "there'll have to be a poem written about it."

"Oh, don't talk, Sir Francis, don't talk!" she said, piteously. "Get him!"

"Yes, that's all very well," he answered her, coolly enough. "But what control do you suppose I have over him, with this bit of stick? I wish the Prince had tried his rotten old rod for himself. There must have been a flaw right in the middle—O thunder !"

This ejaculation, under his breath, was quite inadequate to meet the exigencies of the case; for what happened now was simply bewildering. The salmon, suddenly resolved upon freeing itself from this vicious thing that had got hold of it, rushed np stream for some dozen yards or so; then threw itself thrice into the air, in rapid succession, each time coming down with an amazing report; then it lashed out on the surface—head and tail going—sides gleaming—the churned water flying about in every direction. And still, through all this, the gray line held !—and still it held through subsequent and weariful periods of sulking—and still it held until the fish, roving again, came incautiously near the bank and the crouching John Tod: there was a wary reaching out of the gaff —a quick stroke of the steel—and here, on the stones, lay and struggled a magnificent, brilliant - shining creature—near to thirty pounds, they guessed. Miss Georgie sank down on the heather: she had not breath left for the faintest 'hurrah !'

There ought to have been a reaction after all this wild excitement, especially as they were 'far, far frae hame,' with the afternoon wearing on. Nevertheless, as they made their preparations for the return journey, it was with a light heart; and when at length they set out to seek their way through the woods, and along by the still pools and silver shallows, back to Glen Skean Castle, Miss Georgie had quite recovered her breath and also her considerable powers of speech, while she was unmistakably proud of the share she had taken in this achievement. 'Blithe, blithe, and merry was she'; and the evening was fair, and clear, and golden: when they got through the woods and out

into the open, they found that the distant hills about
Clunes and Glen Loy had become mere roseate transparent films against that glow in the west; only up
by Aonach Môr was there something of a darker bulk
and grandeur, in the sterile shadows facing the east.

"What a story I shall have to tell at dinner to-
night!" cried Miss Georgie Lestrange, her laughing
eyes and cherry lips radiant and smiling.

Her companion was less enthusiastic.

"If you're wise," said the young laird of Grantly,
to his partner in crime, "you'll keep the whole affair
a profound and ghastly secret. And you'll find out
how John Tod can smuggle that fish into the kitch-
en, by some back way."

8*

CHAPTER XII

"WHERE THE DUN DEER LIE"

IT was the religious scruples of the Margravine of Pless-Gmünden that threatened to break up the house party at Glen Skean Castle. For it appeared that a certain youthful Monarch, recently elevated to the throne, had been casting about for a bride; and as chance would have it, his fancy had fallen on the daughter of the said Margravine—the beautiful Alexia; the only drawback being that before any formal betrothal could take place it was necessary that the young lady should change her religion, or at least the outward form of it. She, having a practical turn of mind, was perfectly willing; but her mother, dévote to the last degree, recoiled; while during this period of suspense a considerable section of the King's ministers were secretly endeavoring to get the match broken off altogether, hoping that their master would form a much more important alliance. Now as the Margravine of Pless-Gmünden and the Princess of Monteveltro were known to be bosom-friends—indeed they had been so ever since their school-girl days in Dresden— and as the compelling and resolute character of the Princess was also well known, it was but natural that those whose interests favored the marriage should turn to her, with the idea that her frank remonstrances and her personal influence might induce the hesitating mother to do her duty by her daughter. Hence urgent messages and telegrams—from Buda-Pesth—from Belgrade—from Orsova; insomuch that the poor lass in the post-office at Skean Bridge, laboriously and mechanically spelling out the foreign words, had wellnigh taken leave of her wits.

But on the other hand the Prince was desperately loth to leave, just as the deer-stalking was about to begin. This was the summit of his ambition now : an honest, uncompromising, legitimate stalk : no blazing into detachments of driven animals—with that he was abundantly familiar; but an honest piece of circumvention, and skill, and nerve. He thought he could stand the test; at all events he was anxious to try; and eventually a compromise was effected between the importunate Princess and her dilatory husband. Rumors came in one evening of a large stag—a splendid beast of twelve points or more—having been seen in the neighborhood of the Corrieara burn; it was arranged that the Prince should attempt his first stalk the next morning; while on the following day he and the Princess were to set out on their return to eastern Europe—though, to be sure, they were first of all going round by Grantly on Dee-side, to pay at least a few hours' visit to Aunt Jean.

And thus it was that on this fateful morning, while as yet the great gray building seemed plunged in profoundest slumber, a small procession set forth from the front of the Castle : at its head the red-bearded gillie, Roderick, riding a shaggy brown pony; then there was the stalwart young lad, Hughie, on foot, with a bag slung over his shoulder; and finally came the Prince, mounted on the white mare Maggie, the rein hanging loose on her neck, for Monseigneur was engaged in lighting a cigar to cheer him on his lonely road. And a lonely road it was, when once they had got away

from the Castle and had entered upon the solitudes of
the forest : oppressively and mournfully silent too, for
they had soon left behind them the familiar sounds
of the valley—the continuous murmur of the stream,
the velvet "whuff-whuff" of the peewit's wings, the
startled "coo-ee !" of the long-beaked whaup. None
the less was it an auspicious morning. The sky was
veiled over by a net-work of silvery-gray, the clouds receding in soft gradations of perspective until they almost seemed massed together over the billowy mountains about Glen Loy; and if the interstices appeared to
be widening—if there were further and further gleams
of blue—if the sunlight began to lend a warmer tone to
the rose-purple of the heather—still, there was a cool
air stirring that promised to temper the heat. Above
all, the hills towards which they were bound were clear
to the top ; there was little chance of their being baffled
by slow-descending mists.

What dark premonitions of 'buck-ague'—what stern
resolves—what recurrent misgivings—what wild visions
of a stag Royal—were now warring with each other in
Monseigneur's brain it is unnecessary to guess ; perhaps it would have been better for his nerve if Ronald
the head forester, who was a companionable kind of
man, had been with him ; but Ronald had left long before daybreak on a reconnoitring expedition ; and it
was to the rendezvous he had appointed that they were
now making their way. And so the mute little procession toiled on—across these voiceless wastes of peat-
hag, and bog-myrtle, and heather—until the rude track
they were following began gradually to ascend ; and
now the wise mare Maggie, craning her neck forward,
was left to pick her footing, for ever and anon the
bridle-path would seem to disappear in this rough
wilderness of rock and scanty herbage. Up and up

they went, into the silences of the hills; and the higher
they got the wider and wider grew the great world beneath them, spreading out on every hand to the horizon,
until far in the west the ethereal mountainous ram-
parts were visible all the way from Ardgour to Glen-
garry, and in the east the shadows of Ben Alder had
become of a pale and clear and perfect ultramarine beyond the undulating, intervening straths.

Mile after mile they traversed in this fashion —
splashing through swampy hollows, and climbing up
barren heights—until on the summit of one of these
ridges the gillie on the brown pony began to go more
warily, with whispered communications, in Gaelic, to
his companion Hugh. And then of a sudden, as it
seemed to the startled eyes of Monseigneur, a man
sprung out of the ground—a short, thick-set man, with
bushy black eyebrows and extraordinarily clear gray
eyes; and he was shutting up his telescope-case as he
stepped forward and touched his cap.

"Have you seen him?" said the Prince, eagerly.
"Have you seen the big stag?"

Ronald answered in a slow, and measured, and de-
pressed manner—as if he were speaking of some calamity that had befallen him or his in bygone times.

"Yes, I am thinking that. Anyway there's a grand
beast, along with a wheen more, on the other side of
Ben-na-crasg; but before we could get to them, they
will be lying down, and mebbe they will not be rising
to feed again for hours yet. But there's a lot of hinds
and two or three small beasts just beyond the water-
shed; and we would be going in that direction whatever. Will ye please to get down now, Monsenior?"

So this was the arrangement, then?—the two ponies
were led off by the red-bearded gillie towards some unknown destination; the stalwart young lad put a rifle

over each of his shoulders; the head forester proceeded to lead the way, Monseigneur obediently following.
And little indeed did the hapless Prince know what
was now before him. For first they went down these
steep and rugged slopes until they reached the glen below; then they got into a winding channel filled with
oozy peat-water, and that they followed for half a mile
—sinking into the dark brown mud at every step;
then (after vigilant circumspection) they crossed an
open piece of morass that was more of a quaking bog
than anything else, with patches of bright green that
spoke of holes ready to engulf them; and at last they
found comparative shelter in a rocky ravine, up which
they painfully toiled. By this time the spick-and-span
attire with which Monseigneur had started away in the
morning was in a deplorable condition, and he himself
was little better. He was black up to the thighs; his
face was bespattered (for he had stumbled once or
twice on hidden stumps and come down heavily); his
hair was matted and streaming with perspiration; his
long mustache was now all loose and ragged and forlorn. And yet he held on courageously, with never a
word of complaint; now and again he was forced to
pause in order to take breath and mop his forehead,
but it was with no thought of remonstrance; and not
once had there even been a suggestion as to the opening of a flask.

For over an hour not a syllable had been uttered,
nor was there any uttered now as the deep-chested
forester stopped, took the rifles from Hughie, put cartridges into the barrels, gave one of the weapons to the
Prince, retaining the other for himself, while again
their laborious onward progress was resumed. Presently, however, after a long and cautious survey of the
ground, he left the bed of the ravine, and began to

"LITTLE INDEED DID THE HAPLESS PRINCE KNOW WHAT WAS NOW BEFORE HIM"

clamber up the sheer incline—an operation that was
rendered doubly difficult for Monseigneur, for the reason that he, having some one in front of him, was
bound to keep his rifle in a transverse position as he
clutched and climbed from one stone to another, from
one heather-tuft to that just above. And even here
the same overwhelming silence prevailed. A death-
like stillness: not a bird chirped, not a leaf stirred:
there was a curious impression that one could hear
sounds miles and miles away, only that there were no
sounds to listen to, in this forgotten land. And so it
was that when all of a sudden into this mysterious hush
and peace there sprang an appalling

"BRAH!"

surely that was enough to shake the heart of any mortal man! The terrified Prince grasped the heather to
steady himself, and looked up—for the astounding roar
or snort seemed to proceed from just over his head;
and there for one wild second he beheld on the sky-
line above him an awful creature — a dark creature with large and startled eyes and pricked-up ears
— that was intently gazing down upon him. The
next instant the apparition had vanished—dissipated
itself into air — without a rustle or the patter of a
hoof.

"Was that—a stag?" Monseigneur gasped, with his
heart thumping and thumping as if it would burst out
of his chest.

"Na, na, just a hind," replied the forester, in a low
voice. "I was seeing a good big herd of them close by
here—and mebbe she'll no have frightened them
much—"

"Hinds?—hinds?" said Monseigneur, with impatience. "I do not wish to shoot hinds!—"

"But there's two or three stags I was seeing as well

—smahl beasts—if Monsenior would try a shot before going on—"

"Small—small, did you say ?"

" Oh, yes, indeed, but Monsenior might get an easy shot—"

" Come, come, now, Ronald," the Prince said, imperatively—for he had not suffered all this indescribable torture in order to waste his attention on 'rubbish '—"it's the big stag we're after, and nothing else—"

" As ye please, Monsenior," responded Ronald, coolly. " We'll just haud on then." And therewith their heavy labor was resumed—Monseigneur blindly following, resolved upon enduring to the end, so long as a breath was left in his body.

But at length, towards noon, they had arrived at the crest of a hill, or ridge of hills, overlooking a wide extent of lonely and featureless country—featureless save for a small and sluggish burn that crept noiselessly through these sterile wastes ; and here Ronald, lying on his back, and balancing his telescope on his knees, began a careful scrutiny of the ground. Presently, with his forefinger, he beckoned Monseigneur to worm himself up to his side.

" They're in a terrible bad place—"

" And the big stag ?" the Prince whispered, eagerly.

" Ay, he's there—he's a bit nearer the burn than the others. Take the glass, Monsenior."

It was no easy matter to manage this unwonted instrument ; but eventually, after long searching, the Prince did come upon the herd—hardly distinguishable from the dun hue. of the valley except by reason of their antlers that were here and there in motion, lazily flicking off a fly. All these stags were lying down, out there in the open ; while the monarch of them, of a somewhat darker color than the others, lay a little distance apart. It was on him, of course, that Monseigneur directed the wavering glass; and it was in an awe-stricken kind of fashion that he turned to Ronald with smothered questions as to the chances of their being able to get anywhere near that splendid quarry.

"They're in a terrible bad place," Ronald repeated musingly, as he scanned every feature of the country and watched the 'carry' of every shred of cloud. "But there's no hinds wi' them; and that's in our favor. And mebbe we could get down to the bed of the burn. Anyway, Monsenior, they'll no be getting up to feed for a good hour or two yet; and you might as well be having your luncheon."

A terribly tantalizing meal this was; and equally tantalizing was the period of weary waiting that ensued —while the cool wind of these altitudes was steadily and mercilessly freezing blood and bone. When finally Ronald deemed it prudent to make a move—lying on his back, and pushing himself feet first down the hillside — Monseignenr could hardly follow his example, so stiffened had his joints become; nevertheless he manfully persevered; and in course of time, by a circuitous route, they managed to reach the bed of the stream, where their progression took another and still more agonizing form. Face down it was now; and water that runs in at one's neck and chest is colder than any other kind of water.

More crawling and spying; and now even the professional Ronald was beginning to betray a little subdued excitement.

"A grand beast!" he muttered, dipping down again from one of those guarded surveys. "Just a famous head! And they're all up and feeding now—if they draw over the ridge, ye ought to have a chance, Monsenior. A grand beast—thirteen or fourteen points, I'm thinking—and a fine span : a noble beast indeed."

Monseigneur could hardly listen : he knew that the crisis of his life was approaching. And as it happened, at this perilous juncture, they were favored by singular good fortune; for as they stealthily got nearer and nearer, slouching along by the bed of the burn, they found that the herd were slowly withdrawing over the ridge, while the big stag, with two smaller ones, seemed rather inclined to keep to the valley. And at last the fateful signal was given. Monseigneur, his head scarcely raised above the sandy grass and the knobs of heather, drew himself forward, pushing his rifle in front of him ; he paused to take breath, for he was like to choke with apprehension ; warily he crawled on again ; and now he could make out a little plateau, russet-hued in the warm afternoon sunlight, and quietly feeding there a magnificent and graceful creature with great wide-branching horns. He raised himself slightly on his elbows. He put the rifle to his shoulder. He tried to steady the trembling barrels ; then he held his breath ; he pulled the trigger—and the dull, soft thud of the bullet into the slope beyond proclaimed that he had missed clean.

What followed now was so sudden, so unexpected, and so brief that it gave no opportunity for consideration. The stag, alarmed by the loud report, and not seeing where his enemies lay hid, dashed forward, and as luck would have it came galloping directly down upon them. Ronald, having no time to think, thrust his head into the heather, and put his arm around the back of his neck ; Monseigneur—well, Monseigneur did not know what was happening to him, as this huge animal came bounding along : the next moment the stag had sprang right over them, and was making straight for the burn.

"Now, sir!—now!" yelled Ronald; and the bewil-·dered Prince mechanically obeyed—he swung himself round—he took aim—he fired—and the stag was seen to go crashing down, right in the middle of the shallow stream. But again the gallant brute was on his legs—he struggled through the pool—he tried and again tried the opposite bank—and that was the end of him : all at once he lurched heavily on to his knees, and then fell of a heap, apparently stone - dead. The face of Monseigneur was of the color of vellum.

The next minute the three men were in the water, splashing their way across to the other side ; but it was Hughie who had first grip of the branching antlers.

"Fourteen points, sir!" he called, with a grin.

"Fourteen points!—du lieber!—fourteen—fourteen points!" And indeed when the Prince got up to the noble prize he had secured (by an infamous fluke) his recent paralysis of consternation completely fell away from him, and he broke into an absolute paroxysm of delight. He went daft. He threw his cap in the air. He was loudly laughing and chuckling. "Fourteen points!" he cried—and he also would raise the massive head, to examine and admire. "I tell you, Ronald, that is fourteen sovereigns in your pocket the moment we get home—and seven in yours, Hughie : so that's a fair day's work for all of us ! A grant beast ?—yes, you were right there, Ronald, you rascal ! And how far away are the ponies now ?—and will you be able to get him down to the Castle to-night ? Why don't you cry hurrah, man ?—why don't you cry hurrah ?"

"Monseuior," said Ronald, shyly, "if there was a smahl tasting of whiskey that no one would be caring for—"

Monseigneur got out from the luncheon - bag his capacious flask.

"There," said he, with sovereign magnanimity,
"take what there is — divide it between you — I shall
not want a drop—not a drop.   Only, Ronald, I rely on
you to get this splendid fellow down to the Castle to-
night."

It was just about this time of the afternoon that the
young laird of Grantly, Miss Georgie Lestrange, and
John Tod were returning from a fruitless expedition
up the river, and they had arrived at the mouth of the
Corrieara burn, when it occurred to Frank Gordon
that if Tod were to be sent off home with the fishing
impedimenta, these other two—Miss Georgie and himself, that is—might go for a bit of a stroll into the forest to meet the stalking - party on their way back to
the Castle.   Now there was nothing that the blithe
damsel with the pince - nez was not ready for ; the arrangement was forthwith made ; and presently the two
of them were scrambling up through bushes and
bracken until they were in sight of the vast, treeless
plain and the surrounding hills.   But on the crest she
paused, and turned, and in tragic tones she addressed
the river they were leaving behind them.

"Farewell, dear, dear stream !" she said.   "Farewell, farewell !   'No more by thee my steps shall be,
for ever and for ever !'"

"Why ?" asked her more prosaic neighbor.

"Why ?" she repeated.   "Why ?   And you leaving
to-morrow morning with the Prince and Princess !"

"Yes, but there's Lady Rockminster," said he.
"You could go down to the pools with her."

"Honnor has lost all her enthusiasm," Miss Georgie
replied.   "She won't budge a foot while the water's

as low as it is at present. And yet I do think it's so
jolly to sit on the bank — and eat apples — and watch
the big salmon — whether there's any fishing going on
or no." By this time they were crossing the morass,
making for one of the bridle-tracks leading into the
hills. "I say, it's rather nice to be quite by ourselves,
isn't it ?" Miss Georgie proceeded, as she picked her
steps among the rough heather and peat-hags. "I call
it spiffing, don't you ? John Tod is a nuisance. I detest him. He's quite unlike the others — don't you
think so ? All the others—I mean the Highland keepers, and gillies, and servants are so reserved and polite,
and they have so much quiet self-respect too ; but Tod
—Tod considers himself clever, and attempts to make
fun of them—"

"Yes," observed her companion, "and a facetious
Lowlander trying to be humorous at the expense of
the Highlanders is about the most painful sight that
Providence permits in this unfortunate universe."

"And his imitations — imitations, indeed ! 'Her
nainsel's a shentlemans': did ever any one hear a
Highlander talk like that ?" Miss Georgie demanded,
indignantly.

"Stop, stop !" he cried, laughing. "So far I have
refrained—"

"Refrained from what ?"

"From throwing him into the river. You see, it's
a delicate matter. If he were your own gillie, a duck-
ing in the Priest's Bridge pool might have an excellent
effect on his little pleasantries—"

They had now struck upon the rude bridle-path, and
could continue their route without paying so much attention to their footsteps. And if as yet they could
make out no sign of the return of the stalking-party,
they wandered on very contentedly through this golden

evening, the still air around them sweetened with the
honey-fragrance of the heather and the resinous per-
fume of the bog-myrtle. Already, among the lonely
corries of Aonach Môr, shadows of a wan and pale purple were beginning to draw over; but far in the west
the heavens were all aglow; and the hills around Glen
Loy had become almost transparent—they seemed like
huge phantom billows receding outwards and outwards
to the sea.

It was a wild and solitary scene; and the silence was
impressive; but Miss Georgie Lestrange did not allow
herself to be overawed. She was laughing, talking,
jesting, with occasional little touches of pensive sentiment; and if there was any mischief in her mind, her
manner betrayed nothing but a demure and attractive
innocence.

"Where can those people be?" he kept asking; but
her eyes refused to follow his to the distant slopes and
heights: she seemed to care as little for the return of
the stalkers as she did for the shadows slowly gathering on Aonach Môr.

"Say now, Sir Francis," she proceeded, "wouldn't
you like a little souvenir—a souvenir that might sometimes recall to you the happy days we have spent on
the banks of the Skean? I've been thinking, you
know. Do you remember telling me about the keeper
on the Awe, who wanted to dress a new salmon-fly, and
part of the dressing he used was a bit of red hair from
the head of a girl in the neighborhood? Awfully
clever of him, wasn't it? And the fly turned out suc-
cersful, didn't you say? Didn't they call it the 'Highland Lassie?'"

He was hardly heeding her—so intent was his scrutiny
of the remote undulations and gullies.

"They must have gone back by some other way," he

said, "unless they've had a long chase after a wounded stag."

But her next abrupt question brought him to his senses.

"Is my hair red enough?" she demanded.

"Miss Georgie," said he, reprovingly, "questions like that provoke indiscreet answers. Your hair isn't red. I daren't say what I think it is—because you would think me impertinent."

"Is it red enough to put on a salmon-fly?" she persevered. "Because, if it is, you're quite welcome to cut off as much as would dress three or four flies; and then, in days to come, you know, you might think of the happy times on the Skean."

He did not accept her invitation : he was frightened.

"You don't happen to have a pair of scissors?" she asked next, in an off-hand way. "I think I saw a small pair—in your fly-book—"

"Well, yes, I have," he admitted. "But I couldn't clip off any of your hair—it would be a disfigurement—"

"Not at all," she insisted. "Have you your fly-book in your pocket? Very well; take out the scissors. Behind the ears, don't you understand—underneath—you can easily snip bits that will never be noticed."

"But really," said he, "I—I could not take such a liberty—"

"It appears to me," she said, proudly, "that I am as much entitled to have a salmon-fly called after me as any red-headed girl at Taynuilt. Why not the 'English Lassie' as well as the 'Highland Lassie?'"

Well, his fingers were not very steady as he took out the scissors and set about this unnerving task; and he was extremely modest in the exactions he made on

those ruddy-golden wisps and tangles that curled and
clustered about her milk-white neck; but at length he
had put the tiny quantities together, and carefully
smoothed them, and with a religious care had placed
them in one of the pockets of his fly-book. She, also,
seemed to be satisfied as they resumed their walk.

"The 'English Lass,'" she repeated, lightly. "But
no names, mind—no names—should any stranger be
turning over the leaves of your fly-book. A secret is
between two. And you can write and tell me if I have
brought you any luck."

Meanwhile there was no trace of the stalkers; and
the golden glow in the west was paling; and a strange,
clear, metallic-hued twilight was stealing over the
land.

"Come, we must get away back now," he said to
her, with something more of authority; and she was
obedient; so they turned and set out for the Castle—
the gray towers of which were just visible above the
belt of dark green firs.

And yet their solitary walk home was not to be without an adventure, of its kind. As they were following
this rough track across the wild moorland, he stopped
of a sudden, and began to peer earnestly into the
mysterious dusk.

"Do you see them?" he whispered.

Her eyes took the direction indicated; and as they
grew more and more accustomed to the faint haze
hanging over the russet-brown of the plain, she could
make out certain spectral creatures, that were apparently motionless. But they were not quite motionless;
and as she gazed they grew more and more distinct—
seven hinds and a stag, quietly feeding, and wholly unconscious of the presence of any stranger.

"Stand where you are, and watch," he whispered

to her again, "and I will see how near I can get to them."

Thereupon he set out to crouch and steal along by the deeper of the peat-hags, this being the only method of approach possible, the deer feeding right out in the open. Of course, if he had been engaged on a real, instead of an imaginary, stalk, he would have crawled along serpent-wise, shoving his rifle before him; but he was only making a little experiment, out of curiosity, and perhaps, hoping to interest the solitary onlooker.

And still the children of the mist remained unsuspicious of any danger, so that he had ample opportunity of watching them and admiring their elegant proportions and graceful movements. Then, after a while, he rose to his full height. At that, one of the hinds, standing some distance apart from the others, suddenly tossed up her small head, pricked her ears, and 'glowered' at him. She stared for about three seconds; then, with her slender legs scarce seeming to touch the heath, she tripped lightly across to her comrades, and turned, and stared again. But by this time they were all of them on the alert; even the stolid stag had raised his antlered head and shaggy neck, and was fixedly regarding the intruder. This was the point Frank Gordon had sought to reach; and so long as he remained perfectly still, moving neither hand nor foot, they also were immobile, the group of upthrown heads strikingly picturesque in the dim twilight. He knew what would happen next. The moment he turned away to rejoin his companion, they were off like arrows from a bow, and almost instantly had disappeared in the pale blue mists lying along the base of the hills.

Miss Georgie he found seated on a clump of heather, her face somewhat averted: had she not been watching the deer, then, after all ?   She rose as he approached, and they at once set out on their homeward way.

"A pretty sight, wasn't it ?" he said.

There was no answer.

"Didn't the stag look grand when he threw up his antlers and stared ?" he continued.

"Yes—I suppose so—"

There was something unusual in her tone.   He ventured to cast a sidelong glance towards her ; and to his amazement discovered she had been crying.

"Why, what is it?" said he, stopping short.   "What is the matter ?"

"It is nothing," she said, in a low and choked voice. "Only—this is the last day of our being together—and —and I have been looking back—and I know what you must think of me."

"If you knew what I think of you," he said, gravely, "it would be nothing for you to cry over.   I should hope not !—"

"Ah, but I do know—I do know !" she said, vehemently; and then she went on in a kind of half-reckless, half-despairing fashion : "Well, we've come to the end of the game !—the play is played out !—and if you go away now thinking me bad and wicked, it's no more than I deserve.   Sometimes—I thought I would try to amuse you—but—but a plaything is easily cast aside—and forgotten.   Easily enough—it is easy to throw aside—a plaything—and serves her right—"

She burst into tears, and broke away from him, and hid her face.   But he took her hand, and put both of his round it, and held it, as though he would convey to her some pacifying, some reassuring influence.

"I don't in the least understand you," he said, soothingly.   "Why, what can you have to reproach yourself with—you of all people !—"

"Oh, don't speak to me so!" she sobbed. "I have seen all along that you are not like the rest—you are so unselfish—and forgiving—and generous—and that made it all the worse. Never mind! Think of me—what you please: you will soon forget—"

She raised her eyes, tear-filled and piteous, to his; and then somehow—who shall say at whose instigation or under what mad, uncontrollable impulse?—somehow their lips met, in a passionate, delirious kiss. And so two lives were signed away.

There was no further speech between them just then. Perhaps his brain was overmastered by the wild wonder and joy of this unexpected—and unthought-of—conquest and possession; as for her, her maiden fears and vague alarms and foreshadowings might well hold her in silence at such a crisis. They passed through the grounds and entered the Castle: in the hall, as they were about to go their several ways, she once more raised her eyes to his, and there was the strangest wistfulness and questioning in them. He saw her no more that night.

CHAPTER XIII

NORTH AND SOUTH

THE tall limes and the serried firs were black as ebony against the dark, clear skies; but when, having slipped out from the Castle immediately after dinner, Frank Gordon had passed through this belt of trees and entered upon the solitudes of the forest, a faint, spectral, gray mist lay over all the land; while a full white moon was sailing through the clouds that hung in shreds above the sombre vastness of Ben-na-Vân. The air was moist and scented with the odor of the sweet-gale. There was no sound but the soft sh—sh—sh of the distant river; though once he heard a strange cry overhead—the call of some unseen sea-bird to its mate on their way out to the western main. With his head bent somewhat forward, and his hands in his pockets, he strode slowly on, in no wise dreaming what a terrible necessity it was that drove him to argue with himself, and prove to himself, that he was the very happiest and luckiest man in the whole realm of England.

And yet he was able to convince himself, easily and triumphantly enough. Why, where could he have found such another prize? Here—amid these mysterious wastes—in the wan moonlight—he could summon up a vision of her, with all her brightness, her winsomeness, her gay humor, her happy-go-lucky disposition overbrimming with merriment and audacious good-comradeship; and he thought of the radiance, and color, and sunlight she would introduce into the dull old rooms of Grantly Castle. Nevertheless—nevertheless—there was something else haunting him that he could neither understand nor wholly dismiss. Middle age, surveying the future, counts by years, and has a fairly clear perception of limits. Youth, on the other hand, sees nothing but a succession of eternities, filled with boundless possibilities of fascination and glamour ; and when the young man or the young woman, pressing forward into this unknown and entrancing world, is suddenly brought up, as it were, by some crisis that speaks of finality, the shock is apt to be startling. No doubt young Gordon, as he could conclusively prove to himself, was she happiest of men ; but his amazing good luck had been sprung upon him somewhat unexpectedly; and he was bewildered; and perhaps a trifle afraid. There were to be no more vague wanderings and imaginings, then ?—no more pensive questioning of eyes in the dusk of London conservatories ? —no timid, half-wistful words during a homeward stroll through the June lanes ? It was all fixed and final now ; and there was nothing for him but to assure himself, for the hundred-and-fiftieth time, that his auspicious fortune was immeasurably greater than he deserved.

Of a sudden, far away in the gloom lying over the Corrieara burn, he perceived a red spark of fire, and he paused, wondering. That could be no will-o'-the-wisp, for the Corrieara burn comes down through rocky altitudes ; besides the light was crimson, not an opalescent blue. Who, then, could be traversing this voiceless country at such an hour of the night ? And then he began to recall the events of the day—which had been entirely driven from his mind by recent agitations. This must be the stalking-party come home at last. He

pushed forward. Presently, emerging from the profound shadows under Ben-na-Vân he beheld the small
procession—the Prince riding in front, and smoking a
cigar; then the second pony, with the slain stag bound
on to its back, Ronald walking by its head, and Hughie
keeping him company. It was a picturesque little
group that came out of the mirk into the soft wan radiance of the moonlight; but Monseigneur was not
thinking of that; the moment he saw who the stranger
was, he pulled up his pony, and slid to the ground.

"Here, Ronald," he cried, "you take a turn in the
saddle; you've had a long day of it." And then he
eagerly caught his step-son by the arm. "Frank, my
boy, I've something to show you—the grandest four-
teen-pointer that's been taken in this forest for many
a year! What d'you think of that now?—and my first
stalk! Look here, man, look!—look at the span of
them!—what do you call these for points, eh? And
you don't think they'll have gone to bed when we get
back to the Castle?—no, no, surely not!—I've waited
with the men on purpose, to make certain we should get
the stag home—and they can't have gone to bed—the
ladies must come to the hall door—Frank, honor bright,
now, isn't it a splendid head!—"

"It's a fine head," said Frank Gordon, absently: his
mind had been full of other things. And yet, when
the stalkers resumed their journey—Monseigneur now
on foot—young Gordon was not loth to have the whole
story of the wild day's sport dinned into his ears.
Having proved to himself all that he wished to prove,
it might be wiser to accept that conclusion once and
for ever. Why pay heed to any lurking doubts or dim
forebodings? So he tramped along silently, listening
to the wondrous and excited tale; and even in the
smoking-room, later on, Monseigneur's astonishing ad-

ventures so monopolized the talk that the preoccupa-
tion of any single member of the party was not likely
to be observed.

Between one and two o'clock in the morning, while
he was still lying broad awake, he heard a slight rustling noise somewhere in his room, and paid little attention to it, thinking it but the patient endeavors of a
mouse; the next moment, however, there was a knock
at the door—a single rap—and thereafter he thought
he could detect the faint sound of retreating footsteps.
At once he reached up his hand and turned on the
electric light; and then, looking about, he saw that a
white envelope had been passed underneath the door
and was lying conspicuously enough on the smooth
parquetry. He was not long in possessing himself of
this missive; and a very strange document it turned
out to be—written in pencil, and incoherently scrawled
over several sheets of paper.

'You will be going away early in the morning, and
there will be all the people about; I cannot take leave
of you *that* way. Frank, I *did* try to tell you something this evening; but I could not tell you *everything;*
you would have thought too hardly of me. And all
the same I deserve whatever you may choose to think
of me; but then it began with my wishing to amuse
you; and there were too many opportunities for mischief—too many opportunities—and I was silly—and
of course you despise me—and I haven't a word to say
in my defence. Only, it wasn't *all* mischief—Frank,
you will believe that!—I declare on my honor that
what happened to-night was honest and straight, whatever it may lead to—*I swear to you* I wasn't shamming
then. You will believe me, Frank, won't you? I
don't mean about the clipping of my hair—that *was*

nonsense—I confess to that. For I put your fly-book with the scissors into my pocket when Johnnie left us at the Corrieara burn; and then I pretended to find it, and gave it to you to carry, so that you would have a pair of scissors in your pocket when I offered to let you cut my hair. Think of me what you please; but that's the truth; and there's lots more I could tell you; only a girl doesn't like to demean herself *too much*; and besides, you are going away. But the other thing—what followed—was true: oh, Frank, you surely won't imagine I was shamming *then!* I know I have been wicked—for the sake of fun; ever since my brother Percy went to Florida, I've been left to my own guidance, and maybe I've gone over the line a bit now and again; but if you would only consider this, that perhaps I may prove *truer* in the *long run* than some of your *serious* ones, that have such high and exalted notions. No, I won't even say that; I have my pride too; you may despise me as much as ever you like—and I can take it—and no one will find me complain. But, Frank, it wasn't all shamming—it was not all shamming—you won't believe *that* of me! Or perhaps you think I would let myself be kissed by anybody? I know what men—*some* men, I mean—imagine about women. Very well. Think it, and welcome. I don't care. Why should I care? Frank—Frank—I don't know what I'm saying — and that's the truth; but you're not like the others; you are so generous and forgiving—and perhaps—perhaps—you'll be a little merciful in judging. And please don't write—that would only frighten me; just say 'Good-bye' the minute before you start—and I shall understand.   G.'

Indeed he had no wish to judge harshly—or to judge at all—this poor distracted lass, who seemed to be suffering so acutely on account of her venial sins. Mischief ?—the playfulness of a kitten! This scrawled letter, he could see easily enough, was honest through and through. It was even pathetic in its way. What could he do or say to reassure her—in that brief second before the driving off of the four-in-hand ?

Well, it was little more than a moment he had with her on the next morning; for amidst the bustle of packing the luggage she did not put in an appearance; and reluctantly he was almost about to mount into the brake when she came timidly forth from the porch.

"Good-bye," said she, offering him her hand, her eyes cast to the ground.

"Good-bye," said he, much more cheerfully; and then he added in an undertone : "Don't let your head get filled with these absurd fancies. It isn't the least like you !"

" Will you write to me ?" she said, and she managed to raise her eyes a little bit.

"Of course—as soon as we reach Grantly," he made answer ; and then he said good-bye again ; and got into the brake—hoping that no one had noticed that not protracted farewell.

For he had resolved upon keeping this all too happy secret to himself, in the mean time at least, although his mother was on the point of leaving England ; and not even when they had arrived at Grantly, and when he had private speech with his old confidante, Jean Gordon, did he utter a word as to the prospective change in his life. It was Miss Jean who had news for him—news that startled him not a little.

"Frankie," said she to him, when the Prince and Princess had gone away to their own apartments to prepare for dinner, "do you remember an old gentle-

9*

man, a botanist, and his niece, a Greek girl, who came out here last May ?"

"Do I remember ?" he repeated. "Why, how often have I asked you about them ? And never once have I thought of them without remorse—"

"Remorse ?" she said, staring.

"Remorse—and nothing else," he said. And then he went on quite bitterly : "That I should brag to them of Dee-side hospitality ! 'Come as soon as you can, and stay as long as you can ; and that's a Dee-side welcome'! Dee-side hospitality !—a cutlet, a glass of claret, and a shake of the hand at the door—that's Dee-side hospitality ; and you let them go out into the world again—strangers to the country—and you never see them again—"

"My dear Frank, what more could you have done !" Aunt Jean protested. "You were leaving for London the same night—"

"If I could find them now," said he, warmly, "I would at least try to do something to redeem my promise. We may be what you like on Dee-side, but anyway we do not brag of our hospitality, and then sneak out—"

"Frank," said Jean Gordon, gravely, "you need not speak of those two as being together any more. The poor old man died quite shortly after their visit here —I fancy they left Sanchory the next day or the day after—and went in to Aberdeen. Indeed it's a pitiable story : I would have written to you, but I knew you were coming through."

For now it appeared that Aunt Jean, having occasion to dine with some friends of hers in the Granite City, had by accident met Mr. Murray, the Edinburgh law-yer, who had had the settlement of poor old John Elliott's worldly affairs ; and by further accident he

had begun to tell Miss Jean Gordon something about
the old botanist and his niece, when she grew intensely
interested, explaining that she had already met these
two, out at Grantly. So she got all the particulars
which the Edinburgh W. S. could furnish ; and these
in turn she now communicated to young Frank Gordon, who seemed unusually perturbed.

"Her aunt—a Mrs. Elliott—Devonshire Place ?" he
repeated. "And he fears she has been made into a
kind of household drudge ? Aunt Jean, I will go and
see her the moment I get to London !"

"My dear Frank," said the kindly but practical
Miss Jean, "what could you do ? How could you interfere ?—even if all that Mr. Murray says is true—
and he judged merely by one or two casual visits he
had to pay on business. You can't go rescuing distressed young ladies—"

"Dee-side hospitality !" he said, with returning bit-
terness. "And the girl is allowed to go away into a
big and friendless town like Aberdeen—and the poor
old man dies—of a broken heart, as I guess—and then
she is taken away to London—among strangers— Well,
Aunt Jean, I am not in the habit of rescuing distressed
young ladies—it's not my line—I know nothing about
it ; but as soon as ever I get to London I'm going to
call on her—and perhaps make some little apology—
and show a little sympathy, at all events—and I don't
care who says I shouldn't."

"Frank Gordon, ye're a wilful laddie," said Aunt
Jean, shaking her head ; and she rose, for the dressing-
bell had rung. But all the same she lingered at the
door a second ; and she added, in a sort of shy way :
"Well, Frankie, if you're saying a kindly word to
the girl, you might just put in another one as coming
from me."

Dinner over, he got away to his own room, to write to Miss Georgie Lestrange; and this he found to be not such a desperate business, after all. It was a good-natured, simple, natural sort of letter, without any melancholic appeals or poetic sentiment. He made fun of her confessions and her self-reproaches. He was earnest in begging for all of her photographs she might have with her; and he gave her the address of his chambers in Jermyn Street, whither they might be sent. He wanted to know when she was likely to return to London, explaining that he would very soon be thrown on his own resources there, for his mother was extremely anxious to get hold of the hesitating Margravine of Pless-Gmünden, and the probability was that she and the Prince would not remain in town beyond a few days. Would she (that is, Miss Georgie) renew his thanks to Lady Rockminster for the pleasant time he had spent at Glen Skean Castle; and would she write and tell him what luck Sir Hugh was having with the stags. A friendly letter, without pretence or affectation of any sort. Only, he experienced some little sense of relief when he had got it finished, and when the envelope was sealed and directed.

On the very next day the Prince and Princess of Monteveltro left Aberdeen for the south, travelling up to London by the night mail from Perth; and on their arrival in town they drove to Brown's Hotel, while young Gordon went to his rooms in Jermyn Street, which he kept in permanency. Then, when he had thrown into the fire the circulars awaiting him, there came breakfast—the newspapers—dressing; following which he went out to purchase for himself a tall hat, an umbrella, a pair of gloves, and one or two similar articles not usually worn on Dee-side; and presently he found himself, all properly equipped and ar-

rayed, with the whole of London to choose from, on
this cool, bright, sunny morning.   He had no particular plans.   He thought he would stroll up Bond Street,
and look at the latest photographs of the popular ac-
tresses.   Then he went round to Brown's Hotel ; but
the Prince and Princess had already gone out—they
had to make the most of their brief stay.   Finally,
having absolutely nothing else to do, he wandered on
towards Regent's Park, with some vague idea of getting a glimpse at the house in Devonshire Place where
sooner or later he should have to call at a more reasonable hour.

It was a large house, amid houses still larger and of
considerable pretensions ; and he casually noticed that
it might have been improved as to its outer appearance
had the pots of flowers and shrubs in the balcony of
the first-floor windows been a trifle less dingy.   But of
course he could not stare ; some one might be looking
out—perhaps even Briseis Valieri herself ; so he aim-
lessly passed on—possibly thinking in idle fashion of a
certain spring morning on the banks of Dee — of the
speedwells and gorse around the foot of the massive
Scotch firs — of the shimmering sunlight on the rippling stream—of a tall, and slim, and graceful stranger
who seemed to come to him out of the unknown, with
her great, dark eyes smiling, not with embarrassment.
He was thus sauntering on, rather blindly, perhaps,
when in turning into the Marylebone Road he very
nearly ran into what seemed to him a perambulator that
was being shoved along by the customary nursemaid.

"I beg your pardon," a voice said to him.

"I beg your pardon," he said in reply ; and he raised
his hat slightly — for he was of Highland birth and
blood, and his native courtesy did not distinguish between a housemaid and anybody else.

But the next moment something happened.

"Miss Valieri!" he exclaimed.

"Sir Francis!" she said — a little surprised, but in no wise disconcerted.

The small lad in the Bath chair looked wonderingly from the one to the other.

"I was so sorry to hear of the sad news," the sun-tanned young gentleman said — and he turned and walked with her, for they could not block up the pavement. "I did not know until the day before yesterday. We were always expecting to see you and your uncle again at Grantly; and I wrote several times to Aunt Jean — you remember her — and she could not learn where you had gone. It troubled me more than you can imagine—for we were hoping to see or hear of you again — and you must have considered us so neglectful—"

"Indeed, no, Sir Francis," Briseis said, in rather a low voice. "My uncle was taken ill almost as soon as we reached Aberdeen; and of course there was nothing else to be thought of—"

"It was only the day before yesterday that I got your London address," he continued; "I came up to town this morning — and I had been proposing to call on you—"

"Sir Francis," said she, "may I introduce to you my cousin Adalbert—?"

"How do you do?" said the little gentleman in the Bath chair, and he held out his thin, blue-veined hand. "I suppose you are Sir Francis Gordon. Cousin Briseis has told me all about the claymores and the targes in the hall at Grantly Castle."

"And are you interested in such things?" said young Gordon, in a kindly way.

"Oh, yes, yes," the lad made answer, eagerly.

"Very well. Some day or other, when I get back to the north, I will look out one or two and send them up to you. They're rather picturesque things in the hall, you know."

By this time they were in Devonshire Place; and from one of the ground-floor windows a middle-aged, sandy-haired woman, with careworn face and tired eyes, was looking out. The moment she saw the Bath chair, she left the window, and hurried to the front door—for that would save summoning up one of the servants. The lame boy's crutches she had also brought into the hall.

"Shall I lend you a hand?" young Gordon said to this unfortunate chap; and he got him out, and helped him up the steps, and deposited him on the landing. Then he turned to see why Briseis had not followed. Briseis was tugging and straining at the Bath chair, and evidently dealing with a difficult job; so the next moment he was down at the pavement again; he quietly put her aside; and with one arm (only this was the arm accustomed to the casting of a 38-yard line) he had hauled the chair right up to the door. It was an unusual way of arriving at any one's house; and great was the distress of Mrs. Elliott on learning—through Briseis's introduction—that the stranger who had thus played the part of footman was Sir Francis Gordon of Grantly.

"I am so sorry," she said, almost breathlessly; "—so stupid for no one to be about—and my niece is so independent — she is always for doing everything herself. Briseis has told me, Sir Francis, how kind you were to her and my poor dear brother-in-law when they were in the north; and though we cannot offer you Highland hospitality—still, if you wouldn't mind an informal invitation—we shall be having luncheon almost directly—and it would be a great pleasure, Sir Francis, to us all—"

Nay, she pressed him; for this poor woman was ever conscious of her dear girls, and of the letters they would send home to their parents; moreover, might she not secure Sir Francis Gordon of Grantly for her reception on the following Saturday evening—to add a little lustre to that rare and rather expensive form of advertisement? She was persuasive; and the smiling, timid eyes of the Greek girl plainly said, 'Oh, yes, why not?'; so he assented without more ado.

"This way, Sir Francis," said the widow, conducting him along the hall and up-stairs to the drawing-room. "I fear you will find us rather untidy, for we have all been busy making things for dear Lady Hammersley's fancy bazaar—in aid of her Mission to Draymen, you know. Briseis," she continued, as they entered the room—which appeared to contain a perfectly riotous assemblage of half-dressed dolls, unfinished pen-wipers, and embroidered pillow-slips — "do remove some of these things—put them on the piano—anywhere out of sight: the fact is, Sir Francis, my dear girls are so indefatigable in the cause of charity that sometimes they hurry on from one task to another. And, Briseis, if you would be so kind as to tell Olga and Brenda, and the young ladies, to come in here on their way down to lunch? I do hope everything is ready; for we must not keep Sir Francis waiting."

Sir Francis had now the honor of being presented to, in succession, the five young ladies of this establishment; for the rumor had flown from room to room that a baronet had descended among the sons and daughters of men; and they flocked in out of curiosity, if with no more ambitious aims. But Briseis? She did not appear with them. He guessed—for he remembered certain hints he had received from Aunt Jean as coming from Mr. Murray—that Briseis had gone down-stairs to

"THEY WERE IN DEVONSHIRE PLACE"

see that luncheon was in proper trim; and he guessed rightly.

He was further confirmed in his surmises when they had all trooped down to the dining-room, and taken their places. Here he was introduced to Edward the medical student; and conceived no liking for that cadaverous and sardonic youth; especially as he began to notice that his playful little sarcasms were mostly levelled at Briseis. She—gracious, sweet, apparently well-pleased with all the world—did not seem to mind. She settled the lame boy more comfortably in his chair. She fetched the bread-tray, and forked out a piece for each: the solitary maid-servant could not see to everything. Mrs. Elliott's conversation (between anxious glances directed hither and thither) was chiefly about the old families of Scotland; and she managed to intimate to young Gordon of Grantly (what he knew already) that she and her surroundings were connected with the Elliotts of the Lea.

Then, when they had all been served with hot or cold, the parlormaid left the room, and for some reason or another did not immediately return. Mrs. Elliott grew more and more embarrassed and disconnected in her replies; for all the glasses were empty—there was not even a jug of water on the table. At last, growing desperate, she said—

"Briseis—would you mind—I think Agnes has been detained—would you mind handing round the sherry and claret?"

With the utmost cheerfulness and complacency Briseis Valieri got up from her seat, and went to the sideboard, and possessed herself of the two decanters.

"'Serva Briseis, niveo colore,'" murmured the medical student, with a bit of a snigger; and whoever may or may not have caught the phrase, young Gordon did, and thought (with angry eyes) that he would remember. It might be the beginning of a score.

Meanwhile Briseis, having got hold of the wine, was naturally returning to the chief guest of the occasion, to proffer the usual question. But Frank Gordon had been inwardly chafing and fretting; there was a flush on his forehead; besides, he was a 'self-willed laddie,' as Aunt Jean had called him. And so, on Briseis drawing near, he abruptly rose from his place.

"Will you allow me?" he said; and he took the decanters from her; and deliberately went round the table, asking each which he or she preferred, until at length he reached the medical student. There he planked down the two decanters, without any question at all.

"Oh, Sir Francis," said the poor widow, "how could you give yourself so much trouble? I'm sure I don't know what servants are coming to nowadays: I'm always changing them—and changing for the worse, I think."

After luncheon they returned to the drawing-room; and as Briseis at once set to work on the unfinished knickknacks for the fancy bazaar, while the other girls devoted themselves to such desultory occupations as allowed them covertly to scrutinize the handsome young gentleman from the north, Mrs. Elliott had her visitor all to herself. And at once she plunged in medias res.

"I hope, Sir Francis," she said, in her most winning way (the poor, tired woman, with the almost hopeless eyes!) "that you are not engaged on Saturday evening. We have a few friends coming—these dear girls we have with us must have a little society to lighten their studies—and I am sure you would be charmed with Lady Hammersley—she is so bright and clever, and has known so many famous persons in her time.

She has not definitely promised, it is true," the widow
continued—for she preserved her honesty even amidst
these many and sore perplexities and trials—"but when
she sees all these things we have been making for her
bazaar, I am sure she won't refuse ; and I am sure you
would be charmed with her—"

"Oh, but, Mrs. Elliott," said the young man, modest-
ly, "you need not offer me any inducements. I shall
be delighted to come if I can ; the only thing is, that
my movements at present depend on my mother and
the Prince—I don't know when they may be starting
for Buda-Pesth—" And then, seeing that she seemed
somewhat mystified, he had briefly to explain to her
the relationship between himself and the Prince and
Princess of Monteveltro, and the reasons why he should
be at their beck and call during their stay in London.

Mrs. Elliott's heart beat quick, and wild visions swam
before her eyes. A Prince and Princess—a reigning
Prince, too : if she could but secure these distinguished
personages for this one evening—for ten minutes on
that one evening—would not a seal be set on these little
festivities of hers for ever and ever ? Would not this
or that family communicate with others—at rectory
dinners and the like ? Could not a few paragraphs in
the 'society' papers be secured ? Well, to make this
proposal demanded courage ; but the poor woman was
brave ; and much need had she to be brave, during her
long struggle with vacillating fortune.

"Oh, Sir Francis," said she, with a pitiful eagerness
that he could not but perceive, "do you think you
could persuade the Prince and Princess to come with
you on Saturday evening, if only for a few minutes—it
would be such an honor !—"

He laughed, doubtingly.

"My step-papa is rather lazy," he said ; "but as for

the Mater, she will do anything I ask of her; and I am sure—if they are still in town—and if they happen to have no definite engagement for that evening—I am sure it will give her very great pleasure."

"Should I send the Prince and Princess a card of invitation?" she asked, quickly.

"Oh no," he said; "don't trouble. I will ask them this afternoon how long they are to be in London. And that reminds me: if you will excuse me, I must be off to my duties; for I rather fancy they expect me to trot about with them, until they set out for Buda-Pesth."

So he rose to take his leave; and the last of them with whom he shook hands in the drawing-room was Briseis Valieri.

"I must write and tell Aunt Jean I have seen you," he said to the beautiful, tall Greek girl, who regarded him with no conscious shyness, but rather with a pleased and smiling and perhaps grateful friendliness. "I know she will be most interested to hear."

And therewith he left, lighting a cigarette as soon as he was outside, and good-naturedly thinking that he might just as well try to get the Prince and Princess to confer this small favor on the poor widow, as to whose situation and straits and efforts he had formed a pretty correct conjecture. As he leisurely strolled from Portland Place and Langham Place down into Regent Street, he could not help noticing the attractive young English ladies who with their sisters and mammas were crowding round the milliners' windows—fresh-complexioned maidens, with beautiful hair, and pretty bonnets, and sweetly tinted profile of cheek and chin. Very attractive, no doubt— But his eyes, as he knew, were closed now. His fate was sealed. He had conclusively proved to himself that he was the luckiest and happiest of men ; and he could always fall back upon that assured and comfortable conviction ; although, to be sure, at times—at some odd hour—at some unexpected moment—a quick spasm of unknown and unreasoning dread would seize him, with something almost like suffocation of the heart. But then again, these uncontrollable, these irrational flinchings from the future were of short duration ; he put them aside with angry impatience ; nay, at this very moment was he not going calmly and confidently away down to Jermyn Street, to see if the packet of photographs had arrived from Miss Georgie, so that he might make a proud display of them all along his mantel-shelf ?

CHAPTER XIV

A DEPARTURE

THE photographs were not there; but the Prince was; and forthwith young Gordon found himself haled off to a shop in Piccadilly, where he was bidden to choose a complete set of golfing implements, all of the most approved type.

"Golfing in Monteveltro!" he protested. "Well, you won't want for hazards! How many mountain-peaks to the course?"

"Oh, we shall do excellently," said Monseigneur, with much confidence. "I know where will be a very good links. As for bunkers, plenty; as for turf, why you have not in England a better tennis-lawn than Stephenson—you remember, the British Chargé d'Affaires—has adjoining his house. We shall make out a golf-course well enough, do not you fear!"

Next Frank Gordon was dragged off to another shop in Piccadilly, where inquiries were made about a stag's head of fourteen points that had been sent to be stuffed and mounted; and minute instructions were given as to the safest method of transit by which the much-prized trophy could be conveyed to Sattaro on the Dalmatian coast.

And then again they pursued their way until they drew near to Brown's Hotel. Carriages were driving up; and from these there descended to cross the pavement, one after another, a number of distinctly foreign-looking personages, for Madame the Princess was at home this afternoon to certain of her friends.

"Pah!" said Monseigneur, peevishly. "What is it now! They will never get their £15,000 a year pension for King Milan, though they try to talk over each and every member of the Skuptschina, and his wife, and his mother, and his sister. He is a good man, King Milan, and he has done great service to his country, and better than all he is a well-wisher to Monteveltro; but look at their finances—how are they to meet the next coupon?—"

They entered the hotel.

"Frank," said Monseigneur, in an undertone, "you come up stairs with me. We will slip by unnoticed. I wish to show you what Wienerschnitzel and Gurkensalat can do now: Wienerschnitzel, when he lays down the pipe, gives a bark—that is his thanks for the smoke; and Gurkensalat she can get the pipe into her mouth with her paws, putting her head close to the table—"

But of course an affectionate and obedient son could not play such a shameless trick on his mother; so Frank Gordon, not to be seduced away from his duty, at once went into the drawing-room, and mixed among these strange folk, and endeavored to make himself as polite and agreeable as his not very fluent French or German allowed. The Prince had for the moment disappeared—no doubt to make sure, first of all, that Wienerschnitzel and Gurkensalat were not being neglected.

On this evening the Prince and Princess were dining at a certain Embassy—and young Gordon of Grantly had also received an invitation; and it was while the three of them were driving down to Belgrave Square that he got his earliest opportunity of putting in a word for poor Mrs. Elliott.

"You see, Mater," he pleaded, when he had partly
explained the circumstances, "blood is thicker than
water—Scotch blood especially; and the old Scotch
families should show a little clannishness; and not
many of them have better claims than the Elliotts of
the Lea. And you needn't think it's snobbery on the
part of this poor woman; I don't believe there's an
ounce of snobbery in her composition; but one can see
how your going there might give her a bit of a lift,
don't you know; and I think she is in pretty hard
straits—"

"Saturday?" repeated his mother. "It is practically a holiday-night for us, as it chances: we dine with
the Von Hohenecks—and there was a talk of our trying
to see an act or so of *Carmen*—but that is hardly possible—"

"In any case you could look in at Mrs. Elliott's on
your way home," young Gordon pointed out directly.

"What do you say, Michael?" she asked, turning to
her husband.

"If you wish it, yes," he answered, with easy indifference: he generally submitted to be taken about,
wherever she wanted, by his more energetic consort.

"Most likely there won't be any one you know," her
son continued. "But at least I want you to meet the
Greek young lady about whom I told you—you remember—"

"Oh," she exclaimed, with her eyebrows elevated a
bit, "is this, then, the house where the divine one
scrubs the dishes?"

"It isn't that—or anything like that!" he rejoined,
in tones of distinct annoyance. "Why do you put
things so harshly—and so wrongly? You have merely
heard what Aunt Jean had to say about her—along
with some rumors coming from an Edinburgh lawyer.

But if she is in that position, or anything approaching to it, I know the reason: it is simply because she has got a sort of kindly and good-humored acquiescence in her disposition; she doesn't know her own value; she doesn't stand on her rights; she seems so happy in herself that she would take any trouble to do anything for any one." And then he altered his manner altogether. "Well, Mater, I'm not going to insist. You'll see and judge for yourself. But if there was any generosity about you, or sympathy, or a single spark of humanity or fellow-feeling, why, you'd just take this girl away with you, and keep her beside you as your companion and friend; and you could introduce her at Court—Vienna or anywhere; and I don't think you would have much reason to be ashamed of her! I should imagine not! She has every accomplishment; she speaks all kinds of languages; and she's just the most beautiful creature you ever set eyes on, with the most unselfish nature, and a charm of manner that is indescribable— Oh, you may take my word for it you wouldn't have her long on your hands! The majority of men may be fools; but they're not such mortal fools as that. She's fitted to marry into any society; and of course she would marry well—instead of dragging out her life as a drudge in a sort of genteel boarding-house."

"Frankie, my lad," said the Princess, a little more gravely, "I fear my hands are a little too full for me to make any such experiment—at present, at least."

"But you'll be kind to her on Saturday night," he pleaded.

"Oh, no. Certainly not. I will taunt her with her poverty; and ask her by what right she has come up from the kitchen."

"You will, will you?" said he, with a laugh. "Very

10

well, what I know is this : she'll make a poor, soft, ridiculous idiot of you before you've been three minutes
within the influence of her eyes and her smile."

"Frankie," said the Princess, as they were going up
the Embassy stairs, "is this a trap you've laid for me?"

"When and where?" he exclaimed.

"Saturday night," she replied. "Your language is
rather warm about that young Greek lady—"

"Oh, nonsense, nonsense," he said. "I was giving
you a most unbiassed opinion. Mater, wait till you
see. You know Aunt Jean is not very impressionable ;
and yet she just won Aunt Jean's heart away from
her."

But stirring events were to happen before that Saturday night. When he got home from the Embassy,
the first thing he saw on entering his rooms was a tele-
graphic envelope placed prominently on the mantelpiece. He opened it and read the contents—and these
he found to be sufficiently surprising.

"Come down by first train to-morrow morning.
Urgent. Rockminster, Adelphi Hotel, Liverpool."

And in an instant he had jumped to the conclusion
that this mysterious summons was in some way connected with Georgie Lestrange. She had been too shy
to telegraph to him herself ; so she had asked Lord
Rockminster to do that for her—Rockminster who had
been her host and in a manner her guardian at the
date of her last writing. And were these two now in
Liverpool? And why? Well, the only thing that
remained for him was to hunt up *Bradshaw ;* there he
found that the morning train for Liverpool left Euston
at 7.15 ; and then he sat down and wrote a note to his
mother explaining that she must excuse his absence
on the following day—until the evening, at all events ;

he would send her a more definite message as soon as
he could ascertain what was wanted of him. His sleep
that night was restless; and his waking moments full
of uneasy suspense.

It was a little after noon when he reached Liverpool;
and he went straight to the Adelphi Hotel; Lord Rockminster, as he perceived from a distance, was on the
pavement outside, idly looking about him, and smoking a cigarette.

"Awfully good of you to come down," Rockminster
said, when Frank Gordon arrived. "Fact is, I sent
that telegram on my own responsibility—"

"But what's the matter?" the younger man demanded abruptly.

"If you want it cut short, then: Miss Lestrange
sails to-day in the *Barbaric*, for New York; and I
thought you would like to know—I mean, I thought
you might wish to see her before she left— Now, look
here, Gordon, one word of clear understanding," he
went on—for Frank Gordon appeared too bewildered
to put any questions, "I fancy there is something
between Miss Georgie and you; but it is none of
my business; and I don't want to be told anything
about it. You understand? I know nothing—don't
want to know. Only, she has seemed preoccupied and
distressed out of all reason; and I was certain she
hadn't sent you a telegram—mightn't like, perhaps—.
or may have thought writing would explain better—
she's writing now, in the Ladies' Drawing-room; and
last night I thought I would act on my own responsibility, without asking her any impertinent question—
hope I haven't made an infernal mess of it—"

"But what is it all about? Why is she going to
America? Why did she not tell me?" young Gordon
demanded, with wide eyes.

"No time. Everything has been so hurried. Here, come into the coffee-room, and sit down: there won't be anybody about."

And indeed the long and spacious coffee-room was practically empty, save for a passing waiter. These two took seats at a window table.

"You know her brother Percy," Rockminster began, in his usual imperturbable fashion: whatever whirl of incidents might be about was not likely to upset the equilibrium of his brain.

"I've heard of him—I've never seen him," Frank Gordon answered.

"Very nice fellow—clever, you know—awfully good at private theatricals and that sort of thing. But he got tired of loafing about Campden Hill and South Kensington; went to Florida; bought a partnership in a big fruit-growing concern, and was getting on well enough with his figs and oranges and bananas. Been to Florida?"

"Never."

"You may thank the Lord. Consists of oranges and swamps; and on a show of hands the swamps would have it. From this letter of his partner's it appears he was seized with some sort of malarial fever; got it precious bad; then I suppose they flooded him with quinine and bark; eventually they chased out the fever; and looked to his getting all right again as a matter of course. But he hasn't got all right—fearful depression and weakness — nervous system all broken down—cares for nothing—will not try to get up—sinking into a kind of hopeless apathy—cries for no reason whatever—and only asks for rest—rest—until I can see they are afraid of his slipping off into a kind of rest that isn't in the reckoning. And he has been talking about his sister — in his half-delirious state imploring

them to send for her.   Well, of course all this upset
Miss Georgie terribly, and she hardly knew what to do;
when right on the heels of the letter comes a telegram
saying that a Mr. and Mrs. Martinez de la Pena, neighbors of theirs out there in Florida, were returning by
the *Barbaric,* and would bring her along with them if
she were disposed to come.   So you may imagine what
telegraphing, and packing, and travelling has been
crammed into the past thirty-six hours; but here we
are at last — cabin secured, and everything; and all
that lies before us now is an early luncheon and a leisurely getting aboard the tender."   Rockminster had
been lazily playing with the handle of one of the forks.
He suddenly looked up.   "I say, Gordon, if you think
I've put my foot in this affair, by telegraphing for you,
there is time for you to skip out and get back to the
station; and I shall never breathe a word about your
having been here."

"Of course not — of course not!"   Frank Gordon
made answer, almost indignantly.   "I must see her—
of course I must see her.   And I may tell you this,
Rockminster : you're not so far out in your surmise
about her and myself—only—don't you see—nothing
has been formally communicated to any one as yet.
And I think it's awfully good of you to have taken all
this trouble, and come right away down from Iverness-
shire with her—"

"My good chap, what else could I do!" his companion protested, in his half-indifferent way.   "But I
must go and find her now."

He had not to go very far; for at this precise moment Miss Georgie appeared at the door of the coffee-
room, timidly looking round.   When she saw who this
was who was rising to meet her, along with Lord
Rockminster, she stood stock-still—she almost shrank

back — as if she did not know whether to advance or retreat—as if she did not know what to think or what to say to him. And then again she pulled up a certain courage—though her face was flushed and embarrassed in a most unusual manner; she went forward and said 'How do you do?' to him, as if this were quite an ordinary occasion; and then she turned to Lord Rockminster.

"Mr. and Mrs. De la Pena," said she, "are asking when you propose to have lunch; they seem anxious to be in good time on board the tender—"

"We will have luncheon here and now," said Rockminster, promptly — perceiving a chance of leaving these two together for a moment. "Where are the De la Penas?—in the writing-room? I will go and fetch them."

And then as soon as he was gone she looked up.

"How did you know?" she said. "I have been writing to you—most of the morning—but the letter is in my pocket. I did not think telegraphing would be of any use — I could not explain. How did you know to come here?" .

"Rockminster telegraphed to me last night," he answered her, simply enough.

"Lord Rockminster?" she repeated—and the embarrassment in her face did not grow less. "But— but did Lord Rockminster suspect — how did he come to assume—"

"He was quite right in assuming!" her companion said, boldly. "Of course he could not ask you questions you might think impertinent; but if he guessed that you would rather have me come to see you off, he was quite right in sending for me—"

"Oh, Frank, it's so kind of you—you always are so kind!" she said, in a low voice.

" And is your brother so very ill ?" he asked.

" I will show you his partner's letter presently," said she, as she somewhat drew away from him—for Lord Rockminster and the swarthy-visaged De la Penas were now visible at the coffee-room door.

This unwonted constraint and timidity lasted all through luncheon. Perhaps she resented the inferences that these strangers would naturally draw from the sudden arrival of this young man. Perhaps she was secretly wondering if the rest of the people at Glen Skean Castle shared in the assumption that had induced Lord Rockminster to telegraph for Frank Gordon. Or again she may have been tired with the long travelling; her mind was doubtless full of unrest about her brother; and she may have contemplated the unknown voyage and the subsequent journey with some natural nervousness. At all events, she was no longer the light-hearted, gay, audacious Georgie Lestrange; even when they were going out on the brisk little tender, she paid no heed to the eagerly talkative people about her, nor did she care to look at the wide and busy river, with its innumerable small craft darting about in every direction, while the smoky sunlight was splintered in glints and gleams on the tawny surface of the current. She was as one dazed when she got on board the great ship, with its hurrying passengers, its officers, and the long row of stewards marshalled in array. It was Mrs. De la Pena who took her below, and found out her cabin for her, and deposited there the small parcels she had brought with her. And then she returned on deck again.

"Frank," said she, in an undertone, "were you annoyed that — that Lord Rockminster should have guessed ?"

" Good gracious, why ?" said he.

"And—and do you think the other people at the Castle have been imagining the same thing ?"

"I don't know—but they are entirely welcome !" said he, with a decision that ought to have given heart of grace to this poor trembling lass who was half cling-ing to him.

"Here is the letter I meant to post to you," she continued, and she covertly handed it to him. "You will find Percy's address in it, if you care to write to me—"

"If I care to write to you !"

"And, Frank, don't think of me as you see me now !" she pleaded. "This isn't me at all. I'm frightened by the confusion. Long before we reach New York, I know I shall be as merry as a grig ; and when I get to Branch Valley I shall cheer Percy up in no time and set him quite right again. Don't think of me as I am now—"

A bell rang for the second time.

"I must get back to the tender," said he.

She moved with him to the end of the gangway, where Lord Rockminster was waiting to bid her fare-well ; and it was to Rockminster she said good-bye first. Then she turned to young Gordon.

"Good-bye, Frank !" said she—and she lifted her face towards him—her eyes full of tears.

He said good-bye and kissed her—not caring how many commercial travellers, of Liverpool or New York, might be looking on : indeed, these merry gentlemen were mostly engaged in calling messages to their friends on board the other vessel. Then he, too, had to pass along the gangway ; and almost immediately there-after the tender set off for the wharf, while the great ship began slowly and steadily to creep down stream. He stood on the paddle-box, waving a handkerchief

"'DON'T THINK OF ME AS YOU SEE ME NOW'"

until further recognition was impossible. And that was the last of poor, wild, wicked Georgie that he saw for many a long day to come.

Meanwhile an intimation that the Prince and Princess of Monteveltro really meant to honor by their presence Mrs. Elliott's reception on Saturday night was sufficient to arouse a profound if partly concealed excitement throughout the house in Devonshire Place. Even the sullen and sluggish Brenda woke up to the possibilities of the occasion; the intractable spitfire Olga became quite submissive in her appeals for advice and assistance; and the three young ladies from the country secretly and separately telegraphed down to their relatives, announcing the momentous fact, and demanding authority for unlimited millinery outlay. But it was on the poor widow's shoulders that the burden of anxieties fell; insomuch that at times she was almost sinking into despair, and wishing she had never been so audacious as to prefer her breathless request. And then again she would pull herself together, determined to make the most of her great opportunity. She could not now issue invitations "To meet the Prince and Princess of Monteveltro"—for her cards had already been issued; but she could go to such of her acquaintances as had not yet been asked, and in a casual kind of way mention that these august personages were likely to illumine her poor house on Saturday evening, and would Mr. and Mrs. So-and-so, if they happened to have no other engagement, care to look in for a little while? Indeed, she asked everybody she could think of; for she knew that the bigger the crowd the less attention could be directed to worn carpets and shabby furniture. Then she went to a florist, and made a bargain with him about the loan of flowers for the supper table and the staircase landing. She had almost

10*

pathetic conversations with the confectioner about this
or that small economy, and the resulting price per
head. And all through these few and hurried days
there dwelt in her mind a never-ending, rather an increasing, perplexity as to who among her more distinguished guests should take down whom to supper.
Here are some of the solutions that presented themselves from time to time, amid all this wild worry of
preparation :—

> *Sir F. Gordon—The Princess.*
> *The Crowd.*
> *The Prince—Hostess.*
>
> *   *   *
>
> *The Prince—The Princess.*
> *Sir F. Gordon—Hostess.*
> *The Crowd.*
>
> *   *   *
>
> *The Prince—Hostess.*
> *The Crowd.*
> *Sir F. Gordon—The Princess.*
>
> *   *   *
>
> *Sir F. Gordon—The Princess.*
> *The Prince—Hostess.*
> *The Crowd.*

Nay the longer she considered this problem the more
hopeless it became, until in her desperation she resolved
on doing nothing at all. Some accident would happen.
Some involuntary movement among the people would
lead them to choose such partners as were near them ;
and while the crowd, descending to the dining-room,
would swarm along the buffet or occupy the scattered
chairs, the small table at the upper end reserved for
the Prince and Princess, Sir Francis Gordon, and their
hostess would remain secure. She would talk to her
illustrious guests on their way thither, as if not noticing

what had occurred or was occurring. They would drop
into their places as a matter of course; the white-
gloved waiter would open the first bottle of champagne;
and in a few moments a benignant and reassuring clam-
or would everywhere prevail.

And at length the great night arrived; all the gases
and candles had been lit; the flowers arranged; the
supper table laid out in fair display; everything that
mortal could do on scant means and within the strict
confines of solvency had been done by the apprehensive
but indomitable little widow; only—only—as quarter
of an hour after quarter of an hour went by, and her
rooms had got almost chokefull with the murmuring
crowd she knew that if after all she was disappointed
of her exalted guests then her very heartstrings would
crack. She talked to this one and the other; but her
nervous glances invariably returned to the door. She
did not heed what was said to her; she forgot to notice whether her bonny darlings Olga and Brenda were
looking their best; she could not even send Briseis off
on some final errand of decoration: all her thoughts
were concentrated on that empty doorway. And then,
of a sudden, her longing eyes seemed to recognize a familiar face—handsome and sunburnt—out there in the
semi-dusk; there was a tall young gentleman whose
arrival was of the most joyous import; almost by his
side there was a vision of a lady of imposing presence,
all in white satin and lace and pearls; and following
her came a stout gentleman who wore a broad blue ribbon across his waistcoat and a conspicuous diamond
star close to the lapel of his coat. A kind of hush fell
over the general conversation of the room—and that
was in itself unnerving; but the little widow had steeled
herself against this crisis; she advanced to the Princess,
and took her hand, and welcomed her with a few pretty

words; and she was introduced to the Prince; and these two remained talking with her, while young Gordon passed on to pay his respects to Miss Olga and Miss Brenda. All the same, he was looking about a little. Where was Briseis, then? He could see no sign of her. And yet he had brought the Prince and Princess mainly that they should get to know something of Briseis Valieri; and who could tell at what moment Monseigneur, who was a whimsical sort of person, might not insist on getting away home?

And then he went back to Mrs. Elliott, meaning to ask her downright what had become of her niece. But just at this moment there slipped in at the doorway a tall and slim and graceful figure dressed entirely in black; and the new-comer seemed inclined to linger there, to be out of observation, as it were, while she could see all that was going on. Frank Gordon at once went up to her—delight in his eyes.

"I have been looking for you everywhere, Miss Valieri," said he; "I want you to know my mother. Shall I bring her to you?"

"Oh, no, I will go with you."

Indeed it was but a step or two; and the beautiful young Greek girl showed no hesitation in accompanying him: the next moment found her being presented to the Princess and her husband. Then Gordon, considering that Briseis Valieri might well be left to make her impression in her own way, withdrew from that little group, and wandered back to Olga and Brenda, and their chatter about the new pianist whose red head had set all feminine London on fire.

Now in what manner or under what direction her swarm of guests got themselves down to the supper-room, the agitated and all too happy Mrs. Elliott herself hardly knew; but the end of it was that the long

apartment was speedily filled with an amorphous throng
—the dowagers claiming the occasional chairs, the
younger folk foraging at the buffet, or being attended
to in quiet corners; while the Prince and Princess had
been successfully navigated to the small table. They
and their hostess took their places; but young Gordon
remained standing—looking down the busy room.

"Won't you be seated, Sir Francis?" the widow said
to him — she was anxious to have the little party of
four complete.

"Oh, no, thanks," he said. "I would rather make
myself useful—if I knew how—"

"Then go and fetch Miss Valieri," his mother said
to him, promptly. "Here is a place for her—and we
were interrupted when she was telling me about Tri-
coupi—"

"Oh, Briseis?" interposed the little widow. "She
is so very kind! She offered to remain in the drawing-
room, with my youngest son—the poor lad is lame, you
know, Princess, and cannot get about very well—"

With that Frank Gordon moved away. He did not
seem to have any particular aim. In fact, he had to
move slowly; for the place was crammed; and young
men carrying oscillating things on plates were to be
avoided. But at length he got out into the hall; he
ascended the vacant staircase; he reached the landing.
And here he paused.

For the door of the drawing-room was open an inch
or so; and while he stood hesitatingly still there came
to him a sound such as never before had fallen upon
his ears. Piano-playing in general he rather detested;
its mechanical, staccato tinkle-tank produced no effect
on him—except irritation and a desire for quiet. But
this strange melody that now he heard seemed to run
and ripple in continuous cadences: measured, it is true,

for it was clearly a dance—a joyous dance—soft, and elusive, and distant at times, and then again full and glad and clear as a thrush's song on a May morning. Then it ceased ; and there followed a kind of mysterious chant —a solitary voice, as musical as the music, pronouncing the words almost in monotone :

> *The young maidens are merrily dancing,*
> *Out in the sun the young maidens are dancing,*
> *Their hands are linked around the olive-tree :*
>   *Little one, Marianoula, why dost thou weep?*

Again the dance-music : one can almost see the lithe limbs and the flowing draperies, the outstretched arm and swift-glancing foot, in the dappled shade under the olives. And again the low-voiced, plaintive recitative :

> *Her lover came to the well,*
> *With soft words her lover came to the well,*
> *The red and white flowers of her heart were opened,*
> *The red and white flowers of her heart were filled with*
>   *dew :*
>   *Little one, Marianoula, why sittest thou apart?*

But now those running and rippling chords become more buoyant; the passing note of sadness is abandoned ; the sinuous melody weaves itself into a happier strain. And the recitative that follows speaks welcome words :

> *Lo! a stranger upon the road—*
> *The road that comes winding from Zagora;*
> *He bears in his hand a beautiful necklace :*
>   *Little one, Marianoula, the necklace is for thee.*

The music grows louder and more joyous; and then again it droops—it seems to draw near—it seems almost to whisper—it is a whisper that a maiden may understand :

What are the jewels on the necklace?
The jewels are tears, the tears of absence:
Arise, Marianoula, and greet thy lover!
Little one, Marianoula, thou must dry his tears.

Then there were a few notes of farewell—fading into silence.

The strange and extraordinary charm of this composition—the fascination and mysticism of the music, and the impression of dim remoteness, and pity, and tenderness conveyed by that low-toned voice—held him spellbound for a second or two; and he could not move. It was as if sleep were around him—and dreams—and an inexpressible consciousness of the tragedy of human life. And then—for he was here on a mission—he strove to throw off this magic web of entrancement; he stepped up to the door and opened it; and looking into the large and empty room he found that Briseis had turned from the piano and was talking to her boy-cousin Adalbert.

"I have been sent for you, Miss Valieri," he said. "My mother wants you to sit by her—she has kept a place for you—"

"I cannot do that, Sir Francis," she answered, smiling-eyed, "for I have been left in charge. But if you wouldn't mind staying with Adalbert for a few minutes, I should like to go down and get some supper for him—I know the things he prefers—"

Young Gordon accepted the post with great goodwill; and Briseis left the room.

"What was that your cousin was singing and playing before I came in?" he asked.

"Oh, that?" replied the lame lad. "That? That was one of the things she makes out of her own head, you know. You see, she and I go into the

Park every morning at twelve; and she reads to me;
but it would be rather scudgy of me, wouldn't it, to
keep her always at those reports of cricket and football that a girl can't care about? And so I sometimes read for myself; and then I can see that she
sits thinking—but not very seriously either—it's about
the verses, you know—sometimes they're little Polish
songs, and sometimes Hungarian, and sometimes Ar-
menian—but there's always an English version for me.
And although she's kept awfully busy in the house,
now and again the others are away at an afternoon
concert, or something of that kind—and she's generally left at home with me—and she asks me to come
in here for a little while—and she plays—well, did you
ever hear such playing?—she can make the piano
speak—it says anything she wants to say—and then
between she recites the verses—so low—I wonder you
could have heard—"

At this point the door was again opened. But it
was not Briseis who appeared; it was Olga Elliott,
carrying a plate and a spoon and fork; and the moment that Gordon set eyes on her he saw that something was wrong.

"Yes, you may well stare!" said she—and her lips
were pale with passion. "That I should be ordered
to fetch and carry things like a kitchen-maid—sent
away from the room—while Briseis Valieri is singled
out, and taken up, and put at the Prince's table!
The—the upstart! She and her shabby black rags—
when all the rest of us had been at such pains—"

"Cousin Briseis," said the small lame boy, with his
face afire, "dresses better than any of you—and that
always—always!—"

"Here, take this rubbish—and I hope it may choke
you!" exclaimed the scowling-eyed fury, and she

thrust the plate upon him. "A seat reserved for Briseis Valieri, at the Prince's table!—and I dare say she wasn't asked at all—I dare say it was her own downright impudence that made her force her way—"

"Oh, I beg your pardon, Miss Olga," said Frank Gordon—but mildly, for he had never seen a girl of decent upbringing in such an ungovernable rage before, and in fact he was rather frightened. "The Princess sent me to find Miss Valicri—"

"Then does the Princess know in whose house she is?" demanded this sallow-complexioned virago with the flaming eyes. "She was invited here by a family called Elliott. I am an Elliott. I'm not a foreigner. But I've got to go for aspic jelly—I am sent away from the room—while a foreign creature in a dingy black dress is taken to the Prince's table—with everybody looking on!—"

"It is not a dingy black dress—it is the prettiest dress in the whole house!" the lame boy retorted, panting a little.

But this stormy scene had to end; for there were sounds outside, of people ascending the staircase; and the very first to put in an appearance was the Prince himself, who was accompanied by Briseis Valieri—the Princess having been detained below by Mrs. Elliott, to run the gauntlet of introductions. Monseigneur was talking in German; and he was laughing consumedly; and so occupied was he with this subject of Wienerschnitzel and Gurkensalat that he seized two chairs, and made Briseis sit down with him, that he might the better describe to her the irresistible drolleries of his two black poodles. But when the Princess came up, Briseis was released from durance; for Frank Gordon's mother seemed to have a great deal to say to this Greek girl, and to be much interested in her,

and charmed with her, as all this miscellaneous assemblage could clearly perceive.

As they were driving down to Brown's Hotel—and,
indeed, almost as soon as they had left the house—
Frank Gordon said to his mother:

"Well, Mater, what have you to say about the Maid
of Athens?"

The Princess of Monteveltro—as she sometimes did,
for caprice or amusement—lapsed into the Scotch
tongue.

"Frankie, lad, I thought ye were just bletherin
when ye spoke of her; but I find ye were not. She's
just a witch of a lassie, that—with her great, big eyes,
and the smiling daintiness of her, and her pretty voice:
she'll make many a man's heart sore, will that one.
Keep out of her way, Frankie; keep out of her way;
that's my advice to ye."

"I?" he said, in some little astonishment. And
then he added, quietly: "You don't understand,
Mater. I shall be sending you a letter one of these
days."

CHAPTER XV

A FEW days after these occurrences, and between one and two in the afternoon, Frank Gordon drove up to Mrs. Elliott's house in Devonshire Place, jumped out of the hansom, ascended the steps, and rang the bell. After a little delay a maidservant appeared.

"Can I see Mrs. Elliott?" he asked.

"They're at luncheon," she said, looking troubled.

"Yes, I know. But I want to speak to her for only a moment. Will you tell her, please? No, thanks, I won't go up to the drawing-room; I will wait here."

He remained in the hall, while the girl disappeared into the dining-room, leaving the door open. Apparently there was some disputatious argument going on within; but, as he could plainly hear, it was wound up by a contemptuous declaration on the part of the fiery-tempered Olga.

"It's all rubbish this trying to talk French among ourselves!" she maintained, with scornful emphasis. "We ought to be taken over to Dieppe or Boulogne for a month or two months every year—then we might have a chance. As it is, we simply go blundering on without knowing it; and what fools we should make of ourselves if we went to Paris! I wonder what the Parisian dentist thought when the English girl went into his place and said to him: 'Monsieur, s'il vous plaît, examinez mes dentelles,' "

At this moment the much-harassed mother made her appearance; and directly she saw who her visitor was her face—the poor, worn, enduring face—lit up with pleasure and gratitude.

"Won't you come in, Sir Francis?—we are just having luncheon—"

"Oh, no, thank you," he said. "I have called only for a second. But it is to ask a great favor of you, Mrs. Elliott—"

And what favor could he ask that she was not eager to grant? It was he who had assisted her in a higher ambition than any she had ever dreamed of; already, as the fruit of an industrious sowing of little paragraphs, several of the morning journals had announced that on the previous Saturday evening the Prince and Princess of Monteveltro had been present at a reception given by Mrs. Alexander Elliott, of—Devonshire Place; this piece of intelligence, she knew, would be copied into many of the weekly papers, especially those devoted to the doings of womankind; and there was no end to the flattering hopes that had now got possession of her brain. She saw more applicants for introduction to fashionable society; she saw her terms raised from £400 to £600 per annum; she saw her darling girls made much of and asked to go everywhere; she saw Edward the medical student entered for his three years at Caius College. And what indulgent kindness or courtesy should she withhold from the young man who had done so much for her?

"Mrs. Elliott," said he, "I want you to put all your young ladies under my charge for an hour or so this afternoon. An artist friend of mine has just come back from China—been house-boating and sketching there for over eighteen months—and his drawings are now hung in Lucas's exhibition-rooms in Bond Street.

This is the opening day — private - view day, rather — and he's an old friend of mine; I should like him to have a good crowd, to show that there was public interest; and I'm sure, if you will entrust me with your young ladies, I will take every care of them—"

"Oh, but they will be delighted to go!" she exclaimed, cheerfully—it was such an easy way of granting a favor!

"Shall I call for them at three, or half past?" he inquired.

"Perhaps half past three would be better," said the widow — for she knew what a tumult of preparation would shortly prevail throughout the house. Then she hesitated. "Did you say all of them, Sir Francis? There are Olga and Brenda—I know they are free; and Miss Bingham, and Miss Tressider, and Miss Holmes, I'm sure they will be most pleased to go. But as for Briseis — Miss Valieri, you know — she and I had planned out some bits of household work for the afternoon; and perhaps you would be so kind as to excuse her—"

He flushed — flushed like a school-boy; and for a moment seemed quite taken aback. But the next instant he had adventured upon a course that admits of neither palliation nor excuse.

"Oh, but didn't I tell you," he stammered (inventing as he went on) "that my friend Heatherstone has some Scotch sketches too — Aberdeenshire — it was in Aberdeenshire I first met him years ago; and these are almost sure to be on exhibition—perhaps in a separate room—or on screens, you know. And I am certain Miss Valieri would be so interested in them — if you don't mind, Mrs. Elliott—if it isn't putting you about —I should so much like Miss Valieri to renew her acquaintance with the Aberdeenshire hills—"

"Oh, very well, Sir Francis," said the widow, rather wondering at his unnecessary insistence. "But what a handful you will have!"

"I shall be here punctually at half past three," said he. "And thank you ever so much!" And with that he departed—directing the cabman to drive him forthwith to a certain restaurant in Bond Street. It was not of his own personal requirements he was thinking.

And perhaps he had not entered into any minute analysis of the motives that had led him to embark on this project. For one thing, his time was entirely at his own disposal, now that the Prince and Princess were on their way to Buda-Pesth; and then again Mrs. Elliott was a countrywoman of his, and here was an opportunity of paying her a little compliment; and no doubt Fred Heatherstone would be glad of any addition to the assemblage meandering through the exhibition-rooms. But behind and apart from these considerations there was a vague recollection of his having spoken indiscreetly to the old botanist and his niece about a Dee-side welcome; and he wished Briseis Valieri to know that Dee-side folk were not neglectful; generally speaking, he wanted to make atonement—for a wrong that had never been committed. And so he was most exacting in his arrangements with the head waiter at this restaurant; and he had little sprays of flowers provided to be placed on the table, one for each young lady, when they should come out to have tea; and finally, in course of time, he returned with two four-wheeled cabs to Devonshire Place. Then, as the half-dozen girls went three and three into the two vehicles, he had his choice; and he chose that one in which Briseis was seated — perhaps because she was a sort of half-stranger in London and thus especially his guest; or perhaps because her eyes chanced to meet his, and they were full of a kindly pleasure and thanks ; or perhaps because he had got into a way of rather liking to hear the sound of her voice, which was extremely soft and musical. Anyhow he and she sat opposite each other on their way down to Bond Street; and it was mainly to her that he gave an account of his friend Fred Heatherstone, his position in the art world, and the class of people who for the most part formed his patrons.

It was Fred Heatherstone himself who received them — a youngish man of extraordinarily clear blue eyes, a fresh complexion, and clipped brown beard and mustache ; and very polite he was to Frank Gordon's little group—though it was to Briseis that his regard was continuously and covertly returning ; and when a move was made towards an examination of the pictures, it was Briseis with whom he ranged himself, proposing to go round with her.

"The sketches can't tell everything, you know," said he, in a modest, shy way. "And we had a few adventures on the Chinese canals."

As for Miss Bingham, and Miss Tressider, and Miss Holmes, and the two sisters Olga and Brenda, the ever-arriving crowd and the more striking of the costumes afforded them sufficient occupation ; but of course they had to make a perfunctory survey of the framed drawings ; and it was while they were so engaged that Frank Gordon chanced to espy, near the turnstile, a young lady to whom he had been introduced at the Hypatia Club. Being of a bold, not to say reckless, nature, he ventured to approach this damsel, although he knew her occupation, and could perceive that she held a little note-book half hidden in her hand.

"I'm afraid you won't remember me, Miss Caledon,"

he said, as he raised his hat. "It was Miss Lestrange who was kind enough to—"

"Oh, but I've got you down, Sir Francis," said she, with a half-sarcastic smile : she evidently took it for granted that his object in addressing her was to get his own name into the newspapers : she had had an early and sad experience of the ways of the world, had this comely young lass with the wild blond hair and the alert gray eyes. "But perhaps you can help me— would you mind ?—there are one or two whom I don't recognize, though they appear to be attracting some attention. Who is the short, soldierly man with the grizzled mustache—do you see him over there in the corner—the lady with him can't be his wife, for he's so awfully attentive to her—"

Well, Frank Gordon's acquaintance with the fashionable or artistic circles of London was far from being over-extensive ; but at least he knew a number of those present as friends of his friend Heatherstone ; and he did what he could to assist this frank-spoken and pleasant-looking young person. Then she said—

"You brought in quite a big party with you."

"Yes," he made answer—arriving at last at his real object in going up to her. "And there are two of them you might put down in your list, Miss Caledon— it would be so good of you—their mother would be so pleased—"

"Yes, but is there anything special about their costume ?—or have they done anything ?" she said, rather petulantly.

"Oh, never mind about that," he said. "There they are—just beyond the marble figure—Miss Olga Elliott and Miss Brenda Elliott—their mother would be so awfully pleased—"

She scribbled down the names, rather unwillingly. Then she said—

"But didn't that beautiful girl come in with you—that tall, foreign-looking girl who is going round with Mr. Heatherstone? She is carrying everything before her—don't you notice?—every one following her with their eyes whenever there's a chance—didn't she come in with your party?"

He rather drew back in manner.

"Oh—well—yes—she did," he admitted, in a distant kind of fashion.

"Who is she?" was the next prompt demand.

"Oh, I wouldn't put her in your list," he said, uneasily. "Oh, no, never mind!—I'm sure you've got enough down—"

"But I tell you she promises to be the chief feature of the afternoon: I must have her name!" the lady journalist protested — and the little note-book was again opened.

"I've forgotten it," he said, in desperation.

"Forgotten her name? And she is one of your party?" the young damsel exclaimed, staring at him.

"Oh, no, I did not mean that. What I mean is that it is so difficult to spell—Greek names are very difficult to spell in English—changing the *u* into *y* and the *ch* into *x* and all that kind of thing. I really couldn't undertake— But I see my young people are looking about for me—good-afternoon, Miss Caledon, and thank you ever so much!" He shook hands with her, and raised his hat, and turned away to lose himself in the crowd. And thus it was that in the account which appeared in one or two evening papers—to be copied in numerous weekly publications—of the distinguished throng who had flocked to Mr. F. Heatherstone's Private View, there were to be found the names of

11

Miss Olga and Miss Brenda Elliott, but no mention was made of any Greek young lady having been present. Perhaps Frank Gordon could not have explained to himself the origin of this little bit of proud reserve on his part.

In the mean time Briseis, having gone the round of the walls, was now engaged in talking to the artist's mother — a singularly refined-looking old lady, with silvery-white hair and an almost girlish freshness of complexion; and it was at this point that young Gordon came up with the proposition that as he was about to take his small troop of guests to have tea at the restaurant where he had had a table reserved for them, Mrs. Heatherstone and her son might as well come too. The invitation was at once accepted; the girls were noiselessly summoned; and a short time thereafter they were all of them seated together in the tea-room, chatting and laughing as if newly released from bondage. To be sure, there were only six sprays of flowers; but the moment she saw how matters lay, Briseis, on pretense of putting her gloves and catalogue on the window-sill, passed round the table to Mrs. Heatherstone's chair and slipped her own tiny nosegay in front of the old lady. No one noticed—except young Gordon of Grantly; who thought that sooner or later he might have an opportunity of making up to Miss Valieri for that little act of self-sacrifice.

As it turned out, this expedition from end to end proved to be a complete success; and when eventually he had convoyed his charges home, and when he turned away to walk down to his club, he was very well content with the experiment. He did not stay to consider whether there might not be a certain dangerous facility about it. He was in London, thrown very much on his resources; most of his friends and chums and outlying kinsmen were away in the country; he himself did not propose returning to Aberdeenshire until Christmas, for he had several shooting engagements to get through, in Norfolk and Sussex; and meanwhile there was a kind of odd amusement in taking a drove of girls about, while he was doing a good turn to his countrywoman, Mrs. Elliott, in leaving the house quiet for her. The spitfire Olga was almost kind to him; the sulky and sullen Brenda was quite clearly trying to be amiable; the three bucolics were as merry as crickets; while as for Briseis Valieri, her bright intelligence, her serene sweetness, and the compelling splendor of her eyes were obvious to every one, and why should he alone of mortals refuse to yield to their attraction? He treated her as he treated the others—or he thought he did. And at the present moment he was on his way down to the Sirloin Club, where he intended before dinner to write a long letter to Georgie Lestrange—poor Georgie who, instead of wandering round picture-rooms, and looking at pretty costumes, and having sprays of flowers placed for her at the tea table, was now away on the wild Atlantic, with a world of uncertainties before her.

He might have gone down to the Oxford and Cambridge and taken his chance of finding some one he knew; but the Sirloin is a small and extremely exclusive club; no stranger or guest is admitted within its doors; members are expected to talk to each other, if they are that way inclined, whether they have met before or not; accordingly he was sure of having companionship at dinner, even if his neighbor puffed cigarette smoke into his soup—for the one chamber at the Sirloin serves as dining-room, smoking-room, and reading-room combined. As he entered the long and high-ceilinged apartment it looked invitingly snug on this

chill October evening; there was a big fire blazing at
the further end; there were rose-shaded lamps on the
snow-white table; everything seemed neat, and trim,
and well-appointed; and the row of old silver jugs and
tankards and snuff-boxes—the gifts of loyal members
—lent a certain richness of look to the eighteenth-century sideboard.   There were but three persons present
as yet: the ducal founder of the institution was seated
at a small table, scanning the pages of the candidates'
book; a famous musical entertainer lay at full length
on a sofa, perhaps trying to make up for late nights;
a callow youth, elegantly dressed, and chewing a tooth-
pick, was blankly staring at this or the other of the
valuable engravings that were ranged along the walls.
A profound silence reigned: young Gordon of Grantly
would have undisturbed seclusion for the writing of
the letter that was to follow Miss Georgie across the
far Atlantic.

It was a frank and friendly letter—and extremely
sensible: there were in it none of the endearing banali-
ties, the secret meanings, the 'little language' that lovers are used to send to each other.   He said he was anxiously awaiting her telegram from New York; he hoped
she would find her brother much better; he looked forward to the time when he should be walking up and
down the wharf at Liverpool to welcome her on her return.   And then, having finished this communication
—and being still in a dutiful mood—he took another
sheet of paper, and composed a brief note for his
mother.   According to promise, he said, he was writing to her; and the object of his writing was to tell her
that he was engaged to Miss Georgie Lestrange.   Probably, he hinted, it was no great news to her—after the
constant association she must have observed at Glen
Skean Castle; nevertheless Georgie would be so pleased

if the Princess would send her a kindly little message, and he would see that it was duly conveyed to her. When Frank Gordon had closed and addressed these two letters and deposited them in the box, he rose and looked round about him, with something of the air of being a free man.

The first new-comer he noticed was a well-known actor-manager, whose picturesque and effective *Hamlet* was just then the talk of theatrical circles; and this gentleman, when he had ordered the bit of fish and glass of claret he permitted himself on the way down to the theatre, came over to Gordon.

"I saw you leaving Heatherstone's show this afternoon," said he; "there were a lot of you."

"Yes, rather a responsibility, all those girls."

Then of a sudden an idea sprang into Frank Gordon's brain. He had nothing to do in this town of London; and taking those girls about was a kind of harmless frolic.

"I say," he observed to the actor-manager, who was drawing in a chair to the table, "I should like to bring that little crowd to see your *Hamlet*; and it would be an additional point of interest—it would interest them tremendously—if they could be admitted behind the scenes for a minute or two—"

"Against all law and order," was the very definite response.

"But who makes a law can break it," said Gordon, enigmatically. "And I'll let you off easy; I'll bring only three instead of six. And only a couple of minutes—we should not interfere with anybody—"

This modern representative of Hamlet the Dane was a reflective person. He was also an angler; and occasionally he took his holidays in Scotland. Furthermore, he had heard that Sir Francis Gordon of Grantly was the fortunate possessor of some fine stretches of water on the Dee.

"What evening do you propose?" he said.

"Well—to-morrow—or the next—if I find they are disengaged."

"Make it Thursday evening if you can," said the Prince Hamlet, as his frugal repast was being set before him. "Bring the three young ladies to my box—I will leave your name—and we will see what can be done."

It seemed so simple and natural that he should again think of these pleasant companions. And Mrs. Elliott —who was devoted heart and soul to the young man, and ready to do everything he asked—made no objection when he explained to her that on this occasion he could only take Miss Olga and Miss Brenda and Briseis, because he did not wish to overtax the manager's forbearance. When Olga and Brenda learned that they were going to a private box at the famous theatre, and also that they were to be introduced to the mysteries behind the scenes, they were out of their mind with importance and delight; but all the same they were shrewd enough to guess that this was in reality only another compliment to their cousin Briseis, paid her by the handsome young gentleman whose acquaintanceship she had made in Aberdeenshire. And the worst of it was that Briseis—who was not at all a vain person, but who had quick perceptions, along with the fine and subtle sensitiveness of a woman in respect of any attention paid to her by one of the opposite sex— the worst of it was that Briseis thought so too.

Indeed it was this very swiftness of apprehension on her part that in the present stage of their companionship constituted for him her chiefest charm. She seemed to divine what he had to say before he had half said it; she was instantly responsive to the least hint

or snggestion; there was an answering look—a smile of
recognition — as if further words were unnecessary.
And then he never appealed to her, for confirmation of
his own views, or for further intelligence, and found
her wanting.   For one thing she was far more widely
read than he — in many literatures; she had a more
catholic appreciation of the arts (he cared for little beyond landscape, and for statuary hardly anything at
all); young as she was, she had travelled more and seen
more than he; she had more of the accomplishments
and manners of the great world—though indeed his
modesty, and good-humor, and manliness were sufficient to make up for any defect.   And Olga and Brenda
had soon got into the way of leaving these two to their
half-uttered interchanges of confidence and comment.
Here, for example, in the famous actor's box, the two
sisters were well content to occupy themselves with the
glow and pageantry of the stage, while Briseis, in her
curtained corner, could without being overheard talk
to her companion about any feature of the performance
that seemed to call for remark.   It mattered little to
Olga and Brenda whether they had, or had not, been
brought to this theatre really on account of their cousin
Briseis; it was enongh that they were there—and in a
prominent box; and they were making the most of a
great opportunity.

Then came the fateful summons from the lord Hamlet himself; and at once the two girls were on their
feet, and eager; while Frank Gordon got down Briseis's
opera - cloak.   She, however, put up her hand with a
little gesture, and indicated her dissent.

"Aren't you coming with us?" he said.

"Oh, no, thank you; no, thank you," she answered
him, and her eyes gave him one of their sweetest smiles.
"I prefer to remain with the illusion.   Why should I

wish to see Ophelia dabbing her face with a powder-puff? I understand that such things are; but I do not wish to see them; I would rather stay here — to look at Shakespeare's dream of Denmark."

"Oh, do come!" he said, in obvious disappointment: for surely it was for her sake alone that he had begged for this favor?

But she was obdurate, in her suave and gentle fashion. "I am like a child, I prefer illusions," she said, good-naturedly. "And I am old enough not to tear open my toys."

And so, with an unwillingness that he was polite enough to conceal, he proceeded to escort the two sisters as they followed the attendant who was still waiting for them. When, after the lapse of a quarter of an hour, Olga and Brenda reappeared, they were laden with sumptuous boxes of chocolate and signed photographs, and they were quite excited and breathless over the wonders they had beheld.

And so it went on from day to day, or rather on alternate or occasional days: art-galleries, exhibitions, concerts, theatres; and sometimes the bucolics were asked, and sometimes the two sisters, but always Briseis; while as for the poor, tired-eyed little widow, so far from putting in any protest, she was glad enough to see her young people being taken about and amused. Briseis became of importance in this household. To all of them it seemed sufficiently clear that, although Sir Francis appeared to maintain an attitude of easy impartiality, these continuous plans and entertainments were unmistakably so many little presents offered to Briseis; and in private conclave they decided that she also must be well aware of the fact; and perhaps they envied her a lover who could be so lavish of his time and trouble.

Moreover, they could not but observe, as time went on, that there was something gradually being added to the girl's expression. Beautiful she had always been, even in her saddest and loneliest moments; but now that rare loveliness of hers seemed to bask in a sort of sunlight. To kindness of any description she had always been extraordinarily sensitive and responsive; but now the happiness that shone in her eyes seemed a species of radiance, even as she went about her ordinary duties. And she was busier than ever, of her own free-will; anxious to do a good turn to this one or that; as if her whole nature were pervaded by a sort of joyous and secret gratitude, that she must express in some way or other to her fellow-creatures. Of all the bits of embroidery and finery that she had brought with her from Eastern climes, hardly one remained: she had given them all away, to the other girls in the house.

But if Frank Gordon, as he carelessly thought, had preserved an attitude of unbiassed and benevolent neutrality towards these young ladies who had been so kind as to lend him their society, there was one point on which he was desirous of establishing a dark and esoteric understanding with Briseis alone: he wished to get to know more about the mysterious little songs or chants which she was in the habit of composing when she had an idle moment or two, and which for the most part she kept hidden away in her own memory. He wanted her to write down some of these things for him. But she laughingly put him aside.

"It is all plagiarism," she said to him one afternoon as they were walking home from a concert at St. James's Hall: he and she were in front, the three bucolics behind. "I know many of the airs of the folk-songs; and I take one of them, and play round about

11*

it, and make foolishness of it ; and what use would such a rambling kind of music be to you ?"

"I don't so much mean the music : I mean the words," he said.

"And these too are only echoes," she went on. "I know so many of the ballads — Polish, Russian, and Greek especially — and so many of them are alike ; so that if I wish for a refrain, it is easy to put together a few words—a little story—a suggestion—"

"Then won't you write down one or two of them for me ?" he begged of her, renewing his prayer. "Those I have heard are most exquisite — so simple and ten- -der—"

She laughed again, and shook her head.

"Oh, then you wish me to become like the poetess you met at the ladies' club—giving scraps of her com- positions to her friends ?"

"What, Miss Penguin ?" he exclaimed. "Oh, yes, you are likely to resemble the draggle-tailed 'Sappho' in any way whatever ! Besides I hear that 'Sappho' has given up gasping poetry for the present ; her hys- terics have taken another form—infuriated magazine- articles ; and she is raging and howling and lashing the vices and follies of mankind with whips of scor- pions—the gay old spinster that she is !"

"And then, you know," said Briseis, with blithe un- concern, "these songs are all so sad ; and why should one seek sadness unnecessarily ?" Indeed, any passer- by, chancing to notice the happy eyes and the free and buoyant step of this girl, would have found it difficult to associate her with any form of sadness. Youth, and a serene sweetness of look, and the satis- faction of pleasant companionship—these were visible in her face ; but not sadness. It would have been hard to believe that those beautiful, smiling eyes had ever burned hot with tears, or were ever likely to do that. "There is one of the Russian songs," Briseis continued, "that they sing at a wedding—the friends of the bride sing it as a kind of chorus — and that too is sad — why? Why should it be so? The bride is represented as trembling for fear, and she hides for safety in her mother's love — ah, but it is too tragic to be spoken of. And why—why? Why should there be dread and evil presentiments on a wedding-day?"

For a moment something seemed to clutch at his heart. But only for a moment: he had acquired the habit of shutting out the future from him.

"Dread and evil presentiments on a wedding-day?" he repeated, absently. "Why, indeed?"

CHAPTER XVI

AN AWAKENING

THE cold and clear October sunlight shone over Regent's Park ; from the rustling branches an occasional yellow leaf fluttered down and floated on the silvery and shimmering waters of the lake ; the wide open swaths and undulations of greensward were almost empty ; and far away beyond these the encircling belt of chestnut and sycamore and elm had grown dim and distant in the pale blue London haze. In a sheltered nook within this great solitude Briseis and her lame cousin had sought out their accustomed retreat ; and she was reading to him, with that proud thrill in her voice that could make of his tremulous, emotional nature a sort of stringed instrument answering to her every touch :

'Now, God be praised, the day is ours. Mayenne hath turned
    his rein.
D'Aumale hath cried for quarter. The Flemish count is
    slain.
Their ranks are breaking like thin clouds before a Biscay
    gale ;
The field is heaped with bleeding steeds, and flags, and cloven
    mail—"

Some one approached ; and, as was her wont on such occasions, she merely lowered her tones, and continued her reading, without looking up. The stranger was a young man of about five-and-twenty, of a complexion so bloodless that its waxen pallor had a suggestion of green here and there in the shadows; his eyes were small, black, furtive, and abnormally close together; his small black mustache was carefully pointed at the ends; his features were of the degenerate Hellenic type that one frequently observes in the streets of Algiers or on the quays of Syracuse. As for his costume, there was a sort of Bank Holiday display about it; he wore a broad turned-down collar, a pretentiously arranged tie, prominent cuffs with large silver links, and a straw hat with a black band round it: there was also a black band round his arm. He had been surveying this little group of the two cousins before he ventured to draw near; but now he came close up, and stood motionless; so that Briseis was forced to raise her head.

"Andreas!" she exclaimed.

There was neither welcome, nor misgiving, nor alarm in the look with which she regarded him : only blank astonishment, even bewilderment.

"Yes, no doubt you are surprised?" he said, speaking in Romaic. "May one sit down? Thank you. No, I do not suppose you have heard anything of me since the time that Irene was taken away from us. Poor Enie!—poor Enie!" He glanced at the black band on his sleeve. "And yet it was her death that was the beginning of my misfortunes. I had got a very good post in the French consulate at Smyrna; but I had to give it up when I left to administer the family affairs at home; and since then I have—" He threw out his hands with a little expressive gesture. "I have drifted—drifted until I find myself here in London, talking to my old friend Briseis Valieri, as if we were once more on the beach promenade at Phalerum."

She did not seem overjoyed.

"I was very sorry to hear of poor Enie's death," she said, "but she had been suffering for so long, had she not? And you—what are your plans? Have you come to London on business?"

The coldness of her tone seemed to indicate that she was not anxious to detain this young man with the shifty, watchful eyes and the showy neckerchief and cuffs.

"Business?—yes!" he said, slightly shrugging his shoulders. "If so great and rich a city as London can find enough to satisfy the very humble requirements of Andreas Argyriades. But in the mean time—at this moment—I am here on a little friendly errand to yourself."

"To me? Why to me?" she demanded. She could scarcely conceal her dislike—her impatience to be quit of him.

"Your young companion here," he asked, as a cautious preliminary, "does he understand our language?"

"No," she answered, shortly.

"Ah, then, so much the easier," he said, in a suave fashion; and he seemed to settle himself comfortably down to tell his story. "You know, my dear friend, how methodical our poor Enie was—so perfect in all her dispositions; and the same orderliness I found when I had to examine her effects, for that duty also devolved upon me. So that, in going through her escritoire, when I came upon a packet neatly tied up and labelled outside 'The Love-Letters of Briseis'—"

Briseis started. But he appeared to take no notice.

"—I said to myself: 'Ah, then, Irene wished to be an authoress: here is the MS. all prepared and ready to go to the publisher.' Nevertheless, when I opened the package, I discovered that the writing was not Irene's writing, but that of her dear friend and companion, Briseis Valieri; and I said to myself: 'Well, if it is she who aspires to be an authoress, that also is very good.' And I read a little—oh, such beautiful language—such elegant French—such impassioned descriptions of stolen interviews — moonlight — in the groves of Zante — and I said to myself: 'Surely this little book, when it is published, will create some stir: it will show to all the world that our Greek girls of the present day have fire, imagination, enthusiasm?' But when I read further and further, what was my astonishment! These love-letters were not exercises in literature—ah, no!—they were addressed to one whom we all know very well—to George Lamprinos—"

A crimson flush had mounted to her forehead: the little lame boy in the Bath chair, looking and listening and wondering, had never before seen his pale and beautiful cousin so confused and distressed.

"Where are those letters?" she said, in a low voice.

"They are in London," he answered her, gently.

"And in your possession?"

He nodded assent.

"Have you brought them with you?"

"Ah, no—they are too valuable to carry about with one—"

"Valuable?" she repeated, indignantly. "They are valuable to no one! But they are mine; and I demand to have them sent to me at once. By what right do you keep them back for a moment? It was most wicked of Irene to preserve them—" She checked herself—for she was speaking of the dead. "At least she knew they were to be destroyed—"

"But poor Enie was always so methodical," Argy-

riades murmured, as he played with the silver links of
his red-striped cuffs.

"I must have those letters, and at once," Briseis
said, peremptorily. "They belong to me: I demand
that you send them to me at once."

"Oh, yes, truly and certainly, my dear friend," he
responded, in a placid manner. "But consider for a
moment. In this world it is every one for himself;
especially when one is in hard straits, as I am. And
it is so fortunate for you that those letters fell into
my hands—ah, now, if it had been my brother Demetri
who had got hold of them, what a position would be
yours! Demetri has a heart of stone; he would have
said to himself, 'With these compromising letters in
my possession—'"

"They are not compromising letters—as you know
perfectly well!" she broke in, scornfully.

"They speak for themselves," he replied, with a
quiet smile. "But calm yourself, my dear friend.
It is not Demetri who has the letters; it is I. Demetri would have said, 'Here is a rich young lady, who
has rich friends and relatives: with these confessions
in my hands, I can extort what I please: my fortune
is made.' But I am not such as that. No. I only
ask for a little consideration. It has been at great
cost to myself that I have brought these documents
all the way from Athens—"

She had recovered her composure by this time.

"You could not have sent them to me!" she said,
in open disdain. "There is no service of posts between Greece and England!"

"Ah, but the papers were too valuable," he pleaded.

"And if they were so compromising," she continued, "if you thought they were so compromising, it
never occurred to you that you could burn them?"

"But in that case," he rejoined, with an adroit plausibility, "you would never have known that I wished to do you a favor. No, I had to bring them personally—and at great expense. Then there is the further large expense of my being in London : it was long before I could find you, and become acquainted with your habits, so that I could communicate with you in safety. And therefore I recommend myself to your gracious consideration, before I can hand over the letters to you. I have done my best—and at large expense ; and I have no wish you should suffer any exposure—any humiliation—"

Some sudden revolt of feeling got possession of her : she sprang to her feet, her splendid eyes flashing.

"*Ai da!*—enough of this !" she exclaimed. "I know you, Andreas Argyriades. I know you for a liar and a thief. I know that you robbed your mother and sister of every coin they could earn or borrow for you. And now you come to threaten me, because you think I am alone and unprotected. Well, I may be alone and unprotected, but I am not a coward—believe me, I am not a coward. I tell you to do what you like with those letters ! Make whatever mischief you can with them ; but you shall not have a lepta from me—not one single lepta—"

She paused, for she was all trembling, and the quick coming and going of her breath was like to choke her. The terrified lad in the Bath chair could only interfere with a few bewildered phrases.

"Briseis—what is this man saying to you ?—is he insulting you ?—why don't you bring a policeman ?—I wish—I could help you—"

But Argyriades had put his hand on her arm ; and she failed to liberate herself from his grasp.

"Listen," he said, with soft persuasion. "Listen

to reason, my good friend. I have no wish to make
any mischief—not I! But one must live; and these
papers are of value; and if I were to show them now
to some one—some one like the Lord Fragkis Gordon
—ah, why do you look startled?—do you not understand that I have had to wait some time, some good
long time, to find out your circumstances, so that I
could approach you without danger of publicity?
And the Lord Fragkis Gordon, he at least has plenty
of money, and he might be a little curious to see
such beautiful French writing. Come now, sit down,
my dear friend Briseis. It is so much easier to be
amiable. And it is a simple thing for you to regain possession of the package—so very simple; and
never a word heard of it any more; and no risk of
any one misunderstanding what you have written
when once you have put the bundle of sheets into the
coals—"

She resumed her seat; she had grown outwardly
passive; her eyes were intently preoccupied.

"Do I understand you, then," she said, presently, in
a subdued voice—but of course her boy cousin could
not understand a word—"that you will not give me
back those letters unless I pay you?"

"If you wish to put it that way," he answered her,
with another deprecating little gesture.

"How much do you want?"

A gleam of satisfaction, not wholly concealed, shot
into the small black eyes.

"Ah, that is a point now. That is a point to be examined. If it were Demetri—if it were Demetri who
had the management of this affair, he would probably
say five hundred pounds—"

She answered him with a look—of impatient contempt. But all the same she had grown cowed and

submissive, perhaps overmastered by her one desire to get these papers back forthwith and have done.

"I agree with you," said he, though she had not uttered a word. "That is absurd. But you do not know Demetri; he is a man of iron; he flinches from nothing. With me it is different. I wish to treat you honorably. If I were not in hard straits, do you think I would ask you for a single drachma? No, truly! But you are rich, and you have rich relatives; while I am poor; and one must look to one's self—"

"How much do you want?" she said, in the same hurried undertone.

"Fifty pounds," he answered, slowly; and the small black eyes furtively watched her.

"I have no such sum!"

"Thirty?"

"Nor that!"

"Twenty?"

"Perhaps, if I wrote to Edinburgh, I might get as much—"

With an unexpected movement he threw up both hands, as if scattering away from him all this sordid business; and he laughed.

"Come, now, I am about to surprise you," he said. "You give me bad names: in return I will show you what it is to be magnanimous. I will have no further bargaining. The letters shall be restored to you at once; and I leave it to you to send me subsequently what you please—only what you please—exactly what you please—in consideration of my expenses, and my care and trouble—"

"Yes, yes," she said, eagerly. "Let me have them back at once; and I will send you what I can, from time to time—"

"And meanwhile," he said, with a propitiating air, "if I might beg a small loan—"

"I have nothing with me !"

"But at home—in your house," he went on, insidiously. "Two pounds—three pounds—you see how my stay in London has impoverished me; and you can send it to me—I will give you my address."

He took from his pocket a card that had the name of a street in Soho and a number scribbled on it in pencil. He handed it to her, and she quickly folded it up. Then he rose.

"Farewell for the present, my dear friend; and be just when you reflect on the little transaction of this morning. Be just and considerate. Remember how fortunate it is for you to have these papers returned to you without having been seen by a single eye. And in such a friendly manner. Ah, if it had been Demetri now, what a terrible position would have been yours. But as I tell you, Demetri has a heart of iron, of steel, of diamond. Adieu, then, and au revoir !"

He raised his hat, and was gone. But even when she was rid of his presence Briseis was far from being herself again; she was altogether perturbed and shaken; a prey to doubts and anxieties, and conflicting resolves.

"Briseis," her boy-cousin said, with his large eyes full of a vague apprehension of evil, "what did that man want? What is it that has troubled you so? Did he insult you that you were so scornful of him? Of course I could make out nothing—only the name of Sir Francis Gordon—yes—these were the only words I could make out. But if this man has been frightening you, Sir Francis Gordon would—would—kill him !" The lad spoke in panting accents. And then his eyes filled with tears. "You see, Cousin Briseis, I am so useless—so helpless—if any one wishes to harm you,

what can I do ? But Sir Francis Gordon—if you were
to tell him that this man had threatened you—or insulted you—then you would have some one who could
take your part—there would be no more threatening
then, I think !—"

"Hush, hush, Adalbert," she said. "You do not
understand." She rose from the bench, and glanced
swiftly around to see if there had been any on-looker
or eavesdropper : no one was near. "Come, we must
be going home now. And, Adalbert," she added, with
some earnestness of appeal, "I have confidence in you ;
I can trust you not to say a word as to what you saw
or heard this morning—not a word to any living creature. Indeed, it is nothing ; it will all pass away and
be forgotten. Not a word, Adalbert, mind ; it is a
secret I can trust you with ; and yet what a little
secret ! Soon it will be all forgotten." And with that
she replaced the books and newspapers in the familiar
receptacle, and presently they had started off on their
way to Devonshire Place.

Luncheon on this morning was marked by a most
unwonted phenomenon ; the poor little widow had become quite merry and facetious—that is to say, when
she was not occupied in conciliating fractious tempers,
and trying generally to keep the Queen's peace. It
was the strangest sight, and almost pathetic in its way
—the worn face and the tired eyes betraying a sort of
occult gaiety, while she even adventured upon a little
joke or two, as the talk went on. They hardly knew
what to make of this unusual flow of spirits ; but
Briseis was soon to learn ; for as soon as the others
had dispersed she was summoned to follow her aunt to
her own room.

"My dear Briseis," said Aunt Clara—and for once
the wearied eyes looked pleased and complacent, "I

have good news this morning; the telegram came almost immediately you had left with Adalbert; and yet I could not tell them at luncheon, for a reason. But you have a wise head on young shoulders, dear Briseis; you will understand. Well, then, it has been settled that Miss Bingham's younger sister—she is only a year younger, after all—is coming to stay with us, and on considerably increased terms. I would say very considerably increased—only—you need not talk about it to Olga or Brenda; for the poor darlings know so little of the world and its ways, they know so little of the value of money that they might form perfectly wild ideas about what their dress allowance should be. And I will not conceal from you, dear Briseis," continued Aunt Clara, with the faintest color suffusing her pale face, "that it is probable the Binghams may have been led to this decision by—by hearing of the little party that the Prince and Princess were so good as to honor; and how shall I ever be able to thank that dear Sir Francis for his kindness? Of course Ada wrote home and gave a full account; and although you or I may not be influenced by such considerations—for, after all, any one connected with the Elliotts of the Lea is not likely to make too much of rank and titles—still, you know, people in the country who send their girls to town are pleased to hear that they are moving in good circles, however small these circles may be. And now, Briseis, now I am coming to the point," she proceeded, almost excitedly, yet taking care that her voice should not reach out to the staircase. "The younger girl, Carlotta Bingham, will be here in a week or ten days; and I have been wondering whether we could not get up a little dance—a quiet little Cinderella sort of thing—just about that time; and yet not with the appearance that it was given on her account. Indeed, that is why

I did not tell them at luncheon of this matter having been settled : we will arrange about the dance first, if it is practicable—what do you think ?"

"I, Aunt Clara ?" said Briseis.

"You are so helpful—you are so quick with your suggestions. And indeed it is no use giving such a thing at all, however inexpensive we may try to make it, however we may scrimp and save, unless we have a few people of distinction—a few somebodies. And I'm sure our dear Sir Francis will be able to bring his friend Mr. Heatherstone—his name is in all the papers just now, over that exhibition ; but first and foremost we must have Lady Hammersley. And really she owes it to us, after what we did for her bazaar, with your kind assistance, dear Briseis ; and if there is any one who could persuade her ladyship to fix her own evening, I am convinced it is yourself, for I saw the marked way she made much of you the last time we went there. Now do you understand, Briseis—I want to have the dance decided on before telling the girls about Ada's sister ; and if you would only go now, and take a 'bus or the underground out to Notting Hill and call on Lady Hammersley—"

"Aunt Clara, it is only a little after two !" Briseis said.

"Precisely," answered the intrepid little schemer, "and by the time you get there you will find her and her daughter at home—between lunch and their afternoon drive. And if you put it in that informal way—asking her to choose her own evening—and saying pretty things—she won't refuse you—she can't refuse you — it's the very least she can do after what we did for her bazaar."

So Briseis (who was thinking of widely different things) had to undertake this delicate mission ; but

before setting forth she went to her own room and
counted out her small store of available wealth. It
amounted to a little over five pounds; and when she
had bestowed it in her purse, she sat down and wrote
the following note—"Dear Andreas, I am sending you
£5. It is all I have at present. I hope you can post
me the packet of letters to-night, so that I may receive
them to-morrow morning.—Briseis." And then, when
she had left the house, she walked on until she came
to a post-office; and there she procured an order, value
£5; and that she folded and placed in the note she
had written. When the letter had been dropped into
the box outside she resumed her journey with some
slight feeling of relief. She could ill afford to lose the
£5, which was the last remnant of her quarterly allowance; nevertheless she would free herself, once and
for all, from these insufferable menaces.

Her interview with Lady Hammersley turned out to
be wholly successful; the jolly, red-faced, good-hu-
mored-looking woman said she would be delighted to
bring her daughter on such-and-such an evening; and
forthwith Briseis hurried home with the important
news. Then, and for some days thereafter, a profound
if secret commotion prevailed throughout the house in
Devonshire Place. A programme of dances had to be
drawn out and confided to the stationer; a violinist
and pianist were engaged — Mrs. Elliot declaring that
she could not think of asking Briseis to play the whole
evening, especially as she would be so useful in many
other ways; cards of invitation were printed—"Mrs.
Alexander Elliott . . . At Home . . . Dancing from 8
till 12"; and dear Sir Francis was overwhelmed with
gratitude because he had undertaken to bring one or
two dancing-men with him. As for the young ladies,
it is to be feared that *Polyeucte, Minna von Barnhelm,*

and *I Promessi Sposi,* with their respective dictionaries, received but perfunctory attention ; while the masters, calling at the appointed hours, found their pupils incomprehensibly absent-minded. It was milliners rather than masters who were in request now.

Briseis did not sleep much on the night following her encounter with Andreas Argyriades. She was harassed by doubts as to the wisdom of her own conduct. Ought she not to have held by her first impulse, and defied him to do what mischief he might with those letters ? Had she not declared to him that there was nothing in them that could compromise her; why not, then, have absolutely declined any negotiation whatsoever ? She knew what blackmail was; she knew how commonly it was practised in some countries — in France, for example, where the levying of *chantage* has come to be a recognized and generally a safe profession ; the rascally character of Argyriades was as clear to her as daylight ; and no doubt (she said to herself) she ought to have dared him to the end. But then this other way seemed so simple and easy. The payment of a few pounds—the letters back in her possession—and there could be no possibility of further trouble. Thus she lay through the long hours of the night, striving to reassure herself, torturing herself with misgivings, and craving for the coming of the new day and the postman's ring at the bell.

When the bell did ring she was standing by the door, which she instantly opened. There was no packet for her of any kind. But there was a letter ; and that, retreating into the dusk of the hall, she proceeded to read. It was from Argyriades. He began by expressing devout contrition. In saying that the package he had discovered among his sister's effects was now in his possession, he had, he said, erred by anticipation. It

12

had not yet arrived; but doubtless it would be forthcoming within the next few days; failing that, it might
be assumed that it was being held back by his brother
Demetri, who would be expecting a small present. If
she were impatient, and wished to have these documents without delay, would she send him another £5,
to be forwarded to Demetri, who would no doubt respond?—

She hardly read the rest: she knew the man lied.
And with eyes burning with wrath and scorn she went
rapidly to her room, and wrote a note, telling him that
he lied. She demanded to have the letters returned to
her at once. She would give no further £5; she presumed he knew what punishment was reserved in this
country for scoundrels attempting to obtain money by
threats. She wrote this letter in French—so that *chan-
teur* and *chantage* occurred pretty frequently in it.

But no reply came. Then she wrote again, and again
—with a like result. And at last she adopted a proud-
er attitude. She would bother herself no more with
this hound of a creature, who had stolen from his dead
sister's desk. He might do what he pleased with the
letters. She would think no more of them. And she
had enough to occupy her attention at the moment, with
this whole household of girls coming running to her
every now and again for advice and help. Nay, she
herself was looking forward with more than interest to
this joyous little festivity. She wondered at what hour
Sir Francis Gordon would arrive. She would like to
give him the first dance. And she had decided that as
the sole ornament of her black dress she would wear
in her bodice a bunch of yellow roses: he had greatly
admired some yellow roses, on one occasion, when they
were passing a florist's window in Regent Street. And
would he remember?

That proved to be a fateful evening—for one of the persons concerned, at least. Frank Gordon was somewhat late in arriving; as he handed over his coat and hat to the manservant, he could hear the hushed sound of the music overhead; already there were several couples hanging about the upper part of the staircase, either to avoid the infliction of a square dance, or to indulge in a little aimless prattle. And just as he was about to ascend and make his way through these loungers in order to present himself to his hostess, who else than Briseis should come out of the dining-room. She seemed in a hurry; it was by a sort of accident that she turned to see who this latest arrival might be; but the next instant she had stopped short, while the look of welcome and gladness and kindness that leapt to her glorious eyes was surely enough to have turned any young man's head. And in that bewildering moment he thought he had never seen her so beautiful. There was a sort of semi-dusk here at the foot of the stairway; and the dark figure with its bunch of yellow roses appeared all the more effective for it; but the compelling attraction was the smile of her parted lips, with all that that meant of affection and good-will.

"You are late," she said. "I had intended to give you the very first dance—if you wished it—"

"Then let us go up now," he said, promptly, "and we will call the next dance the first dance—"

"Ah, no, no," she answered him, laughing. "I am too busy at present. Aunt Clara can't do everything—"

"And you are not going to give me a dance at all?" he said, reproachfully.

"Oh, yes—perhaps a little later on—when all the shy young ladies have been provided with partners. But very soon I shall have to ask you to take Lady Hammersley down to supper—she says she wants to know

you—she has relatives somewhere in the. Highlands."
And' with that she went lightly and quickly up the
staircase, disappearing into the crowded and brilliantly
lit room ; while he, somewhat discontentedly following,
had to seek out Mrs. Elliott, to pay his respects in due
form.

The strange thing was that until this very moment
he had never even contemplated the possibility of his
being permitted to dance with Briseis. If he had
thought of the matter, he would have told himself that
she must dance beautifully : her perfect figure, the
gracefulness of all her movements, her sympathetic ear
were all assurances of that ; but somehow it had never
occurred to him that on him might fall the entrancement of finding her hand on his shoulder, her head
close to him, while the cadenced rise and fall of the
music carried them away together into a dream-world
of forgetfulness.   He had come to this chance little
party in a perfunctory sort of fashion.   Mrs. Elliott
had been kind to him ; he considered that he ought to
put in an appearance ; and he was quite ready to pilot
Miss Olga through the Lancers, or teach the livelier
Miss Ada the latest evolution of the Highland Schot-
tische.   But that his fingers should be clasping Briseis's
fingers—his arm partly round her lissome and yielding
form—the yellow roses so near to him that he could
perceive their fragrance : this wondrous happening
seemed hardly to be in the nature of things.   With
all her sweetness and charm, and frank generosity,
he had always felt that there was something mys-
teriously unapproachable about her ; she was not as
other girls, with whom one could be easily familiar ;
when a goddess appears, smiling and benignant-eyed,
prostration is the natural attitude.   *Serva Briseis* she
was not—to him ; rather Vrysaïs—Vrysaïs, the unknown

queen whose dim memory still lingers about the Lesbian shores.

He was startled out of his reverie by Briseis herself. She came up to him in a brisk and bright and friendly way, not in the least suggestive of forgotten queens and haunted towers overlooking the far Aegean seas.

"The next is a waltz," she said, glancing at her programme. "I promised it to Professor Drewer — a friend of Edward's; but he is not in the room—perhaps he has left—"

"Will you give it to me?" he said, rather breathlessly.

"I must wait a minute or two — two minutes at the outside—and then—"

The soft and melodious strains of the waltz began; Briseis was looking down the long room; and Gordon, with dim apprehension, had half turned towards the portière concealing the staircase, when there appeared (whence he had come it was hard to say) a tall, thin man of about thirty with a pale face clean shaven save for short black whiskers.

"This is ours, I think," he said politely to Briseis; and she — well, perhaps there was the least deprecatory raising of her eyebrows as she parted from Frank Gordon—she had to receive the new-comer with a little smile of greeting. She put her hand on his arm; he led her through the nebulous crowd; and presently they had gained the central open space where several couples were already moving swiftly and rhythmically to the undulating pulsations of the music. And then these two also glided away.

And now it was that Frank Gordon's punishment began — a punishment for long afternoons and days and weeks of happy, careless, thoughtless self-indulgence —a punishment the sternness and magnitude of which

were not yet to be imagined.   For of course it was no
mere pang of mortification over Briseis having been
carried off from him; the loss of a dance was a common ballroom incident; he bore the man no ill-will
whatever.   But as he stood there looking on, watching
with hungry eyes that ever-reappearing figure—so slender, so graceful, so bewitching in its allurement of sinuous motion, there was a cruel pain at his heart.   And
why?   Any of the other girls might go whirling past
with looped-up skirt and clinging hands and arms; they
were welcome; he had not a thought for them.   But the
black figure with the yellow roses: why did the ever-
recurring glimpses of her cause a dull, indefinable aching, a deadened and hopeless sense of the unattainable,
while the vibrating tones of the violin spoke of nothing
but sadness, and renunciation, and wild farewell?   As
yet, standing there, he had no real conception of the
tragic circumstances in which he had become involved;
but at least he knew that this vague suffering, this dark
and unreasoning jealousy, this blankness of despair,
were strange and unforeseen things, that might have
consequences he dared not contemplate.   And in the
mean time?   Well; he was near the door; and in a
blind kind of way he pushed aside the curtains and
got out upon the landing at the top of the staircase,
whither some straggling folk had wandered to breathe
a cooler air.   His main intent was to find some plausible excuse he could leave for Briseis and Mrs. Elliott,
and then to seek the seclusion of his own rooms, to
discover for himself what he had now to face.

It was at this moment that he was seized upon by his
hostess, who introduced him to Lady Hammersley, and
asked him to take her down to supper.   The roseate
dame with the banked-up white hair was a talkative
companion; when, in the room below, he had got a

couple of chairs, and procured some refreshment for her, she proceeded to entertain him with a voluble discourse on many and diverse matters — her mission to draymen, her love of horses, her abhorrence of divided skirts, and her desire to visit Scotland.

"And you, Sir Francis," she said. "I suppose you will soon be returning to Dee-side?"

He seemed to wake up as if out of a dream.

"I?" he said. "Oh, no—no. I think—I think I must take a little voyage across the Atlantic, first of all."

CHAPTER XVII

"NOW ALL IS DONE"

"BRISEIS," said her boy-cousin, here in Regent's Park, "did you see any one as we were leaving the Inner Circle ?"

"No one in particular," she answered him, carelessly. "Why ?"

"I suppose I must have been mistaken," he said— and with that she resumed her turning over the leaves of his MS. book, to choose some piece for recitation.

But nevertheless he remained restless and dissatisfied ; he kept glancing down the dim blue vistas between the trunks of chestnut and sycamore ; indeed he was so preoccupied that at first he did not notice what this was that she had begun to read. And then of a sudden he became conscious.

"Don't !" he said, quickly, his face burning red with confusion. "Don't read that, Briseis ! I did not know it was there. I'm awfully sorry. I beg your pardon. I forgot it was there, or I would have torn out the leaves. I beg your pardon—"

"But what harm is there in Lord Byron's 'Isles of Greece'?" said she, wondering.

"It is a reproach against your conntry—a long reproach from beginning to end—and—and I don't want you to imagine—that any English person would think anything like that — or say anything like that to you—"

"Indeed," said she, smiling, to this sensitive small gentleman, "it is no reproach at all, but an exhortation; and it may have had its effect, you know, Adalbert. Anyhow, Greece has won her independence; and she ought to be the last to resent anything Byron ever wrote about her—"

"Give me the book, Briseis," he said, and she handed it to him; "I will look out for something else."

But even now he did not turn at once to the MS. pages.

"Cousin Bry," he said, "you remember the man who spoke to you one morning last week?"

"Oh, yes," she made answer, lightly enough.

"Is it to avoid him that we have taken to coming here?"

For the truth was they had forsaken their familiar retreat, where aforetime they had been half surrounded by bushes; and they had sought out another secluded spot, also overlooking the lake. At this present moment they were seated in a sort of open enclosure; above their heads the spreading branches of an elm; in front of them a breadth of greensward sloping down to the margin of the water; then the wide space of calm surface; and beyond that, on the other side, a row of tall trees that did not stir a leaf on this windless morning. Under that bank of foliage the oily, olive-green shadows were still and dreamlike—until a swan came breasting along, cleaving the liquid mirror, and leaving behind it two flashing divergent lines of silver. Placid and silent was this haven of rest, though there was a distant rumble of omnibuses, and though a faint film of smoke telling of the great city rose into the mingled white and azure of a cirrhus sky. These surroundings of theirs were no doubt common enough; and yet there was a certain sense of remoteness; even

12*

the rumbling of the omnibuses had at times a suggestion of the sea.

When Briseis was asked whether she had chosen
this isolated refuge in order to escape from Andreas
Argyriades, she laughed—a little uneasily.

"Why, what do you take me for, Adalbert?" she
said. "Do I look as if I were afraid of him? Have
you seen me watching for him—and hiding? But
then, you know, there are sometimes horrid things to
be met with, like black beetles, and mice, and earwigs;
and although one isn't actually afraid of them, one
would rather keep out of their way—"

"For if it was the same man," her cousin continued,
"that I saw as we were leaving the Inner Circle, he
appeared to be following us—"

"So much the better—so much the better!" she responded, with blithe assurance. "We shall get our
interview over all the sooner. And you understand,
Adalbert, that we must be back in good time this
morning: Sir Francis is coming to lunch, to take some
of us to the theatre—the *Mother-in-law*—very amusing
they say it is—and it is a great chance, for there is
such a run on the piece—but he said some time ago
that he would look out. Adalbert, did you ever know
any one quite so kind, and thoughtful, and generous
as he is?" Her manner had completely changed, and
her expression too; her beautiful, great, dark eyes
were full of a happy light; there was a soft and lingering music in the low tones of her voice whenever she
chanced to speak (which was pretty often) of Frank
Gordon. "And then he is so modest!" she went on.
"Why, if I were he, I should be so proud—oh! so
proud as to be unendurable—I should want everybody
to know, not merely that I was Sir Francis Gordon, but
that I was Gordon of Grantly. And I should expect

every one to know the history of the clan, and all the
battles and fights of the old time. Why, when I was
at Grantly Castle, he seemed to make light of everything—the family portraits—the weapons in the hall—
the ancient building itself; he seemed afraid to be
thought a *poseur;* he seemed to laugh everything
aside, and to consider his visitors as all-important.
But there," she said, with a sudden peevishness, "what
is the use of my talking? I know what your opinion
is: I know you detest him!"

"Oh, yes, of course I do," said her cousin. "Only
—only I wonder where else you would find a grown-up
man like that—one in his position—taking notice of a
lame boy like me."

"There now—that's what it is!" she broke in, eagerly. "That's just where it is! He is generously disposed all round; there is no time-serving and respecting of persons; look at the trouble he must have been
at to get you the Highland dirk, and the broadsword,
and the targe—"

"Of course, Briseis," her boy-cousin said, "every
one understands why he is particularly kind to any one
in our house — why he comes to the house at all.
Every one knows: it is to see you."

But at this she drew in a little; and there was a
touch of color on her forehead as she replied—

"You must not say such things, Adalbert. They
might be very much misunderstood."

Some short time thereafter, happening to raise her
eyes from the MS. book, she saw that Andreas Argyriades was approaching by one of the paths: even at a
certain distance she knew who this was by the green-
white waxen pallor of his face and the furtive and
watchful look of his small black eyes, to say nothing
of his jaunty costume, now supplemented by a cane and

a pair of yellow kid gloves. She betrayed no surprise
—took no notice, indeed. She resumed her reading, if
in lower tones—

> 'Strike! and drive the trembling rebels
> Backwards o'er the stormy Forth;
> Let them tell their pale Convention
> How they fared within the North.
> Let them tell that Highland honor
> Is not to be bought nor sold—'

"I beg your pardon for interrupting you, my dear
friend," Argyriades said, in Romaic, and with a cere-
monious bow he took off his straw hat.

She looked up; the recognition she accorded him
was of the slightest; but he on his part deliberately
went to the foot of an adjacent tree, got hold of one
of the small green-painted chairs standing there, and
brought it back with him, seating himself beside her.

"Now, my dear friend Briseis—"

"I do not wish to hear anything you may have to
say," she interposed, calmly and coldly.

"Again I beg your pardon," he said, with studied
politeness, "but it is necessary you should. It is of
great importance to you—greater than you imagine. I
did not answer the hasty notes you sent me; no, for it
is always unwise, it is useless, to reply to what is written in anger. To consider the situation quietly is the
better way—"

"I do not wish to consider any situation," she retorted, with some greater warmth. "You know well
how the case stands between us. You stole from your
dead sister's writing-desk certain letters belonging to
me. You offered to hand them over to me if I paid
you; and foolishly I sent you the money you demanded.
Then you lied; you refused to return them, hoping for

more money; and now you come here, again hoping for more money. But, sir, you have made a mistake. I tell you, you may do what you like with those letters. Show them to whom you like! They are perfectly harmless, as you are aware—"

"Perhaps—perhaps," he replied, with absolute equanimity. "Perhaps I might think so; perhaps another might not think so; it matters nothing. But in my present hard straits, if I cannot come to you now and again and ask you for a little friendly help—if I am forced, greatly against my will, to come to you in a different manner—I do not propose to avail myself of that packet of letters at all. .Oh, no. I may myself burn them; they are of little use to me; though I had hoped they might be the means of inducing you to give a little aid to an acquaintance of former times and a fellow-countryman. It was not to be so. Very well. But I have other resources. Indeed I may say that I have means whereby I can very easily secure your consent to any arrangement I choose to propose—"

"Ti thauma!" she exclaimed, scornfully; but she was startled all the same; his manner was so tranquil and confident.

"Oh, yes, truly," he continued, crossing his gloved hands the one over the other, the cane being between. "Do you know why I did not answer the hurried and angry notes you sent to me? Because I wished to have more of them — indignant, demanding, imperative, so much the better. But on reflection I have enough. And it is with these, not with the others, that I propose to secure your kindness, my dear friend. I can dispense with the passionate adorations of our good Lamprinos; I can even burn them. But what have I in their stead? My dear friend, you do not appear to perceive the situation in which you have placed yourself. Supposing that I take only the first of these notes to any one particularly interested in you, and I say, 'Sir, behold here is a communication to me from the beautiful Miss Valieri; and you will see that she pays a first instalment of £5 to procure back to herself certain letters : it is for you to judge whether these letters were likely to have been compromising or not ?' My dear friend, you say I can work no harm. Is not that a little harm ? Is not that a revenge, a just revenge, in the case of your being implacable and refusing me assistance in my hard straits ?—"

Her look had changed. She saw how she had been entrapped ; and for a moment or two she was fear-stricken and palpitating.

"But the truth is stronger !" she said, breathlessly. "Even if you tried such a base and wicked thing, the truth would defeat you ! For any one would immediately answer you, 'Produce, then, the compromising letters'—"

"And if these were destroyed ?—or missing somewhere in Greece ?" he said, placidly. "If there remained only this plain and evident testimony that you were so anxious to get them back that you paid a first instalment of money—"

At this moment there chanced to come along one of the workmen of the Park, carrying some garden implement in his hand. As soon as he was near enough, Adalbert Elliott, who had been watching his cousin's face with the intensest scrutiny, and who was almost voiceless, indeed, with excitement and indignation—Adalbert managed to call aloud from the Bath chair—

"Gardener—gardener—come here for a moment ! Or will you go for a policeman—will you send a policeman here—there is a lady being terrified by this rascal—"

The British workman does not like meddling in matters which he does not understand. The official in mole-skin stood staring with bovine eyes at the members of this little group, looking from one to the other, saying nothing, asking nothing. But Briseis herself addressed him hurriedly—

"No, no, it is all a mistake. Never mind; it is nothing. We were merely talking. This gentleman is my friend."—'God, what a friend!' she said to herself, as the gardener went leisurely on his way.

"What does your young companion wish?" asked Argyriades, calmly, with a glance at the lad's flushed cheeks and panting breast.

"He wishes a policeman to be sent for," was her instant retort.

"What, for me?" he said, elevating his eyebrows slightly. "Ah, that would be impolitic. You surely do not court exposure, my dear friend? If there is any exposure, if there is any lamentable result, then it is owing to you, not to me. Besides, what am I doing that is against English law? Here I am sitting quietly, advising an old acquaintance as to what is best in her own interests. Not a single threat even—everything amicable. Now if it were Demetri that you had to deal with, ah, what a position would be yours! Demetri recognizes that in the implacable fight for life it is every one for himself; and he is merciless, relentless— relentless, merciless. Whereas I come to you and show you what danger you are in; I wish to be your friend; I wish to help you—"

"Then give me back every one of those notes I sent you!" she said, imperatively. "Keep the letters! And keep the money! Or if it is money you want—" She hesitated. "Yes—to have done with you I will give you ten pounds—I will give you twenty pounds—

for everything—everything—everything !" Then again she said : " No, I will not !—not a farthing! Oh, I don't know what to do !" she exclaimed, almost wildly. "But this I do know, that if your brother Demetri is a meaner, a more contemptible scoundrel than you, then I am ashamed that my country should have given birth to such a pair !"

She rose to her feet, as if by some physical effort she would throw off the coils she felt inevitably gathering round her. And Adalbert, who had been looking on in the greatest distress, struck in.

" Briseis, is it not about time we were getting back home ? If Sir Francis Gordon is coming to lunch, we must not be late, you know—"

" Yes, yes, yes," she said, quickly, and she placed the M.S. volume in the leather pocket.

" And may not I accompany you for part of the way ?" Argyriades said, blandly. " There are so many things I wish to make clear to you while I have the opportunity. It is not always safe to write, in delicate negotiations—"

" Then you are afraid of the magistrate, after all !" she said.

" Ah, no, no, not in the least," he responded, as he set out walking by her side. " For what am I doing ? In a language that no one around understands I am offering you a little advice—nothing more. I show you how you are situated ; and I ask you not to push me to extremities. I am not revengeful ; though you have refused help to a countryman, and called him many hard names. These I do not heed ; these do not hurt. No, I give you my word of honor, I am not revengeful ; and I do not propose to show any one your written en-treaties to me, if you will be considerate, if you will give me a few pounds from time to time, until you can give me the large sum that is to redeem what you call everything—everything—everything. I am not merciless, like Demetri ; I am reasonable ; but above all I am poor, and in hard straits—while you are rich."

"I am not rich !" she answered him—but with some despairing consciousness that answering was of no avail. "My small fortune was lost, altogether lost ; and the little I have to live on now—"

"Ah, I know," he said. "I know something of that. But you have rich relatives, and rich friends, and, still more, you have rich expectations : do I not understand something of that too ? Reflect, then. Might it not be worth your while to consent to some arrangement — some equitable arrangement — which would benefit me and harm none other—"

"I have no money—I gave you all I had !" she said, desperately.

"Ah, but how easy for you to obtain it ! There are always guardians, trustees, relatives who can be appealed to ; they advance assistance, because of the rich expectations—how easy all that is !"

And so he went on explaining her position to her, and defending his own conduct, with an insinuating and subtle ingenuity ; while her revolted judgment had hardly a word in reply—or perhaps she did not deign to reply. In this manner they left the Park, and crossed over, and got into Devonshire Place ; and still he hung on to her, with his crafty plausibilities carefully avoiding any distinct introduction of a threat. But just as they were nearing the house, Adalbert called out—

"Briseis, there is Sir Francis !—won't you wait for him ?"

Her eyes lighted up with pleasure and welcome—perhaps with some assurance of safety too. As for

Argyriades, he also seemed to recognize the new-comer.

"You will let me hear from you?" he said to Briseis, in an undertone. "Adieu!" And therewith he raised his hat, turned away, and made off in the direction of the Marylebone Road.

During the next second or two something strange and bewildering occurred. She was standing there, ready to put into words the more than friendly greet-ing that already shone in her face, and having no fur-ther thought at all of the baneful influence from which she had just been freed. As Frank Gordon came along she could see that his look was following the figure of the man who had so suddenly slunk away at his ap-proach. That was but natural. He may even have been surprised; people do not usually beat so hasty a retreat; it was enough to court observation. But what she was not prepared for—she who had studied, who knew, his every shade of expression—was the grave and reserved fashion in which Gordon, who ordinarily was so light-hearted and off-handed, received and returned her welcome. Was he in trouble, then? It could not be that in an instant he had grown suspicious of her! Only—and all this happened with incredible swiftness—as he helped her as usual to get Adal-bert and the empty Bath chair into the house, her heart sank somehow. With some strange and vague alarm she felt that he and she were not as they had been. And she did not know what wrong she had done.

Nor was it with much lightness of spirit that he now ascended to the drawing-room, leaving Briseis and her boy-cousin below. He knew that this must be his last visit—or at least one of the last—to a house whither he had been drawn by an unsuspected but all too powerful attraction. It is true he might have made some excuse and escaped from this theatre-engagement also, thereby enabling him to sever the connection at once and finally ; but he did not wish to do anything that would provoke remark. He would rather with-draw gradually. And he would take scrupulous care to show, on the one or two occasions on which he might still have to meet Briseis, that his attitude towards her differed in nothing from his attitude towards the others. He could keep his own secret—and dree his own wierd.

But in those hours of anxious self-examination that had followed his startling discovery, during which he was asking himself whether he had unwittingly been guilty of exhibiting any special favor towards Briseis, there was one point that pricked him hard. In making up the successive small parties for concerts or picture-galleries or theatres, while Mrs. Elliott's convenience, or the size of the box, or some such consideration might rule out this one or that of the other girls, Bri-seis was always included. It had come to be a general understanding. It was 'Briseis—and who else with her ?' And now, at the last moment, here came an op-portunity of showing that he had never meant to treat Briseis differently from the rest. The box he had se-cured at the theatre was for four : if she—by some arrangement apparently accidental—were to be left out, would not that be a demonstration of impartiality ? Surely she would not feel hurt ? Surely she could not imagine that any slight was intended ? The other girls were accustomed to be left at home from time to time. And he knew that he was no traitor to Briseis in so scheming, in so acting ; it was what he was in honor bound to do ; and then—thereafter—let come what might !

> 'He gave his bridle-reins a shake,
>   With adieu for evermore,
>   My dear,
>   And adieu for evermore.'

Nevertheless it was in no gay mood that he now entered the drawing-room, to receive the usual welcome from these gabbling girls. And at the very outset they noticed the alteration in his demeanor. Could this be Frank Gordon, who was always so full of fun, and devilment, and wild projects? Why, so preoccupied and ill at ease was he that he even condescended to talk about the weather. Beautiful morning — looking like a change, though—dark clouds gathering in the east—coming up against the wind—uncommon to have thunder at this time of the year— But at this moment the little widow made her appearance, smiling upon her favorite as was her wont.

"I'm very sorry, Mrs. Elliott," he said to her, presently, "but the only box I could get for to-day holds only four. Now I don't think it was quite settled—perhaps you could tell me who are going to be so kind as to make up the party—"

"Really, Sir Francis," said the widow—and her tired and troubled face looked quite sympathetic and pleased as she regarded the young man—"they are all so much indebted to you; but this time I do think my dearest Olga and Brenda were mentioned—I wouldn't dictate —it is for you to say—"

"Oh, but that's all right," said he. "That's all right." And then at this point he hesitated, and very nearly broke away from his resolve. He felt as if he were about to strike Briseis—and that she would quiver under the blow. However, he went on. "There is the fourth place, Mrs. Elliott—?"

She looked at him with some astonishment.

"Oh, yes—of course—I had assumed you would be taking Briseis—"

"But haven't we been rather neglectful of Miss Cinderella ?" he suggested. "There shouldn't be a Cinderella in any house—it isn't fair—"

Carlotta Bingham, who was known by this nickname, and who was the youngest and latest addition to the household, colored up when she heard herself mentioned in this connection : she had not hitherto participated in any of these little festivities.

"Oh, our dear Carlotta ?" exclaimed the widow, with instant approval. "That would be so nice ! That would be so kind of you, Sir Francis. I'm sure you will be such a happy party. They tell me that *The Mother-in-law* is just too laughable for anything." And so that matter was settled ; and as the gong now sounded they all of them trooped down to the dining-room, where Briseis had just established her cousin Adalbert at the luncheon table.

To Frank Gordon this was a sombre meal : it seemed to be in consonance with the mysterious darkening of the day all around them, caused by the creeping up of the thunder-clouds that now hung overhead. There was plenty of chattering at the table, it is true ; but to him it sounded as if it came from a distance. He instinctively knew that at times Briseis's eyes sought his face, questioning ; and he did not dare to meet any of those timid glances. He rather tried to listen to the trash that the anæmic medical student was talking : it appeared to be some kind of cheap cynicism—perhaps sufficient to overawe a company of girls.

"What does a man do when he's drunk ? Why, he don't know ! If he's got a stiff dose of rum into him, he'll turn his hand to anything. He'll quarrel with a policeman, and knock off his helmet; and that means

a five-shilling fine the next morning.   Or he'll run out
from an earth-work and under heavy fire he'll pick up
a wounded comrade, and carry him back into safety;
and that means that next day his colonel tells him he's
going to recommend him for the Victoria Cross.   It's
all a toss-up—whether it's to be a five-shilling fine or
the V. C.; and when he gets sober again he finds out
what has happened!"

The fond mother looked admiringly at the pallid
youth; and with unmistakable pride she turned to her
neighbor.

"Well, Sir Francis, what do you say to that?" she
asked, with a smile.

"There's a good deal of scepticism going about nowadays," he answered her, with careless irrelevance.
"Very soon they'll be saying that Balbus never did
build any wall."

In fact he was paying but little heed to all this aimless strife of tongues; he was thinking rather of the
moment when Briseis should discover that she was to
be left behind, and he was wondering how she would
take the unexpected change.   As it turned out, some
chance remark of one of the girls, as they rose from
table, revealed the truth; but he resolutely kept his
eyes away from Briseis's face.   Probably, he said to
himself, she would show no sign at all; she was not a
school-girl; and if there was any little surprise or disappointment, the general sunniness of her nature would
soon throw all that aside.   When, a little while thereafter, they parted at the front door—for she had come
to see the theatre-goers off—she shook hands with him
and bade good - by to him just as usual; and if she regarded him with something of grave inquiry — perhaps of proud and injured and pathetic injury—it was
mayhap as well that he did not notice.   He was glad

to get away and bury himself in this four-wheeled cab.

It might have been a hearse, as far as he was concerned; and black as his thoughts were the louring heavens overhead, that looked all the more heavy and ominous because of the steely half-light shining along the house fronts. Fortunately the girls kept jabbering among themselves; and he was left alone in peace. What he was mostly thinking of was this— Had the last farewell been taken ?—and in that manner ?

The four of them got into the box just as the play began. It was one of those farcical comedies the hero of which courts the laughter of the audience by exhibiting himself as a helpless imbecile in all sorts of impossible situations; and in this case he was neither better nor worse than his kind; the house, from stalls to gallery, roared at the poor man's perplexities and fatuities — even though at times there was a sort of startled hush as the thunder growled overhead. But what Frank Gordon saw was the strangest thing: a phantasmagoria with no laughter in it at all — with no meaning even: a series of scenes without connection: an appearance of figures that had apparently no relation to each other. A fat, elderly gentleman was vociferously irate about something; two young women, with tragic gestures, wept hysterically; the distracted tomfool tumbled in on the stage with his coat half torn off his back; there was a wild conference of relatives, all of them in evening dress and all of them undoubtedly insane : in short, the fun grew fast and furious, and the audience kept up a continuous chorus of laughter, in spite of that low, muttering growl above the roof. And then, once and again, there was a sudden light in the upper parts of the theatre — a pale and livid flash that made the other lights look orange; then a space of silence followed by an alarming rattle that seemed to shake the gewgaw building and all its canvas simulacra; and after that a fierce hissing of rain that sounded as if it were descending in sheets.   It was the oddest kind of accompaniment to this tangled web of nothingness that was being produced on the stage; perhaps it was some consciousness of this overweighing war of the elements that distracted his attention; at all events these figures were to him as figures in a dream; and when at length he had to see about getting his companions safely taken home, he had not the faintest intelligible idea as to what had been passing before him.   He had been present at the performance of a mystery.

When they arrived at the house, the girls would have had him go in with them, for tea; but he declined; he resumed possession of the cab, and was driven down to the Sirloin Club, which snug little place he found he had all to himself.   So he drew in an easy-chair to the fire; and called for a reading-lamp to be placed on the small table; and took from his pocket a number of letters that he had merely skimmed over in the morning.   There was one from the Princess, who had remarkably little to say about her future daughter-in-law, and a great deal to say, of a comical kind, concerning the worldly-pious waverings of the Margravine of Pless-Gmünden.   There was one from Lord Rockminster, containing an invitation for the first fortnight in December.   There was another from Lady Adela, informing him that she was about to send him her new novel, and he was 'honestly—*honestly*, now,' to tell her what he thought of it, and how many of the people he could recognize.   If he knew of any free libraries, in the north or elsewhere, that would accept a copy, she would be delighted to send one; and would it be considered a greater compliment if she added her autograph ?   But of course the all - engrossing communication was that from Georgie Lestrange—one of the first she had written after her arrival at her new abode; and these pages he pored over, and read again and again, as if he were striving to learn something about the writer—something more than was possible to be learnt during their lad-and-lass skirmishing among the hills and moors and river-valleys of Inverness-shire. Curiously enough, it was to these wild neighborhoods that (as soon as she had said what she had to say about her brother's condition) the longings of her soul seemed to return.   Already Miss Georgie was grown nostalgic. The sky of Florida, she declared, was too palely and uniformly blue, and it was too far removed away from the earth.   She wanted clouds that came into the picture — that were part of her surroundings — that lent light and shadow to the dappled straths, that gave splendors of color to the sunsets, and brought majesty into the moonlight nights.   All of which considerations naturally led up to reminiscences, of a more or less pathetic cast.

" Do you remember," wrote this ingenuous student of art and landscape, "one morning you were fishing the Priest's Bridge Pool ; and I was reading a book ; and when I began to read I thought the skies were perfectly fine and flawless.   Then in a little while I happened to look up, to see what you were doing ; and lo and behold ! there had stolen into the sky, staring over the crest of the opposite hill, a great mass of white cloud, not shaded with any perspective, but a bolt-upright mass, a blinding white against a blinding blue, and glaring at you as if it had come jumping out of another world.   And then such keenness of color ; the purple slopes of heather, far off as they were, had come

13

quite *near*—you would have thought you could touch
them with your parasol, which was all very remarkable
and admirable; but in five minutes the heavens were
black, and the rain was whipping the Priest's Bridge
Pool into smoke, and I was hiding my wee self under
an alder-bush . . . Was that the day we startled the
heron down by the Silver Pool, on our way home ?   Oh,
the gorgeousness of that evening !—the hills out in the
west like violet velvet against the gold ; and all the
tops of Aonach Môr burning in crimson ; and then down
in the still pools, beside the green alders, the crimson repeated again on the smooth water.   And there was that
gray phantom of a creature ; and we crept up behind
the bushes; and he was out on a stone ; and I think
you could have touched him with the point of your rod,
before he stretched out his great wings and went away
down the river as silently as a moth . . . But best of
all were the moonlight evenings — you remember ? —
when we went a little way up into the open forest, and
listened for the belling of the stags, and there was a
golden moon just over Ben-na-Vân, and a mist all along
the moorland, and Lady Adela, and Rose, and Sibyl—
the White Sisters — like three ghosts, and not a single
word said because of the stillness.   And once we heard
the pipes—oh ! so far away—a faint, *unearthly* cry—
I never heard the like of it before—it was the ban-
shee ! Do you remember the magical nights with the
moonlight coming through the trees on to the lawn,
and the scent of sweet-gale, and the murmur of the
stream down in the valley ? — do you remember ? —
do you care to remember? — are you as anxious as I
am to remember and recall? Well, well, it's no use.
Only, I'm sick of blue skies — skies that are monot-
onously and uninterestingly blue ; and my heart flies
away back to a country that I know—a country where

there are clouds, and wild seas, and rain, and silver, and glorious sunsets, and mystic nights among the hills.

Dahin, dahin,
Möcht' ich mit dir, O mein Geliebter, ziehn!"

Why, this was quite a burst of eloquence on the part of Georgie; and for the moment he, too, experienced an upraising of heart in recalling their boy-and-girl escapades. Surely it was none so tragic a fate to which his honor had bound him; that happy-go-lucky companionship in the northern wilds would lead naturally enough into the more serious, the life-long, companionship that lay before him. And all would be well.

But there was something haunting him, even amidst these optimistic resolves and hopes: it was the recollection of a house in Devonshire Place—the front door open—and a last look from which he had turned away his eyes.

CHAPTER XVIII

A RESOLVE

Now hardly had Frank Gordon and the three girls driven away to the theatre when the indefatigable little widow, seeking to console those who had been left behind, proposed that she and they should pay a visit to the Brewers' Exhibition at the Agricultural Hall. Perhaps, strictly speaking, this could scarcely be called introducing the young ladies to polite society —at least, to any great extent; but the entertainment was cheap; much information might be acquired; and there was a Highland piper playing outside one of the distillery stalls. And so, despite the threatening weather, a cab was sent for; and Miss Ada, and Miss Holmes, and Miss Tressider were bidden to get ready.

"I'm very sorry we can't take you as well, dear Briseis," said the widow. "The cab only holds four, of course. And besides I know you are anxious to get on with those dining-room curtains; for I wouldn't let any one else touch them; they might spoil your design; and it was so clever of you to think of a stem of maize and the simple leaves; the gold thread on the dark green cloth is so effective; and such free, bold drawing—where did you learn to do all these clever things?—or is it just a natural gift all round? I'm so sorry we can't take you—"

"Oh, but I would much rather get on with the

curtains, Aunt Clara," said Briseis. She had looked dazed and scared all during luncheon—perhaps no one had noticed; and now she seemed chiefly anxious to get away and be alone. But she remained in the hall, to help the girls on with their jackets and capes.

The cab came up; the bustling, loquacious party got out upon the pavement—with many exclamations about the thunderous look of the skies; then they drove off; and the house again grew still. Briseis went into the school-room. Her cousin Adalbert was lying on the sofa, absorbed in reading football news; but as soon as he saw her, he threw aside the paper.

"Briseis," said he at once, "have you and Sir Francis Gordon quarrelled?"

She hesitated. What was the use of a boy confidant? And yet she was sorely distraught; her mind was all tempest-torn with fears and conjectures; to speak to any one was an immeasurable relief. And the lame lad had always been her chivalrous friend and champion.

"What makes you think that?" she asked, evasively.

"He never left you at home before, when others were going."

"Oh, that is nothing—that is nothing," she answered him. "Some one must remain behind—why not I? I have had more than my share of those concerts and theatres. He has been very kind to me—very—"

"He hardly spoke a word to you at luncheon," her cousin continued.

"There was so much talking!" she said.

"Well, then, when he first saw you—I mean outside—when he came along the pavement—and the other man was going away—"

Her expression instantly changed.

"Ah, did you notice that, Adalbert?—did you notice that? Was it so obvious that any one could notice it? Indeed I knew I could not be mistaken! And what had I done? Why should he be angry with me? Yes, I saw him look in that curious way after Argyriades; but why should he blame me if any one speaks to me? Why should he have changed so suddenly—why should he regard me with coldness and distrust? And yet I cannot believe that he could suspect me—that he could be so unjust as to accuse me merely because he saw a stranger going away! No, no; there must be something else," she went on, with growing excitement. "Adalbert, what is it that I have done? What wrong can I have done? Why did he not tell me if I was to blame?"

She was standing by the table, her fingers tightly clasped in front of her; her lips were trembling, and her eyes had filled with tears. It was a strange thing for the helpless lame boy to witness. Ordinarily the demeanor of this beautiful, tall cousin of his was marked by a perfect self-possession—a self-possession sweet and serene and well-wishing: now she was like some frightened child, who had been reprimanded or punished for an unknown offence. Yet how could the poor lad help her? He had no wit or skill in such matters. Indeed, of late, when Briseis seemed to be in trouble, it had always occurred to him that it was to Frank Gordon himself she ought to appeal.

"Briseis," he said, almost at random, "what does that man want who has come twice to threaten you? I cannot understand a word of what he says; but I know he threatens you—you are so scornful and indignant—"

"Ah, that is quite another thing," she answered

him, quickly. "That is a question of money; that is
a trifle; I am not so concerned about that, except at
the moment. It is not of threatening or of money that
one thinks when— And yet—and yet," she went on,
after a second or so, "there are such strange possibilities. If Argyriades has already tried to make mischief
—who can tell? It is all a bewilderment to me—and I
have no one to guide me—no one at all. And if there
was any chance of mischief, don't you think it would
be better to sacrifice anything—anything—to get rid of
that man? Don't you think so, Adalbert? If it is
only a question of money, what is money?—what is
any sacrifice to get rid of such a threat? I have no
money—none at all at present; but perhaps my trustee
in Edinburgh could get some for me. Don't you think
I ought to buy this man off at any cost, to make sure
—to make sure?—don't you think so, Adalbert?—
don't you think so?"

In her agitation she was really talking to herself;
she did not wait for any reply; and her cousin, embarrassed and conscious that he was incapable of advising
her, dared not speak. But she seemed to have made
up her mind. She cleared a portion of the table. She
fetched some writing-materials from the top of a chest
of drawers. And then she sat down and hastily wrote
two notes: the first of them, addressed to Mr. Murray,
the Edinburgh W.S., begged him to advance her five-
and-twenty pounds, if that was within the scope of his
powers; the second conveyed a curt intimation to
Argyriades that she would meet him at a quarter to
twelve on the following morning, at the corner of York
Terrace and York Gate, while she added that she hoped
he would come prepared to state explicitly what sum he
would take in return for all communications from her
in his possession, including the one she was now pen-

ning. These two letters, for safety's sake, she herself carried to the nearest post-office box; thereafter return-ing to the tranquil embroidery of golden stems and joints and leaves on the breadth of dark green cloth. Her boy-cousin, furtively regarding her from time to time, guessed that her mind might not be quite as tranquil as her occupation; but he was too diffident to interfere, even with a shy word of sympathy.

The day wore on, and she grew more and more sick at heart, because of all this doubt, and questioning, and anxious surmise. Frank Gordon's change of man-ner towards her had been so sudden, so unexpected, so inexplicable. 'Why—why?' she kept asking herself. Surely he could not suspect or scorn her simply because a stranger in the street had slunk away at his approach? Or had Argyriades been attempting to find a better market for his stolen wares? Perhaps a sample had been shown? And she was to be condemned unheard —by the one human being on whose opinion and regard she had come to set such perilous store.

And then she drew a cloak of pride around her. Why should she be solicitous about any man's esteem? It was for her to award favor, if she should so choose; that was her prerogative; they who valued her ap-proval, even to the extent of a good word or a friendly look, would have to come for it. The old ballads had told her what the Gordons were—gay, gallant, and fickle; 'he turned about lightly, as the Gordons does a';' and this one, the most careless-hearted of all the race of them, if he had suddenly resolved to become grave and serious and distant, was welcome so to do. Nay, if he believed her capable of this or that folly or infamy, it was not for her to defend herself. The world was wide enough for them both; and she was no Lady Jean Melville, to take to her bed, and lie there pale

and wan, because another of the gay Gordons had turned
on his heel.

That night was wet; the rain kept softly pattering
on the window of her solitary little room, up in the at-
tic; when she looked out, and down, she could see the
lamps throwing reflections of quivering gold on the
streaming black pavements. She had been crying a
little, from time to time. For her cloak of pride had
brought her but small comfort, and had long ago been
discarded; an anguish of dull foreboding held possession of her; sleep was out of the question; she was all
unstrung; and she was abjectly penitent—for she knew
not what. Now and again she went to her mirror;
perhaps with some pathetic desire to convince herself
of the splendor of her youthful beauty; perhaps merely out of dread that this unresting grief might leave
traces that she would find it difficult to explain on the
morrow. At last, hardly conscious of what she was
doing, she opened her writing-desk, and turned up the
gas a little, and sought for and brought forth a sheet
of M.S. scrawled and dotted over.

On more than one occasion Frank Gordon had expressed himself as greatly interested in her reminiscences of Slavonic and Romaic folk-songs, and in the
singular faculty she had for improvising, while she was
seated at the piano, some little story of the same fashion, and adding to it a wandering, capricious accompaniment by way of mystical refrain. He had even
begged her to give him one of these compositions; but
she rarely committed them to paper; perhaps she was
afraid that by accident they might come under the eye
of some professional critic. Nevertheless, his request
had remained in her mind; and happening one afternoon to find herself with a brief and unusual space of
leisure she had roughly jotted down the haphazard lines

13*

and notes of a fragment; and that she had put away in her desk, and forgotten. But now, as she took it out, she thought she would make a fair copy; and she thought she would send it to him—as a timid kind of propitiation, if there was any unknown cause of quarrel between them : in any case, by his manner of receiving this poor little peace-offering, he would show how he still regarded her. And thus it was that the proud-hearted Briseis brought herself to humble contrition (for she knew not what); and in the dark and still hours of the night she proceeded to copy carefully and clearly the irregular verses and the accompanying ripple of melody, though at the outset she spoiled three sheets of paper, because of tears that fell.

It was a simple enough story that she had heard or read of somewhere : the story of a small band of brigands overtaken by the soldiery, and in the forefront of the fray the young wife of the chief of the brigands, a peasant girl whom he had abducted not many months before. This was how it began—

Saddest bride is the stolen bride, and Eleänaia is weeping.
Happiest bride is the stolen bride, and Eleänaia smiles.
Proud she stands by her husband's side, at bay in the mountains,
Proud when the gendarme's bullet speeds straight to her heart.
(Creep closer, child, the moonlight is white in the forest.)

And then it went on to tell how the brigand, when his band had escaped, disguised himself, and went down to the nearest village, to try to obtain a permit that his wife should be buried in consecrated ground ; and how his disguise was discovered, and himself taken and shot. But it was not of Eleänaia and her brave and luckless husband that Briseis was thinking as she went on with her transcription, scrupulously correcting here, and expanding there. Surely Frank Gordon could not be offended by her sending him this scrap of ballad-music, amateurish as it might be?. He had asked for it, indeed—though that was awhile ago. And anyhow it would establish some kind of link between them; he would surely write in reply; perhaps there might be an explanation. He could not take it amiss!

Next morning it was still wet; but ere any of the household were up, she had been out and along to the pillar letter-box, despatching her wistful, half-reluctant, tentative appeal for reconciliation. And still it rained, on and on; and hourly London became more gloomy, and squalid, and hideous. When it drew towards noon, there was no thought of the lame boy going out in his Bath chair; the day was too distressing; so he had to content himself with a seat at the window, and a bundle of those journals which he had found by experience gave the most dithyrambic accounts of the deeds of his heroes, whether on the muddy football field or on the windy and sea-haunted links of the north.

And so it was that a little before twelve Briseis was enabled to steal forth alone and perhaps unobserved to keep her appointment with Andreas Argyriades. Protected by water-proof and umbrella she made her way through the swimming streets; and at the corner she had mentioned to him she found her compatriot—looking very miserable, indeed, for though he also carried an umbrella, it had proved inadequate to shield his Bank-holiday attire, and he now presented a somewhat damp and bedraggled appearance. Nevertheless his spirit was calm and unruffled; his self-confidence had suffered no abatement; and he received Briseis with a profound courtesy, watching her all the while.

"Have you brought an answer for me, and a definite answer?" she asked, abruptly and coldly.

"Pardon me, my dear friend, it is not so simple as perhaps you think," he replied, in his usual suave manner. "There are many points to be regarded. For example, I have just learnt that my brother Demetri is coming to this country. Very well. When he arrives, what is the first question he will ask of me? He will say—'Andreas, my son, what have you been able to make out of the Valieri-Lamprinos affair?' He is so mercenary, is my brother Demetri! Then if I tell him some paltry sum, he will first laugh at me for a fool, but afterwards he will stab me. Ah, he is terrible—terrible—a famished wolf is merciful compared to him; he spares no one; and you—have you no fear for yourself if he is angry?—"

"Children's tales!" she responded, with contempt. "Do you think you can frighten me with such foolishness?"

"Akousate me!" he pleaded, in silken speech. "I wish to be your friend; and you will need a friend—when Demetri arrives. And how can I give you a definite answer: how can I tell you the exact value he might place on all these papers? No, no; my dear young lady, be guided by me; furnish me with a small sum at present—ten pounds—twenty pounds—what you please—which will be a pacification for Demetri; then subsequently we will consider—"

"We will not consider!" she retorted. "Why should I give you anything? Why should I give you a single drachma? It is only to get rid of you, once and for all; and if you refuse to agree to this conclusion, what is the alternative? The police, Mr. Argyriades!"

He shook his head, almost mournfully.

"Ah, no, you could not be so unwise," he said. "What have I pointed out to you before?—that I have done nothing—"

"You have asked for money; you have threatened me; you have threatened to show these letters—"

"Where is your evidence, my dear friend? Have you a scrap of my handwriting as proof?" he said, in a kind of compassionate manner. "Ah, no, have done with that idea! If you appeal to your police—to your English law—I can suffer nothing; but you—you will have to suffer the publicity, the exposure; and perhaps your story will be believed, and perhaps it will not. It is so much better to be amicable! Give me twenty pounds—in the mean time—for pacification—"

"I have not a farthing!" she exclaimed.

"Ah, then we are wasting time," he said, a little more sternly. "Shall I put the matter plainly to you, my dear friend? I have certain goods to sell; and they must go to the highest bidder. I have given you the opportunity; but you allow one day after the other to pass, and you do not provide yourself with the necessary funds, though you could easily do so. Well? Well, I must go to another market, that is all. I know who will redeem those compromising documents — oh, yes, and at the figure I ask — and if I have already shown him a little sample, to tempt him—"

"Have you—dared?" she demanded, with her cheek grown a trifle paler: some wild fancy had shot through her brain that here might be the true key to the enigma that had been torturing her through the long dark hours.

"I do not say yes or no, for I do not wish to commit myself," he answered her, calmly. "But at least you will consider what I have it in my power to do, at any moment. Oh, I confess to you that at first I was not so sure, when I was waiting and observing; for there are several young ladies in the house, and the Lord

Fragkis Gordon he might be interested in one or the other : perhaps — shall I say it ? — it was some little touch of expression on your part, when the name was mentioned, that convinced me I was on firm ground. For you understand, my dear friend, that though all the world must recognize that you are extremely beautiful — beautiful with a youthfulness and a freshness and an animation that not all of the prettiest of our Greek girls are happy enough to possess—all the world must see that ; but all the world may not know how quick a tale-teller is the expression of your face, to one who has the skill to remark. So perhaps it was yourself who confirmed my earlier surmises ?—but that is of little consequence ; what I wish to make clear to you, perfectly clear, is that I am on assured ground. Those letters that you sent to me, are they not my property ? May not I do what I choose with them ? May not I sell them to whoever will give most for them ? Therefore you cannot harm me ; but I might harm you—if you were so imprudent as to drive me to extremities. Only, you will not do that. I am sure you will not do that. No ; you will take into consideration many things : your own position ; the serious costs I have incurred ; and the advisability of pacifying Demetri. Is it not so ? You will be wise and reasonable ; and a wise and reasonable person accepts what is inevitable. Now, my dear friend, I cannot keep you standing here in the rain—it is dreadful : tell me, what can you give me that will propitiate Demetri when he arrives ?—"

"I have nothing to do with him," she said, hurriedly—but her attitude was less defiant. "I want back the letters you have of mine ; and I ask you, once for all, what I must pay for them, to have an end. At present I have no money, as I told you before ; but I have written to my trustee in Edinburgh, to see if he can let me have twenty-five pounds—"

"Yes; twenty-five pounds?" he repeated, in an encouraging way. "That would do very well to pacify Demetri—"

"I have nothing to do with Demetri!" she broke in again.

"But if he is bringing with him the Lamprinos letters?" he said, insidiously.

"And you said you had them here in London!"

"Ah, yes, I may have been a little premature—but that is nothing," he said, coolly enough. "Well, then, let us say that so far it is arranged : twenty-five pounds to propitiate Demetri. And after?"

"After?—not one lepta ! No, nor one atom of communication between you and me ! I must have the whole of the letters—every one of them : I will verify them myself; I will burn them myself; and then— nothing between you and me !"

"And all that is to come about for twenty-five pounds !" he said, elevating his eyebrows in affected surprise. "Really, if it were not so serious a matter, one might laugh. My dear young lady, you do not seem to comprehend : one does not undertake such trouble as I have encountered for a miserable twenty-five pounds—no, nor anything like that !—"

"What can I do more !" she cried, in a desperate kind of way—for the ingenuity of his arguments had confused her amidst her vague alarm and distress.

"But no, it is not for me to dictate !" he said, blandly. "As I have told you, you have rich friends—and they must know of your great expectations—and if you wish for money, why—"

"I cannot get more than that !" she protested—but more humbly now.

He shrugged his shoulders.

"Ah, well, there is then the alternative. If one will not pay, the other must. I have only to show these letters to the person you are thinking of at this moment, and I have only to say to him 'If you are interested in the young lady, would it not be generous of you to pay a considerable sum to withdraw such compromising documents from being handed about ?'—"

"And you say you do not threaten !" she interposed, scornfully.

"Pardon me," he answered her. "What I said was that you had nothing to show that I had threatened. — But come, come, my dear friend, I do not wish to threaten at all. Why should we quarrel ? We are quite harmoniously agreed so far. You will send me the twenty-five pounds, to make the best bargain I can for you with Demetri. That is the first step—"

"And the last," she said. "It must be first and last — or none. And if I send you the twenty-five pounds, how am I to know that you will return me the letters—every one of them ?"

"You cannot trust me, then ? Ah, that is the worst of having to do with one like Demetri," he proceeded, in a regretful fashion. "If it had not been for him, you would have had the packet long before now. But Demetri, he is insatiable. Never mind. You have done well. You have left me to deal with him. Do not fear. I will defend you against Demetri. Consider me the protector of your interests. You will send me the twenty-five pounds; and I will make the best bargain I can for you; and there will be no need to show these very strange letters, these very damaging letters, to any other person. You have done well, my dear friend, rest assured. It rejoices my heart to find you so placable, so reasonable. I give you my word of honor that you have resolved wisely. For what is the matter of a few pounds? What is a trifling matter of money to a beautiful young girl when her good name might be called in question—"

"My good name?" said Briseis—with a flash of her eyes.

"Ah, no, no—I meant by those who did not know her," he replied, softly. "That is a precious possession for a young girl, her good name; and of course you have acted with discretion. And it is so much pleasanter to have these amicable relations established. Need I tell you that if it had been war between us, it would have been a somewhat serious war? The famished wolf has no time to think of scruples; and here am I, in the most desperate of straits, and with Demetri coming over to demand explanations. But that is all past now. All is to be amiable and pleasant. And when, if I may ask, do you expect to receive the twenty-five pounds?"

"To-morrow, perhaps, or next day," she said, almost mechanically — for her brain was perplexed and bewildered by the ingenuities of his representations.

"Ah, that is well," said he; "and may I as a last word congratulate you, my dear friend, on the wisdom of your decision? You have done well. Confide your interests to me; and I will secure you against Demetri Argyriades. Adieu, then — for the rain is terrible. Within the coming day or two I shall hear from you; until then—adieu!"

"Sas proskunō," she answered him, absently; and the next moment she found herself alone, standing there in the midst of this wet and dismal London.

The following two or three days were for Briseis
Valieri little else than a prolonged agony of suspense
and dim apprehension. Every ring at the door-bell
caused her heart to jump; but the posts came and
went, morning, noon, and evening, and not even a line
arrived from Frank Gordon to say that her little propitiatory offering had been received. And then her
heart would grow hot, and her cheek would tingle
with maidenly pride and shame. Had she humbled
herself, only to be spurned? Had she placed herself
in the position of a suppliant, when indignant reserve
and silence would have better become her?

The Edinburgh W.S. had promptly replied, enclosing his own cheque for the amount she had mentioned,
and politely adding that it gave him pleasure to com-
ply with her request. But she hesitated about sending the money on to Argyriades, not because of its
value, but because she had a sort of despairing consciousness that it would not really and finally free her
from the terrorism which he was endeavoring to establish over her. Nay, it might even more hopelessly involve her in the toils he was obviously trying to wind
round her. It was only when he was talking to her—
when he was exercising a devilish cunning in describing to her the helplessness of her position—that she
felt ready to give him anything, to promise him anything, in order to get rid of him at once and forever:
when she was outside the influence of his plausible
speech, she could see clearly enough that whatever she
might give or promise would only place her more completely within his grip. Unhappily she had already
gone too far. She had sent him money; she had written urgent notes demanding the return of certain
papers; she had referred to interviews, and made ap-
pointments. And how was all this to be undone by

her forwarding to him the sum of money she had just received from Edinburgh ? It would but place another weapon of coercion in his hands.

However, that disquietude, harassing as it might be, was now eclipsed by a greater that in a way arose out of it. When day after day passed and nothing had been heard in answer to her timid little presentation of the Greek ballad, she began to convince herself that Argyriades, in some measure at least, must have carried out his threat. Had he, then, gone to Frank Gordon, and, without actually showing documents, intimated that he had secrets to sell ? Or had he taken with him one of the letters and produced it to see if he could find a purchaser for such compromising wares —one who, from magnanimous friendship or from any other motive could be induced to buy these things that he might destroy them ? And what, she asked herself, in such circumstances would a straightforward young Englishman be likely to do ? Why, without doubt, he would forthwith kick the scoundrel out at the door. Yes ; but the knowledge would remain ; and might be dwelt upon, and perhaps magnified. And who could wonder if this same clean-minded young Englishman should decline to have any further association with a girl who appeared to have doubtful antecedents, whose correspondence was passing about as bank-notes in the hands of blacklegs and blackmailers ?

All this fretting and guessing may have unhinged her judgment a little ; but gradually she became possessed with the resolve, at once piteous and imperious, that at any cost she must set herself right with Frank Gordon. Whatever had happened, she must know the truth ; whatever had happened, he also must know the truth. And she would go direct to himself. It was an unusual, perhaps an unmaidenly,

thing to do; and it might involve a certain abasement;
but it was too late to take such minor considerations
into account. She would go direct to himself—and
find out with her own eyes.

CHAPTER XIX

FACE TO FACE

THE bronzed November sunshine was streaming into a spacious and lofty apartment in one of the Northumberland Avenue hotels ; and up at the end of the room stood Lady Adela Cunyngham and Frank Gordon, talking to each other, and looking down the long tables that were laid out for luncheon, and that presented quite a pretty spectacle with their silver and fine linen, their glossy menu-cards, and their floral decorations of chrysanthemums and old-man's-beard.

"So kind of you to come and help me !" said the handsome young matron. "What should I have done —a poor lone woman arriving all by herself in London —not even Rose or Sibyl turning up to lend me a hand ; and as for Sir Hugh—I suppose Sir Hugh will think he has fulfilled his part when he pays the bill. But I had no scruple about asking you, when I learnt you were in town ; for you know, Sir Francis, we look on you as one of the family now, ever since we heard of your engagement. And by-the-way, when is Georgie coming home, if her brother is so much better ?"

"Soon, I believe," he answered her. "I have offered to go over to New York, to bring her back ; but nothing definite has been settled."

Lady Adela cast another surveying and satisfied glance along the brilliant tables.

"Well, I think all is right now ; and we may as well

go into the reception-room. Oh, one moment, Sir Francis," she said. "I ordered the wines you mentioned; but I did not say anything as to quantities. Now, you know, Sir Hugh is the most generous of men; but he is businesslike as well; and assuredly he will look into the account; and with regard to those wines, how is one to know what has been used—how will there be any check?"

"There will be Sir Hugh's cheque," he said, with a school-boy grin.

"I really do think I should have accepted the hotel proposal—so much a head—"

"Not at all!" he said, promptly. "There won't be any wine drunk—none to speak of. Do you think the Hypatians are likely to take wine at luncheon? If one of them should break out into wild carousal—a furious Maenad—she may put two lumps of sugar into her tea; but the orgie won't go further than that. Oh, there is Aunt Jean," he added, as he saw some one pass the door.

Accordingly the two of them went into the reception-room, where Miss Jean Gordon was found to be the first comer.

"These milliners and their charges will just be the ruin of me!" said she—for she had come south to pay a series of visits, and was busily preparing for the same.

"Now, Aunt Jean," her nephew proceeded—for Lady Adela had turned away to receive the new arrivals—"I'll tell you about some of the people you are to meet—"

"But if they are as celebrated as you say, surely I'll recognize them by head-mark?"

"Well, yes, they are celebrated," he replied, somewhat evasively. "They are celebrated, certainly—but —but it's mostly amongst themselves they are cele-

"'SO KIND OF YOU TO COME AND HELP ME!'"

brated. I don't know that their names have travelled
as far as Dee-side. Anyhow, they are extremely important people ; and mind, when you're talking to any
of them, to put in a good word for Lady Adela's new
novel—"

"Merciful me, laddie, I have not read a word of it !"
cried Aunt Jean.

"No, nor has anybody else, for it isn't published
yet," her nephew explained to her. "But why should
you not be supposed to know all about it ?—and these
writing-people will put paragraphs in the papers, and
make a stir—don't you understand that ? Have the
Dee-side folk got so little gumption as not to understand that ?—and why this elaborate entertainment is
given ? Now don't forget, Aunt Jean : the title is
Faded Jonquils ; and all kinds of well-known personages figure in it ; it is a brilliant picture of society ;
the disguises are delightfully thin ; if you're anybody
at all, you'll recognize the whole crowd. One or two
most distinguished critics have seen the proof-sheets,
and are charmed ; and she'll get a testimonial from
Mr. G. or she's not the woman I take her for. Now
let me see : I'd better tell you whom you'll sit next.
On your left will be a Mr. Quincey Hooper—he's the
London correspondent of an American paper ; nothing
to alarm you about him ; he's rather like an ostler, and
he'll probably tuck the corner of his table - napkin
under his chin, and he'll certainly talk all the time
about lords : nothing worse than that. Then on the
other side you'll have a Miss Penguin. She's a poetess
— a great, wild, fearsome poetess. But you won't
mind. She's a giddy old crock ; and she'll tell you
strange stories about a set of people whom she calls the
aristocracy. She doesn't know anything about them ;
but that's neither here nor there ; and she's a playful

old kitten : you'll find her great fun. Oh, here's my beneficent Miss Caledon—I must go and speak to her" —and off he went to welcome the intrepid young lady-journalist, whose extremely pretty gray eyes appeared at this moment to have something of demure amusement in them.

Now if it was by way of a trick that Frank Gordon had foisted the Passionate Poetess on to poor, innocent, unsuspecting Aunt Jean, he was well served out. For when by-and-by this large company had sedately filed into the luncheon-room, and when they were engaged in finding out their appointed seats—and while the zither-choir from the Black Forest was playing 'Alle Vögel sind schon da, alle Vögel, alle !' so that it seemed as if the birds of innumerable spring-times were hovering around and thrilling all the air with their vibrant melody—in the midst of this hum of confusion young Gordon became aware that a dowdy, pompous, over-dressed woman was bearing down on him. He could not understand this at all, for he himself had written out the cards and placed them along the tables; but the next moment the explanation came from Miss Penguin, who now confronted him.

" I wished to have a little chat with you, Sir Francis," said she, "and I took the liberty of transposing one or two of the cards—"

" Well, I'm hanged !" he wrathfully said to himself —which was improper, and also most impolite.

But there was no escape for him ; her baleful eye was upon him ; and the very first question she asked of him, as they sat down, was the identical question with which she had challenged him at the Hypatia Club.

" Have you read my *Mirrorings* ?"

He desperately hunted about for a lie—in vain ; and then he blurted out—

"I really don't know what the circulating libraries are coming to. You write to them for the best books, naturally; and they send you nothing but trash. And so—that is—the inexcusable reason—"

"I see," she observed, calmly. "You have not read my book. Consequently you have no answer to my indictment."

"Your indictment?"

He vaguely remembered that on that previous occasion this frowsy old frump with the pale protuberant fringe and the tattered finery had occupied herself chiefly in slandering her fellow-countrywomen, when she wasn't engaged in hacking and slashing at their husbands and brothers and sons; and also that she appeared to hold him, Frank Gordon of Grantly, responsible for all the ill doings and infamies of the 'aristocracy' of Great Britain.

"Yes, my indictment," she proceeded, and she held him with her inexorable eye. "Perhaps you will allow me to repeat at least a portion of it."

"Lord help us!—I'm in for it again," said young Gordon to himself.

And he was. Worse still, he found himself between two fires; for while he had this infuriate spinster at his elbow, on the other side of the head table, and not more than a yard or two from him, Octavius Quirk, in his frothily tempestuous fashion, was describing to Lady Adela and any others within ear-shot his doughty deeds in the field of journalistic criticism.

"Such a responsibility!" murmured Lady Adela, softly and sweetly. "Such an important newspaper—"

"The Moulinet—that's what I should like to call my department," continued the flabby-cheeked creature with the boiled gooseberry eyes. "I want my lads to understand that they must have a free shoulder-swing!

14

And we're doing excellent service, Lady Adela—oh, I assure you ! The weekly log-rollers have got a fright : there's a good deal less croaking and calling of the frogs to each other since we began to heave bricks into the pond. And the puling poets in the Government offices —stealing the Queen's stationery to write their miserable magazine-verse on it : we've made one or two of them sit up. But the two tribes that we mean to slaughter—the two tribes that are to have no mercy— are the Cuttle-fish and the Worms—"

"I'm afraid I don't quite—"

"The Cuttle-fish—who fling ink in the face of the public, and hide themselves in a sham profundity. I'm an Englishman ; I want English ; I want the English of Milton, and Shakespeare, and Dryden ; I don't want leerings, and twistings, and divings into the mud of obscurity. And then there are the precious people— the posturers—strutting in front of a literary mirror and admiring themselves : well, we mean to thrash the saw-dust out of their taffeta phrases, their 'three-piled hy-perboles, spruce affectation, figures pedantical' ; and we may be able to bring back something of the 'russet yeas, and honest kersey noes.' 'He speaks not like a man of God's making' : then he'll have to change his tune ; or we'll drum the dandified ass out of exist-ence—"

The wind-bag paused for a moment—for the zithern had begun to play 'Es steht ein Baum im Odenwald' ; but he soon ignored this interruption.

"Ah, the Worms, Lady Adela—I was almost forget-ting—"

"Yes ?" responded Lady Adela, in her pleasantest manner ; while Gordon inwardly said to himself 'O what a price one has to pay in England for puffs and paragraphs !'

"The Worms—the invertebrate literary things that live upon dead men's reputations — and the greater the reputation the better. 'Hallo,' cries one or other of these nonentities, 'let's get out another edition of So-and-so; he has been dead a hundred years; and there's no one to hinder us.' And then the Nonentity brings out the book of the big dead author, and claps his own little name on the title-page, cheek by jowl with the big name, and the public doesn't resent his impudence; no, the good, easy public buys the new edition; and the parasite comes in time to be recognized as a man of letters. Good business—living on dead authors! Well, we mean to make things lively for the Worms!" continued Mr. Quirk, with boisterous hilarity. "Since they are so determined on publicity, we mean to make them dance a little. Cuttle-fish— Worms — Posturers — Bardlets in search of a laureate-ship: we intend having a bit of amusement down our way! My lads are ready—" And so the Jabberwock held on; while Lady Adela paid him the tribute of a mute sympathy and reverence; when she had to pay a price, she paid it without stint.

A voice rose above the varied din—a girl's voice, rather hard and metallic, it is true, but clear and penetrating, and harmonizing admirably with the zither accompaniment. 'Von meinem Bergli muss i scheiden, was so liebli is und schön'—this was the old familiar strain; and Frank Gordon, who was sick-tired of journalistic chatter, and still more tired of hearing an exasperated unmarried female denounce the iniquities of husbands—young Gordon was glad to turn away and listen, entranced. Nay, as soon as the 'Abschied vom Dirndel' was finished, he left his place and made his way round to the small table at which the Schwarz-walder—three men and two girls—were seated; and there he made bold to take a vacant chair that happened to be next the young lady who had just been singing; and he was proceeding, with many apologies, to tell her how every one was grateful to her, when the damsel with the big, gentle eyes (he made sure her name was Anneli) interrupted him.

"Wie meinen Sie, mein Herr?" she said.

This was for a moment disconcerting; but he had some courage; and so with the best German he could muster he paid his compliments; and then he added—

"Sie kennen vielleicht irgend einige griechische Volkslieder?"

"Das glaube ich nicht," she answered, "will aber fragen."

And with that she addressed herself to the grave-eyed, black-bearded man at the end of the table, who, in turn, answered young Gordon direct and in English, explaining that they were very sorry they did not know any Greek folk-songs. But this inquiry had formed a sort of introduction; and next Gordon said, in a straightforward and friendly way:

"Well, I have heard the zither played many and many an evening, in the Black Forest and the Tyrol; but never, as far as I can remember, without there being something on the table. Would you mind—if I tried to rectify a little mistake that I see has been made?"

And thereupon he went off and got hold of a waiter; and in a few moments he had returned, the waiter bringing with him a couple of bottles of Zeltinger, some green glasses, and a basket filled with comfits and sweet biscuits. The wine was poured out; the cakes were handed to the timid-eyed Fräulein; while young Gordon coolly and calmly resumed his seat—for he had a frank and boyish way of making himself at

home that stood him in good stead among strangers.
And indeed he found the society of these honest
Schwarzwalder a good deal more congenial than that
he had recently quitted. They drank his health, in
a serious manner; he responded with the toast of
'Deutschland über Alles!' and the Fräulein laughed
as they sipped a little of the wine; then the leader of
the choir, glancing round the table, said in an undertone 'Compagneia,' and forthwith the glasses were
shoved aside, and each zither had resting on it ten
nerved finger-tips ready for the signal.

'Ich nehm' mein Gläschen in die Hand'

he rolled out in a strong bass voice; then his companions came in with their chorus

'Vive la Compagneia!'

—and whether the general Compagneia over there at the
long tables listened or did not listen was of little consequence to Frank Gordon. He had escaped from the palpitating Sappho; he had escaped from the blustering
wind-bag; he was among decent, kindly folk, who, in
the intervals of their professional duties, became more
and more friendly with the young Englishman who appeared to be well acquainted with their country and
its homely customs. And truly they gave him of their
best. It was for him they sang 'Mariandel ist so
schön, Mariandel ist so treu,' and 'Herzig's Schatzerl,
lass dich herzen,' and 'Im Aargau sind zwei Liebi,' and
'Von allen den Mädchen so blink und so blank'; and
then when the smoking began—for Lady Adela knew
the ways of many of her guests, and was an astute and
tolerant hostess—he had cigars brought for the beard-
ed members of this little company; and altogether he
and they got on very well.

And yet, notwithstanding the occasion and this good comradeship on which he had accidentally happened, he was heavy at heart. Some of these Volkslieder have a pathetic note, apt to awaken memories. And there was another folk-song, lying in his desk down in Jermyn Street, that would keep recurring to his mind, accusing and reproaching him. A dozen times he had taken out the sheet of MS. intending to write and say he had received it; and again and again he had shrank from employing the cold and distant terms which alone were permissible to him. And what would Briseis be thinking of him now? Perhaps her wounded pride had stepped in to protect her: probably she would not deign to waste another thought on one who had used her so discourteously.

By this time the large luncheon party had become in a measure nebulous—moving hither and thither and forming new groups; and the handsome young mistress of the feast could now pay a little more attention to her guests generally. Winning, gracious, and graceful, she went from one to the other, with an adroit word and a smile ever at her command; and if, during these random conversations, any reference was made to the forthcoming publication of *Faded Jonquils*, it was always with a modest deprecation on her part, as if her poor little book were not fit to be mentioned before all these wise and clever people. Amid this prevailing movement and clamor of talk it was easy for any one to slip away unobserved; and Frank Gordon —having ascertained that Miss Jean was returning to her dressmaker, and would rejoin him in Jermyn Street later on — said a word of apology and good-by to his hostess, and left.

When he reached his rooms he put his despatch-box on the table, and opened it, and drew in a chair. But

it was not factors' reports he was after.   He took out
the large sheet of paper on which were copied so carefully and accurately the words and accompaniment of
the Greek folk-song; and at these he sat staring absently, as he had done too often before.   The music,
it is true, was far too intricate and elaborate for him
even to guess at the sound of it; he was thinking
rather of the patient labor and the neat handwriting;
and of the desperate task that lay before himself.   And
yet he could not remain altogether silent.   Nay, might
not he be able to introduce into this note that had to be
written—that he must write now—something of a farewell character?   A formal and restrained farewell—
that was what was demanded of him: though again and
again his fingers had refused to pen the words.

It was just about this moment that there drew up
at the corner of Jermyn Street a four-wheeled cab,
from which a young woman descended.   Her tall and
elegant figure was dressed mostly in black; she was
veiled—though the texture of her veil was thin enough
to show that her complexion was somewhat colorless;
and she had a preoccupied and hurried air.   As soon
as she had arranged with the cabman about waiting for
her, she turned and went quickly along the pavement,
giving no need to anything around her, but glancing
up from time to time at the number of this or that
lodging-house or private hotel.   At last she arrived at
the one she sought.   The outer door was open; the
inner door, partially glazed, was about a yard or so
within the hall; and it was with hardly a second of
hesitation that she stepped into this shallow entrance,
and was about to ring the bell.

And then all of a sudden she withdrew her hand as
if the bell-knob had burnt her with fire; she stood
paralyzed with confusion and fear and shame; her face

was suffused with hot blood; her heart panting as if it would suffocate her. What was she here for?—she seemed to ask herself. Could this be the proud-spirited Briscis Valieri, come humbly and servilely to the door of a young man's dwelling, to beg for the re-establishment of her good name? Was this what she was here for?—to explain—to excuse—to vindicate? Her father —her mother—even the poor old man with whom she used to go wandering among the Scotch hills: what would they have said could they have foreseen? And then it swiftly occurred to her—might she not even now escape? Had no one observed her through those oblong panes of glass? The bell had certainly not been rung. And so, the next moment, she had vanished out of that entrance-way; and little did she know of what had befallen her until she found herself staring into the window of a perfumer's shop, her whole frame tingling and trembling.

She gradually recovered control over herself; her face resumed something of its natural hue; a passer-by would merely have thought that this tall and distinguished-looking young lady was regarding those hairbrushes and scent-bottles with an unusual fixity of attention. For indeed what she had now to consider was the alternative that lay before her—a return to the hopeless suspense and misery of these past days and nights. She had strung herself up so far; and this wild endeavor of hers, the product of despair almost, had within it some gleam of hope; and now to abandon it—to go away back to the long brooding hours of anguish—that seemed a kind of impossible thing. She could not go back. She must have some assurance. She must know what had occurred. It was not a mere vindication of herself that was driving her on: it was as though all the coming years of her young life were calling to her, making a more imperative demand. And so, looking neither to the right nor to the left, she returned hastily to the entrance, and rang the bell.

A manservant appeared.

"Is—Sir Francis Gordon—at home?" she managed to say.

"I think I heard him come in, ma'am," the man said; and he knocked at an adjacent door.

The next moment the door was opened; and Briseis found herself—she did not know how—advancing into a room the sole occupant of which, on seeing her, had instantly risen to his feet. And there she stood confronting him—unable to utter a word—dreading what she had done. It seemed at this crisis as if the proud heart must straightway break, in the depth of her humiliation. And yet she looked at him. Had he nothing to say to her? Would he understand that a girl was imperiously bound to clear her good name?

And as for him: well, this sudden and actual bodily presentment of her had at once swept away all the dreams, and musings, and tempered resolves of the preceding days; and a passionate longing arose in him to go forward to her, and place his hands on her shoulders, and say to her: "Briseis, let me guess why you have come here! Do not speak: it is for me to speak: and all that I have to tell you is, I love you!—I love you!—I love you!" Nay, the magnetism of her presence was overpowering; and her agitation— the appeal of her look—surely that was more than mortal man could withstand: why should he not take her to him, and kiss her hair, her cheeks, her lips, with "I love you! I love you!" told again and again to her upturned eyes. And he would say to her: "You are disturbed—you suffer: let me shield you, then; let us forget everything else in the world, and

14*

be a world to ourselves; let us go through life together—you and I, together !"   And then, under the
magic charm of youth and youth's response to persuasive caresses, there would come into her softened
eyes some sign of yielding, of wistful self-surrender—

But this wild impulse, that thrilled him to the very
soul, had to be sternly restrained; pale, resolute,
reserved, he stood before her, awaiting her commands;
whether she knew or not, there were chains of honor
binding him, as cruel as steel.

She found speech at last.

"You will forgive my—my coming here," she said,
in a low voice.   "I had not heard from you—"

"I was about to write to you," he said—and he
glanced towards the table: if her eyes followed in that
direction, they could not fail to see the sheet of MS.
music lying there.

"And—and I was alarmed," she continued, rather
brokenly.   "Because — because I have been threatened—"

"You—threatened ?" he repeated.   "By a man or
a woman ?"

"A man."

"That might be made awkward," he said slowly.

"I was alarmed because—because he threatened to
come to you, and show you some letters," she went
on ; and though outwardly she maintained her self-
control, there was a suggestion of tears in her voice.
"And when you did not write, I thought he had been
to you—I thought you had believed him—that you
suspected me—"

"Who is this man ?" he asked.

"Andreas Argyriades.   You saw him one morning
in Devonshire Place, just as you came up.   And he
has not been to you ?"

"Not at all."

"Nor written to you?"

"I have had no communication with him of any kind—I never heard of him before!" he exclaimed. "But whoever he is, do you imagine I would believe any story or report or rumor against you brought by an ill-wisher of that kind? I think the reception he would meet with would convince him of the extreme unwisdom of his attempt."

"Oh, yes—yes—I am certain of that," she said, in an almost incoherent fashion; and she seemed half-stupefied, and distraught, and unstrung. For these assurances of his, grateful as they might be to her ears, contained no explanation whatever of the graver mystery of his change of demeanor towards her. And how was she to ask for that? There was a limit even to her piteous abasement. "Only," she continued, in this nervous way—"only—I wished you to understand about Argyriades—I wished you to know—about Argyriades; and if he should write to you—or call upon you—"

"Then he shall have his answer," Gordon said, with firm lips. "And perhaps it will be an answer that he will remember throughout his life."

"And you will forgive—my coming here—and interrupting you. I know I should not have done so—but I was troubled—and you had not written—"

"I am exceedingly sorry I did not write before," he said. And in truth at this juncture he had need of all his self-command; for the sight of her distress and a certain touch of pathos in the tone of her voice were wellnigh overmastering him: it seemed so natural that, throwing all other considerations to the winds, he should go to her, and clasp her to the shelter of his arms, and soothe her shaken spirit with tender and com-

forting words.   But he held back : if there must needs
be an explanation, this was not the moment : her mere
presence here, in this room, was all too bewildering a
thing.

"Good-by, then," she said, and she extended her
hand.   "You will forgive me for troubling you — for
coming — but I was in great doubt and perplexity —
about Argyriades—"

He held her hand in his : so much he could not
deny himself.

"Do you remember Aunt Jean at Grantly ?" he said
to her, in a very gentle fashion.   "She is in London at
present ; and I expect her here every moment.   Won't
you stay and see her ?—she would be so glad."

"Oh, no, I cannot—I cannot," Briseis said, hurriedly.   "I must go."

But if it was her wish to get away unobserved from
this embarrassing situation she was foiled ; for just as
he was opening the door into the hall, there came a
ring at the outer bell.

"That must be Aunt Jean," he said.

CHAPTER XX

DER EWIGE GESANG

IT was a disconcerting and even a perilous moment for all three; a single false note of hesitation might have been disastrous; but the sagacity, the womanly instinct, and the native kindliness of Jean Gordon triumphed: in a second she was mistress of the situation.

"Dear me," she said to the girl, "to think that you are just the one person in the town of London I was most wishing to see—and you were going away! Na, na; you'll just come up to my own little parlor, and we'll have a chat together: why did not my nephew here tell you I was to be in directly? Come along now —dear me, to think I might have missed you!" And therewithal, in some mysterious manner, Briseis found herself conducted to a moderately small apartment on the next floor, which turned out to be Miss Jean's sitting-room.

But although she might be temporarily unnerved, Briseis Valieri was too proud to have anything to do with false pretences. She remained standing.

"I must tell you, Miss Gordon," she said, almost as a kind of challenge, "that I did not know you were in London."

"You did not? Well, well!" was the placid answer —though the shrewd gray eyes were attentive.

"I did not," Briseis went on, striving to be perfectly calm. "I came to see Sir Francis; and I expected

to find him alone. I came to learn from himself if he
had been told anything about me by—by a countryman
of mine. It was a wrong thing for me to do. I know
that. I know that perfectly well. But—but I was
desperate; and perhaps—perhaps, Miss Gordon—if you
heard the whole story, you would not think so badly of
me—"

Indeed there was no thought of evil in those kindly
and scrutinizing gray eyes; there was nothing but an
obviously affectionate interest; and it was in the gen-
tlest fashion that Miss Jean persuaded her unexpected visitor to remove her cloak and sit down. Then
came the inevitable suggestion about tea; but that Briseis put aside; she was too anxious to tell her tale, and
explain how she had been induced to place herself in
so ambiguous a position. And as that tale, rapid,
eager, and rather piteous, was being told, a somewhat
remarkable thing occurred. Aunt Jean had taken up
from the table a Japanese paper-knife, and at first she
had merely occupied herself in idly passing her fingers
over the metallic figures; but as the story of Argyriades
and his proceedings went on, she got hold of the instrument in both her hands, and she was unconsciously
bending it this way and that while she was earnestly
exhorting her companion to exercise an absolute self-
control.

"Yes, yes, my dear—there is no use in anger—you
must be cool and collected," she said, in little gasps of
sentences, while her double grip on the paper-cutter
did not cease. "And I may tell you you've come to
us just in time. That scoundrel was only beginning
to get a hold over ye. I can see his intention. I'm
older than you. It was not five pounds—or fifty—that
he wanted; he wanted to bleed ye like a leech, and to
terrify ye into going on your knees to your friends, for

"THERE WAS NO THOUGHT OF EVIL IN THOSE KINDLY AND SCRUTINIZING GRAY EYES"

more, and more, and more. Oh, the scoundrel !—yes, and he thought he could get money from Frank? Well, he'll get something from Frank. My word, he'll get something from Frank ! For ye've just come to us in time, my dear young lady, before he got complete hold over ye : oh, ye did right to come—I maintain ye did right to come : a young girl's good name is everything to her : it's her very life : and if she thinks she has been slandered, is she not likely to be driven desperate ? But then, you see, in such a predicament —face to face with such a treacherous scoundrel—one must take care to keep perfectly quiet and cool. Anger will not do. Indignation will not do. And some of us Gordons about Dee-side—I mean the menfolk of us—are said to be rather quick in the temper ; and it never serves to let temper loose. No, no. We must be quiet and cautious in dealing with a smooth-tongued miscreant like that. I confess," Aunt Jean continued —and the short sentences were becoming more and more vehement and envenomed—"if I were myself to see him—I might be tempted — to say a word: I suppose—I suppose—a smack across the face—from a woman's hand—would not hurt him— But no, no—as I tell ye, that would not do—we must give ye good advice—cool and calm advice—and ye see that, even in talking of the infernal rascal, I can keep quite easy and collected—"

The metal knife could no longer withstand this nervous bending; with a sudden snap it sprang in two ; and Jean Gordon looked helplessly at the fragments.

"Dear me," she said, "they're useless things : I forgot I had it in my hand"—and once more she endeavored to impress on Briseis the supreme importance of remaining scrupulously tranquil and calm-blooded, if Andreas Argyriades were to be encountered on equal terms.

For the last few moments Briseis had been plunged in profound abstraction.

" Miss Gordon," she said, at length, " it is very kind of you to think of trying to help me against that man ; but—but I would rather not trouble Sir Francis any further in the matter—"

" What ?" exclaimed her warm - hearted partisan, " are you going back into slavery ? Are ye deliberately laying up for yourself years of misery, until this blackguard finds there's nothing more to be squeezed out of either your friends or you ?—"

" Oh, no," Briseis said. " I am less afraid of him now. Sir Francis has assured me he will not believe one word Argyriades has to say, whether he calls or writes—"

" Bless me, Frank Gordon is not the whole world !" Miss Jean protested. " And a young lady cannot afford to have a number of her letters—well, I'll not use the word compromising—but private and confidential letters, I suppose—she cannot afford to have such things in the possession of a man who is determined to make an ill use of them."

" Compromising ?" Briseis repeated, with a rose-red flush appearing in her pale and exquisite complexion. " You must not say that, Miss Gordon. They could only be considered compromising by some one quite ignorant of the circumstances. Love-letters they are, that is true—silly and romantic love-letters ; but any one ought to be able to see that they are merely a heap of school-girl nonsense. A school-girl prank it was ; for we all pretended to be in love with George Lamprinos — he was the music - master ; and I wrote these letters for mischief mostly, confiding them in se-

crecy to my chief friend and companion, Irene Argyriades, on the understanding that she was to read them
and destroy them. Lamprinos never saw a single line
of any one of them—of course not!—he would have
laughed, and understood well enough: school-girls are
always playing such tricks. And then Irene, instead of
burning these scrawls, appears to have kept them; and
then her brother finds them, and thinks he can make
money—not so much out of them, perhaps, as out of
the other notes I wrote to him, demanding their return.
But I am less anxious now—"

"They must be got back," said Miss Jean, firmly.
"And it's Frank Gordon must get them back for
you."

"Oh, no, you must not ask him—please do not!"
said Briseis, hurriedly. "It is not necessary. I will
get them back myself—"

"You—to deal with a vagabond like that!" said
Aunt Jean, in kindly scorn. "It's somebody with a
stronger nerve than either you or I have must take up
this affair; and though my nephew Frankie is just as
easy-going and good-humored a lad as ever I met with
in all my life, still he's got a most merciless temper—
I will admit that—he's got a perfectly heathenish temper if there's been any wrong-doing or underhand dealing where those next him are concerned: I'm thinking
if your Greek gentleman knew who was after him, he
would be up and off and out o' this country in two
skips and a jump. So you'll just give me the man's
address, and I'll jot it down; and, my dear young lady,
you'll put all these fears and apprehensions out of your
mind—for well can I see what ye must have suffered."

Then Briseis rose to go, and as her last word she
said, rather wistfully—

"Then—Miss Gordon—you do not blame me—for

having come here alone—when I was in such great
trouble ?"

"Blame you ?" said Aunt Jean, and she took the
girl's hand in hers, and kissed her on the cheek as an
elder sister might have done. "I think I should find
it difficult to blame ye for anything ! But whatever
happens, if you should be in want of a friend, just you
come to Jean Gordon, and ye'll not find her to fail ye."
And again at the door below she reiterated these ex-
pressions of affectionate sympathy, in a way altogether
unusual with her, for most folks considered her rather
a cross-grained and sharp-tongued woman. Then
Briseis took her leave ; and after that Aunt Jean remained for a minute or two in the hall, considering,
before she would enter her nephew's room.

When at last she opened the door, she found Frank
Gordon pacing to and fro in great agitation; but at
sight of her he stopped short.

"Frank, lad," said she, in an unwontedly grave fashion, "what is all this ?"

"Oh, I don't know, Aunt Jean," he said. "I don't
know !"

He took another restless step or two up and down,
and again he confronted her.

"What do you think, Aunt Jean ? I want you to
tell me what I'm to do ! Things were bad enough before—when I thought I had only my own mischance to
face—but now—"

"Ay, and is that the way the land lies ?" she said,
regarding him curiously. "You as well ? Frank, lad,
you don't mean that ! Mercy me, what is going to
happen to us all ! But you don't mean that !—"

"Yes, yes ; and you've got to tell me what I am to
do, Aunt Jean — that is the first and foremost
thing—"

She paused for a moment or two, to collect herself. Then she said deliberately—

"Well, Frank, there's many would say I ought to have no skill of such matters. But I have seen something of the ways of young folk; and I have kept my eyes open; and what I am certain sure of is that that girl's coming here by herself to-day can mean but the one thing—that she is wildly in love with you. There's no other accounting for it: the fear of having been miscalled to you seems to have driven her fairly out of her mind. And even then I can hardly understand it —now that she's away—for when she's near you there's a kind of glamour about her, she's so bewitching with her beauty and her pleading eyes that you're ready to swear a white-winged angel is a poor kind of creature compared with her; but now—but now when one thinks of it—that she should have risked being suspected of making a confession—confessing the secret that a girl keeps deepest down in her own heart—that she should have run such a risk even remotely is hard to comprehend, unless she's been just driven frantic by that man. For of course she knows you're engaged to be married?"

"Oh, no, she doesn't," he replied, hastily. "At least, I suppose not—there was never a word said about it—"

Aunt Jean uttered a little half-stifled cry.

"Frank Gordon, what do ye tell me! what have you done? She does not know? The poor lass!—the poor lass!—now I can see why she came here this afternoon —she felt that it was the happiness or the misery of her life that had to be settled. And it's the misery, I suppose. I suppose it's the misery. What have you done, man!—what have you done! Why did you not tell her—long ago—"

"Why, how could I tell her, Aunt Jean!" he responded, almost angrily—for his conscience seemed wholly to acquit him. "Bethink yourself, Aunt Jean! How was I to imagine that it could concern her in the least? If I had dared to assume such a thing, then perhaps I might have told her. But such an assumption—the impertinence of it!—the insolence of it!—it never entered my head that it could matter a brass farthing to her whether I was engaged to be married or not. Only, when I found, of a sudden, that I had grown too fond of her, then I did what was left for me to do: I gave up going to the house; and I was trying to pave the way for our becoming absolute strangers to each other. It appeared to me that was all I could do; and I had hoped to dree my own wierd without any human creature being a bit the wiser. But as for explaining to her that I was engaged to be married: why, there were other girls in Mrs. Elliott's house besides Briseis Valieri: was I to go to each of them, or to all of them together, and say to them 'Look here, I consider myself such a transcendently fascinating person that I must warn you beforehand that I am not to be captured.' That would have been a modest precaution! ·Indeed there was no nonsense of the kind in the air. We were amusing ourselves—theatres, concerts, a bit of a dance now and again: who was to imagine that any tragedy was to spring out of it all?—"

He was silent for a space. His whole being seemed rent asunder with conflicting passions; on the one hand his heart kept whispering to him in secret and delirious exultation 'Rejoice!—rejoice!—the woman you love loves you: the crowning glory of life is yours'; while in response to that the calmer pulses of his brain would keep repeating the old, inexorable burden 'Renounce!—renounce!—to you also has come the common lot of mortal man — *Entbehren sollst du!*—

sollst entbehren!' And at last he threw himself into a chair, his clinched fists on his knees, his head somewhat bent forward, his eyes fixed on the floor.

"I suppose I've been to blame, Aunt Jean," he said. "Take it that way—and tell me what I am to do. I am ready to bear the penalty—if there's anything that can be undone, if there's anything that can be put right. What am I to do? Is there any atonement—any sacrifice—"

"Frank, laddie," said Aunt Jean, "you're not the first that has found his word given one way and his heart turned another; and ye need not seek for more sorrows than ye're likely to meet; for it's a sore strait to be in. And as for blaming you, that will I not. I'm beginning to suspect there's a simple enough explanation why you never told her of your engagement; and it's just this, that you were in love with her all the time, or drifting into being in love with her—unknown to yourself—and that's why ye could not bring yourself to tell her—"

At this he looked up quickly: Miss Jean's shrewd guess seemed to have struck home.

"Then it is all due to my blindness," he said, slowly, and as if to himself. "And there is no recalling—no reparation. . . . Aunt Jean, would you go to her, and speak to her? Will you tell her why I have recently kept away from the house—why I did not answer her letter? I know it is a great deal to ask; for it is a terrible business; but it is just maddening to think that she may consider herself slighted — imagine such a thing!—Briseis Valieri—slighted and left aside!"

"Yes, but that's what may be in her heart, and likely to remain there all the days of her life, unless you go to her yourself, Frank," said Aunt Jean, calmly.

"I? She would be insulted!"

"You must go," said Aunt Jean. "You cannot part with her forever—I suppose it is forever, according to the chances of the world—without a last word of good-by, surely. That would be strange conduct towards a girl that has been none too well treated—I don't mean by you, Frank—I don't mean by you—I mean almost ever since we got to know of her existence. And who would have thought it? Do you remember her that day at Grantly? She looked as if all the world around her were laughing in kindness towards her. She looked so young, and winning, and splendid; she seemed to shed a kind of delight whichever way she turned; and she was so willing to be pleased—so grateful—not presuming on her great beauty, as many a girl would. Who could have prophesied anything but the fairest of the earth for her. She seemed born to happy circumstances, and tender guidance, and loving-kindness from those around her—which she could well repay—which she could well repay, I will say that. And now—poor lass!—poor lass!—"

And at this point Aunt Jean rose, and turned away from him, and remained standing there for several seconds, with her handkerchief up to her eyes. It was a most unusual break-down for her, and she was ashamed. When she came back to her place, she spoke in a very different key.

"Frank Gordon," she said, "there's one thing you've got to do, to show the man that's in you. You've got to call that scoundrel to account."

"Oh, that's all right—that's nothing," he said, impatiently. At this moment he had no thought to waste on Andreas Argyriades. It was of Briseis he was thinking; and his heart was full of pity, and remorse, and an unspeakable longing and yearning and solicitude.

"But it's not nothing—it's something," said Miss Jean, hotly. "Perhaps ye do not understand under what terrorism that girl has been living of late?—perhaps ye do not think of what she must have suffered before she underwent the humiliation of coming here, to defend herself? Is that nothing? Is that to be passed over? Consider what she must have gone through before she brought herself to this door—before she rang the bell; and is there to be no punishment for the blackguard that brought her to such a pass? Is there to be nothing done? Ye're not going to leave it to me to take a horsewhip? Am I to find him out? Am I to lash him?—the scoundrel—the scoundrel!—"

"Aunt Jean," he said, in answer to her passionate invective, "that's all easy enough. If everything else were as easy! Thrashing Argyriades will not put matters straight."

"But thrashing Argyriades is the first thing that lies before ye," she persisted, in her indomitable way. "And I want to know how and when ye mean to set about it."

"There won't be any difficulty," he said. "Only I suppose I shall have to telegraph to Wentworth to send me up my thickest shooting-boots."

"Ay," said Miss Jean, eagerly, "and ye'll kick him across the street—and ye'll follow him—and kick him back across the street again—"

"I can try," her nephew said. "Unless he varies the performance by kicking me."

Aunt Jean pulled herself together.

"No, no—there must be no folly or rashness," she said, severely. "It's what I've just been maintaining —we must keep quiet and cool if we're to deal wi' this sleek-spoken rascal. It'll not do to land yourselves both in the police courts, and have names mentioned,

and a story for people to gabble about. Oh, he knew
well what he was after, that miscreant, when he laid
his plans. The letters he got—letters written by one
school-girl to another school-girl, for mere mischief's
sake—these were harmless enough, and useless enough
to him; but when he got other letters demanding them
back—and when she was foolish enough to send him £5
as a beginning—then he had a better hold. Frankie,
lad, it's for you to make him let go—but discreetly—
discreetly. If he's got his fingers on the gunwale of
the boat, chop them off, or give him a clout on the
head: only, there must not be a ripple on the water afterwards. No police proceedings. The public are quick
to believe the worst: how are they to know that these
letters were but a piece of mischief-making between
two school-girls—about a music-master—who never saw
a single line of them—"

She had gradually weaned him back from wider and
more distracting thoughts to this bit of business immediately on hand: he began to take an interest in it.

"What you say is quite right, Aunt Jean," he answered her, presently. "There must be no police proceedings. We must catch him some other way—and
give him a dose that will last him for the rest of his life.
Of course the animal was counting on impunity; they
all do that; they reckon that their victim will suffer
anything and sacrifice anything rather than face a
public scandal. It comes to this, Aunt Jean, that the
blackmailing of an innocent person is the one crime the
law cannot punish without hurting the innocent person more than the guilty one. Very well: when the
chance offers we must step in and assist the law with a
little private enterprise—"

"Ay, now ye're talking sense, Frankie, lad!" she
said, with obvious and extreme gratification. "And

what will ye do? Ye must serve him well! What are ye thinking of doing?"

"That must be a matter for careful and pious consideration, Aunt Jean," he answered her. "But as he appears to have been dealing in terrorism, I propose to give him a sample of his own wares—something just about sufficient to frighten the soul out of his body, as you might say. And in the mean time I will take a run up to Oxford, this afternoon or to-morrow morning: I know one or two of the lads there who would like to join in a little frolic. This is his address, is it? Soho, of course. I suppose he'll have a knife about him. However, we must try to keep out of the police courts—anything short of that."

Indeed for the time being he seemed to welcome this definite action demanded of him as a relief from the distressing perplexities that lay ahead; and while Miss Jean remained with him his brain was busy with projects by means of which he might outwit the wily Greek. But when she left (there had been a ring at the door, and she judged that certain of her purchases had arrived) he relapsed into contemplation of a future that appeared black and hopeless enough. His imagination was haunted by two figures: the one that of the proud - spirited Briseis, now wounded to the quick, and hiding herself away in her humiliation and shame; the other that of the light-hearted Georgie, soon to be coming gayly home, and little guessing that she would be received by an unwilling lover, who, to save his pledged word, must become a hypocrite husband. How, he asked himself again and again, had such a state of things arrived? Who was to blame? And what was to be done, by way of reparation or atonement, if any such thing were possible? Should he meet Georgie Lestrange with a frank explanation, and

15

beg of her to forego her claim ? Why, that were the very depth of meanness and disloyalty and cowardice ! Should he go to Briseis and say "I love you : you love me : let us break and cast aside all other bonds !" But was the proud Briseis likely to accept a dishonored and dishonoring passion ? Whichever way he turned, he saw no guidance or ray of hope ; and all the while his heart, in its wild desire and despair, was secretly urging him to let his honor go ? How many minutes would it take him to drive to Devonshire Place ? Would he find Briseis alone ? If he held her hands in his, and forced her to meet eyes with eyes, surely she would listen to the fervor of his appeal ! Love would as ever be supreme and triumphant—even at the cost of a broken troth ; and in the exultation and delirium of a new-found happiness, who was to remind them how it had been come by ? These were agonizing temptations : in mere self-defence—to gain some quiet for his overtortured spirit—he compelled himself to turn to Argyriades and the possible methods of overreaching him. This was an immediate duty— and so far right welcome.

And in the mean time Jean Gordon had gone up stairs to her own room, her alarm over these tragic happenings being almost lost in the unholy and vindictive joy of knowing that soon, and effectively, retribution was about to fall on the creature who had driven Briseis Valieri to desperation. As she opened these packages of finery, she was crooning to herself an aimless little song—a Dee-side song—that certainly had not much to do with the graver matters that had just come into her life :

O fair was the dawning and fair was the day
When I met with young Donald in Cambus o' May ;

He called me his dawtie, he called me his dear,
He asked if I'd marry, without any fear.

When the sugar was bought, and the tea, and the meal,
I should have gone home to Kincardine o' Neil ;
But Donald's old mother she asked me to stay,
And consent to a wedding in Cambus o' May.

Three pipers came down from Pannanich Wells ;
They fired off the cannon ; they rang all the bells ;
O the march to the church it was gallant and gay,
When us two were married in Cambus o' May.

And now I'm a widow, gray-haired and alone ;
And the folks in Glen Muick are hard as a stone ;
And I sit by the fire, and I think of the day
When young Donald met me in Cambus o' May.

It was a simple song, of simple people, living away by themselves in the remote Aberdeenshire valleys ; it had apparently but little connection with any plans and schemes of vengeance to be visited on a Greek blackmailer, here in this teeming town of London.

CHAPTER XXI

JUDGE AND JURY

OF a sudden a shaft of light shot through this impending gloom : it was a letter from Georgie, who wrote in the blithest of spirits, vaunting herself as a physician and healer of men, and forgetting all about her sham nostalgia in view of her approaching voyage home.

"The fact is, I had to jeer him into convalescence!" Miss Georgie proceeded. "My diagnosis of the case was that in the weakness following the fever he had allowed his nerves to multiply themselves upon themselves (if I knew Greek I would give you a name for this process that would convince you at once); he had even begun to think about dying ; and I had the greatest difficulty in persuading him that dying was the very stupidest thing that any one could do, and that thinking of it was next door to an invitation. The doctors had half-murdered him with drugs. Why *will* they go on like that ? They're awfully nice men ; and at dinner they can tell you most amusing stories when they choose ; instead of which they go about the country breaking the sixth commandment. I know I'm an awful fool (it's quite sweet to call yourself names, and to think that no one else dare) but I saw what was to be done with Percy ; I stopped those abominable fluids, and fed him on things that gave his rebellious gorge a little rest ; and I jibed at him and jeered at him ; and then he had to waken up to answer me according to my cheek. And now he vows and swears he will never let himself sink into that condition again ; so I am going home with a light heart. And it's *awfully* good of you, my gallant chieftain-boy, to offer to come over to New York ; but it isn't in the least necessary ; for I'm going back under the wing of quite a company of young folks that the de la Penas know, and what's more to the purpose I calculate that we're likely to have a ripping good time. The party is ultimately bound for Algiers and other Mediterranean places ; and consists of Miss Madeline Phayre and Miss Janie Phayre, sisters, Miss Romanes, Mr. S. F. Quentin, of Chicago, and Mr. Algeciras, of this neighborhood— along with a Madame St. Roche, who is to play duenna ; and as the two gentlemen are engaged respectively to the two sisters, I imagine that Miss Romanes and I may have *a little fun* during the voyage—never mind, all property kidnapped or stolen during the passage over to be honorably restored to the legal owner on the steamer's arrival at Liverpool. But you will be at Liverpool, I suppose ? And you won't scowl if they hint that we've been having games ? Because it's *so hideously* dull on board ship—unless there's a little quiet skylarking afoot."

And so she went on, in a tone and fashion that reassured him exceedingly. For he had been looking forward with an indefinable dread to that first meeting with Georgie Lestrange, whether it was to take place in Liverpool or New York ; he had begun to fear she might discover what had happened, and might scornfully reject the only atonement he could offer. But these gay, rambling pages once more brought the real and living Georgie before him, and seemed to say to him that he might lay aside his vague apprehensions. She was not likely to prove exacting as regards romantic sentiment. Exalted moods—the language of passion, simulated or true—would only make her laugh. How it was—he reminded himself, as he was walking quickly through the crowded thoroughfares of London, in the direction of Soho—how it was that an evening saunter into the solitude of a deer-forest should have suddenly melted Miss Georgie into tears and brought about a mute confession that had bound their two lives together, he had never been able quite to determine. Nor could he clearly understand why, ever since that engagement, he had found himself under the necessity of arguing with himself and proving to himself that he was the luckiest of men. However, these demonstrations and conclusions remained. They were as sound now as ever they were. And the merry, and mischievous, and happy-go-lucky young minx who had thus buoyantly written to him would not be too exigent in the matter of love-making; her audacious spirit would take little heed of trifles; and all would go well. Yes, all would go well—except in one direction: of which he dared hardly think.

When Frank Gordon reached his destination in Soho, and rang the bell, the evil-visaged harridan who answered the summons informed him, in reply to his question, where he would find Mr. Argyriades, but did not offer to accompany him; accordingly he ascended the dusky stairs alone, he knocked at a certain door, and then, hearing some unintelligible sound, he made bold to enter. The first object that met his eyes, in this squalid little room, was the figure of a young man in shirt sleeves and stockinged feet, who was seated on the edge of a bed, and who was engaged in carefully varnishing a pair of patent leather boots; the next thing he perceived was that this young man, looking up from his employment, suddenly grew livid—his pale and

unwholesome skin changing to the hue of one of the
lighter-colored jades. It was but a momentary exhibition of fear ; Argyriades made a desperate effort at re-
gaining his ordinary coolness and assured demeanor ;
and if that peculiar tinge still remained in his face, his
manner betrayed no immediate alarm.

And as for the tall, handsome, fresh - complexioned
lad who now stood at the door of this vile - smelling
den, he also had need of all his self-command. For it
would have been so easy to step forward, and seize this
coward creature by the neck, and shake him like a rat ;
and indeed, for one hot moment, the temptation—seeing the scoundrel face to face—and thinking of the
story that Briseis had told — was almost irresistible.
But Frank Gordon had vowed vows. He was going (the
guileless English youth !) to be as coldly diplomatic as
Miss Jean herself could have desired. He had come
to circumvent a blackmailer ; not to ply cudgels, and
have names mentioned in a police-court. Hands off
was his watch-word ; though the natural man within
him was tingling.

And so he said, with a careful politeness—

"Your name is Argyriades, I believe ?"

By this time Argyriades had put aside his boots and
the blacking-pot.

"Please," said he, in broken English, "the Lord
Fragkis—speak French."

This was a contingency that Gordon had not faced,
or he would have framed some judicious sentences beforehand ; so that he had now to blunder on as best
he might ; and at no time was his French too fluent.

"I understand," he said, "that you have some letters belonging to a lady—whose name need not be mentioned."

"Monsieur has been misinformed," was the instant

and suave rejoinder. "These letters are in the possession of my brother Demetri."

Again young Gordon was disconcerted—at the very outset. It seemed so much more simple (and desirable) to take this fellow by the scruff of the neck, and heave him about the room. But vows are vows.

"At all events you know where they are," he resumed, "and I take it you could get hold of them and hand them over, for a consideration : is not that so?"

The young man with the café-and-toothpick complexion shrugged his shoulders.

"It is possible," he said.

"How much of a consideration?"

"But Monsieur is a little too brusque. I have not undertaken to sell those letters—no; I come in as an intermediary, to establish amicable relations; I know the inexorable nature of my brother Demetri, and I wish to mitigate his demands. It is as a friend that I offer my services—"

"Oh, drop that—" And again Frank Gordon stuck fast. For the life of him he could not remember the French equivalent for 'rot,' if there is any French equivalent for that bit of English slang. At last he fell back on *bêtise*. "Oh, drop that stupidity!" he exclaimed. "I have heard all about your brother Demetri—and your admirable disinterestedness. It is a familiar farce, my friend; but we are not infants. What I want to know is this—Can you put your hands on those letters, and bring them to me, guaranteeing that not one is missing ; and if you can do that, when will you do it, and what will your price be? Of course you know that you have already put yourself in a very serious position—"

"I have guarded myself, Monsieur," the young man answered, with the faintest trace of a smile.

" If there were a prosecution—"

" There will be no prosecution."

" And so you think you are safe?" Gordon said, regarding him in an apparently dispassionate manner. You are of opinion you can do this sort of thing with impunity. You subject a perfectly innocent girl to a brutal terrorism; you extort money from her; you threaten, if she does not get you more, to compromise her in the eyes of her friends—"

" Your proofs of all this?" Argyriades said, quietly.

Another exasperating pause. It would have been so much easier to have settled this matter with fists! But still he sternly stuck to his diplomacy.

" Enough of words," he said. " Listen, if you please. I am going down to Henley this afternoon, and may be there some time. If you can get possession of those letters and bring them to me the day after to-morrow—take down the address—Red Lion Hotel, Henley on Thames — then I will give you a fair price for them. Do you understand?—Henley—Red Lion Hotel — you go from Paddington station — the Great Western—"

Argyriades reached over for his coat, took out from one of the pockets a soiled envelope, and, with a little assistance in the way of spelling, managed to jot down the address.

" And—and what may one expect, Monsieur, in recompense for these valuable papers?"

" I said a fair price," was the impassive reply.

" Monsieur is no doubt generous, as are all the English milords. Nevertheless, one would prefer to be a little more exact—"

" I said a fair price."

" Yes, perfectly—but still—"

15*

"Then perhaps you yourself would have the goodness to name a figure?"

Argyriades looked up quickly.

"Five hundred pounds."

There was neither protest nor scornful rejection.

"Five hundred pounds is a large sum," Gordon said, slowly.

"Perhaps — but look at the value of these papers, Monsieur!" Argyriades made answer, with unwonted eagerness. "Consider their value. Consider the harm they might do — if they were to fall into unfriendly hands. My word of honor, it is not too much to pay to shield a young lady's reputation! Consider the position in which she has placed herself—the testimony these letters bring against her—"

In an instant all the situation was changed. Gordon sprang to his feet and strode forward a step—his eyes burning and glaring.

"Another such word—you infamous cur—and I will choke the life out of your miserable body!"

"Monsieur!—Monsieur!" Argyriades exclaimed — and strangely enough he picked up his boots and hurriedly put them on. "If there is to be violence, I must go out and seek help. Of what use is force—is rage? You cannot compel me to give up the letters unless I wish. I appeal to the magistrate for protection—if you wish for an exposure, very well—"

By this time he had got on his coat too— But Gordon at once passed to the door, intercepting him.

"No, you don't leave this room until we come to some arrangement—of one kind or another—"

"Very well, Monsieur, very well," Argyriades replied in an injured tone. "I am indeed willing to come to an agreement—it is Monsieur who is so headstrong and liable to anger. And why? I have been doing my best for the young lady—I have done what I could to protect her—"

"You?" said Frank Gordon, with his eyes glaring again.

"From my brother Demetri—"

"Oh, to the devil with your brother Demetri ! Have done with that farce. I want to know if you can bring me those letters the day after to-morrow, at the address I have given you. Understand, I don't want the school-girl letters : you may keep those—and publish them if you like : I mean the letters written to you—including the one enclosing you money—"

"Monsieur, I will bring every one !" said Argyriades, with an expression of devout sincerity. "Solemnly, on my heart, I declare to you that I will bring every one. You, I know, will be a faithful guardian : in the interests of the young lady herself, to whom could I better entrust them ? Then my duty will be done—as mediator — as the protector against Demetri. Only, pardon me, Monsieur the Lord Fragkis — the sum was not precisely agreed upon—"

"I said a fair price," Gordon reiterated.

"Five hundred pounds, then !" Argyriades said, with an air of finally and satisfactorily closing the bargain ; and then, after a few more directions as to how he was to find his way, these two separated — for the time being.

A couple of days thereafter, and towards three o'clock in the afternoon, a smartly - dressed young gentleman might have been observed loitering about in front of the Red Lion Hotel, Henley. He was a lad of prepossessing appearance—well-featured, fair-skinned, light-haired, and blue-eyed ; and if his figure was somewhat short and slight, at least he had an upright carriage and set of the head : indeed, good looks were part of the boy's inheritance, for this was Lord Alec Ross, youngest son of the Duke of Kintyre, and the Kintyre family have been famous for generations for their handsome men and beautiful women. As he strolled up and down, he was idly gazing around him — though there was not much to see; for Henley in winter time is a dull and deserted place; and on this particular afternoon the cold and pallid sunshine could hardly muster up a gleam on the leaden surface of the river; an east wind had brought a faint mist to hang about the wooded heights; while the wide main street, the old stone bridge, and the banks showed hardly anywhere a sign of human life. It was mostly in the direction of the railway station, however, that the yellow-haired lad sent his occasional and expectant glances.

Presently, from that neighborhood, there hove into sight a young man who, judging by the way he examined the houses as he came along, appeared to be a stranger. In due course he found himself confronted by the sign of the Red Lion, and straightway he made for the door of the hotel. And by some kind of accident the ingenuous - eyed youth who had been loitering about drew near at the same moment.

"I beg your pardon, Monsieur," the latter said, in very excellent French, "but perhaps you have a desire to see Sir Francis Gordon?"

Argyriades did not answer at once. Whether he resented this intrusion, or whether he was disconcerted at being so readily recognized, could not well be gathered from his look.

"I have an appointment—at this hotel—"

"Certainly. Quite right. But Sir Francis wasn't exactly sure as to the moment you might arrive; and he is engrossingly busy in his house - boat — you comprehend ?—a house-boat—a house built on a boat—it's only a little way up the river; and he said he would be infinitely obliged to you if you would come along and see him there—"

"But, Monsieur," said Argyriades, rather drawing back, "it was at the hotel I had an appointment—"

"Oh, it's all right," said the young lad—and his clear blue eyes wore an expression of entirely super-human innocence, while his speech was offhand and matter-of-fact. "The house-boat is a favorite resort of Sir Francis's—for study, you understand—the Univer-sity of Oxford is just along this highway here; and then it is convenient sometimes to get away from one's companions, you doubtless agree with me. And now have the goodness to accompany me, Monsieur; we will drop into a boat; and I will pull you up to the isl-and—a few minutes only—I will myself take you to Sir Francis—"

After a second of hesitation Argyriades appeared to overcome his reluctance—or annoyance. He said—

"Thanks, Monsieur, if you will be so kind"—and therewith he allowed himself to be conducted along to the landing-stage, and under direction he got into the stern of a dingy old skiff, while Lord Alec took the oars and proceeded to pull up stream.

And now the Oxford lad, seated opposite his com-panion, had an excellent opportunity of scanning his appearance; the result of the scrutiny being an inward ejaculation—'I wonder what the Duke would say if he saw me taking this dilapidated dandy out for a row on the Thames!' But the remarks that he addressed to Argyriades himself were of a different character.

"I understand that you come from Greece, Mon-sieur," he observed, with airy good-nature. "It is a land which has given the youth of this country a great deal of trouble, particularly in their earlier years; but

they don't bear any malice—not at all! Have you any
house-boats on the Eurotas? No?—you surprise me!
Any pike-fishing—on the Alpheus, for example? The
tastes of Monsieur do not lie in that direction, perhaps.
But at least you have bobbed for gold-fish in the Fountain of Arethusa, in among the reeds, you know?—
pardon me, I forgot; that is in Sicily. There must be
other amusements, however. Have you any foot-ball
in Athens?—"

"Balloons, Monsieur?" repeated Argyriades—but
suspiciously, for the lad's girlish blue eyes were almost
too artless.

"No, no—foot-ball—the game. The ball is a ball of
leather, not of great value; but two sides fight for it,
furiously; and then when the fight is over anybody may
have the ball. Ah, you have not seen it?—how unfortunate! But at all events you have cricket—the
game of cricket—no doubt you could find an excellent
pitch on the Plain of Marathon—"

"Ah, Monsieur!—see!—see!—" cried Argyriades,
in greatest alarm, for apparently the bow of the skiff
was about to crash into the side of a house-boat that
was lying alongside a small and willowy island in midstream. But Alec Ross knew what he was about:
with a glance over his shoulder he dug his left oar into
the water, shipped his right at the same moment, and
the skiff glided quietly under the gunwale of the house-
boat, and came to rest. The countenance of the Greek
resumed its wonted composure.

It was a strange place for a rendezvous—this forlorn
and dismantled house-boat lying in among the pollard
trunks and withered herbage of the solitary island;
but Lord Alec did not give his companion much time
for observation; he hitched the painter of the skiff to
the gunwale of the boat, got on board, and invited Ar-

gyriades to follow. The Greek, whatever he may have thought, obeyed in silence; his eyes were on the alert, however; and when young Ross, descending a couple of steps into a sort of shallow cockpit, opened a door in front of him and politely asked his guest to enter, the latter paused. And yet there was no sign of any ambush or beguiling; indeed there was no indication of life anywhere; a profound silence reigned; and he himself had noticed, on drawing near this isolated house-boat, that not a curl of smoke issued from its stove-pipe, though the day was cheerless enough and cold.

"I beg you to proceed, Monsieur," said young Ross. "It is somewhat dark—but if you step forward—and push aside the curtain—"

Almost at the same moment the curtain was drawn aside, from within; and there broke upon the Greek's senses a scene well calculated to shake even the firmest nerves. For before him there was a long and barely-furnished apartment, all the windows of which were closed and shuttered; three lamps, suspended from the roof, shed a yellow light; at the head of the table sate a figure wearing a black mask; on each side of the table were two others, similarly disguised; a sixth stood sentry by the arras; while on the board before the conspirators lay a couple of fencing foils with the buttons off, and a pair of old-fashioned cavalry pistols of formidable aspect. Perhaps Argyriades did not grasp all these details in this one wild second; but at least he perceived that he had been trapped; and instantly he turned to escape—only to find that the yellow-haired youth had shut the door behind him and locked it on the outside. He tugged and struggled desperately—and in vain: then a hand was laid on his shoulder.

"It is useless," said the masked figure who had been standing by the curtain—which had now been drawn wholly aside.

For a moment Argyriades attempted bravado. He confronted this black-visaged company.

"What is the meaning—of this outrage?" he demanded. "I will appeal to the magistrate—" But here he happened to catch sight of the weapons displayed on the table; and his courage seemed to fall away. "Gentlemen," said he, pitifully, "what is your intention? What do you wish with me? What have I done?"

The person at the head of the board rose in a slow and deliberate manner, and remained standing.

"Attend, sir, and listen to what I have to say," he began; and if his French pronunciation may have left something to be desired, at least he spoke methodically, so that there should be no mistake about his meaning. "Andreas Argyriades," he continued, "we have been informed, and we have reason to believe, that you have been guilty of attempting to extort money by threats, and also of harassing and persecuting a countrywoman of your own, who ought rather to have had a claim on your sympathy. The crime of black-mailing is punishable by English law; but unfortunately, in the case of such offences, justice is done at the expense of the innocent as well as the guilty. You therefore thought you could act with impunity. You erred. We here assembled mean to assist the law, without that publicity which you reckoned to be your safeguard. And yet we do not intend to take advantage of our numbers. You are completely at our mercy, as you must perceive; but you shall have a fair field and no favor; you shall have your choice not only of these weapons but of your antagonist; we only demand that you make reparation for the evil you have done, and the worse evil that you contemplated—"

The pale face of Argyriades had grown ghastly.

"Gentlemen—sir—I beseech you !" he managed to articulate ; and in the extremity of his dismay he appeared to shrink back from those hideous objects lying before him. "It will be murder ! I know nothing of these weapons—no—I tell you it will be murder ! Gentlemen, I beg of you !—listen to me !—I have an explanation. Gentlemen, I am a friend of the young lady —an old friend of hers—my sister and she were schoolfellows. Gentlemen, one of you must be the Lord Fragkis Gordon ; he will assure you that I have declared myself her friend, her devoted friend. And now, gentlemen, this is the truth : it was my brother who found these letters ; and when I discovered the evil use he wished to make of them, I determined to save the young lady. Gentlemen, it is the truth—on my honor —on the honor of my mother, it is the truth ! I determined to save her. I came all the way from England to protect her—for I knew that if my brother showed these letters to any one, then her reputation would be blasted forever—"

But at this one of those present—the one nearest Argyriades—sprang to his feet, and tore off his mask, and flung it on the table.

"You damned liar and coward !" said Gordon, with his eyes blazing ; and with the back of his hand he smote the Greek across the mouth. "Will that make you fight, then ? I knew you wouldn't face these weapons—they were only put there to scare you—you miserable cur ! Here, you fellows," (this in English) "haul his coat off for him—hold him up—haul the beast on to his legs—and I'll give him the wholesomest thrashing he ever had in his born days !"

For by this time Argyriades, beside himself with terror, had literally sunk upon his knees, and with trembling hands he was opening a packet of papers that he had pulled from his pocket.

"See, gentlemen!—see, Lord Fragkis!—I give them to you—every one—and I do not ask for a centime! What more, gentlemen? I give you them—every one —and not a centime—only let me go! Gentlemen, have mercy!—have pity!—and I swear solemnly I will not say a word of this that you have done—"

"Haul the beast on to his legs!" Gordon cried again, furiously.

But the leader of the band came along.

"I say, Gordon," he muttered in English, "you can't fight that fellow—I wouldn't soil my boots with kicking him. See if the papers are all right; and then we'll pitch him into the river, or fling him ashore somehow. Good Lord, I've often heard of blue funk, but never saw green funk before!—look at him!—green, by Jingo, green!"

Whereupon Gordon got hold of the bundle of letters; and it was those addressed to Argyriades himself that he was most particular about; so far as he could judge by what Briseis had told him, the collection was complete. And then there only remained to bundle this abject wretch out of the boat and into the skiff: he appeared hardly to know what he was doing—fear had paralyzed his brain.

"I hope, Monsieur," said Lord Alec Ross, as he put the oars in the rowlocks, "that your interview with Sir Francis Gordon proved satisfactory. And may one ask where you would like to be landed?"

"To the shore—to the shore—anywhere," gasped this green-faced creature, whose horror-stricken eyes seemed to be thinking back.

"Because I don't propose to take you down to Henley, for reasons that I have," continued Lord Alec. "I would rather, if you don't object, land you on that other bank there ; and—and—well, if you strike across country, you'll come to a railway-station in time, you know—"

"Anywhere—anywhere that you please," was the almost inarticulate response.

"You are extremely obliging," said Lord Alec ; and in requital of this courtesy he took some trouble in choosing a convenient landing-place, so that Argyriades should get ashore without difficulty. The Greek did not look behind him as he left.

A short time thereafter a party of seven young gentlemen had assembled in a private room in the Red Lion. A brake was at the door below, waiting to convey six of them to Oxford ; but in the meantime they were refreshing themselves with five o'clock tea— which consisted of brandy and soda and cigarettes ; and there was a great deal of talking and laughing. In the midst of the hubbub one of them happened to glance at an early edition of a London evening paper that the waiter had just brought in.

"Hallo, Gordon," he cried, "what the dickens is this ? Doesn't this concern you?"

He handed over the pink sheet ; and the first headline that caught Frank Gordon's eye was sufficiently startling—'Attempted Assassination of the Prince of Monteveltro.'

CHAPTER XXII

'LOVED I NOT HONOR MORE'

REUTER'S telegram briefly narrated how the Prince of Monteveltro, walking home on the previous evening from the Club at Sofia to his hotel, in company with the British Diplomatic Agent, had been shot at by some one unknown, but had fortunately escaped, the bullet just grazing his ear. It was a clear moonlight night; and the British Agent, having ascertained that his friend was but slightly wounded, had started off in pursuit of the assailant, who, however, could not be found, though one or two bystanders aided in the search. It was impossible to say whether the outrage was of political origin; but it was well known in Sofia that the Prince of Monteveltro had been on intimate terms with the late M. Stambuloff. So far Reuter; and the telegram from the Princess which Frank Gordon found awaiting him on his return to his rooms was even more laconic—'No cause for alarm'; but the letter which in due course followed gave him more ample information.

"It was really most provoking," the Princess wrote. "You can't imagine how vexed and irritated he has been by this trifling affair. Not that he was or is frightened—not in the least. I don't believe a Montenegrin is capable of the sensation of fear—unless when he sees somebody about to open a soda-water bottle. But the Prince is *annoyed* and *indignant* beyond measure ; it is just as if a small boy had hit him with a pebble—a small boy out of the range of his whip ; and this bit of plaster on his ear keeps him in a constant state of fret. Why did we come to Sofia? Why were we in Bulgaria at all? Why couldn't we let other people's affairs alone? Not only that, but because his ear tickles him he has been threatening to abdicate — in favor of his brother George! Think of it!—abdication! —*just now!*—JUST NOW!—when the Great Partitioning is clearly on the horizon. Of course Prince George is a very worthy man ; he makes an efficient Commander of the Body-guard ; and he is a good soldier and drill-inspector ; but if he were to come well out of the general scrimmage, his very highest ambition would be to get our frontier extended across to Obribazar. Abdication! — just because somebody or something gave him a little clip on the ear ; and we are to give up the Great Game that is being played out here just now ; and we are to go and rent a place in the Highlands— some place like Glen Skean, I suppose, where Heaven is to be represented by a perpetual stalking of stags. I won't deny that this attempt on his life may have arisen out of political feeling ; for the last time we were in Sofia he made far too open a parade of his acquaintanceship with Stambuloff—playing baccarat every other night with him at the Club, and so on ; and all because Stambuloff professed to be interested in the antics of Wienerschnitzel and Gurkensalat. A most imprudent parade ; as I warned him at the time ; and it is quite possible that some of the fanatic friends of Panitza's may have him down on their list ; but to talk of abdication because a bit of sticking - plaster worries the lobe of your ear is really too absurd!

"Besides, even supposing that some crazy lunatic or association of lunatics cherishes a design against the

Prince, that can only be through a mistake, and the
mistake will be set right directly, when the Prince's
true position and probable sympathies will be declared
to all Europe.   For what do you think is going to happen ? You need not proclaim it in the market-place—
not at least until the news has got into the St. Peters-
burg papers — but I learn on very excellent authority
that the Czar is about to present to his faithful ally,
the Prince of Monteveltro, a cargo of munitions of war
—hill-guns, rifles, cartridges, dynamite, etc., etc.; and
if this significant gift does not keep those Bulgarian
Russomaniacs quiet, what can ? Instead of taking a
chance shot at him from behind a ruined wall, they
will be more likely to invite him to become a candidate
for the throne of the Principality, in the almost certain
event of the porridge-pot boiling over one of these
days.   And to think of going off in a huff to the Highlands of Scotland ! Yet S. A. is a self-willed man,
just once in a while : from January to December as
easy-going a person as ever you met ; and then on some
29th of February he puts his foot down—and *le Prince
le veult*, with a vengeance ! And what, then, if we were
to bid a long farewell to all our greatness, and end by
settling down somewhere about the Grampians, becoming your neighbors as soon as you have married your
ruddy-haired enchantress ? I suppose S. A. imagines
that deer-stalking and salmon-fishing last all the year
round ; and that he'll always have the Bourne girls to
play Beethoven for him ; and Lady Rockminster and
Lady Adela to dance Scotch reels in the evening when
the men come down from the moor. But no—but no !
He is peevish and out of temper just now, merely because a wasp has stung him ; and we will not allow
him to give up the Great Game because of so trifling a
circumstance. And I know him. I know when the

first bugle sounds—and sound it will ere long—the old
war-horse will answer with his neigh.   And it is *not*
Prince George who will be consulted about the rectifi-
cation of frontier-lines."

Frank Gordon had made the waiting for this letter
an excuse for delaying his visit to Briseis — that visit
of explanation and farewell that he looked forward to
with an immeasurable dread and pain.   He had persuaded himself that he must have full details of the
attempted assassination ; at any moment he might be
summoned away to the East ; he must remain at his
mother's beck and call.   But now that he knew all
there was to be known, he could no longer shelter
himself behind these pretexts.   He had to undertake
this terribly delicate mission, come what might, though
the suffering it would cause he would have heeded less
if he could have borne it alone ; it was his thought of
Briseis that was the origin of this almost insurmount-
able shrinking and reluctance.   If Aunt Jean had but
consented to act as intermediary !   And then again he
argued with himself that Aunt Jean had been of true
judgment in this matter ; it was the more manly thing
for him to go straight to the girl herself ; and if she
treated him with proud anger and disdain—if she
was pitiless — well, that she had a perfect right to
do and to be ; and he would carry his punishment
with him through many and many long years of remembering.

He was a very unhappy lad as he walked up to Devonshire Place ; but he experienced some relief on
finding that Briseis was not in the drawing-room when
he was shown in.   Mrs. Elliott was, however ; and she
rose with effusion—and with some touch of color in
the tired and pathetic face—to welcome her visitor.

" My dear Sir Francis, I was beginning to think we

should never see you again—and then that dreadful
affair out there in the East—you cannot tell how upset
we all were by the news, and how we have been sym-
pathizing with the poor Princess. My bonny darlings
were out at afternoon tea when the evening paper was
brought in—they are such tender-hearted, unselfish,
generous things, and so anxious to help in the chari-
ties that dear Lady Hammersley has under her charge
—and I assure you there was quite a scene when the
announcement was read aloud about the attempted
murder : they are so extremely sensitive and sympathetic—their concern about the poor Princess was
quite affecting, so I am told. The poor dears had to
come home in a cab—though they know well that I
expect them to practise the strictest economy ; and
Brenda especially—she is of such a nervously suscepti-
ble nature—she was quite overcome, and lay down on
a sofa, and we had to administer port-wine again and
again before we could get her calmed and soothed. And
what are your last tidings of the dear Princess, Sir
Francis ? I suppose she is completely overwhelmed—
such a narrow escape !—such an awful calamity just
averted by the finger of Providence—I hope she is
bearing up well—"

"Oh, yes, pretty well," the young man replied.
"Indeed she seems to look upon the whole affair as
rather a humorous incident. You see, it wasn't her
ear that had a bit taken out of it."

"And the poor Prince—I do hope he has quite recovered from the shock !"

"I don't know about the shock," he said, "but I
do know he is extremely annoyed and angry. And it
is no great wonder. He doesn't want to be dragged
into all these political imbroglios. He wants to be let
alone. He is not a quarrelsome man at all; he likes

to amuse himself with his two black poodles; and naturally he resents being flicked on the ear in consequence of other people's disputes. The sooner he gets back to the mountainous security of Monteveltro the better."

He had been talking almost at random — with an ever-present consciousness that at any moment the door of this room might open. And if these polite questions and perfunctory answers formed a sort of respite for the time being, he knew that it could not avail for long; nay, he at length grew impatient and desperate; he was forced to interrupt this idle conversation.

"Mrs. Elliott," said he, "may I ask if Miss Valieri is at home?"

"Oh, yes," replied the widow, blithely. "Oh yes. She was so very good-natured as to insist on remaining behind, when all the others were going off to Madame Reichenwald's concert; for her cousin, poor boy, is in bed with a bad cold, and he won't have any one but her to read to him; and she is the dearest creature—so ready to sacrifice any little pleasure of her own—and so cheerful about it, too—"

"For to tell you the truth I called to see her," he said, bluntly enough; and then he continued, in a more hesitating manner: "The fact is, I was entrusted with a small commission—perhaps I ought to say I undertook it on my own responsibility; and if you don't mind, Mrs. Elliott—if it is not an inconvenience to you—I should like to see her for a few moments—by herself, I mean—"

Aunt Clara rose with much good nature.

"I will send her to you at once. But," she added, as she was leaving, "I must see you before you go, Sir Francis. My darling girls would never forgive me if

16

there were not some proper message of sympathy sent
to the poor dear Princess.   So *au revoir !*"

For two or three minutes he was left alone in this
silent room, in no enviable state of mind.   And then the
door opened; and here was Briseis—somewhat pale, perhaps, but as beautiful as ever, so overmasteringly beautiful, indeed, that of a sudden his heart cried aloud to
him 'To me—to me—to me! Take her—enfold her—
that is the one woman in all the world!' But the next
moment that passionate cry was stilled.   He became
conscious that the Briseis standing there and confronting him was not the Briseis with whom he had so recently parted — all unstrung and unnerved, piteous,
half-humiliated, appealing.   This Briseis was cold, distant, and of a perfect self-command ; the calm, straightforward regard she fixed on him was not questioning—
nor yet repellent—but only attentive, in a proud kind
of way ; sweet and serene as she looked—as she could
not help looking—she appeared to have become in some
strange fashion remote.   And a singular thing was that
she had not advanced to greet him in the usual manner ; perhaps neither he nor she noticed the omission ;
it was hardly a time for formalities.   But this outward
impassivity of hers chilled and disconcerted him ; this
was not Briseis at all ; this was a beautiful stranger,
distinguished-looking, noble-looking, courteous, com-
plaisant—and ten thousand miles away.

There was no awkward pause of silence ; for he had
a message to deliver.

"I have brought you the letters Argyriades got possession of," said he, "and I do not think he will trouble
you any more."

He took out the packet and placed it on the table.
She betrayed neither surprise, nor joy, nor gratitude ;
but she came forward a step or two.

"Won't you be seated?" she said. "I wish you to read those letters."

He had not expected any such proposal; he looked disappointed and pained.

"Oh, no—no," he said, rather stiffly.

"But I wish it," she rejoined.

"Then I refuse," he said—his forehead flushing.

"I have been told that these letters would compromise my good name if they were shown to any one," she proceeded, in a deliberate manner, "and I wish to know if that is true."

"And by whom were you told!" he answered her, with scorn. "By a miserable wretch trying to extort money, and ready for any amount of brazen lying. Well, he is not likely to repeat that performance—at least where you are concerned."

Then in somewhat set terms she thanked him for having secured and restored these papers; and she even went the length of asking, in a more or less direct way, whether he had paid anything, and how much, to Argyriades. And Frank Gordon could only say to himself, bitterly enough, that if she chose to shame and insult him, she was within her right in doing so.

"What did I give him?" he said. "I gave him a stroke across the mouth; and he took it submissively. That was all he got; but it appeared to satisfy him; I don't think he will deal in threats and menaces for some time to come. And perhaps I ought to tell you that I did look at some of the letters—those that you wrote to Argyriades—I wanted to see if he had brought all of them back—according to what you told me; and I think you will find they are all there."

"Yes; but there are others: I wish you to read them," she said, coldly.

"Why should you persist in taunting me?" he answered her, in accents of reproach.

"Taunting you?"

"Yes, indeed. You are telling me that I need to be convinced of this or that, with regard to you! And that is what you think of me! Well, the poorest opinion you can have of me is better than I deserve, I know that. I know that—"

All this time he had hardly dared to meet her eyes, so banished from her had he been by the studious dignity and courtesy of her demeanor; and the wild desire there was within him to beg for forgiveness—to beg for friendliness—for anything that would restore something like their former relationship could find no words whatever. His heart was passionately urging him to speak; and yet a kind of hopelessness had overcome him; her manner—her tones—even the poise of her head, that in other days he had so much admired— seemed all too plainly to say to him: 'You—you are but as one of the other strangers whom I find surrounding me. You will judge as they will judge. If, then, you have heard anything against my good name, read these letters for yourself; and when you have been convinced, go. Having cleared myself, I have no wish to continue any further association; and you may return and take your place amongst the crowd.'

"Well, yes," he resumed, after a moment, "the poorest opinion you can form of me is no doubt the just one; and if you think that I could be influenced by anything that such a fellow as Argyriades might say— or if you think that I should want to read anything in order to have my faith in you confirmed or re-established —let it be so. Let it be so. But there are one or two points that I should wish to explain, before saying good-by—"

"Yes, before saying good-by," she repeated—almost relentlessly, as it appeared to his wrought-up imagination ; and the pallor in the perfect and exquisite face, that, too, seemed to speak unmistakably of a final farewell.

"I gathered, partly from yourself, partly from what Aunt Jean told me, that you had been disturbed—surprised, perhaps I should say — by one or two small things : my remaining away from this house, my not answering your letter for some days, and the like. Well, when you came to me, fancying that perhaps Argyriades had been the cause of this conduct on my part, I told you he had nothing whatever to do with it. But I did not give you the true explanation. And as it is to be good-by, I should not like you to look back and believe that I had been guilty of any intentional discourtesy—"

Then he lost his head somewhat.

"Briseis, do you not know—can you not guess—what forced me to give up a friendship that seemed so beautiful a thing, and so harmless to every one concerned ? Do you remember our first meeting—that morning on Dee-side—when you came down alone to the river ?—do you remember how easily and simply we got talking together ?—it appeared to be so natural that we should know each other. I was free then ; my life was not pledged away to any one ; and indeed I was not thinking of such things—though Aunt Jean would have it, when she saw you, that here was my great chance, for she took to you from the very first, and would tell you now that she has never seen any one like you. But I could not be so presumptuous ; and besides, you and I were no more than merely acquainted, even after you had been out to Grantly ; and then I went away to the South—and—and other things happened—and my life was no longer my own. But all the same, when I heard you were in London, I wanted to see you; and the oftener we met the further did our slight acquaintance-ship grow into a friendship that was about my most valued possession. I saw no harm in it; for I was blind; and the passing hour was too delightful to be sacrificed. But during all this time I was getting to understand you better and better: you were not merely the beautiful stranger I had met on Dee - side — nor yet the charming visitor who had brought a kind of splendor with her into the dusky old rooms at Grantly; you had become—well, you had become the Briseis that I know now—the Briseis that I shall hold in my heart while I have life."

He ceased for the moment; and his brows were knit together, as if from some mental pain.

"I did not consider; I was too confident and care-less," he went on. "If I had dreamed of any danger, I should have looked upon my being engaged to marry another woman as a sufficient safeguard. But I did not think; and one fascinating hour followed another; and always I was getting more and more into communion with the winning subtleties of a nature the sweetest and purest that I have known on earth. Oh, do not im-agine I seek to excuse myself. All the blame is mine. And there was self-deception too. I deceived myself— I refused to look at consequences—so long as there was another chance of listening to the rustle of your dress on the stair, of seeing you come into the room, of sub-mitting once more to the glamour of your voice and your eyes. And then there came the awakening. It was at a dance—here in this house—you wore yellow roses with your black dress, do you remember?—and that was the night I made the discovery, that I loved one woman while my honor bound me to another. It was a terrible discovery; but at least I could hope that the punishment for any mischief that had been done would fall on my head alone; and I resolved to withdraw myself—not perhaps all at once, but so that no one should guess what had occurred. Briseis, think as badly of me as you will; I deserve the worst; but—but don't imagine I meant any slight—"

While he was pouring forth these pathetic, blundering, boyish utterances, the face of Briseis had undergone the strangest transformation. Her cold impassivity of look had changed into an eager interest and wonder; and wonder had given place to joy; and joy had found its expression in an ineffable happiness; though, to be sure, before he had come to the end of his story, her eyes—the soft, dark, eloquent eyes—had their conquering beauty all bedimmed with tears. She went quickly towards him. She held out her hand.

"My friend, for ever!" she said—and her grasp was as firm as his own.

The grandeur of her magnanimity—and her unconsciousness of it—amazed him : this was not the disdainful dismissal that he had expected, and that he felt he had earned. Her wet eyes were affectionate and kind; she held his hand for a second or two; and then she strove to put into words some explanation of this sudden change in her attitude towards him.

"Ah, you do not understand, then—you do not understand that the treasure of a woman, all through her life, is the remembrance that the one man she has loved has loved her—yes, for a moment. She may not have what is thought to be happiness; she may not marry the man she loves; but that secret she carries with her, to her dying day—and it is her treasure and her pride. No, no," she continued, with a sort of wistful smile— and her speech was broken and uncertain, almost to incoherence, "you cannot understand—and I cannot explain. But—but you have given me my treasure to keep—and I am more grateful than I can say: what it would have been if we had parted for ever and no word of revelation! I am content. Dear friend, do not think I am envious of any one! If—if circumstances seem hard, then it is some other one who is the happier.... I wish her well.... In time your love will go to her—it is the way of the world—it is right to be so. And you will forget—the Greek girl—to whom you were kind....Good-by, dear friend—good-by — God bless you and her—"

He caught her in his arms, for he thought she would have fallen.

"Briseis — it is not good-by!" he said to her, in a low voice—in a voice so intense that her eyes shrank away from him. "It shall not be good-by! I love you—you love me: is not that enough? It is the highest law—"

She freed herself from his embrace.

"Except honor," she said, with so much of her usual sweet serenity that he stood rebuked and abashed, ashamed of his momentary madness, and despairing of the fetters that bound him. As for her, she was clearly struggling to recall her proud self-command, that had nearly broken down; and yet, as she gave him her hand for the last time, there was the greatest tenderness in her regard; and she suffered him to kiss her on the forehead, in mute token of farewell. Then she went from the room; she had borne herself bravely; whatever of anguish and tragic renunciation may have been in her heart was not for him to see.

And indeed all that afternoon, while she was engaged in her ordinary domestic duties, and in her customary intercourse with Olga and Brenda, with Miss Ada and

"HER COLD IMPASSIVITY OF LOOK HAD CHANGED"

Miss Carlotta and the rest, she was in no wise cast down; for there still remained some afterglow of the gladness with which she had heard the man she loved confess that he loved her, and perhaps also some lingering trace of that exaltation of feeling with which she had bade him go to redeem his pledged faith. But in the solitude of her own room at night, this high courage fell away from her. The dark was filled with pictures — a succession of scenes; and it seemed to her that her life had been but a series of bereavements; and this last not the least cruel of these. For now she was altogether alone. One after another had departed from her; and now he who in happier circumstances — such as fell to the lot of other women — might have been her lover, he also was taken from her, through the merciless decrees of fate. And what remained? She contemplated the long years before her with a shuddering dread; she would rather have the end, and that soon. In those black hours of the night — her strength all gone — her pillow wet with tears — she went wearily back, as aforetime, to seek for solace and soothing in the old, familiar lines —

> *Over all the mountains*
> *Is peace ;*
> *Along the far summits*
> *Hearest thou*
> *Hardly a breath ;*
> *The birds are hushed in the forest.*
> *Wait thou only, and soon*
> *Thou also shalt sleep.*

But it was a wider sleep that her aching heart yearned and prayed and sobbed for: a wider and larger sleep: the sleep, sound and beneficent and dreamless, that shall endure through the making and changing and dying of worlds.

16*

CHAPTER XXIII

'SWEET NELLIE O'REE'

IT was about this time that one evening found Miss Georgie Lestrange and her brother Percy the sole occupants of a private sitting-room in the Waldorf Hotel, New York—a room of considerable size, for the brightly-decorated dinner-table was laid for a party of eight. Percy Lestrange—a young man of irregular features and red hair—was staring contemplatively into the fire; his sister, clad in a sea-going costume of serge, was standing on tiptoe to bring herself on a level with a slab of mirror in the over-mantel, so that she might arrange her necktie. The necktie was of a dark green and blue tartan, with a slender line of yellow running through it—the Gordon tartan, in fact.

And, as usual, the pretty and pert-nosed damsel was talking away recklessly and at railway-speed.

"I do call it a horrid nuisance, this starting off in the middle of the night—don't you? So unnecessary. Why, what's the use of it? I should have thought they'd want all the daylight they could get to steam down the bay—shouldn't you? Never mind. There are compensations. For you do have moments of sense, Percy—haven't you?—and it was just snip-snap of you to think of this little send-off, and getting Madame St. Roche and the rest of us on board all in good humor." She turned from the mantelpiece and looked along the brilliant table, with evident satisfaction. "And I, for

"'THERE ARE COMPENSATIONS'"

one," she remarked, with some significance, "seeing as how strange things may eventuate during the next day or two, I, for one, sha'n't be sorry to have a jolly old tuck-in."

"Really, Georgie," he said, in a peevish manner, "your language is too awful! And why will you keep on asking questions, when you don't expect any answer? It's perfectly maddening! Why can't you state your opinions, without challenging assent — on perfectly immaterial points? Why that perpetual 'don't you?' and 'haven't you?' and—"

"Now, now, Percy, enough of that," she broke in, with an air of authority. "That's all part and parcel of the nervousness and irritability of your breakdown; and you undertook you wouldn't give way to it again. And you're not going to quarrel on the very last night of our being together—are you? As if I hadn't enough to worry me! I think it was most inconsiderate of Lady Adela, don't you? To have this wretched book of hers waiting for me, and to expect me to spend my only day in New York in hunting up this Caspar Sprigg, to woolly-lamb him, and get him to promise a review! It's too bad! Well, I can't now, anyway. You'll have to, Percy—to-morrow or next day, before you go back south."

"Let her look after her own woolly-lambing!" said the convalescent, crossly. "Besides, how am I to find out this fellow?"

"Oh, he's a Professor of something or other," said Miss Georgie, as she took up the *menu* and regarded it with imaginative eyes. "Anglophobia, as likely as not—Caspar Sprigg, Professor of Anglophobia, University of Braggingsville—mightn't that fetch him? I remember the creature — one night at Lady Adela's — hideously ugly—no chin— Oh, I say, Percy, I call this just a ripping spread !" But here there was a noise of newcomers outside ; and Miss Georgie, not to be thought a greedy young person, quickly replaced the *menu* on the table, and assumed her most correct deportment.

However, as it turned out, these were not the expected guests ; the sounds gradually died away ; and then it was that Percy Lestrange, looking up from his reverie, addressed his sister — with some slight hesitation in his tone.

"I say, Georgie : I have been considering whether I ought to tell you—as a warning beforehand—or whether I should let you find it out for yourself. After all, it's of no great consequence—you can treat him as a perfect stranger—"

She was not paying much heed. She had picked up the *menu* again ; and her eyes seemed to be pleased with the prospect—bouchées à la Montglas—faux-filet au cresson—aubergines à la Provençale, and the like.

"Are you listening ?" her brother said. "It may interest you, you know. When I was down at the steamship company's office this afternoon, I saw the completed list of passengers, and among them—well, you would make the discovery sooner or later—is the name of Jack Cavan—"

The *menu* fell from her fingers, fluttering down to the floor.

"You don't mean that !" she exclaimed—with dismay in her voice.

"But I do. John Philip Cavan. There's not the least doubt about it."

"Then I won't go !" she said, passionately. "I won't sail in that ship. I won't submit to this abominable persecution. It's done deliberately. It isn't a coincidence—not a bit of it ! Of course he knew I was in America; I was perfectly aware of that; but who could have imagined he would be so mean as to plan this voyage! And it's all a part of the same system. The last time I saw him in a theatre, whenever there was anything insulting said about women, in the piece, he would turn round and level his opera-glass at me. Oh, the ingenuity of the fiend is perfectly devilish!—there's no other word for it—"

"Well," said her brother, with a languid air, "if young women will go playing games—"

"It's never the men, of course!" she said, contemptuously. "It's never the men who lead them on, and get them into scrapes—of course not! And as for Jack Cavan, he deserved all he got—he was paid out for his temper, and his high-mightiness and his fine airs: only, if he thinks he's going to persecute me all the way across the Atlantic, he's very much mistaken. I won't go in that ship, Percy. I will forfeit my berth. When does the next steamer of the same line sail?—surely they'll let me change—"

"Oh, what's the good of going on like that!" her brother said, fretfully. "You can't make a fool of yourself before these people—refusing at the last moment. What explanation could you offer?—"

"You could have a relapse," she put in, adroitly.

"Don't talk rubbish. The fact is, you behaved very badly—and now you are in a blue funk. It isn't Jack Cavan that's pursuing you; it's your conscience. And it isn't Jack Cavan, it's you conscience that will haunt you all the way across the Atlantic. How can Jack Cavan harm you? You'll have these half-dozen people surrounding you from morning till night. By-the-way, I suppose you told Sir Francis all about that old story?—"

"Tell Frank Gordon?" said she, blushing a rosy-

red. " No, I did not. Of conrse not. Certainly not.
There was quite time enough for bygones to be bygones : quite time enough—if only that spiteful fiend
would let me alone—" But at this point the door was
thrown open ; and Miss Georgie's companions for the
voyage did at last make their appearance—Madame St.
Roche, Miss Madeline Phayre, Miss Janie Phayre, Miss
Romanes, Mr. Algeciras, and Mr. S. F. Quentin of
Chicago—all of them, as they came into the room,
laughing and talking at once, so excited were they
over this little reunion and the larger prospect ahead
of them.

Indeed it was the ordinarily vivacious Georgie who
alone sate thoughtful and preoccupied—for spaces at
least—during this merry banquet: perhaps she was
considering the various devices to which she might
resort in view of the contingency that had so unexpectedly been sprung upon her. At all events when
they did at length drive away down to the dock and
get on board the steamer, she was not much in evidence; and when, finally, the great vessel moved
away out into the dark—a darkness that was all a-
throb with lights, red, green, and electric-blue—it was
found that Miss Lestrange had disappeared altogether ;
she had escaped from the usual foregathering in the
saloon to the solitude of her state-room ; and as it was
surmised that she might be busy opening her cabin-
trunks, her friends refrained from disturbing her.
And thus it was that Miss Georgie started upon her
voyage—with such a night's rest as her not too tender
conscience might allow her.

Next morning, when the grey of the dawn was
visibly declared in the porthole, she reached up her
hand to the top of her berth and pressed a button ;
and in response to her summons the stewardess ap-

peared—a tall, gaunt, sandy-haired woman with, on occasion, an Irish twinkle in her eyes.

"Oh, stewardess, I'm so ill!" said the young lady, in a panting and most piteous manner. "I'm so dreadfully ill. I didn't ring for you—out of consideration for the others; but I can bear this no longer. What must I take? Tell me what I must take. My brother said champagne, and plenty of it, from the first thing in the morning; but that would be too awful, wouldn't it? Then there's brandy, but that's more horrid still, isn't it? I'm sick enough already; brandy would only 'mak sikker.' That's a joke. That's a Scotch joke. You may think I'm not very ill if I can try to make fun of it; but it's no laughing matter; and I knew all night I should be ill—I dreamt of it—"

"Sure I'm very sorry, Miss," said the stewardess, gravely. "What can I bring for you?"

"Yes, that's just it," she moaned. "I don't know. It's so horrid to be ill, and not to know what to do. And yet, after all, the boat is not pitching so much—"

"Oh, no, Miss!"

"Nor rolling either—"

"No, Miss, and for a very good reason too," said the stewardess. "Sure we're at anchor!"

"What?" exclaimed the invalid, suddenly looking up.

"Yes indeed, Miss; we're anchored in the bay. There's a thick fog."

"And we haven't been to sea at all?"

"Oh, no, Miss; we're not near as far down as Sandy Hook."

For a moment Miss Georgie—thinking back over her apprehensions of the night—looked annoyed and angry; but there was really no use in quarrelling with

the sardonic stewardess; so she merely said, with a
certain petulance of tone—

"Well, you can bring me a cup of tea and a biscuit.
I'm not going into the saloon for breakfast this morning."

Now for how many hours or days, and under what
pretexts, Miss Lestrange might have proposed to herself to remain shut up in her cabin, it is impossible to
say—perhaps all the voyage over; but the girl-friends
who were travelling with her would not permit anything of that kind; they came swarming into the
small stateroom, insisting that she must get dressed
and go on deck to see the strange sight.   And a strange
sight it was—this huge living hive of a vessel cut off
from all communication with the rest of the world;
or rather there was a sort of communication, of a dim
and mysterious kind; for through the opaque, motionless white fog that encompassed them, they could hear
voices calling beneath, voices hailing from certain
small boats that had crept out from the shore.   Nothing
could be seen of these visitants or their whereabouts;
sometimes their remarks and replies sounded quite
close at hand, at other times they were hollow and
remote; but whatever advice or information they were
tendering, it was universally conceded that until this
dense fog lifted there was not the slightest chance of
the ship venturing to crawl across the bar.

And meanwhile Miss Georgie, though she pretended
to be engrossed in gazing over the side of the vessel,
and listening, had been keeping her eyes alert, and
that in a tremulous and agitated mood.   But no one
came near.   Perhaps the person she dreaded to meet
was having his morning cigar in the smoking-room, or
playing Nap, with some fellow-passengers.   And at
length the girls, tired of looking into the mystic white

profundity, proposed that they should all adjourn to
the music-room; and to this Miss Georgie eagerly assented; she knew she would be safe there, for none of
the men-folk were likely to come to listen to Chopin
and Mendelssohn, in the wan light of day.

The hours passed until two bells struck, and then
there was an adjournment to the saloon for luncheon.
And now it was that the hapless Miss Georgie encountered her enemy—ran full tilt against him at the foot
of the companion-way, for her anxious eyes had failed
to warn her of his approach. He was a young man of
about six- or eight-and-twenty, clean shaven, of sallow
complexion, and with a look about his firm and intel-
ligent features as of one who was not likely to suffer
much trifling at the hands of a wicked and wilful young
lady. As he drew near, he gave no sign of recognition;
but he regarded her—with a cold, and pitiless, and in-
different scrutiny; while poor Georgie, frightened out
of her senses, and blushing furiously, could only make
a wild effort to appear as if she were continuing a conversation with one of her companions—

"Oh, serge, did you say?—blue serge?—yes, I quite
agree with you—there's nothing so neat and serviceable—I always use it myself, though my things shab so
quickly on board ship—and I'm too poor to bring
trunkfuls of dresses with me—"

He was gone—and she drew a long breath to still
her panting heart; and then again when they had entered the saloon and taken their places, she found to
her immense relief he was seated so far away from
them that she had not so much to fear from his relentless eyes. And fortunately not one of her friends had
noticed her confusion and alarm.

Well, the fog lasted all that day, and all the next,
and the next—three days and nights the great steamer

remained in that strange white isolation; and although
certain critics — mostly commercial travellers in the
smoking-room—grumbled and alleged that the captain
might have got out if he had shown a little more daring, the bulk of the passengers resigned themselves to
their fate, and contrived to pass the time somehow by
dint of various amusements.   The ladies who had first
obtained possession of the piano were practically allowed to retain a monopoly of it; and this boudoir-
like apartment formed a snug and happy retreat; in
especial was Miss Georgie glad to find safety there—
for reasons she did not choose to reveal.

But on the morning of the second day of the fog, Miss
Janie Phayre came along to Miss Lestrange's cabin.

"I say, Georgina," she observed—for only so far had
their intimacy progressed—"do you know anything of
this?   I have just found it amongst my music; and I
am perfectly certain it was not there last night.   It
must have been put there this morning, sure.   And
yet it's not for me—these are not my initials—"

Miss Georgie was leisurely finishing her toilet; but
she turned, and perceived that her visitor was holding
in her hand a sheet of paper, that had a couple of
verses written on it in pencil.   When she took the prof-
fered page she started slightly, as if recognizing the
writing; then as her glance followed down these lines,
her vague surprise gave way to a very different emotion: her cheeks and forehead were flushed red, and
her eyes were indignant and angry.   For this was the
taunting rhyme that she found 'respectfully dedicated
to Miss G. L.':

> *I gave you my life, what more could I do,*
> *And you swore and you swore you would ever be true;*
> *But summer is short; the leaf falls from the tree;*
> *And women are changeable, Nellie O'Ree!*

And do I upbraid you?—oh no, and oh no ;
The world is the world ; and things will go so.
And you need not recall, 'mid your laughter and glee,
That you broke a man's heart, sweet Nellie O'Ree!

"Do I know what it means?" she said, hotly.
"Yes, of course I do! The insolence of it !—the insolence !—"

She tore the paper in four pieces, and crushed them
together, and flung them wrathfully on the floor.

"Oh, what is it, dear Georgina!" her astonished
visitor cried, in instant curiosity. "Is there anything
going on on board ?—what is it ?—do tell !"

"There's an impertinent man on board, that's about
all !" said Miss Georgina, scornfully. "Is that anything new? You'll meet with plenty of them before
you're much older. But I would rather not say any
more."

She sate herself down on the couch, her eyes still
burning; and as it was clear that she did not wish to
give any explanation, Miss Janie, after a brief farewell
message, withdrew—no doubt hoping to hear something further of this mystery later on. The moment
she had left, Miss Lestrange picked up the crumpled
ball of paper. She unrolled it and pieced together the
fragments. She read down, carefully and thoughtfully, the touching little ballad of 'Nellie O'Ree'; and
then for a little while she let it lie in her lap; and
then she proceeded to tear the fragments into still
smaller fragments, and these she scattered out at the
open port. When finally she was ready to leave her
cabin, there was a look of very definite resolution on
her face.

She did not go to the music-room, or anywhere near
it. She went straight up on deck, her eyes outstrip-
ping her in their peremptory search. And she soon

found what she sought : Mr. Jack Cavan was taking
his morning promenade, alone as it chanced, and muffled up in a capacious ulster, for the mist was raw and
cold.

Without a second of hesitation she went directly towards him ; and he, perceiving that she did not mean
to let him pass, stopped short.

"How dared you put that thing among the music—
how dared you !" she demanded, with a flaming glance.

He turned very pale, even to the lips.   But he did
not flinch.

"I wished you to see it," he said, deliberately.

"Yes, and the others !" she retorted.   "And the
others too, of course !   You wished them to see it
too, no doubt !   It was for them to draw their own
conclusions from its — from its — from its untruth !"
She paused, to get her breath—or perhaps not knowing how to express the vehemence of her anger.   And
then she blurted out : "Well, thank goodness I know
some one who would not do such a thing !"

This appeared to sting him ; for after all he was but
mortal.

"The raw-boned Scotchman, I presume !"

"Frank Gordon is the handsomest boy that ever
came to London," said she, warmly.   "And what's
more, he has the manliness to be forgiving.   I say he
has the manliness to be generous and forgiving.   He's
the kind of man who would forgive anything to a
woman—"

"That is a convenient kind," he remarked, with an
air of disdain.

"—if he cared enough for her," she went on.   "Yes.
If he cared enough for her, he would show himself
manly and forgiving—not—not revengeful and insulting—"

She stopped again.

"Have you anything further to say, Miss Lestrange?" he asked.

"No, I have not!"

"Then I will bid you good-morning," he said, respectfully enough, and he raised his hat, and walked away.

Miss Georgie went down below. At the foot of the companion she lingered for a second, to apply her handkerchief to her eyes. Then bold and erect of head she marched down the length of the saloon, and entered the music-room, where the usual little coterie was assembled around the piano.

"Georgina, dear," cried the elder of the Phayre girls, "what is all this about a mysterious piece of poetry?"

"A piece of poetry?—a piece of trash!" replied Miss Georgie, with scorn. "I threw it out of the window. Oh, there's no secret about it," she continued, loftily, as she found that these curious maidens were regarding her. "None. Why should there be? No secret whatever. There is a gentleman on board whom I once—once knew a little; and—and—he took this way of recalling himself to my recollection. Stupid, wasn't it? He might just as well have come frankly up and spoken, mightn't he? I call it a stupid trick. But you needn't speak of poetry—poetry!—a silly little Irish song—of no consequence whatever. At least I suppose it was Irish—I forget—I threw it out of the window. He's Irish himself, of course. That explains his writing verses. There's not an Irishman born that doesn't think he can write verses and throw a salmon-fly better than anybody else in the world. Only, I wish they wouldn't bother one with their silly songs!"

So that was the end of the episode, for the present —though one or two of Miss Georgie's companions may at odd hours have ruminated over this obscure transaction, and speculated. However, after the weary days and nights of waiting, the great ship-full of folk at length discovered that they were to be released from their chill imprisonment; the welcome throb of the screw was felt once more; they began to creep down towards Sandy Hook, and in due course of time got out into the open Atlantic. Not only that, but they found themselves sailing into the most lovely weather—calm seas and cloudless skies—blue above and a shining blue all around; and this delightful transformation seemed to produce a corresponding change in the spirits of everybody on board. Whither had fled the grumblers? There was a universal kindliness and cheerfulness and goodwill; confidence in the captain was entirely restored; the passengers said nice things about each other—knowing they would be repeated; rope-quoits and shovel-board were started; and of course the music-room was quite abandoned, for who could remain away from the charming promenades on deck, in the bracing air and sunlight? And perhaps the general amiability had got into Miss Georgie's heart; or perhaps the having continually to avoid Jack Cavan on these marchings up and down was beginning to prey on her nerves; at all events, finding him on one occasion alone, she again went up to speak to him. As before, he was all attention—and as frigid as ice.

"Couldn't we," said she, valiantly, "couldn't we agree to be friends, for the voyage over at least?"

He regarded her for a moment, and said quite gravely—

"Yes, if you wish it."

"Oh, if that is the way," said she, proudly, "—no, thanks!" And at once and haughtily she returned to her friends.

There came a night : a full moon was sailing through the tranquil heavens, and on the slumbering and slowly-moving waters there lay a pathway of silver, widening here and narrowing there, until it reached the immeasurable and unknown horizon. It was late, and yet a number of people had preferred this magical white scene to the golden comfort of the saloon ; and Madame St. Roche was a lenient chaperon ; she and her little party were all on deck, huddled cosily together, chatting the one to the other, or gazing contemplatively out on the entrancing beauty of sea and sky. And now it was that there stole into the silence—for the continuous lapping of the waves, and the familiar throb of the engines, formed almost a silence — there stole into the silence a sound so sweet, so clear, so distant that it seemed to come from nowhere at all, it seemed rather like the echo of a flute heard in some remote and mystic fairyland that one has visited in a half-forgotten dream.

"Oh, isn't it too beautiful," murmured one of the girls.

"It's a cornet," said one of the gentlemen : "but where the dickens is the player ?—is he some Ariel in the rigging, or flying in the wake of the boat ?"

"That darling Purser—he has planned this for us," said another of the girls.

"Hush—hush !" said the most sensible of the group.

And well indeed they might listen to this soft and silver-toned strain that had for its accompaniment the half-heard whisper and rush of the moonlit waves. It was an Irish air—it was 'Farewell, but if ever you welcome the hour'—and it was exquisitely played : no wonder they listened. But meanwhile something had happened to Georgie Lestrange. She was seated next Madame St. Roche ; and the moment the clear notes of the cornet began to steal through the witchery of the night, the elder lady felt the girl grasp her arm. It was an involuntary action, probably; anyhow the hand remained there, fixed and trembling ; and the figure of the girl was trembling too. Nay, as Madame furtively perceived, tears were running down her cheeks ; and as her agitation grew greater and greater, it was clear she could stay here no longer. She tried to slink away unobserved — with uncertain gait and head bent down. Not a word was said by any of her companions—perhaps in the dusk they had not noticed; but Madame rose and swiftly and discreetly followed.

She tapped at the door of the cabin, and got no answer ; but she heard a sound as of wild sobbing; and so she made bold to enter. She found the unhappy girl in a perfect passion of crying ; she lay at full length on the couch, her face downward ; and in the agony of her grief her hands were clenched into the cushion, while her whole frame quivered and shook.

"Georgina, dear !"

"Oh, my God, it's too cruel—it's too cruel !" she moaned, in the intervals of her frantic sobbing. "I cannot bear it—I cannot suffer this torture any more— he wants to break my heart—and I think he has done that now. Ah, Madame St. Roche, you do not know— you do not know—that was the air he used to play for me when we were at Glengariff—it was his last goodnight to me—every night when I had gone into the hotel —and he was out in the bay—and then when my people wouldn't let him come to see me—that was at Wicklow —after the quarrel—he used to play those Irish airs— and they were a message from him to me—oh, it's too

cruel !—it's too cruel !—but—but he has had his revenge sure enough—oh, yes—sure enough—for I will
never reach Queenstown alive—"

"Merciful Heaven, what do you say !" cried Madame,
and she drew in a chair to the couch, and released one
of the girl's hands and held it.

"No, I will not !" she sobbed again. "I will not. I
have made up my mind. Long before we get to Queenstown—there will be an end—and he will have his revenge sure enough—" But here she burst into another
flood of tears that for a time completely stopped all
utterance.

"My child, you are mad !" exclaimed Madame. "I
see all the situation of affairs—it is not revenge—it is
to win you back to him that he plays the beautiful air
—it is to recall tender scenes—"

"It is not—it is not !" she said, passionately. "It is
to taunt me—to reproach me—to accuse me : it is for revenge. And—and—Madame—what more revenge can
he want ? The moment I set eyes on him—on board
this ship—I knew that I had thrown my life away.
You see—you see—I have been absent from England
for a time—and able to look at things—and then—
then when I saw him—all the old-time came back—
even though I was mad-angry with him—or he with
me—I don't care which—and then—then he goes and
plays this air—knowing it would just cut my heart in
two—"

"Yes, yes, child," said Madame, "and he made a
very effective appeal to you, as any one can see ; and
it will all come right—"

"Come right ?" she repeated, and she struggled upwards from her recumbent position, and sate there de-
jected and hopeless, making some effort to get the tears
away from her cheeks and eyes. "Come right ?—yes

17

—when I throw myself overboard—then it will come right—and he will have his revenge at last. That will be the end—and there will be no need—of any more reproaches—"

And so they continued the argument, the one comforting, the other despairing; until finally Madame persuaded her young charge to go to bed, to see if the night might not bring rest to her suffering soul.

Next morning Miss Georgie did not make her usual appearance on deck, nor was she present at luncheon. In the afternoon, a gentleman, hitherto unknown to her, came up to Madame St. Roche, and said he hoped that Miss Lestrange was not unwell.

"She is rather ailing to-day," was the reply.

"Will you be so kind as to tell her that I am exceedingly sorry to hear it?" said he. "My name is Cavan."

Madame (with rapid thoughts of her own) immediately took the message below. Miss Georgie was lying on the couch in her state-room, partly dressed, with plenty of rugs thrown over her; and very listless and languid she looked after the long night's sleepless suffering. However, when she heard what Madame had to tell, she roused herself somewhat.

"But how did he say it, Madame?—that is the point. Formally, of course. A mere formal message, that is all. An ordinary piece of politeness—"

"Ah, no, not at all," said Madame; "it was most friendly and sincere. My child, I fear you have been hard towards that young man."

"Hard?" the poor invalid repeated bitterly. "Hard? You may think so—but you don't know *him!*"

After a little while she said—

"Madame St. Roche, do you ever go up the staircase leading from the fore-saloon?—there is an archway at the head of it where there are seats for two or three—would you mind sending the stewardess to see if that corner is vacant ?—and if it is she might ask Mr. Quentin or Mr. Algeciras, either of them, to come down and lend me an arm : I could be ready in a few minutes, and it would be more interesting than lying here."

All which was duly done ; and Miss Georgie found herself esconced in this sheltered spot, whence she could look out on the deck and the rigging if she was so disposed. But she was not yet satisfied.

"Mr. Quentin," she said to her escort, "do you know a Mr. Cavan who is on board ?"

"By sight only."

"I wish you would go and tell him, please, that I want to see him."

A few moments brought Jack Cavan to her side, while the sensible Quentin, remembering a familiar adage, made some sort of excuse and disappeared.

"Sit down, Jack," said she, in a softened and troubled voice, "I want to speak to you."

Obediently he took his place by her, and these two were now the only occupants of this shadowed recess, with but little fear of interruption.

"Jack, I want to ask for your forgiveness," she said, "and if you refuse, you'll be sorry some day, and perhaps sooner than you think. Haven't you had enough of revenge ? I know now that I have made a wreck of my life—isn't that enough revenge for you ?"

"I don't want revenge," said he, bluntly. "I want you, Georgie."

"Ah, but that's all past and gone," she answered him, in a sad and resigned fashion. "When you've made your bed you must lie on it. That's all over now. You shouldn't have quarrelled."

"It was you who quarrelled—you and your people—"

"Ah, well, you need not bring all that back again," she said, with a bit of a sigh. "It's all over and done with now. But oh, Jack, Jack, what made you play that song of Moore's last night—it recalled all the old times—the old times—the old times—"

She began to cry a little; but presently she dried her eyes again. "If you had a scrap of courage, Georgie," said he, "we might easily bring back those old times to both of us."

"What do you mean?" she said, suddenly looking up: then her eyes fell. "Oh, yes, I know. I know what you mean. But I couldn't. Oh, I couldn't—I couldn't! He's such a dear fellow—and it would be so dishonorable—"

"It would not be dishonorable at all," he said boldly. "It would be quite the reverse. I suspected you hadn't forgotten the old times, Georgie—oh, didn't I know it quite well! And if I have vexed you and angered you, then you must forgive me: it's you that must forgive. And you needn't talk about anything dishonorable: after what you have just said, it's the only honorable thing you can do, by him, and by me, and by yourself—"

"Oh, Jack, it's just dreadful to say it—so mean and contemptible—I feel so thoroughly mean and contemptible—but—but—do you think he would let me off?"

"I take it, he is a gentleman!" her companion exclaimed. "He wouldn't force a girl into marrying him that doesn't want to marry him. Besides, when he hears the whole story, he will see that I have the prior claim. I have the first claim on you—"

"Oh, Jack, I couldn't do it!" she still protested. "I couldn't do it. I couldn't face him. Think of his coming to meet me at Liverpool—how could I face

him ?   He's so frank and straightforward himself—and
I should feel so deceitful and sneakish and despica-
ble—"

"Nothing of the sort !" he maintained, vehemently,
"I tell you it's the straight thing to do.   Georgie," he
went on, in a most insidious manner, "will you leave it
all to me ?   Will you let me arrange it ?   Will you leave
it all in my hands ?"

"Y—yes, Jack—if you think you can—"

What now occurred took place in a recess, as before
described, at the top of the fore - saloon companion,
which was rarely used at this time of the day, while
any passer-by going along the deck would hardly think
of peering into this obscure retreat.   So that there was
no tale to tell throughout the ship—or to be set down
here.   When Miss Georgie next spoke it was in a soft
and purring and happy fashion — and singularly blithe
seemed this poor invalid wrapped up in the fur cloak
Lady Adela had given her.

"You see, Jack, it was this way.—now I'll tell you
honestly how it all happened in the Highlands—for
I've as good a right as any one to make excuses, haven't
I ?—and you wouldn't condemn me unheard, would
you ?   It was like this, you see—you see, it was like
this—well, perhaps it's not so easy to explain—"

"Don't explain anything, Georgie," said he, with a
certain grimness.   "I know your ways."

"Ah, now you want to quarrel again !" she retorted,
instantly.   "And you don't appear to care a straw
whether I come back to you with a clear and white
conscience—as I could prove to you if you'd only listen.
Now, Jack, do listen !   It was like this, you see.   He
and I were the youngest of the house-party up at Glen
Skean Castle, you know; and naturally we chummed ;
and he was awfully nice, and kind, and forgiving—not

like some people. And of course there was a little
skylarking; only he was as bad as I was—I declare to
you he was as bad as I was; he used to take me away
for long excursions with him; and he would dry my
back-hair when it got wet with the rain, and pin it up
again; or he would bathe my wrists with eau‑de‑Co‑
logne when they were bitten with the midges; and he
made me drink out of the same glass with him—like a
couple of children — like Paul and Virginia; and he
cut off some of my hair to make salmon‑flies with.
And tricks of that kind. You see how honest I am.
Any other girl would conceal all that nonsense. And
then it got rather more serious—not really serious, you
know, but there was a kind of appearance of serious‑
ness about it, don't you understand—and my head got
all bewildered, what with the moorlands, and the mists,
and the red deer, and the wild nights among the hills
—and—and, in short, we blundered into an engage‑
ment. What made me do it, I cannot imagine. But
I thought you were a brute—in fact, I knew it—and I
know it now; and he is just the nicest boy that ever
was born, and that's what he is. You won't mind my
saying that, will you? You wouldn't be scudgy and
mean and jealous, seeing what has happened? And
he was such a dear boy, and so good-natured, and hand‑
some, and ready for any mad mischief that you might
put into his head. I mean, that might come into his
head. And then, Jack, you must remember this: I
have never thought much of myself, or put any value
on myself; but I might have been Lady Gordon of
Grantly, and the daughter-in-law of a Princess as well.
Only, Jack—only—I will confess it—it would have
been with a broken heart. I knew that the moment
I set eyes on you on board this ship. Then I knew
what I had done. And I was in such despair that

I told Madame St. Roche I would throw myself into
the sea before ever we should reach Queenstown. Perhaps I didn't quite mean it, but I was pretty miserable
all the same—"

"Georgie," he said, interrupting her for a moment,
and speaking rather gravely, "don't make any mistake : I understand well enough that you are giving up
a good deal."

"Ah, but I've got you, Jack!—oh, darling Jack, I've
got you! And what would anything else be to me,
if I had to go through life with a broken heart?" She
paused for a second, and then resumed, in a somewhat
altered key. "At the same time, Jack, I shouldn't
like Frank Gordon to think that I had thrown myself away, as they call it. I don't want him to consider me a sentimental idiot. There wasn't much of that
kind of nonsense betwixt him and me, and I shouldn't
like to have him laugh at me now. I'm not moon-
struck, am I? I'm not a lunatic?—though it is awfully
nice to be sitting close and snug beside you, Jack.
And this is what I meant to say—though it's rather horrid—since you are going to explain matters to him, if
you could bring in some little mention of Kilcrana
Abbey—then—then he might understand I wasn't a
stage-struck school-girl. Of course it's horrid to talk
of such things. I know it's horrid. And I do honestly
believe, Jack, that if you had been a poor man, I could
have sacrificed everything for your sake—but it's better
as it is, I dare say. And oh, dear Jack, if you should
really think there's been the least bit of sacrifice—the
least tiny little bit of a sacrifice—I'm sure you'll remember it to me, and be kind to me, and pet me — for you
know well enough you've got a brute of a temper—"

It was at this moment—the afternoon having drawn
to dusk—that the electric lights flashed into existence

all around them. She sprang to her feet, very nimbly for an invalid.

"My gracious, what will Madame think of me ! Jack, you must come and be introduced to my friends, some time before dinner. Can you tell lies ?"

"I can try."

"How many could you muster, do you think ?"

"About fifteen thousand."

"It'll take about all that to explain the situation to these people. So go away and think. I will say nothing till I hear from you. Good-bye !"

"Au revoir !" said he ; and their parting was most discreet, for they were afraid of that blue-white electric glare.

And again that night the moon shone gloriously, this time riding through long and fleecy streaks of cloud ; and Madame St. Roche proved to be the most sympathetic of chaperons ; and Jack Cavan had discovered another secluded nook that the constructor of the vessel would seem to have specially designed for a pair of happy lovers. They were sitting together, these two ; and they had a great deal to say to each other, serious or the reverse of serious, with regard to the future ; but of a sudden Miss Georgie broke in with a low, smothered croon of delight—

"Oh, Jack, kiss me again, and tell me it's all true !"

CHAPTER XXIV

'SEEMED ATHENS AS A PARADISE'

ATHENS lay under snow—snow trampled and brownish-yellow in the main thoroughfares, but a wonder and a splendor far up among the lonely pillars of the Acropolis, and still further away, along the shoulders of Hymettus, a solid white against the deep pellucid blue. Down here in the city, the air was still, and clear, and bitterly cold; the passers-by looked miserable, and the scraggy little horses shivered; while the occasional wearer of a fustanella appeared to be conscious that the garment was entirely out of keeping with this kind of climate. But in the salle-à-manger of the Hotel of the Tower of the Winds, in the Palace Square, there was another tale to tell; the long and lofty apartment had been well warmed by the stoves; and indeed the two travellers who had just taken their places at the central table found themselves in comfortable case; for at this hour there were no other guests, the assiduous waiter was displaying before them a most excellent lunch, while the proprietor himself was opening for them a bottle of Santorin.

"Well, Aunt Jean, you've done me many a good turn," said the younger of the two—who seemed restless and preoccupied, and would hardly look at the food set before him—"but never one like this: the long railway-journey—in mid-winter—"

"Toots, toots, laddie," said Jean Gordon, with her

17*

usual good-humor — and she at least paid sufficient attention to the cutlets and macaroni—"it's been nothing but a bit jaunt! And it's not for Aberdeenshire folk to complain of a whaff of snow—"

"There was no one else I could ask for advice or help," he went on. "You are so wise, and shrewd, and kindly; and then you have her confidence already; she won't be frightened when she sees you—if you can get to see her. But the whole situation is so desperately difficult. You know how proud she is—proud and sensitive. And if I had come away out here by myself, and gone direct to her, her whole nature would have been up in revolt against the assumption—the assumption—well, that she was to be had for the asking. She would have shut herself up still more completely—"

"The foolish creature," put in Aunt Jean, "to run away and hide herself in this fashion!"

"As for that," said he, "I can easily understand her desire to get away from England: she had not been too well treated there; and I suppose she thought she would seek a refuge with the people amongst whom she had been brought up. And I dare say she wanted to leave everything behind her, and cut off all communication with what was bygone. But if there was any intention to keep her whereabouts a secret, then my blessings on that pudding-faced Olga Elliott for blurting it out! Of course it was spite that prompted her. 'A maid-servant!' says she. 'Gone to be a maid-servant in an asylum for orphan girls in Athens!' And then I knew in a moment! I knew in a moment! Why, dozens of times I had heard Briseis talk of that institution, and of the Patronne being an old friend of hers, and of the extraordinary beauty of many of the young girls there. That was how it first came about—that was how she first spoke of it: she was telling me that

any one arriving in Athens as a stranger, and expecting
to see the creations of Phidias or Praxiteles walking
along Hermes-street, would be awfully disappointed
with the look of the people—the women in especial;
but on the other hand, she said, many of the young
girls were just divinely beautiful creatures; and then
she told me all about this institution, and about her
often going up at the play-hour to have a romp with
the grave-eyed small goddesses. 'Oh,' says I to myself,
the moment Olga Elliott blundered out with the truth,
'we're all right now—if only Aunt Jean will come along
and be the wise counsellor. But the fearful long railway-journey—and the crossing from Brindisi to Patras
in mid-winter.'"

"Get on with your lunch, man!" said Aunt Jean.
"And I wish you'd see if they cannot get some seltzer-
water with just a bit of a sparkle in it: this is as dead
as last Hallowe'en."

"Here, garçon!" he boldly called to the waiter. "Ça
ne marche pas — cherchez une bouteille qui marche!"

"Ye see, Frankie, lad, I'm rather fidgeting to get
through," said Miss Jean, in an undertone, "and I'll
tell you the reason, though maybe I shouldn't. Do you
remember a young officer coming up to speak to me in
the railway-station at Brindisi?"

"Yes, I do."

"Well, that was an aide-de-camp of Prince George's.
And he had come all the way across from Monteveltro
on a special mission; and while you were looking after
the luggage he explained the matter to me, and gave
me a small box addressed to you, and a letter from
your mother addressed to a certain young lady; and
in the event of everything going right, I was to deliver both. But bless ye, laddie, how can I sit still and
eat in peace while that casket is in my dressing-bag—

up-stairs in my room—in a foreign hotel?—I'm just on tenterhooks till I get it handed over. The young brigand with the great mustache and the glaring eyes warned me of its value—"

"It's a pity you shouldn't have your luncheon in comfort, Aunt Jean," said he, humanely. "Shall I go and fetch down your bag, and you can have it put on a chair, and keep it under your own eyes all the time—"

"The very thing!" said Aunt Jean. "Away ye go. Number eight is my room, and the bag is up at the window."

In due course the dressing-bag was brought down and placed on the chair at her side; but still Miss Jean was not satisfied; perhaps some natural feminine curiosity had to be taken into account.

"What I can well understand," she said, "is that your mother and the Prince might wish to send the young lady a little present, as a kind of congratulation on her engagement—if engagement there is to be; but what I cannot understand is why, seeing they are in Vienna, they should not send it from there—Vienna, the very place for such things! But to put all this trouble on Prince George, and have that mustachioed brigand come across from Monteveltro, at this time of year, when the mountains are usually snowed up— Frank," she said on a sudden impulse, "I'm going to give ye the casket now: I'm going to take it for granted that all will be well—"

"Aunt Jean," he remonstrated, almost despairingly, "if you take anything for granted you will ruin everything! You don't seem to know with whom you have to deal. Briseis Valieri may look very serene in manner and self-possessed, but she's as easily startled as a fawn, and sensitive beyond expression. I tell you,

you must assume nothing! We are travelling for pleasure—we came here by accident—oh, any excuse you like!—but for goodness' sake don't make it appear as though you had come right away from England to capture her and carry her off. If you knew how proud she is—and—and—apprehensive—"

"Leave her to me, laddie," said the shrewd Miss Jean; and then, not to be balked of her little gratification, she unlocked her dressing-bag, and got hold of the casket, and handed it over. "'Take off the wrappers, and let me see."

It was worth inspection: even the cover of it—the lid of the casket—with its dark-green transparent enamel ornamented with filigree-work of faded gold, was a piece of exquisite art; but when he took out the inclosed treasure—a bracelet it was, of Byzantine design, of elaborate and intricate craftsmanship, and all encrusted with uncut precious stones — Jean Gordon's covetous eyes were staring.

"I'll wager that's from the family jewels!" she exclaimed. "And that's why it came over from Monteveltro. Frank, lad," she added, significantly, "your mother didn't persuade the Prince to send you anything of that kind when she heard of your first engagement. There was not so much approval then."

"Poor Georgie!" said he, half-laughing. "She was about dead with terror when she landed at Liverpool—and just wild with gratitude when she found I wasn't going to cut her throat for jilting me."

"Now will ye sit down in quiet and let a body finish her luncheon decently," said Miss Jean; and he did as he was bid; whereupon she proceeded with the pastry, and fruit, and sips of Santorin; but sho kept on talking all the same. "I'm not to assume anything? Very well. But I know what your mother has in her mind—that you should take your bride to Vienna, and spend the remainder of the winter there with them, before they go back to the Principality. And a sensible plan too. Dee-side is bleak at the beginning of the year. Better wait till the primroses and the hyacinths come out in the woods : that's the time to show the young wife her new home. And ye'll not find me there. I declare to you ye'll not find me there—"

"We'll see about that, Aunt Jean," said he—himself trapped into an assumption.

"Na, na; I've been long enough prisoned up in that tower, and never a knight of them coming prancing on his steed, and blowing his bugle, to release me. I'll be off to Edinburgh. There's the Leslies, and the Kirkpatricks, and the Ramsays—plenty of company ; and although they used to say 'dinna misca' a Gordon in the raws of Strathbogie,' there will be quite enough consideration for a Gordon of Grantly a wee bit farther south than Strathbogie. And then I'll be seeing you from time to time, Frankie, to notice if marriage has made any change. Sometimes it does, mind. I'm sure you've heard of that roystering, blustering, blethering idiot, Maceachran—the savagest pulpit-thumper in the north of Scotland—he's like Fin Mac Cowle

'That dang the devil, and gart him yowle'*

—and he keeps his wife, and his family, and his elders, and his congregation just in trembling subjection to his thrawn temper and his down-drawn mouth. Dear me, I remember him when he first came to Sanchory —a pale, whitey-faced divinity-student, as gentle as a pet-lamb, and as shy as a school-miss—"

* 'That beat the devil, and made him howl.'

"And has that fearful change been produced by marriage?" her nephew asked of her.

"No, I rather think it's been original sin developing," said Aunt Jean, thoughtfully. Then of a sudden she looked up. "And now, Frankie, before I set out, give me complete instructions."

"Not I," he answered her. "I can trust you, Aunt Jean. You always say and do just the right thing at the right moment—"

"Very well, then: the one point settled is that if I can find the runaway, I am to ask her to dine with us this evening. And we are merely two distinguished travellers, passing through Athens—is that the proposition?"

"I leave it all to you, Aunt Jean," he said, nervously and anxiously.

"Frankie, lad, your simulations won't be the least bit of good. She'll suspect something, the instant she sees me—"

"I leave it all to you, Aunt Jean," he maintained, doggedly.

"And while I am racing and chasing about this unknown town, what are you going to do with yourself?"

"Oh, I don't know," he said, absently, "I suppose I may as well climb away up to the top of the Acropolis, to have a general look round. Perhaps I may get a glimpse of the island of Aegina—that was Briseis's home, you know, when she was quite a young girl."

"Well, I suppose the sooner I'm off the better," said Miss Jean, rising from her chair. "And while I'm getting ready you ought to go and lock up that precious casket in your portmanteau: I'm glad it's out of my charge."

A short time thereafter a carriage was drawn up in

front of the hotel, and Frank Gordon was pacing to
and fro at the foot of the staircase, waiting for Miss
Jean to come down.   When she did appear, she was
buttoning a pair of furred gloves.

> "'O little did my mither think,'"

she said, as she drew near

> "'That day she cradled me,
> What lands I was to travel ower'

—and the idea of my adventuring into this strange
place—all by myself—what is to become of me ?—"
   "Oh, you'll be all right : you've got a good French
tongue in your head, Aunt Jean," he said, encour-
agingly.   "Every one knows that.   With all her experience of Courts, the Mater doesn't speak French
near as well as you do, and with such a perfect accent—"
   "It's you that are the fine judge, Frankie!" she
said, mocking at him; and then she stepped across
the swept pavement, and took her place in the carriage,
and nodded good-by to him, and was driven off.
   And as they went swiftly and noiselessly through
the muffled streets, Jean Gordon had very little attention to bestow on what she was passing.   She knew
that this was a much more delicate and difficult mission than she had been willing to confess; and it was
not on every one's behalf she would have undertaken
it; but there was little she would not do for her be-
loved nephew Frank.   In any case, she had now little
time for plans and preparations; the distance was not
great; and just as she had made up her mind that
she must trust mainly to luck the carriage was pulled
up in front of the institution she was in quest of—a
large building with something of architectural preten-

sions, situated in a quiet and rather outlying part of the city.

She let herself down from the vehicle, and stepped across the pavement to the gate; and there she stood stock-still, for through the railings she beheld a scene that had a sudden and unexpected interest for her. The entrance to the institution was not in front, but at the side, and some way along; and around this sheltered door-way, and in a little bit of a verandah adjoining, were scattered groups of young girls—from seven to fourteen or fifteen their ages might be—who were engaged, rather timidly and in a kind of unwonted fashion, in picking up handfuls of snow and flinging them, with little cries of exultation, at a solitary figure out in the open. Something seemed to catch in Jean Gordon's throat. For the figure was that of a young woman, tall, and slim, and of a wonderful, agile grace; and from among the stunted and leafless trees in the strip of garden she also was picking up handfuls of snow and hurling them back at her enemies—one against thirty was the unequal contest; and she was laughing merrily —so merrily that every now and again, through her parted lips, the sunshine gleamed on her perfect teeth. Moreover, the reflected light from the snow had robbed her face of its natural shadows, so that there was a kind of glorification there; and the brisk exercise had brought a rose-leaf tinge to the pale olive of her cheek; and her eyes, large, and dark, and lustrous, were laughing as well as her laughing lips.

"Bless me," said Aunt Jean to herself, "there's no man alive could withstand the witchery of that creature!"

But when Briseis chanced to notice the newcomer, her expression instantly changed—not to fear, but to simple amazement. She advanced quickly to meet her.

"Miss Gordon—in Athens—and all alone !" she exclaimed. And then her heart seemed to sink within her. "You—you do not bring ill news ?"

"Not at all—not at all !" said Miss Jean, as she took the girl in her arms and kissed her affectionately on both cheeks. "And I'm not alone : Frank is with me—"

Inadvertently and almost imperceptibly Briseis appeared to draw back a little bit.

"And—and who else ?" she asked.

"Why, no one ! We are just by our two selves. And of course we don't know a soul in the place ; and we thought it would be awfully kind of you if you would come and spend the evening with us, at the hotel —the Hotel of the Tower of the Winds—"

"All by yourselves !" the girl repeated, in great surprise, and yet apparently well pleased. "But come in —come in—you must let me introduce you to my good friend the Patronne, and she will let me off for the rest of the day ; and I will be your cicerone ; I must show you the Stadion—that will interest you, you know, because of the revival of the Olympic Games—" And therewith she called aloud a few words, in a tongue that Miss Jean could make nothing of, and straightway the small Greek maidens began to troop into the house, but not before Aunt Jean had assured herself that what she had heard of the exceeding comeliness of many of these youthful daughters of Attica had in nowise been exaggerated.

When they went into the apothēkē they found that the Patronne was engaged with two Italian ladies who were examining the sewn - work and embroideries wrought by the elder girls in the institution ; accordingly they had to wait ; but when all the purchases had been made, and the visitors had departed, Briseis

experienced no difficulty in obtaining her freedom—
though with kindly warnings against standing about
and getting her feet wet. So that in a brief while she
was seated in Aunt Jean's carriage, and presently these
two were on their way towards the time-worn Stadion.

"Isn't it rather a shame," said Miss Jean, tentatively,
"that that poor lad should be left by himself, while I
am getting all the benefit of your instruction?"

"We will call for him at the hotel if you wish it,"
said Briseis, promptly.

"Well, he isn't there, just at present. He said he
would wander away up to the Acropolis, to have a look
round—"

"The Acropolis? Oh, then, he is brave indeed!
For I fear the steps of the Propylaea will be very slippery
with the half-melted snow; and on the top there are
snow-drifts among the broken pillars—one might meet
with an accident—"

"Couldn't we go up and find him there?" suggested
Miss Jean, who was not much afraid of any such twopenny-halfpenny snow-drift as the town of Athens was
likely to produce. "He would be so glad to see you—"

"Oh, very well, then," said Briseis, good-naturedly,
and she addressed a word or two, again in that mysterious tongue, to the driver. "You will have a
glimpse of the Stadion in passing, and we will go right
on to the Acropolis."

And now it was that Jean Gordon, despite of all her
nerve, knew that her heart was in her mouth; and
little heed did she pay to the Stadion, nor yet to the
Olympieion, nor to the temple-crowned, snow-powdered
heights beyond. Furtively, underneath the rug, her
hand stole to the hand of the girl, and held it fast.

"Briseis, my dear child," said she, "I told you I
brought no ill-news. And that is true. But I bring

news. I don't say that it concerns you—I would not presume to say that. Perhaps it does not—perhaps it does not concern you in the least; and you must not think me impertinent—"

"But what is it, Miss Jean?" said Briseis, wondering.

"Well," said Aunt Jean, after a moment's desperate hesitation, "when you were in London, my nephew Frank was engaged to be married. You knew that, of course. But the engagement is all broken off now: he is a free man: and—and he thought you would rather hear of it, in a roundabout way, from me—"

For a second the girl did not seem to realize all that this implied, though at the mere first mention of the news she had grown deadly pale; then suddenly she said, in a sort of breathless fashion—

"Miss Jean, Miss Jean, I would rather go back! You won't mind, will you—some other time I will go to the Acropolis with you—some other time—the children—the Patronne—will be expecting me—" And then she herself appeared to see that this was some kind of admission; and she made a wild effort to regain her self-control. "Oh, yes, we will go on," she managed to say. "Why not? The Propylaea steps may be a little difficult; but that's nothing. They may have cleared a pathway even—anyhow—anyhow—it will be a singular spectacle for you—you must not miss it. And so you tell me Sir Francis is not to be married after all!—well, well—" But with that her heroic effort to appear unconcerned failed her; and except for a mechanical sentence now and again she relapsed into a silence that Jean Gordon was too considerate to attempt to break. The girl seemed afraid.

And meanwhile Frank Gordon was away up on the summit of the solitary hill, stumbling about among the

broken pillars, or surveying the wide prospect around
him, from the white-clad range of Parnes to the blue
waters of the Gulf of Aegina. The luck of this fellow!
—to have come to Athens for the first time and found
it all a marvel of snow-radiance and azure sea. As for
his inspection of the ancient monuments, that was of
a quite ignorant and perfunctory character; perhaps
his imagination was busy elsewhere; and unmistakably
he had to attend a good deal to his footing—for the
wind-driven snow had covered over not only the deep
seams and fissures in the rock itself but also the spaces
between the tumbled and shattered columns, so that
everywhere were treacherous holes. But in the roofed-
over portion of the Erectheum there was less of drift;
and here the beautiful scroll-work of the cornices was
clearly exposed to view; so that he lingered in these
precincts for a long time—thinking and thinking—
perchance of egg-and-dart, and key, and honeysuckle:
perchance not.

Voices broke in upon his reverie—a strange sound
on this lonely and snow-hushed height. They drew
nearer; and not wishing to be caught in a corner, as
it were, by strangers, he withdrew from this sheltered
spot, and passed out by the tall Ionic pillars. When
he got into the open, Briseis was standing there. She
was standing there, waiting. There was no pretence
in her eyes now, as she regarded him. For the moment her attitude was not unlike that of the restored
Caryatid in the portico hard by—just as noble, and
simple, and gracious; but this living and breathing
figure was of flesh and blood, as was evident enough in
the color of her face and in the shrinking and maiden
wistfulness of her look. To him it was all a vision—
a flash: the next instant his outstretched hands had
seized hers, and drawn her to him.

"My own!" he said—and she had no word in reply.

By this time Jean Gordon had gone away. The fact is, as the gardeners at Grantly Castle knew to their sorrow, she had a trick, no matter in what outlandish part she might be—or the more outlandish the better —of collecting roots, slips, cuttings, and the like, to try if these could be got to grow in Aberdeenshire; and now, close by the Temple of the Six Virgins, she was industriously engaged in brushing away the snow from certain clumps of withered weeds and thistles, seeking for some prickly bulb of seed that she might carry off. Also she was much interested in the figure of the replaced Caryatid, for the mutilated original is in the British Museum; and she was saying to it: 'Yes, you are indeed very beautiful, and serene, and sweet, but you have not the magnetism and the witchery of the laughing girl I saw half-an-hour ago throwing snowballs in the orchard.' She left the lovers to themselves.

And thus it was that on this spacious plateau, which through so many centuries has been the cynosure of all the civilized world — on this lofty plateau that looks abroad on surroundings sufficiently august—Pentelicus, Hymettus, Aegaleos, and the shining blue of the Bay of Salamis—here it was that a betrothal took place, of two souls that had thought themselves sundered for ever, but had come together at last. And truly it was a fitting day for such a betrothal, a day altogether auspicious; for it is not every morning that the City of the Violet Crown arrays herself in her bridal robes of silver and white.

THE END

Sir WALTER BESANT'S WORKS.

Mr. Besant wields the wand of a wizard, let him wave it in whatever direction he will. . . . The spell that dwells in this wand is formed by intense earnestness and vivid imagination.—*Spectator*, London.

There is a bluff, honest, hearty, and homely method about Mr. Besant's stories which makes them acceptable, and because he is so easily understood is another reason why he is so particularly relished by the English public.—*N. Y. Times.*

ALL IN A GARDEN FAIR. 4to, Paper, 20 cents.

ALL SORTS AND CONDITIONS OF MEN. Illustrated. 12mo, Cloth, $1 25; 8vo, Paper, 50 cents.

ARMOREL OF LYONESSE. Illustrated. 12mo, Cloth, $1 25; 8vo, Paper, 50 cents.

BEYOND THE DREAMS OF AVARICE. Illustrated. 12mo, Cloth, $1 50.

CHILDREN OF GIBEON. 12mo, Cloth, $1 25; 8vo, Paper, 50 cents.

DOROTHY FORSTER. 4to, Paper, 20 cents.

FIFTY YEARS AGO. Illustrated. 8vo, Cloth, $2 50.

FOR FAITH AND FREEDOM. Illustrated. 12mo, Cloth, $1 25; 8vo, Paper, 50 cents.

HERR PAULUS. 8vo, Paper, 35 cents.

KATHERINE REGINA. 4to, Paper, 15 cents.

LIFE OF COLIGNY. 16mo, Cloth, 30 cents.

SELF OR BEARER. 4to, Paper, 15 cents.

LONDON. Illustrated. 8vo, Cloth, Ornamental, $3 00.

ST. KATHARINE'S BY THE TOWER. Illustrated. 12mo, Cloth, $1 25; Paper, 50 cents.

THE BELL OF ST. PAUL'S. 8vo, Paper, 35 cents.

THE HOLY ROSE. 4to, Paper, 20 cents.

THE INNER HOUSE. 8vo, Paper, 30 cents.

THE IVORY GATE. 12mo, Cloth, $1 25.

THE REBEL QUEEN. Illustrated. 12mo, Cloth, $1 50.

THE WORLD WENT VERY WELL THEN. Illustrated. 12mo, Cloth, $1 25; 4to, Paper, 25 cents.

TO CALL HER MINE. Illustrated. 4to, Paper, 20 cents.

UNCLE JACK AND OTHER STORIES. 12mo, Paper, 25 cents.

PUBLISHED BY HARPER & BROTHERS, NEW YORK.

R. D. BLACKMORE'S NOVELS.

PERLYCROSS. A Novel. 12mo, Cloth, Ornamental, $1 75.

Told with delicate and delightful art. Its pictures of rural English scenes and characters will woo and solace the reader. . . . It is
charming company in charming surroundings. Its pathos, its humor,
and its array of natural incidents are all satisfying. One must feel
thankful for so finished and exquisite a story. . . . Not often do we
find a more impressive piece of work.—*N. Y. Sun.*

A new novel from the pen of R. D. Blackmore is as great a treat
to the fastidious and discriminating novel-reader as a new and rare
dish is to an epicure. . . . A story to be lingered over with delight.—
Boston Beacon.

SPRINGHAVEN. Illustrated, 12mo, Cloth, $1 50; 4to, Paper,
25 cents.

LORNA DOONE. Illustrated. 12mo, Cloth, $1 00; 8vo, Paper,
40 cents.

KIT AND KITTY. 12mo, Cloth, $1 25; Paper, 35 cents.

CHRISTOWELL. 4to, Paper, 20 cents.

CRADOCK NOWELL. 8vo, Paper, 60 cents.

EREMA; OR, MY FATHER'S SIN. 8vo, Paper, 50 cents.

MARY ANERLEY. 16mo, Cloth, $1 00; 4to, Paper, 15 cents.

TOMMY UPMORE. 16mo, Cloth, 50 cents; Paper, 35 cents;
4to, Paper, 20 cents.

His descriptions are wonderfully vivid and natural. His pages
are brightened everywhere with great humor; the quaint, dry turns of
thought remind you occasionally of Fielding.—*London Times.*

His tales, all of them, are pre-eminently meritorious. They are
remarkable for their careful elaboration, the conscientious finish of
their workmanship, their affluence of striking dramatic and narrative
incident, their close observation and general interpretation of nature,
their profusion of picturesque description, and their quiet and sustained
humor.—*Christian Intelligencer,* N. Y.

PUBLISHED BY HARPER & BROTHERS, NEW YORK.

☞ *The above works are for sale by all booksellers, or will be sent by the
publishers, postage prepaid, to any part of the United States, Canada, or Mexico,
on receipt of the price.*

www.ingramcontent.com/pod-product-compliance
Lightning Source LLC
Chambersburg PA
CBHW030951110726
47900CB00004B/1226